Praise for
Catherine Wheels

"I read good novelists to keep our great words—*holy, salvation, hope, trust, miracle, saint*—specific and *lived*. Not abstract. Not churchy. Leif Peterson's *Catherine Wheels* does this convincingly: One after another, men and women who have quit on life are led back to life by a nine-year-old, saint-christened girl, each one a believable Christ-resurrection that could be, and probably is, taking place in your neighborhood right now."

> —EUGENE PETERSON, translator of *The Message*

"Leif Peterson tracks the unfolding consciousness of three generations as they search for connections to one another and find themselves touching the edges of what lies beyond the ordinary."

> —Virginia Stem Owens, coauthor of *Living Next Door to the Death House* and board member for *Books and Culture*

A Novel

Catherine Wheels

LEIF
PETERSON

WATERBROOK
PRESS

CATHERINE WHEELS
PUBLISHED BY WATERBROOK PRESS
12265 Oracle Boulevard, Suite 200
Colorado Springs, Colorado 80921
A division of Random House, Inc.

Scripture quotations are from the author's own paraphrase.

The characters and events in this book are fictional, and any resemblance to actual persons or events is coincidental.

ISBN 1-57856-894-3

Library of Congress Cataloging-in-Publication Data
    Peterson, Leif.
Catherine Wheels / Leif Peterson.—1st ed.
        p. cm.
    ISBN 1-57856-894-3
    1. Girls—Fiction. I. Title.
PS3616.E8433C38 2005

                                                              2005008470

Printed in the United States of America
2005—First Edition

10 9 8 7 6 5 4 3 2 1

When the day is done, there's one place I want to be...

This is for Amy.

*I*n Spokane, we built our own field of dreams.

My brother and I were living there the summer my mother died. I'd just finished my junior year at a small college nestled on the north end of town in an oasis of towering ponderosa pine. Normally I went home to Baltimore for summers and holidays, but that summer I decided to stay. I got a job at a sporting-goods store and joined the softball team it sponsored. Stephen painted houses. He'd just finished his first year at General Theological Seminary, but his fiancée, Mary, was in Spokane. We lived with our friend Perry Palmer in a little house in the heart of Dog Town.

We had a large, fenced backyard that was covered in landscaping bark. During the first weeks of summer, Perry converted the backyard into a Wiffle-ball field. He shoveled up the bark and hauled it away, then brought in sod for the infield. We laid the sod on a Saturday afternoon, cutting the pieces with a kitchen knife. Perry dug dirt from a flower bed at the front of the house and built a pitcher's mound. He extended the fence posts and put up lights for night games.

Summer days in Spokane are hot and dry, the evenings long, and the nights cool and starry. After work we'd play Wiffle ball while a sprinkler on the neighbor's lawn ticked back and forth. We'd play late into the evenings long after it got dark, the sound of the bat on the ball, plastic on plastic, hollow and sharp like exclamation marks.

But it was during a softball game that my mother died. I'd just hit a shot over the right fielder's head. By the time he got to it, I was rounding second. It was an easy triple, but I thought I could stretch it into a home run.

I rounded third and glanced to right field where the fielder was winding up to throw home. He seemed to move in slow motion, part of another dimension. A gust of wind blew and kicked up clouds of dirt. The sound of the field was dampened, everything muted. Halfway down the third-base line, I had a vision of my mother. She was walking on a dark city street in a neighborhood she shouldn't have been in. She was wearing a black cape, walking between parallel sidewalks toward a distant vanishing point. I got the distinct impression she was walking away from *me*. I wanted to yell to her, but before I had the chance, she disappeared, enveloped in a fog.

I've often wondered if I made it safely home, but I have no memory of the rest of the game. That evening, Perry and I were in the backyard playing Wiffle ball when I thought of my mother again. She'd been scheduled for a minor surgery that day. It was so minor and so routine that I didn't even remember what it was. Still feeling a little unsettled by the vision, I told Perry that I thought I should call home. I went inside, but before I could get to the phone, it rang.

I picked it up and listened as someone from my parents' church tried to explain to me that my mother had not come out of the anesthesia. At first I thought she simply meant that my mother hadn't yet woken up, and I couldn't understand why she was calling. When it dawned on me that she was dead, the vision replayed itself—my mother on a dark street of an unfriendly city, dressed in black, walking away. I put the phone down without hanging up and looked around the room. All the furniture was mismatched and worn, typical college stuff, handed down, not bought. Outside it was getting dark. The rhythmic clicking of a sprinkler from the neighbor's yard serrated the stillness of the night.

The back screen door opened and Perry came in. "What's wrong?"

His voice was dull and matted; the air in the room gauzy.

"What's wrong?" he repeated.

"My mother died," I said. "I need to find Stephen."

*T*wice in my life I've heard something that at the time I took to be the voice of God. Both times it was just one word, and both times it was the same word: *Move.* I have no way of knowing that what I heard was the voice of God, but I have no other explanation for hearing an audible voice when I was completely alone. And there's this: In my limited experience with God, he doesn't speak that often. So on those rare occasions when he deems it necessary, it seems that he might choose to be succinct.

When I was eleven years old, I ran away from home. I don't remember the reason for it any longer, only that I felt hurt and unappreciated, and I thought I'd teach my family a lesson by depriving them of my presence for the rest of their lives. I got about a mile away before my resolve dwindled. I was already getting hungry and wondering what my mother might be making for dinner. I decided I wouldn't run away, but stay away long enough to be sure they were good and worried and wouldn't make the same mistake again. Maybe I'd stay out all night. I settled down under a large white oak in an otherwise open, grassy field and closed my eyes. Then came the voice telling me to move. I opened my eyes, but there was no one there. I sat up and looked behind the tree. There was a thick smell of something like ozone and a tangible presence of something in the air. I stood up and ran home while a summer thunderstorm erupted behind me. Back at the house no one had even noticed my absence, but by then I didn't care. I'd heard God speak, and I'd obeyed.

That night, right after getting into bed, I fell into a deep, dreamless sleep, but after what I guessed was only ten or fifteen minutes, my eyes suddenly popped open. Outside the rain had stopped, and on the screen of my open bedroom window were three white moths. I thought they were beautiful, brilliant white with wings like angels. I was suddenly tired again, and I closed my eyes thinking, *Maybe they are angels. Three little angels.*

A few weeks later my brother Stephen and I were riding our bikes past the same field. It was a humid August afternoon. I was ahead of Stephen, but when I saw the oak tree, I skidded to a stop, and Stephen crashed into me.

"What's the *matter* with you?"

He glared at me as he righted his bike and dusted off his pants.

I pointed to the tree.

"So what?" he said.

The oak had been split down the middle as if with a giant celestial cleaver, and the insides were charred black.

I stood and stared.

"It got hit by lightning," said Stephen. "So what? It happens all the time."

I told Stephen about running away from home weeks earlier. About lying under the tree. About hearing the voice of God.

If it'd been anyone else, I would've kept silent. But I knew Stephen would appreciate what I was saying and not tease me about it. He'd known since he was four that he was going to become a priest. He took God stuff very seriously.

"Tell me again," he said. "And don't leave anything out."

I told him again as we walked around the base of the tree. Stephen listened like a scientist or detective searching for that one hidden clue that would reveal the truth. He ran his finger along the charcoaled innards of the tree and tasted his fingers.

"This didn't happen recently," he said. "It could've happened several weeks ago. It could've happened right after you left."

We were silent on the ride home, but as we put our bikes away in the garage, Stephen put his hand on my shoulder.

"Don't take this lightly, Thomas. Don't think this kind of thing happens to everyone. God has a plan for your life, and you better not ever forget it. I wish it had happened to me, but maybe that would have been too obvious. Maybe you needed a wake-up call."

He dropped his hand from my shoulder and stared down at his shoes. When he raised his head, I saw that his eyes were brimmed with tears.

"Don't ever forget it."

Twenty years later I was standing in the rain in front of the wrought-iron gates of an asylum in the lush forest of La Honda where my fiancée had gone to escape me and our wedding. At some point in the afternoon, the rain became heavier, and the gate guard left his booth to approach me.

"Thomas," he said. "Go home. It's almost Christmas. You've been here for weeks. What's it proved?"

I put my hands on the bars of the gate and squeezed the cold iron.

"I can't, Terry," I said. "She needs me here."

He shook his head, then reached his arm through the gate and handed me half a Reuben sandwich wrapped in waxed paper. He looked at me and turned back to his booth.

"You may be as crazy as she is," he said.

Then I heard the voice again—*Move*. It wasn't Terry. If I hadn't heard it when I was eleven, I might have wondered, but there was no question. It was the same voice. It was God. A flash of lightning lit the surrounding hills, leaving behind the dense smell of ozone. I heard Terry mutter from the warmth of his booth, "Imagine that. Lightning in December."

That night at the kitchen table in my apartment in South San Francisco, I hatched a plan to rescue Karen from the asylum where she'd cloistered herself. God's word to me was clear enough. I needed to do something. All the weeks of standing at those gates in the rain now seemed ridiculous. Despite everything Karen's doctors had told me, despite their warnings that my presence was not helpful, despite the fact that she had given orders that I not be admitted, everything had become clear. What Karen needed was not resolute patience, but action. She needed someone to *do* something. She needed me to move.

Gaining access to Karen's room was surprisingly easy. At some point as I walked unnoticed through the asylum, all my careful planning began to appear superfluous. It was Christmas Eve and almost midnight, so there was only a skeleton crew of staff on duty. I encountered no one as I slipped through a rear kitchen door, propped open by a brick for staff on cigarette breaks.

The industrial kitchen was quiet and dark, a shimmer of blue moonlight on the stainless-steel countertops. I walked down a long corridor that led to the lobby. At the receptionist's desk was an old woman who looked as if one good shout would send her into cardiac arrest. According to plan, I waited in the men's bathroom until I heard the receptionist's soft steps pass by and enter the bathroom next door. I walked to the vacant desk, typed Karen's name into the computer, and her room number appeared on the screen like a tiny constellation.

Karen's room was lit by the blue glow of her television. The flickering light bounced off the papered walls like moths. She was standing at the window staring out into the starless night. I stepped into the room silently, I thought, but Karen turned and viewed me with such apathy that for a moment I thought she'd been drugged. The room seemed void of oxygen, the walls made of thick, uncaring steel.

"What are you doing here?" she asked, not at all surprised to see me, but perhaps only a little peevish, as if I'd gone to her apartment on our wedding day and seen her in her dress before the ceremony.

"I'm here for you," I said.

Karen stared, without quite looking at me. She lapsed into Latin and delivered my final sentence with a slight flick of her hand, dismissing me.

"Acta est fabula."

Even if I hadn't known the meaning of the words, it wouldn't have mattered. Because she delivered them so void of emotion, tinted only by annoyance. Because her eyes were so blank, so empty of affection, this time there could be no room for misunderstanding.

It's all over. The drama has been acted out.

I stared at her for a moment more, still unwilling to believe we'd come to this. Karen's face was a ghostly blue, as expressionless as a stone. I turned and left as silently as I'd arrived.

Moments later I was walking away across the dark lawns of the asylum through a silken rain. I took one last look up at the third-floor window, which I believed to be her room. Even then there remained a trace of hope that she would be there, her dark silhouette waving me back, glad of my rescue.

Without even returning to my apartment, I began driving toward Montana and Perry. Without Karen, there was no reason to stay in San Francisco. Now the offer Perry had made on my wedding day seemed less like a backup plan and more like a determined course of action.

"You know where to find me," he had said, touching my shoulder and giving it a squeeze, then ducking into a cab that took him to the airport.

Because it was Christmas, almost no restaurants were open, and the food at the gas stations looked indigestible, everything waxen and withered under domes of thin plastic. So I ate nothing, my drive a self-imposed fast that further contributed to my newfound sense of clarity. At the time, this transition from one life to another seemed elementary, as if I could simply walk through a threshold from one world to another, and as I did the world behind me would vanish.

I drove through the night and passed Mount Shasta at dawn. The morning sun turned it a brilliant yellow in my rearview mirror.

Late that day, when I crossed the Columbia River at McNary Dam and entered Washington, I had one of those rare moments of clarity when the quiet solitude of the water seemed to reach up from the gentle current and beckoned all ill feeling, all anxiety to float away along the meandering curves, eventually out to sea. I left the stark ocher banks of the Columbia and drove through a universe of wheat fields lying fallow with last season's stubble and a light dusting of snow. It was desolate but also full of promise and potential. A Bible verse from my childhood kept running through my head: *The old has passed away...all things have become new.*

When I reached I-90 and turned east, the sun dipped below the horizon behind me, and the Eastern Washington desert turned phosphorescent gold. I thought about the first time I'd kissed Karen, then immediately felt guilty for faltering in my resolve, as if even thinking about her was something I'd given up for Lent.

Somewhere between Ritzville and Spokane, as the road ahead of me darkened into that awkward transition between light and dark, I pulled off the highway and crawled into the backseat. I thought I would fall right to sleep, but instead a vision of my wedding day began playing like a movie in my head, and I was too tired to fight it off.

Karen is late. As the minutes tick off the clock, there's a great deal of good-natured ribbing from Perry and my brother. We are standing in a small anteroom at the front of the church. Every few minutes I poke my head out to see if there's any indication that Karen has arrived. My father is sitting in one of the front pews looking tired, my mother's absence conspicuous. It occurs to me that this is the first time I've seen him in a church since my mother's funeral. I don't even know if he goes to church anymore. I wish Ellen weren't a bridesmaid so she could sit with him. He looks as if he's holding up all right, but it's hard to tell.

Time passes, and the joking turns awkward. When the reality can't be ignored anymore, there's nothing but silent pity. At last, when the guests can't be kept waiting any longer, someone drives to Karen's apartment and, shortly after, a solemn exodus from the church begins. I feel a strange urge to position myself at the front doors and make apologies to everyone as they leave, but my brother and Perry take my arms and lead me out a side door. My head seems full of water. The external world has suddenly taken a step back, as if I'm contagious.

As we leave the church and head for my brother's car, we pass three middle-aged men standing on the sidewalk smoking. Although I don't recognize any of them and don't know how they could have come across such information, I hear one of them say something about a wedding dress, how it's still hanging on the back of her bathroom door. They shake their heads in mock sympathy as I pass, their false pity raining down like burning hail.

Moments later I'm sitting at a bar. Perry is on one side of me, my brother on the other, both of them pretending not to watch me in the mirror behind the bartender. I rub my palms across the smooth surface of the bar and wonder what kind of wood it is. Drinks magically appear before me, and I drink them. I've entered a fog, but I'm still conscious of the pity that hovers like mist in the room. Even the bartender seems aware of my desperation and places drinks before me with tenderness. Beyond this I'm aware only of Perry's silent disapproval as I get up between drinks and call Karen's apartment from the pay phone at the back of the room. There's no anger or malice in the brief messages I leave on her machine—only weak pleadings.

I awoke freezing, my bladder full, thick frost on the car windows. The sky was black and starless as I relieved myself on the farmer's field where I'd parked hours earlier. As I peed, the strangeness of the present rose up like a cresting wave. How did I end up in this barren wheat field? I scraped the frost from the front windshield, backtracked to the highway, and again headed east.

I crossed into Montana at dawn and by midmorning had arrived in Perry's little town. A blanket of low clouds covered everything, obscuring the mountains, threatening snow. I went into a busy café and sat at the counter. A waitress with enigmatic eyes served me a plate of eggs with hash browns and toast. I watched her as I ate. There was something odd about the way she moved—graceful yet careful and intentional. Later I thought again about her eyes. I wondered if they'd been colorless or a rare deep black like onyx. Had she been beautiful? I tried to picture her face when I'd asked her about Perry's castle, but the details of her features, like a half-remembered dream, had already faded. Her voice was all that stayed with me: quiet, whispery, and delicate, as if she'd borrowed it from a bird.

"Simple," she said so quietly that I leaned closer. "Follow the signs to the ski resort. When you get to the turn for the resort, keep going straight and you'll end up at the castle."

She tilted her head.

"It's privately owned, you know. They don't do tours or anything."

"I know," I said, paying my bill. "I'm going to live there."

She cocked her head again and smiled. "Then I imagine I'll see you again."

"I imagine."

When I left the café, large, wet flakes of snow were falling. As I ascended the winding mountain road, they gradually became fine and prolific. I passed the turnoff to the ski resort, and the road narrowed. The snow became even heavier, as if the castle itself were generating the storm. I turned on my headlights and slowed to a crawl, aware at some point that it might be faster and safer if I got out and walked. I continued on for fifteen or twenty minutes. At last a huge structure darkened the horizon, and I passed through the castle's gatehouse only seconds after seeing it.

I parked in front of a carriage house and walked across a small courtyard toward the main doors of the castle. A narrow wooden footbridge crossed what at first I thought was a moat, but from the center of the bridge, I could see that it was merely an elongated pond stretching across the front of the castle, frozen now, already covered with several inches of fresh snow. Although it was only late morning, the sky was dark with the storm, and the castle itself was black and quiet; no lights inside or out.

I stood like a dwarf before the huge doors and knocked, knowing already that Perry wasn't inside. A chill wind had come up, blowing fine, icy flakes down the collar of my jacket, swirling them like dust devils around the stones at my feet. Retreating across the footbridge, I decided to walk around the castle, hoping to find an unlocked door or unlatched window. I passed through a trellised gate at the side of the carriage house and walked into a large garden bordered on three sides by a high hedge of juniper. Attached to the castle wall, there was a small stone building that served as a toolshed, and next to it, an ornate steel door that I somehow knew would be unlocked. I pushed against the cold steel and entered a long tunnel leading into the castle.

Except for the absence of the wind, it was no warmer inside than out. I jogged back to my car, fished out a flashlight from under the front seat, and returned to the tunnel. As I walked through the darkness, I thought that even if Perry had abandoned the castle, I was sure to find a bedroom with blankets and a fireplace so I could at least get some sleep before deciding where to go next.

At the end of the tunnel, I entered a huge industrial kitchen with doors leading in several directions. For a moment I was struck with a childish desire to explore, but at the same time I was aware of the damp cold that was working its way into my bones. I flipped on some light switches, but when no lights came on, I chose a hallway that looked as if it would lead to the heart of the castle.

It was a labyrinthine floor plan, but I stuck to what seemed to be major arteries. After a few minutes I pushed open a door at the end of a long hallway and walked into a dim room. It felt thirty degrees warmer than the corridor. I reached out my hand to the wall at my side and found a panel of switches. When I flipped several of them on at once, the room filled with light.

I made a cursory inspection of the room, then walked through a set of double doors into an expansive library. It seemed clear now that what had once been the great hall of the castle had been chopped up and made into Perry's apartment and this library. There was a leather sofa, the deep color of claret, in front of a large fireplace where kindling and logs had been laid. I found matches on the mantle and lit the fire, and sat down on the couch. The leather of the sofa warmed around me, and I began to feel the exhaustion I'd been holding off for weeks. I pulled a blanket from the back of the couch and fell asleep to the crackling of the fire.

When I awoke, the fire had burned down to embers, and the room was dark. I didn't know how long I'd slept, but it seemed to be sometime in the middle of the night. I got up and walked into the apartment and stood in front of a set of french doors that led off the kitchen. When I flipped on an exterior floodlight, a flagstone patio and the edge of an empty swimming pool appeared in the waxen light. It was still snowing. The wind was blowing the flagstones clean in some places, leaving silvery piles and drifts of snow in protected corners and pockets. Occasionally the wind howled around a corner of the building in a low, personified moan.

I knew Perry hadn't been gone long because everything I found in the refrigerator was fresh: salami, gorgonzola and pepper-jack cheese, kalamata olives, even pâté. I made myself a turkey sandwich and hoped that Perry was out fishing and not in the hospital.

After throwing another log on the fire, I slumped back on the couch and ate the sandwich while I stared into the flames. It occurred to me that the long sleep I'd just experienced had been dreamless. I hadn't slept well for weeks, my nights plagued by dreams of failed weddings, failed rescue operations, failed everything. I wondered if it was exhaustion, or some power the castle possessed, that had unburdened me. I watched the flames lick over the logs and let my mind go blank—something else I'd not been able to accomplish for a long time. I wondered what kind of bargain I would have to strike, and with whom, to keep this state of mind indefinitely. What a warm comfort it would be to think nothing, to know nothing, to remember nothing.

When I awoke again, the room was filled with shrill morning

sunlight, and Perry was sitting in a nearby chair watching me. He waited for me to sit up and rub my hands over my face before saying, "So you finally came to your senses."

There was a hint of self-satisfaction in his voice. Perry was kind and one of the most generous people I'd ever known. There was a childlike vulnerability to him that was refreshing, but there was also a stoic reserve, a holding back. I felt an overwhelming assurance that I'd made the right decision in coming to the castle.

Perry watched me with a flicker of amusement in his dark eyes. He was wearing thick wool pants and a turtleneck that looked as if it might swallow his head. His face was tanned and leathery from years of playing hard in wind and sun. It didn't look like the face of someone who was dying.

I rubbed my eyes and said the only thing that came to mind. "What time is it?"

Then from the kitchen came the smell of percolating coffee.

*P*erry had two mythically large Rottweilers. After he died I learned he'd written them into his will. On that second morning at the castle, after breakfast, I stood at the french doors and looked out at the dogs on the patio. They were huddled up close to the glass, their eyes narrowed against the blowing snow. They'd spent the last three days with Perry at a nearby mountain lake, lying side by side on the wind-blown ice while Perry fished. Now they seemed to be thinking that they'd paid their dues and someone should have compassion and let them in, even if it wasn't normally the practice.

Perry had gone back to sleep, so instead of letting them in, I put on one of his jackets and stepped outside. The dogs stood up and sniffed at my pants. When I started across the patio, they fell in step behind me. They seemed to think that whatever the weather, taking a walk was better than staring into a warm room.

I walked around the empty pool. Dead leaves and debris were locked into the ice at the bottom. A low stone wall bordered the patio. I leaped over it, and the dogs followed. We walked through a small grove of cottonwoods to the tall stone wall that surrounded the bordering convent—Perry's only neighbor for miles. As we began to follow the wall, the dogs ran ahead. They would come back periodically to make sure I was still following, then race ahead again. The sky had cleared, and the new-fallen snow was dry, squeaking like a child's toy under my boots with each step.

Even with the fresh snow, I could make out a faint path or deer trail that looked as if it might circle the entire convent. The dogs were familiar with it, so I let them guide me.

The convent wall was made of porous stone, lichened and worn, rising ten or twelve feet from the ground. We left the glade of cottonwoods and entered a thick fir forest where the snow was only a dusting on the trail. Later, when we emerged from the woods, we came into a clearing that looked out over the valley floor. Because of the storm the day before, I hadn't realized how far up the mountain we were. Looking at the lake below, I experienced a moment of vertigo, as it seemed to drop away, diminished through the unclouded space. The small town on its south shore, where I'd eaten breakfast the day before, was nothing more than a handful of spilled bread crumbs on a fresh white carpet. To the east on the neighboring peak, slightly higher than ours, I could see the ski resort, its runs distinct scars etched down its face, but the skiers merely downward spiraling dust motes.

One of my first dates with Karen had been to a small resort in the mountains above Boulder, Colorado, where Karen and I were attending grad school. I awoke that morning to a foot of fresh snow, and with only one class that day and nothing to teach, I called her and suggested we skip our classes and go skiing.

It was early enough in our relationship that we hadn't yet kissed. I remember this because all day I longed to kiss her. I was already infatuated. Otherwise I might have noticed the red flags she threw up. Red flags I ignored—or never saw—that said wait, slow down, I can't and won't do this.

I know I began to love her that day, to love her independence, her bravado, her intelligence, her devil-may-care attitude, her disregard for convention, her motivation to succeed. I'd only learn in stages that at the root of all her personality traits was an intense harbored anger.

* * *

For lunch Karen and I sit outside the lodge at a picnic table. The snow has stopped, the clouds are beginning to dissipate, and streaks of sun are lighting up patches of the mountain like spotlights. I've brought along a cooler of cheese, bread, and salami. Because we've ascended several thousand feet from town, when Karen opens the mustard, it explodes onto her face and hair. I laugh, but it's apparent that I shouldn't have. My laughter has injured her. I want to wipe the flecks of mustard from her cheeks and hair, lick my fingers clean, and make some advance in our intimacy, but I'm not willing to risk her wrath. I'm afraid of losing any of the precious ground I've gained over the past weeks.

The rest of the day I try to atone by backing off a little, but in truth, Karen gives me little opportunity to do anything else. She takes advantage of her superior skiing ability and disappears down the mountain seconds after getting off the lift, no longer even waiting for me at trail junctions. I find her at the base of the lift, already in line, holding my spot—somewhat reluctantly—and we ascend through the dissipating clouds in silence.

On the drive home, however, after drinking beer in the lodge, I sense a degree of forgiveness. Karen roots through the tapes in my glove box, teasing me about my terrible taste in music.

"Billy Joel?"

She tosses the tape over her shoulder into the backseat.

"This is something we're going to have to work on."

I'm happy beyond measure that she's willing to work on one of my character flaws.

She puts in some Tracy Chapman and sings along. I can't help smiling. To me her ridicule is like flirting.

Over the following weeks, as we spend more time together, this dichotomy in Karen's personality becomes more apparent. There are clear signs of progress, sweet moments of vulnerability, adolescent flirtings, but then, often, an almost immediate withdrawal tainted with animosity and resentment, as if she's already aware of an inevitable betrayal. But if anything, this complexity makes her even more desirable.

During my reverie, the dogs sat patiently at my feet. When at last I made a move to go, they leaped up and raced along the convent wall.

As we circled back toward the castle, I realized how large the convent must be. I guessed that the wall might be over a mile around and the grounds inside enormous. Then it occurred to me that, so far, I hadn't encountered a gate or door or any way to get in or out. But moments later, as the castle's main tower came into view above a row of colossal spruce trees, I neared a pair of wrought-iron gates, as if my mere thinking of them had caused them to appear. I expected there would be some sort of plaque announcing the name of the convent and the order of the nuns, but there was nothing. Even the view from the gate was unrevealing. The winding road onto the grounds was bordered on both sides by tall arborvitae, and nothing was visible beyond the second sharp bend. The dogs sniffed at the base of the gate and whined.

But as I turned to leave, I looked up at the rock archway above the gates, and noticed the words *A Cruce Salus* etched into the stone. I suddenly had trouble taking a full breath. It wasn't the meaning of the words that affected me, because I'd never seen them before, but the language itself.

Latin. It was Karen's language. It was the language that had brought us together but now could do nothing but remind me of our failure.

* * *

I meet her in the foreign-language department where I've gone on other business. She's arguing with the department head, both of her hands flat on the counter. I'm immediately taken by her. It's not her physical beauty, although she is pretty in a boyish, simple way. What I'm taken by is her composure. I realize from the start that she's full of self-confidence approaching arrogance—someone who knows she's smarter than everyone around her and yet knows she's stuck in a world in which she has to play by other people's rules.

I walk up behind her as the argument continues. The Latin class she was supposed to teach has been canceled because no one has signed up. She's making a plea for an extension, asking how many students she needs.

"Just one," says the department head. "It's a fellowship position. The funds are there, but you have to have at least one student."

I step up next to her, and a secretary asks if she can help me. I tell her I'm there to sign up for Latin.

Karen turns and smiles, suspicion flooding her eyes. I glance at her, then turn to the form I've been given and start filling it out.

"Well," says the man Karen's been arguing with, "there you are."

All week I'm anxious for our first class, imagining myself alone in a room with her as she chalks ancient, unknown words and phrases on the blackboard, revealing in her dry voice their mystery. But it never happens.

The week before our first class, Karen appears at my office door in the low-ceilinged attic of the English building. She leans against the doorjamb, holding several notebooks and a file folder against her chest.

"How do your students find you up here?" she asks.

"Some never do," I say.

She narrows her eyes and looks around the room. I don't think she approves of my office.

"I came by to tell you I drummed up some recruits for my class. So you're free to drop it."

I cock my head, but I already know she's got me figured out. Knowing how weak it will sound, I say, "But I want to take your class."

Karen smiles. "You might change your mind if you had all the information."

"Like what?"

"Like I never date my students."

When I returned from my walk around the convent, Perry was still asleep, so I decided to explore a little on my own. From the gates of the convent, the main tower of the castle had caught my eye, rising high above the battlements. It appeared to stand adjacent to the apartment, situated near one of its interior corners.

I stepped into the dark hallway where I'd first entered the apartment and found a thick oak doorway that led to the stairs of the tower. I climbed the spiral steps in the darkness and stopped at a landing where there was another door. I checked the door, but it was locked. I continued up to the next landing where there was yet another door, but it was also locked. Beyond this there were no more doors, but the stairs ascended through several more rooms within the tower itself. These were mostly empty, although some had been used for the storage of broken or unwanted furniture, boxes of old magazines, chests of yellowed clothing. There were narrow windows throughout the tower. Whenever I came across one, I looked out. I gained views of the lake on the valley floor, the neighboring ski mountain, and the range of mountains to the south, but the windows were never in quite the right position to see into the interior of the convent, which was what I was most interested in.

The uppermost room of the tower was empty, except for a rocking chair facing one of the windows. I sat down and looked out over a sea of snow-covered mountains, range upon range, one behind the other, finally disappearing into a haze that I imagined was over Canada. I wondered which of Perry's relatives had sat in this chair and looked out across the same ocean of mountains. His Canadian grandfather, nostalgic about what he'd left behind? His grandmother, longing to return home? Maybe his mother or father, bored with the parties and missing the civilized world? Or perhaps Perry himself, gazing out onto another country, another ethereal world, wondering what would come next?

As I descended through the darkness of the tower, I reasoned that Perry's apartment, with all its windows and light, lay just on the other side of the tower's wall. The apartment was a bright cocoon of warmth in an otherwise cold and abandoned monument of stone. At one time his family had used the entire castle. But over the years, as its vastness became daunting and the heating costs impractical, rooms and eventually entire wings were closed up. Finally his own father had turned the great hall into what was now Perry's apartment, shutting off power to the rest of the castle. The castle's history was such a fitting metaphor for Perry's life that I thought it appropriate to the point of comfort that he had come here to die.

That night before dinner, Perry led me down a narrow stone stairway to the basement. When he turned on the lights, I saw that the walls were lined with rough-hewn timber racks filled with hundreds of bottles of wine. While Perry searched for a bottle, I strayed across the dirt floor and discovered that one wall of the basement was covered with rows of small doors fastened with heavy brass hardware.

"What are these?"

Perry joined me, a bottle of wine dangling from each hand, and with no inflection whatsoever said, "Catacombs."

I looked at him to see if he might be joking.

"Graves?" I asked. "You mean your ancestors are buried here?"

"As far as I know, they're all empty," said Perry. "I'll be the first Palmer to be buried here. Probably the last."

I looked at him again but saw nothing to indicate that he wasn't serious. This is the way Perry could be. He didn't always make things easy. There was a new awkwardness between us, like old lovers who split for a time and have now decided to give it another try. How long before the awkwardness dissipates? How long do you sleep in separate beds? How long before you can again attempt intimacy? As we went back up to the apartment, I wondered at Perry's remark, wondered if it might be an invitation, a handful of crumbs extended to coax something nearer.

Back upstairs I sat at the kitchen bar and opened a bottle of Margaux while Perry filleted a large whitefish he'd caught the day before. He laid it on a sheet of parchment paper and began dicing an onion. I wondered if over the next few weeks we would confide in each other or if we would choose to live together perpetually surrounded by our own aloneness.

I watched as Perry sautéed fennel, onion, and garlic in a skillet. I wondered if it mattered. What difference would it make? Perry was dying. Nothing was going to change that. Why not eat, drink, and be merry until the end? Maybe the best thing we could do for each other was simply be present.

Perry had introduced me to cooking. In college he'd taught me to make bacon (the secret to good bacon is slow cooking). Later he taught me how to make a Thai curry, a decent martini, then sushi.

He went to the liquor cabinet and added a splash of Pernod to the skillet. Then he poured the mixture over the fish, sealed it in the parchment paper, and placed it in the oven.

After dinner we took the remaining wine to the library and sat in front of the fire.

"So how're you holding up?" I asked.

He took a long sip of wine and stared into the fire.

"Physically or emotionally?"

"Both, I guess."

For a long time he stared into the fire. When he spoke he seemed to be concentrating on each word.

"It's an interesting thing, knowing that you're dying. It's both a curse and a gift. But it's not a matter of choosing to think of it as one or the other. It's both. All the time."

He took a drink of wine and smiled. "Do you believe in ghosts?"

I looked at him, then into the fire. "I don't know."

"It might be nice to have a few around. So the place didn't feel so empty. Before you came, I sometimes wished the place were haunted."

"You've never seen a ghost?"

"No," said Perry. "The only ghosts in this castle are the ones you bring with you."

It was Perry's grandfather who'd come to Montana from Canada and used his life savings to buy thousands of acres of land at $1.25 an acre. Later, when the railroad came through, he made his fortune. The castle had been built for Perry's grandmother, probably in an attempt to appease her. She missed Canada and was always threatening to return. She hated the castle and spent only one summer there before carrying out her threat, telling her husband that she was going home and he could follow if he wished. He stood his ground for another six months, but in the end the staff was let go and he returned to Canada.

For years afterward, the castle was used as a vacation house. After his grandfather died, Perry and his father and mother spent entire summers there. His father was an editor for a publishing house in Boston and his mother was an English professor at Radcliffe. Perry's primary memories of those summers were of the extravagant parties his parents threw. Almost every weekend guests would arrive: writers, literary agents, other editors, and sometimes people who, as far as Perry could tell, had no connection with publishing or education. They didn't even appear to be friends. For days the castle would be alive with voices and laughter. From late afternoon each day when the guests appeared from their rooms until early into the morning, the castle was transformed into a living thing, a beast that possessed all the sordidness and vulnerability of a real creature.

Perry would awaken each day and leave his room to explore, anticipating what new mystery of human nature he might discover. He once walked into an open bedroom and saw a naked woman lying face down on the bed, her ankles tangled in the sheets. On the back of her thigh was a tattoo of a rainbow trout. More than her naked-ness, the trout aroused Perry's curiosity. He stepped to the side of the bed and reached out to touch it, but when he heard a man clearing his throat in the bathroom, he turned and ran.

Another time, early in the morning, Perry ventured into the ball-room where there'd been dancing the night before. The polished par-quet floor was dotted with cocktail napkins and the occasional errant pistachio. The pale light in the room was flaxen. At the far end of the hall was a man about his father's age standing in front of a tall win-dow, watching the sunrise.

He seemed at peace. When he turned and saw Perry, his face didn't show any surprise. He smiled and then looked as if he'd just remembered something important and left the room. It didn't seem strange to Perry at the time that the man had had a revolver in his hand. Years passed before Perry realized that the man had been planning to kill himself, and Perry had interrupted.

Then, as suddenly as they'd come, the guests would go, and the castle would again become an uninhabited shell. Were it not for the dirty martini glasses left on nightstands and the occasional personal item forgotten under a bed, Perry would have thought he'd dreamed those parties.

"Of course," Perry told me, "I may have been drunk myself much of the time. There was never a shortage of half-full glasses of champagne and scotch left forgotten on almost any available surface. My parents were always far too busy and drunk themselves to keep tabs on me. So it makes sense it would all seem a dream."

At some point the parties ended, and entire wings of the castle were sealed up. Then one spring Perry's father had the great hall converted into an apartment and the library. The sprawling rose garden was uprooted to make room for the pool and patio, and the rest of the castle was forgotten.

Not long after this, during the summer Perry turned sixteen, his father's publishing company moved the family to Europe, and for years the castle sat empty. Perry returned to the States two years later to attend college, and that's where our two histories converged.

But something had happened in Europe. Something I was never told. There'd been a falling out, an estrangement. I was sure Perry's parents knew that he was living in the castle. They were aware of his illness. But as far as I knew, they hadn't spoken to him in years.

When I awoke the next morning, the room was light. I was still lying on my back, just as I'd fallen asleep. I didn't think I'd moved all night.

I marveled at how rested I felt. I lay still and felt the warmth and plushness of the bed around me. My body felt heavy, almost drugged. I moved a finger and scratched a spot on my thigh. From deep below my room came the distinct smell of frying bacon, and I thought, *Slow cooking.*

Another morning. Again the weighty, narcotic feeling of deep, uninterrupted sleep. Again the smell of frying bacon. I tried to think how long it had been since I came to the castle. Three days? A week? Several weeks? How many times had I walked around the convent with the dogs? How many bottles of wine had Perry and I drunk? How many meals had we shared?

I looked at the ornate wrought-iron handle of the heavy door of the bedroom, and it didn't seem unfamiliar. I had none of the detached feelings you experience in a hotel room in which all the objects seem foreign.

Downstairs I sat at the kitchen bar as Perry slid a plate of bacon and eggs in front of me.

"Happy New Year's," he said.

Later that day I was standing at a window in the library, the book I'd been reading dangling in my hand. A soft snow was falling outside. A pair of red-shafted flickers chased each other from spruce to spruce through the dimming afternoon light. I was startled by the ringing of a telephone. It was the first time I'd heard it.

Moments later Perry appeared at the door and held out the phone with a look on his face that said, *Who knows you're here?*

A picture of Karen swept into my head. An image of her standing in the lobby of the asylum dressed in a hat and scarf and long coat belted at the waist. There are two identical suitcases at her feet. She stands with her feet together, the phone to her ear, and waits for me to come on the line.

When I didn't move, Perry came to me, the phone extended like a foreign object. It took me a moment to understand who I was talking to—it was the rector at the Episcopal church where my brother worked. The room fell away for a moment while he talked. I found myself clutching the neck of a nearby floor lamp. I held the phone to my ear mechanically and gave habitual responses. Outside the flickers had alighted on the ground. I remember thinking how odd it was to see a flicker on the ground and tried to think whether I'd ever seen it before.

"There's a letter here addressed to you," I heard through the phone. "If there's anything I can do…"

I spoke without breathing, managed to ask about Mary and Catherine, and thanked him for calling. I told him I'd be on the next flight to Seattle, and I let the phone drop.

I turned around and saw that Perry was still in the room.

"My brother's dead," I said. "Apparently he killed himself."

I turned back to the window. Outside the flickers were pecking at something ashen in the snow. Something moved at the edge of my vision, and I saw one of Perry's Rottweilers crawling beneath a hedge, stalking the flicker. Time stopped, everything frozen in tableau. Suddenly the dog leaped back into time, and I was sure he'd catch the bird, but in a burst of powdery snow, it rose straight up to the sky, unscathed, like a phoenix.

*M*y perception of Seattle winters is that at some point every fall, a chill rain begins to mist from the sky and continues unabated until the Fourth of July. The sun makes only a handful of appearances, enough to remind everyone that they don't live in hell, merely earth's most accurate facsimile. But when my plane landed in the darkness at Sea-Tac, a loud crashing rain was pummeling the skylights of the airport. Outside, taxis and shuttles pushed through inches of standing water, approaching the curbside like gondolas on the canals of Venice. The wind was blowing so fiercely, so willfully, that I couldn't help thinking of it as personified—the wrath of an angry god bent on vengeance. People scurried to vehicles like frightened animals, bent at the waist, shielding their eyes with newspapers and forearms. As my taxi pulled away from the curb, I saw several women holding their dresses pinched between their knees, their hair blown and matted across their faces.

It was after midnight when I arrived at my hotel. Without even brushing my teeth, I undressed and fell into the king-size bed. But the moment I closed my eyes, my thoughts began to spin like a pinwheel, unprotected even here from the gusty storm.

I thought about Stephen sitting in his idling car in his garage. What do you think about when you know you're about to die? It was nothing more than a coincidence, but for me it certainly didn't help that my brother had chosen the same method of self-destruction as Karen's mother.

Of course I recognized what a selfish thought this was. Wasn't

Stephen thinking of me when he decided how he was going to kill himself? But I supposed I should be allowed a little selfishness. Wasn't Stephen being selfish? What is suicide if not the ultimate act of thinking solely of yourself?

But the key difference between Karen's mother's suicide and my brother's was that my brother had placed no one else in danger, so perhaps he'd shown concern for someone other than himself. Karen's mother, on the other hand, came very close to taking the entire family with her.

Sprawled in the king-size bed, I massaged my temples and tried to push away the storm of thoughts, but like ripples in a pond, they grew in ever-widening circles. I got up and drank three miniatures of scotch from the minibar and lay back down. I could hear the dull murmur of a television coming from the room next door and tried to decipher what they were watching. I'd decided it was a late news program when I heard three distinct gunshots followed by the shrill whine of a siren.

When at last I fell asleep, I dreamed of the night Karen's mother killed herself. Karen had spoken of it only once and hadn't provided many details, but in my dream everything was vivid, as if the whole thing were a well-crafted story.

I'm a ghost wandering through a dark split-level house in a suburb of Denver. Everyone in the house is in bed. I wander up a half flight of stairs and enter a bedroom where Karen is sleeping. She's twelve and still sleeps with a doll, something I realize even in the dream that she would now consider weakness. Her breathing is heavy, and there's something strange about her face that I can't quite define, but then I realize she's happy, perhaps for the last time in her life. I reach out and touch her face, pushing aside some strands of hair that have fallen across her cheek.

Then the pace of the dream quickens, taking on a sudden urgency. Without walking there, I'm back in the hallway. Karen's mother walks past, her body partially passing through me. My heartbeat accelerates, knowing what she plans to do but also aware that I'm of another world, viewing things that have already happened. I have no powers of persuasion. I follow her to the garage, where, without any hesitation, she gets behind the wheel of a station wagon and starts the engine.

She sits there for some time, her hands on the wheel, staring ahead at the garage door. Realizing that the process will take longer than she expected, she turns on the radio and inserts an eight-track tape. The soft drone of "The Red River Valley" fills the garage, and I watch as she drifts off, not yet knowing if this is fatigue or the lethargic effects of the carbon monoxide.

I feel a certain peace watching her sleep. The eight-track changes tracks in the middle of the song, and I'm aware that the car's fumes are traveling through the ventilation system to the rest of the house. I go back to the bedrooms and am able to watch simultaneously as Karen and her two brothers and father begin to toss in their beds, their faces etched with discomfort. An hour seems to pass. Though in waking life I'm aware of the actual outcome of these events, in the dream I'm convinced that the whole family is already in their deathbeds.

At last Karen's youngest brother wakes up, rubbing his face with the palms of his hands. He goes to the bathroom and pees, squinting at the bright light, then goes to his father's bedside and begins shaking his shoulder. When the father wakes and asks what's wrong, the boy finds it difficult to speak. He only wants to crawl into his parents' bed and go to sleep. He manages to mumble that he has a headache and, when he does, the father realizes he has one too.

Karen's father notices that his wife is not in bed and, already suspecting what has happened, begins throwing open the windows and rousing the other children.

"What are you doing?" Karen asks her father, annoyed at being awakened in the middle of the night and having a headache on top of it.

"Go outside," he says. By the tone of his voice, she knows she must obey. She also knows that the whole family has passed in their sleep through an unnamable threshold, that everything in their lives will now be divided by this night into before and after.

When I awoke, the events of the dream were so fresh in my mind, so vivid, that it took me awhile to recollect that it was my brother who had just killed himself, not Karen's mother. I showered and dressed, then called my brother's church and arranged a meeting with the rector (he insisted I call him John) who'd called me the afternoon before. It took a few minutes of speaking to his secretary, who I thought was rather blundering, before he came on the line.

"Sorry," he said. "You gave my secretary a shock."

"How's that?" I asked.

"It's just that when she first heard your voice, she thought for a moment that it was Stephen."

"I see," was all I could think to say.

"I'm sorry," he said after a long silence. "Over the phone you're the spitting image."

"Wait till you see me," I said.

Next I called Stephen's wife, Mary, and told her I'd be by to see her later that morning. I asked if there was anything I could bring.

"No," she said. "I can't think of anything we need. We're fine."

Meaning, I knew, that there was nothing I could provide by stopping at a store on the way. Nothing that could be bought or acquired, nothing at all I could bring that would in any way make a difference.

"It'll be good to see you," she said before hanging up.

"You, too," I said, but I could think of nothing good about it.

As I stood beneath the hotel's canopy, waiting for the doorman to hail me a taxi, I was relieved to notice that the night's storm had passed and had been replaced by the relentless misting rain synonymous for me with winter in Seattle. I stuck my hand out from beneath the canopy and let the rain hit my palm, but it was hardly rain at all, more like a thousand invisible fairies dancing on my skin, their pirouetting feet wet with morning dew.

Although we were two years apart, Stephen and I were often mistaken for twins. When we got older and both grew mustaches, it became even harder for people to tell us apart. I saw this faux twinship as an arena of opportunity, especially when we attended the same college, but Stephen was far too moral to have anything to do with a deception, no matter how innocent it may have seemed.

Once, however, we used it to our advantage, and to my delight at the time, it had been mostly Stephen's idea.

It's the beginning of a new semester. I return from lunch one day to find Stephen standing in my dorm room holding a textbook I've bought for a class in natural science. I don't have any interest in the class, but it looks like the easiest way to fulfill my science requirement.

"You taking this class?" he asks.

"Under protest."

I guess that he's taking the class too and figures we can save money by sharing the textbook, but what he has in mind is much better. He proposes that we take turns attending the class. By taking notes in a single notebook, we can study together for tests and pass the course by attending half the sessions. Because it's a large class and the professor is on exchange from Hong Kong, it seems likely to work. And it does. The only hitch is that Stephen ends up getting a C in the class, and I a B. He feigns annoyance with me for weeks, complaining that my notes weren't as good as his.

So I wasn't surprised when I stepped into the church secretary's office and she screamed. Later, when we'd situated ourselves at a small sitting area in his office, Father John had to apologize a second time for his secretary, but again he felt obliged to mention that the resemblance was uncanny. He offered coffee, but I declined, afraid that the secretary would be asked to bring it.

I thought I had dozens of questions, but I was only able to ask the most obvious—"Do you have any idea why Stephen might have wanted to take his own life?"—before the meeting was abbreviated by the production of the letter, something I had somehow forgotten.

Father John's eyes narrowed as he withdrew the envelope from his breast pocket. He handed it to me and said, "Actually, we were hoping you might be able to tell us."

I studied the envelope, turning it over in my hands as if the exterior might reveal something. After a moment John said, "He left that on his office desk. No one else knows about it. I thought you should see it first, but I'm sure the police will want to have a look at it as well."

"Of course," I said, but his words were above my head, and I wasn't even sure what I was agreeing to.

We sat there for a few more minutes, a tangible anticipation growing in the room, as if we were children at play winding the handle of a jack-in-the-box, knowing what was about to happen, but not knowing when. And yet we both knew that I wouldn't open the letter there.

In fact, when I returned to my hotel room later that evening, I still hadn't opened the letter. It fell to the floor when I threw my coat over the back of a chair, and I realized that I'd again forgotten it. Although *forgotten* isn't entirely accurate. All afternoon at Mary's, I'd known it was there, but I thought if I refused to acknowledge it, it might go away. I was reminded of a time in Colorado when I'd done the same thing.

Karen and I have only been seeing each other for a month the first time she breaks up with me. Although we've decided to keep our relationship discreet inside the grad school, it is at an English department function that she chooses to do it. It's a going-away party for one of the department secretaries who's getting married and moving east. Although we've come to the party together, once there we part ways, not wanting to arouse suspicion. I'm in a bad mood because my class that morning went poorly—the discussion never got off the ground, and none of the students bothered to read the assignment.

At some point Karen walks up to me and whispers in my ear.

"We have to talk."

Something about her eyes has changed, and I know she wants to break up.

For the rest of the party, I either avoid her or surround myself with others so she never has the opportunity to get me alone. It's avoidance of the worst kind. I convince myself that if she can't say it, she can't do it.

I did the same thing with Stephen's letter. The whole afternoon at Mary's had a dreamlike quality to it. I didn't feel present, more as if I was walking through a memory. On the drive over I passed a stranded motorist and for a moment considered stopping. Stephen would have stopped. Stephen was addicted to helping people in trouble. He was always on the lookout for broken-down cars or hitchhikers. He seemed to have the ability to attract them with a mysterious sort of magnetism. Mary used to accuse him of inventing errands on the weekends so that he could drive around and find someone with a steaming radiator or a flat tire.

When I got to Mary's, a woman I didn't know opened the door and said, "Oh, God!" then took a step backward. Her reaction dominoed through the half-dozen other faces in the room until Mary appeared and led me inside by the arm. She kissed me on the lips, something she always did very naturally but I'd never quite gotten used to. This time, however, I thought I noticed an instant of hesitation, a gram of effort behind her kiss.

No one else in the room was capable of subtlety. Mary led me to the dining room where a table of lunch meats had been arranged. She introduced me to people along the way, and none of them were able to mask the shock that registered on their faces. After being introduced to one woman, I distinctly heard her say "Lord God" under her breath.

All afternoon a constant parade of people wandered in and out of the house, the casseroles stacking up on the kitchen table and countertops like rubble at a demolition site. I eventually ended up alone with Catherine in her room, both of us seeking sanctuary from the reek of empathy that filled the rest of the house. I couldn't see how Mary was doing it.

Of course Catherine was unaffected by the likeness I bore to her father. I suppose that's why I sought refuge with her. We sat on the floor of her room and built a castle out of LEGOs.

"I live in a castle," I said.

She didn't look up from the bridge she was building over the imaginary moat.

"You were supposed to get married."

"Yes, I was."

"Life isn't always fair, is it?"

"No. I guess it's not."

I watched her working on her bridge, and we didn't say anything else for a while. I went back to adding machicolations to the top of the curtain wall. I didn't have much of a relationship with Catherine, but I'd always gotten the impression that she was smart beyond her years. She often had a knowing look on her face, the hint of a smile that let you know she knew more than she was letting on. I wondered what was going through her head just now. How does a little girl make sense of the death of her father?

"How old are you?" I asked as she was putting the finishing touches on the tower.

"You're not a very good uncle, are you?" she asked.

"Nine," I said.

"Lucky guess. When's my birthday?"

Normally I wouldn't have gotten this one, but Catherine had been born on December 31, near midnight. I remember the jokes Stephen and I had made about his getting the tax break for the year. But when I recited her birth date, I realized I hadn't sent a present. Catherine looked at me. She'd been waiting for this realization. She shook her head and went back to work on the castle, as if to say, "Uh-huh, I thought so."

It struck me that my brother had waited until the day after Catherine's birthday, until the first day of the new year, to kill himself. All over the country people were waking up with hangovers, and yet with a vague optimism, that clean-slate feeling for the year ahead. And my brother was dead behind the wheel of his idling car in the garage he had built the summer before, unable to wipe his slate clean, unable to bear another year of contradiction.

* * *

I left Stephen's letter on the floor where it had fallen, while I took a bath in a tub I could have shared with a manatee. As I soaked, Catherine's words "You're not a very good uncle, are you?" kept replaying in my head. This heartbreaking statement should have filled me with a resolve to be a better uncle, to be the best uncle a girl ever had. Instead, I was overcome with a weary feeling of defeat, which only strengthened my resolve to jettison my old life, disappear within the walls of the castle, and resume a cloistered existence. If Catherine couldn't have a good uncle, then better no uncle at all.

When I climbed into bed, I took the letter with me. On the outside of the envelope Stephen, in his efficient handwriting, had written: *For my brother, Thomas.* I opened it and read with an odd tranquillity, the way I might read a recipe or an interesting article, not in the frame of mind that one would normally read a suicide note.

Dear Brother,

Let me tell you a story. Several years ago a young man from my parish came to me for counseling. Although his dilemma was simple, I believe my counsel was quite astute. Sitting in my office with his head bowed, rarely meeting my eyes, he seemed shy, or shamed. He told me that for the last six months, he and his girlfriend had been sleeping together ("Going all the way," I think, was the phrase he used), and it was causing him intense feelings of guilt. He believed that premarital sex was a sin, and yet he continued; thus the problem.

    I told him that one of two things would soon happen—that beliefs and behavior cannot be at odds with each other for too long. Eventually he would either change his behavior or (much

more likely, I told him) he would stop believing that what he was
doing was wrong.

I didn't realize then that there was a third option for
resolving such a dilemma, the one, of course, that I've chosen
for myself.

Thomas, I don't know if it's possible to be born into a voca-
tion. If it is, then I've certainly been a priest since I took my
first lungful of air in that Baltimore hospital. I know you'll not
argue with that. I think you've always understood that it's not
just what I do, but who I am.

So I hope you will also understand the impasse I've come
to. How can I be a priest and not believe in God? Are you
shocked? Probably not. I know that Mother's death has caused
all of us to wrestle with what all our lives we've been taught and
shown and seen for ourselves to be the truth—a foundation of
stone that has now crumbled.

If I weren't a priest, I might have other options. You and
Ellen and Father can amend your belief system, rearranging it
so that it doesn't include God. That's not possible for me. I'm a
priest, and a priest must believe in God. I ask your forgiveness,
but there are no other roads for me to follow.

I leave it to you to discern who should have the information
contained in this letter. It might help some; for others it might
only make things worse. I know you'll be able to tell the difference.

Your brother,

Stephen

The next morning I awoke feeling disoriented. My sleep had been
riddled with fragmented dreams, and for the rest of the morning, I
tried to sort out dream from reality. I got dressed and ordered coffee

and scones from room service, then decided to take a quick shower, even though I'd bathed the night before.

When my breakfast came I opened the door to a porter. He was talking with a chambermaid standing across the hall next to her metal cart stacked with linens. They'd been laughing at something (I thought perhaps me), but when I appeared they stopped. The chambermaid's face turned sorrowful. She dropped her eyes and picked up some bed linens from her cart. The porter held out the tray and said, "Your breakfast," but I thought he said it with a good deal of pity, as if it was common knowledge that the rest of the hotel's guests would be breakfasting at the huge buffet downstairs, but this pitiful offering of coffee and scones alone in my room was the best I could manage.

I drank the coffee by the window at a table that had a map of Seattle under its glass top. It struck me what a fragmented city Seattle was: Kirkland, Bellevue, Renton, Kent, even Federal Way. They all fell loosely under the heading "Seattle," connected by a maze of highways and ramps, having their own separate identities but creating no cohesive whole. It had a feeling of messiness and vulnerability. There was no safe center, no refuge anywhere. Nothing but a random smattering of buildings and highways filled to capacity with cars and people, none of it having any purpose.

It was in this frame of mind that I called Ellen to tell her that our brother had killed himself. I'd tried her once from the airport, right before getting on the plane, but her message said that she was in the Hamptons with friends for the holiday and wouldn't be back until the second. This time, after only one ring, she picked up.

She was out of breath. I imagined she'd just come in the door.

"Thomas?" she said.

Her voice had that quizzical-yet-concerned tone. I saw her standing in the corner of her spacious New York loft, tilting her head, a mannerism she had that conveyed "That's odd," no matter what she was saying. I could almost hear her thinking, *Well, what a surprise. I haven't heard from you since your wedding, or nonwedding, or aborted wedding...*

"What's the occasion?" was all she actually said.

I hadn't planned what I was going to say. "I'm in Seattle."

"What are you doing there?"

It occurred to me that Ellen knew nothing about my life. I thought it might help to bring her up to date but realized that no context would soften the blow of Stephen's suicide.

"I don't know how to tell you this, so I'll just say it. Stephen's dead. He killed himself."

I heard Ellen put the phone down and walk away. I imagined she'd gone to her window and was looking out over the serrated skyline of the city. After several minutes her voice came back on the line.

"Tell me what to do. I don't know what to do."

*M*y father, quite a good chess player himself, was a devoted Bobby Fischer fan. I remember how often dinner conversations would turn to Bobby and his latest superhuman chess feat. Because of my father's gift for detail and repetition, for years I almost believed I'd been to Herceg Novi, Yugoslavia, where Bobby Fischer won the World Speed Chess Championship in 1970. Even today I can lie in bed at night and close my eyes and see Fischer after the tournament, reciting to a reporter from memory, in order, every move of the more than one thousand from his twenty-two games. And although it happened before I was born, I will always associate Kennedy's assassination not with the loss of a great president but with the postponement of Fischer's exhibition at the Astor Hotel, where he was to simultaneously play (and defeat, according to my father) four hundred opponents. And then, in a home that was alcohol-free, I remember the night in 1972, when I was seven years old, when my father produced a bottle of champagne and poured glasses for all of us. It was, of course, the night we learned that Bobby Fischer had defeated Boris Spassky in Reykjavik, Iceland, for the world title.

My own fascination with Bobby Fischer had more to do with his disappearance in 1975 than with his chess-playing coups. After a dispute over how the world-title tournament had been conducted, Fischer forfeited the title, and it was awarded to the Russian challenger Anatoly Karpov. After that, Bobby withdrew from the world of chess (and, as far as anyone knew, from the world itself) for seventeen years, until he reappeared in 1992 and challenged his rival Spassky to a rematch, a match that Fischer won.

I'm not sure what is at the root of my fascination with disappearing, but it's a fascination—or character flaw?—that I shared with Stephen and Father and, I suppose, Ellen, too. I'd been so caught up in the flotsam of my own life that I hadn't thought of it before, but now it was obvious. Since our mother's death we had all performed our own versions of Fischer's disappearing act. We had our own distinct styles—suicide, a ruined Caribbean resort, a castle in Montana, and perhaps least obvious, hiding out in the anonymity of New York and rarely answering the phone—but in the end we'd all chosen to leave rather than stay. My mother had rooted us all in faith, but in her absence, faith wasn't enough to save us.

Ellen flew out to Seattle for Stephen's funeral, arriving and leaving that same day. What to do about our father had been the main topic of conversation as I drove her back to the airport, but we hadn't been able to come to any decision about whether one or both of us would go tell him. Finally, as the boarding calls were being announced for her flight, Ellen kissed me on the cheek and said, "You'll have to go. I just can't swing it." She kissed me again and boarded her plane.

During what was supposed to be a short layover in Houston, I called Perry and told him I'd decided to visit my father on his little island in the Caribbean and wouldn't be returning to the castle as soon as I'd planned.

Only a month after my mother's death, my father, with brutal efficiency, had put all his domestic affairs in order. He purchased a long-unused, run-down resort on a small island off the coast of Puerto

Rico and moved there with no plans to return. During the years since my father's move, I'd received sporadic postcards from him updating me on his progress in restoring the resort, which, as far as I could tell, was very little. He still had no working telephone, and since a postcard informing him that his son had killed himself was out of the question, I had, by Ellen's abdication, been elected to make a personal visit.

My flight out of Houston was delayed, delayed again, then canceled for mechanical reasons. I ended up spending the night in a hotel room so close to the airport that there were times during the night when I thought I could hear boarding calls being announced.

The next day my ears plugged up on the descent into San Juan and didn't improve on the short flight out to my father's island. I'd retrieved my suitcase from baggage claim, stepped out into the tropical Puerto Rican heat, and climbed into a taxi in front of the tiny airport before it occurred to me that I didn't know where I was going. I was overdressed in a long-sleeved shirt and cotton sweater, and these details, juxtaposed against the tropical landscape, made me feel detached and out of place.

My taxi driver, a black man whose skin really was black, drove away from the airport without my saying a word. He had such a laid-back posture that I wondered if he cared whether I wanted to go somewhere specific. Once clear of the airport, however, he glanced at me in the rearview mirror and caught me yawning and swallowing, trying to clear my ears. I took this as an invitation for some kind of direction.

"I'm looking for my father," I said. "He owns an old resort."

As soon as the words were out of my mouth, I realized how absurd they sounded, but the driver showed no sign that I'd said anything unusual. He drove on, never again looking in the mirror. He hummed as he drove along a narrow, shoulderless road lined with scrub oaks and rickety barbed-wire fences. The combination of the humming and my stopped-up ears ungrounded me, as if I'd entered a world where the gravity was not as strong.

After about twenty minutes we pulled up in front of a villa that at one time must have been quite genteel but was now broken and forgotten, unattended to since the last hurricane. Most of the windows were broken or missing, and paint flaked from the eaves and trim like peeling skin. The stucco walls were pocked and discolored, and some kind of climbing ivy entwined posts and downspouts—thin, green fingers reaching up from the ground, trying to pull everything down in one grand act of entropy.

I walked through the french doors into the tiled lobby, and a gangly black man appeared.

"Master Thomas," he said. "Welcome to Casa La Verdad. My name is Martin." He took my suitcase and led me across the lobby. "We were expecting you sooner. I trust you're well."

I nodded but couldn't speak. I followed him through a dim bar and out onto a flagstone patio partially covered with a rotting pergola and more of the omnipresent ivy. In order to ground myself, I tried to discern his age. When he'd met me at the front doors, I'd thought he might be in his late sixties, maybe seventies, but now in the bright afternoon light, with the briny sea breeze in our faces, he looked younger. He was black, as black as the cab driver had been, but his hair, tied in a ponytail, was long, straight, and thick, which gave me the impression that he was part Indian.

"My father…" I managed.

Martin pointed up the beach, and I recognized my father's distinct silhouette in the distance. He was walking hand in hand with a woman in a yellow bikini who looked to be half his age.

"Can I get you something from the bar?" asked Martin.

Even from afar I could tell that there was a lightness in the way my father and the woman interacted, like new lovers blind to each other's shortcomings. But as they drew nearer to the resort and I recognized the woman, I realized that it wasn't the giddiness of young love, but the infection of reunion. My father seemed younger than when I'd last seen him, his face lean and tanned. And although I'd seen her two days before, my sister seemed already renewed by the strange tranquillity of my father's ruined resort.

I ached to go to my father and embrace him, but instead I followed Martin back inside and sat at the bar. I watched Martin make me a gin and tonic and felt the beads of sweat running down the sides of my face. Above the mirror behind the bar hung a carved wooden plaque that said "Sorrow also sings when it runs too deep to cry." I wondered if my father's sorrow ran deep enough now that it could sing. There was something about the resort that made me think that was the case. But what if still more sorrow were heaped on? As I sipped my drink and waited for my father and Ellen to return, I figured we'd soon have the opportunity to find out. I didn't know what had changed Ellen's mind about coming, but one thing was clear, she'd not yet told our father of Stephen's death. In true Ellen form, she'd left that to me.

That night Ellen and I shared a meal with our father for the first time since our mother's death. Martin brought us each a plate with a whole, clawless lobster on it, then whisked them away the moment we were done and replaced them with blackened tuna steaks and slices of fresh mango. My father drank wine with the meal, something I'd not known him to do before. He drank quite a bit too, Martin appearing unbeckoned to refill his glass whenever it was empty. I kept waiting for him to ask us why we were there. I wanted him to ask. He must have known we weren't there for a vacation. He would have known that nothing short of death would have brought both Ellen and me to his resort. *So why rush it?* I thought. He would have the rest of his life to grieve over Stephen. Why not delay the impact for a little while and have one last enjoyable meal with his remaining children?

After dinner, while Ellen helped Martin with the dishes, Father and I stepped outside and wandered toward the water. It was a hot, breezeless evening, and the sky was filled with stars. Down on the beach, we stopped and looked at the river of moonlight reflected on the water.

"How're you doing?" I asked.

My father looked at me. "Do you have something you need to tell me?"

"I'm not very good at this sort of thing."

"Is it Stephen?"

"Yes."

"Is he dead?"

"Yes."

I was going to say more, but he held up his hand. He turned and walked away down the empty beach. I watched his silhouette shrink and shrink, glowing in the moonlight.

It was only then that I realized I would never see my brother again. I would never again look into his eyes. I would never again hear his infectious laugh. I hadn't cried when I heard Stephen had killed himself. I hadn't cried at the funeral. Now I sank down in the sand and the tears spilled out. I cried for Stephen and I cried for our mother and I cried for what I knew this would do to our father.

I didn't see my father return that evening. Later, Martin took Ellen and me to our bungalows. He carried a flashlight and pointed out places on the cement walkway that were cracked and uneven. He showed Ellen her bungalow first, then led me next door to mine. I stood on the little front porch for a moment after he'd left and waited for Ellen to come out. There was a large rubber tree at the edge of my porch, and I thought I saw something crawling through its branches. In a moment Ellen reappeared and joined me.

"I don't think I want to sleep alone tonight."

I put my arm around her and kissed the top of her head. Her shoulders were thin and bony, like a little girl's.

As a child, and even into her teens, Ellen had been plagued by night-mares. Over the years she'd seen a calico mixture of doctors, psychia-trists, and dream therapists, but no one had been able to give her any relief, nor had anyone been able to offer an explanation for why she had them in the first place. During the day she was a happy, well-adjusted kid, living in a comfortable home with a loving family. It was so odd that such a child would have nightmares that one doctor even suspected a brain tumor and conducted a series of CAT scans.

Maybe because I was the closest to her in age—Ellen was born eleven months after I was—or maybe because our bedrooms shared a connecting door, Ellen chose me for comfort in the aftermath of her nightmares. Several times a month—during the worst times, several times a week—the door between our rooms would creak open in the middle of the night, and Ellen would pad across the carpeted floor and slip into my bed. She'd curl up next to me, and I'd be able to feel her heart pounding like a piston. Sometimes she would fall back to sleep. Other times she would tell me the details of her dreams. She was almost always being chased by a man with some sort of weapon. It was always apparent that her pursuer was enjoying her terror.

Once when we were in high school, I got up in the middle of the night to use the bathroom and heard someone in the living room. There I found my mother pacing the floor in her nightgown, her hands to her face, deep in prayer. I watched for a long time, crouched

at the entrance to the hall, forgetting that I had to go to the bathroom. It wasn't unusual for my mother to pray. She prayed in the
mornings before she emerged from her room, and she prayed
throughout the day. She was the kind of person who prays for parking spaces. Once I heard her say in the midst of baking a cake, "Oh,
shoot, I forgot we're out of eggs." I'd been reaching into the refrigerator for a pitcher of juice, and there behind it, where it shouldn't have
been, was an egg. I handed it to my mother, and she said, "Well,
praise the Lord for that." I remember this because of the strong reaction I had to it. I remember leaving the kitchen thinking, *I don't think
God had anything to do with that egg being there.*

I watched for a long time as my mother paced and prayed. The
room was filled with moonlight, casting everything in blue shadow.
Her bare feet made no marks on the carpet. I wanted to grab her, to
hold her to this world, but I feared my arms would pass through her
and she would dissipate into dust.

Weeks later I made the connection. I was awake in the middle of
the night, having trouble getting back to sleep. I was picturing a grove
of aspens quaking in a mountain breeze when Ellen walked into the
room and slipped into my bed.

"Nightmare?" I asked.

"No. I just couldn't sleep."

Then, as if it was occurring to her for the first time, she said, "I
haven't had a nightmare for weeks."

I realized then what my mother had been praying for.

"I don't think you will anymore," I said.

But although Ellen never had another nightmare, she would still
sometimes crawl into bed with me in the middle of the night. Even
during college, when we were home for vacations or holidays, she
would often slip under my covers, complaining that she couldn't sleep,

then soon drift off. Other times she would talk at length about the hassles of her job, her latest ex-boyfriend, how the superintendent in her building had it out for her.

My bungalow had a queen-size bed, and we lay on our backs and stared at the mottled stucco ceiling. Outside the waves crashed onto the beach. Ellen inched over so that our arms and legs touched.

"Do you mind?" she asked.

I told her I didn't and slipped my hand in hers. Minutes later her breathing had become deep and regular, but when I thought she was asleep, she spoke.

"This is so strange."

I thought there were any number of things she might be referring to.

"Yes, it is," I said.

The next morning I woke up and got out of bed without waking Ellen. I walked the hundred or so yards back to the main villa. The chatter of unfamiliar bird song filled the trees above me. I found Martin sitting at a small wicker table by the empty swimming pool, reading the paper. He leaped up when he saw me, as if he'd been caught at something.

"Master Thomas," he said with a slight bow, "I wasn't expecting anyone to be up so early."

"Please sit," I said.

There was an insulated carafe on the table. I pointed to it and asked if it was coffee, and Martin was on his feet again.

"I'll get you a cup."

Before I could stop him, he was striding across the patio on his long, gangly legs.

After I'd made it clear that I required nothing beyond coffee, Martin settled back into his chair. He was uncomfortable, not knowing whether he should resume reading his paper or offer me a section.

"Is it going to be hot today?" I asked.

Martin looked up at the sky. "Like yesterday."

"You seem very loyal to my father," I observed.

Martin looked at me and smiled. He was polite to a fault, but I could tell he wouldn't give me any more information than politeness demanded.

"He has been good to me."

What was Martin's relationship to my father? Was he servant? employee? friend? caregiver? I learned over time that he was all of these. I've seen Martin washing my father's feet, kneeling before him on the hard flagstone patio with bucket and rag after pulling shards of coral from the arch of his foot. I've also seen Martin refuse my father a glass of wine when he thought he'd had enough, then suggest that he go to bed. Martin was that enigmatic employee—or servant (I never knew if he was paid)—who defied boundaries. But of one thing there could be no question: To my father he was loyal.

I learned this from my father. When he showed up at Casa La Verdad (having bought it sight unseen), he found Martin living in the basement of the main villa. My father gathered, in the midst of incessant apologies, that Martin had worked for the previous owners. When they left (they had actually been arrested for some tax illegality), Martin had stayed, not knowing what else to do. He'd planned to stay only a few weeks until he found somewhere else to go, but in the end, staying was easier than going. His few weeks turned into eighteen years.

"What did you do?" my father asked. "What did you eat? What did you do for money?"

Martin smiled for the first time, showing a little of his pride, and gestured to the ocean.

"The sea is generous," he said. "I have eaten well."

When Martin gave him a tour of the resort, my father learned that in addition to provender from the sea, the resort's pantries had been well stocked at the time of its closure. One day it was business as usual, then there were police, arrests, a general exodus. The resort was wrapped like a gift in police tape, and Martin and the resort were forgotten until the day my father showed up.

"He still had toilet paper when I got here," my father said. He laughed when he said this, a deep, resonating laugh that made me want to hold him. We were walking on the beach. "Later we decided that it was fortuitous that I came when I did, because on the day I arrived, he'd pulled the last roll off the shelf." My father laughed again.

It didn't escape me that my father had used the word *fortuitous,* derived from the Latin *forte* meaning "by chance." It hung in the air before us like a swarm of gnats, in stark contrast to the word he would have used before my mother's death—*predestined.*

There'd also been the matter of the brandy, which added to this sense that fate (another nice, godless word) had somehow joined their lives. For eighteen years Martin had allowed himself a single glass of Armagnac before going to bed each night. The night before my father arrived, he'd poured himself the last glass from the last bottle.

Martin again leaped up from the table when Ellen appeared. She approached like a debutante, wearing cat-eye sunglasses and a cotton robe. As she walked the robe shifted, and I could see bits and pieces of her yellow bikini. When Martin offered her coffee, she asked if it would be possible to get a Bloody Mary instead. Without hesitation, Martin said, "Of course," as if the resort were often full of urbane women who ordered cocktails for breakfast.

When Martin returned with Ellen's drink, our father approached from the other side of the patio and pulled a chair up to our table. He told us good morning, then looked at Ellen's glass and said, "That looks good. I think I'll try one of those." And again Martin was up.

Ellen started each day with a Bloody Mary, then shed her robe and spent the day on a wicker chaise longue by the empty pool. She alternated between reading a mystery and sleeping, but she was always tanning. Ellen tanned beautifully, her skin having some subtle pigmentation that Stephen's and mine lacked.

After a few days, her pale, New York skin had turned a coppery bronze. At dinner in the evenings, she would show up with a sundress thrown over her bikini. Her skin glowed, always warm to the touch. When she sometimes joined me in bed at night, I would throw back the sheets. On the mornings after she'd slept in my bed, I'd awake to the faint smell of vodka and pepper.

Father spent his days taking long walks on the beach, so long that I thought he must be doing more than just walking, that he must be going somewhere, doing something, perhaps spending time with someone—a woman? But Martin assured me that he only walked, that he'd been doing it every day since his arrival, although, Martin admitted, since my arrival the walks had grown longer. He would leave after breakfast, sometimes heading north, sometimes south, and we wouldn't see him again until late in the afternoon.

"It's a terrible thing to outlive your children," said Martin.

As for myself, I couldn't stand to be so idle. I fixed several leaking faucets, rehung a screen door that was askew, and wiped down the walls of the dining room with bleach where mildew had speckled the paint like age spots, but after a while these little tasks felt tedious. So I started looking for a more substantial project.

After considering the rampant ivy that entwined everything (still too tedious), the cracked tiles on the floor of the lobby (a bit beyond my know-how), and the sodden drywall that needed to be replaced in all the bungalows (more than I could accomplish in a week), I settled on the rotting pergola that covered a portion of the pool area. It was the perfect project. It was something I could complete from start to finish within two or three days, and it was outside in the fresh air, where I would rather be working. It would be easy work, and the end result rewarding.

I tracked down Martin and told him I would need to go into town to order supplies. I asked if there was a vehicle I could use.

"We have no vehicles," said Martin. He seemed offended that I would make such an assumption. He turned toward the bar and said, "I will call Simon."

Using a radio behind the bar, he talked with Simon, then told me that he would be along soon. I went back out to the patio with pencil and paper and calculated what I would need to replace the pergola. Ellen was in her usual spot on the other side of the pool, sleeping. I looked up and down the beach for a sign of my father, but except for some seagulls fighting over something in the sand, the beach was deserted.

After about half an hour, I heard a horn sound out front. I walked out to the cab and saw with pleasure that Simon was the same driver who'd picked me up at the airport.

When I returned from town, I found Ellen right where she'd been when I left. The only difference was that her skin glowed a deeper shade of bronze. Father had returned from his walk and was talking with Martin in the shade of the rotting pergola. When I approached, Martin nodded and walked away.

"Martin tells me you're planning to fix the pergola," he said.

"Replace it is more like it. I don't think any of it is salvageable."

My father looked out to the ocean. "Ellen mentioned there was a note."

"Yes."

For a while we just stood there. When I first arrived I thought my father had looked younger, more fit than I remembered. Now he seemed old. I wondered if what I had mistaken for fitness was decay. I wanted to reach out and touch him, but I was afraid I would find his skin cold.

"It's in my bungalow," I said. "I'll get it."

My lumber was not being delivered until the next day, so I spent the afternoon stripping the wiry vines from the old pergola, then piece by piece, tearing it down and stacking the decaying wood off to the side of the patio. I glanced out to the beach in front of the resort, where Father had gone with Stephen's letter. After reading it, he let it drop to the sand at his feet; then he waded into the water and stood there for a long time with the waves breaking at his thighs.

When he waded in further, Ellen got up from her chaise longue and walked over to where I was working. She wrapped her arms around my elbow and rested her cheek on my sweaty shoulder. We watched as our father dove into a breaking wave and swam toward the horizon. As he continued to swim and swim, I could feel Ellen's pulse in her fingertips. He stopped far out in the water and floated on his back, rolling with the waves.

When he started swimming toward shore, Ellen pointed to the water's edge where Stephen's letter had been picked up by a wave and was beginning to float out to sea. I didn't move. I'd shown it to Ellen and Mary on the day of Stephen's funeral. Now that Father had seen it, I couldn't think of a reason to save it.

I watched my father swim toward shore, knowing that with each stroke, he was attempting to push out of his mind the invading memories of his wife and her senseless death.

It took me three days to resurrect the pergola. The first day I set my posts and hung my beams; then for the next two days I worked on top, setting the rafters. From this crow's-nest I had a clear view of the whole pool area and a long stretch of the beach in front of the resort. As I set rafter after rafter in neat parallel lines, I noticed a subtle repositioning of the characters in the tableau below me.

The second day began status quo—Ellen in her chaise longue, facing the sun by the empty pool, the yellow of her bikini and the red of her Bloody Mary like perennials pushing up through the cracked concrete. Martin was at his wicker table reading the paper, looking up after every sentence or so to make sure neither Ellen nor I required anything. Soon, Father appeared from the french doors of the villa, waved to us, then turned toward the beach for his walk. Then there was a quiet shifting. The breeze changed directions and grew warmer. I noticed Ellen was up on one elbow, watching our father recede toward the beach. She relaxed again, and I thought she might only have been trying to decide whether to signal to Martin for another drink. But she raised herself on her elbow again. This time she stood up and jogged after our father. She caught up to him, and they stood facing each other for a moment. They exchanged a few words, then joined hands and turned up the beach. I watched their joined figures grow smaller and smaller on the brilliant white sand. I felt a faint emptiness like hunger growing in my gut. But I didn't kid myself for long—I'd had a full breakfast.

This twinge of jealousy led to thoughts of Stephen, and as the top of the pergola grew, fragmented memories of him replayed like drug-induced flashbacks in my mind. Ellen was closest to me in our family, but Stephen was a mama's boy.

I remember a day near Halloween when I'm ten years old. My mother and Stephen are in the kitchen together. She is standing at the counter in a yeasty apron kneading bread; he's sitting at the kitchen bar with a sketch pad, keeping her company. I've spread fake blood all over one of my hands, and I burst into the kitchen with terror on my face. I scream that I've put my hand through a window pane on our front door. My mother about faints at the sight of all the blood, but pulling from that mysterious reserve of strength that all mothers have, she's able to grab a towel and rush to my aid. But before she can reach me, Stephen intercepts her. I'd expected him to join in conspiratorial laughter with me, but he pulls her aside and tells her in the calmest of voices that it's all a joke, that there's nothing wrong with my hand, but that maybe my head should be examined.

"Oh, Lord," my mother says at last, turning back to her bread. "Why would you do such a thing?"

Stephen pushes me out of the kitchen into the dining room and whomps me on the side of the head so hard that I think he may have given me an aneurysm. When I've regained my senses enough to look at him in disbelief, he takes my arm and squeezes my bicep so hard that I have fingerprint bruises there for a week.

"If you ever pull a stunt like that again," he says, "I will bury you alive in the backyard."

Another flashback: We're in college together in Spokane, Washington, and we've decided to hop a freight train to Seattle for the weekend. We've packed sleeping bags and food in rucksacks and are waiting under an overpass for a westbound train. It's October, and the ground is snowless but frozen. Suddenly the railyard's security man, the Bull, is standing in front of us asking what we're doing. As obvious as it is, I know I would attempt a lie. Stephen, however, simply tells the truth: "We're waiting for a train to Seattle." Impressed by his honesty, the Bull nods and tells us that he can't allow us to wait on railroad property. He points to a spot no more than fifteen feet behind us and says, "You'll have to wait over there." The implied message: I know you're not doing any harm, but I have to do my job. And further implied: You're free to get on that train, just don't let me see you doing it.

The ride to Seattle is glorious. We sit most of the way in the open door of an empty boxcar. First the sullen desert of Eastern Washington, then the lush forests of the Cascades, ablaze with fall colors, pass us by. Except for an incident in the Seattle trainyard when I come close to losing a leg—I'm crawling across a track, and the train above me begins to move—it's the perfect trip. I suppose the excitement of almost losing a leg only adds to its perfection.

When we return to our dorm at the end of the weekend, we are tired and dirty, our clothes and hair stinking of diesel. I want to fall into bed and sleep twelve straight hours before my first class in the morning, but Stephen insists that we call our mother and tell her we're all right.

"She doesn't even know we went," I say.

"Yes," he says, "but once we tell her, she'll be glad to know we're all right."

I'm too tired to argue, so I relent, asking him not to mention that I came very close to losing a leg.

Of course, he does tell her, but as with the Bull in the Spokane yard, his honesty wins her over.

"I'm glad you told me all this after you got back and I knew you were all right," she says before hanging up. "It makes me feel fortunate somehow."

I realize that this has been Stephen's intent all along, that he knows the news of our safe return, after the fact, will have this effect on her. I marvel at how well he knows her, knows the intricacies of a mother's love and fear for her children.

During the three days I had been erecting the pergola, Ellen hadn't made any appearances in my bedroom at night. The day after I finished, however, I'd spent the day idly by the pool, for the first time not arguing with Martin when he offered to refresh my beer whenever he saw that my glass was empty. That night, after crawling into bed, I heard the door to my bungalow ease open, and in a moment I felt Ellen's warm body next to mine. She didn't speak. I thought that this was one of those times when she simply wanted to be near me while she slept. But then she spoke.

"What's your next project?" she asked.

"I'm done," I said. "I'm going home. I think tomorrow."

"That's what I thought."

We were quiet for a while. Ellen inched a little closer, pressing her pelvis into my hip.

"What about you?" I asked. I already knew what she'd decided.

"Simon took me into town this morning, and I called my boss. I told him to consider the rest of my vacation my notice. I'll stay here and help Father with the restoration. I think I'll enjoy it."

I didn't believe, nor do I think Ellen did, that our father would ever finish restoring the resort and open it again for business, but it was a comforting rationalization, a purpose for waking each day.

We didn't talk after that. I lay awake for a long time, and I think Ellen did too. I stared at the ceiling where large flakes of paint clung like dead leaves to late-fall oak trees. Outside the bungalow an unfamiliar tropical bird was singing a mournful song. Over the slight smell of vodka and spices from Ellen's warm skin, I thought I detected the smell of bread baking. I was sure it was Martin in the villa's kitchen, baking something for tomorrow's breakfast, but I couldn't help thinking of my mother. She would always come into our rooms at night, after we'd gone to bed, to check that we were sleeping well. Often a distinct smell of yeast came with her, a smell that followed her like a guardian angel.

*B*ack in Montana I stepped outside the airport into a bright winter's day. There'd been a recent snow, but now the skies were clear, the air cold and crisp. It was such a stark contrast to my muddled emotions that I felt mocked.

I got into a cab driven by a woman with rounded shoulders and cold sores on her thin, colorless lips. There was a bump on the bridge of her nose, and her skin was sallow. It wasn't hard to imagine the kind of life she'd had. Yet at the same time, she seemed happy enough. The kind of person who takes adversity in stride and laughs when things go wrong. Someone who has no time for self-pity. When she asked me where I wanted to go, I felt self-conscious. I wanted to tell her that I wasn't always like this. That once I was open and friendly and hopeful and funny. That once I'd been more like her.

I'd thought that all I wanted was to get back to the castle and sleep, but as we passed through town, I spied the little café. I wondered if all I needed to become my old self again was a cup of coffee. Maybe it was that simple.

I asked the driver if she would mind waiting while I went in and had a cup of coffee.

"I don't mind," she said. "Not if you bring me a cup when you come back."

"Okay," I said. "How do you like it?"

"I like it hot. As hot as they can get it."

"Hot. Okay. I'll try my best."

I sat at the counter, and the waitress with the mysterious eyes waited on me. As she poured my coffee, I was half expecting her to comment on my tan. Then I noticed what I'd been too tired or too disoriented to notice on my first visit—she was blind.

Her movements across the short distance between the kitchen window and the counter were graceful, but slow and calculated. When she poured coffee, she picked up the mugs, unlike the other waitresses, who filled them where they were.

This realization rattled a philanthropic bone in my body, made me want to take care of her. I imagined walking with her through town, guiding her by the elbow, describing the icicles that hung from the rooftops while I studied her face, the faint pools of freckles beneath her eyes, to see if she was pleased with my descriptions.

Fortunately, I recognized what an inept savior I would make. My motives were messianic and self-serving, not altruistic. It was condescending and unattractive.

I ordered extra-hot coffee to go and left. Back in the cab I leaned over the front seat and handed the driver her coffee.

"You look like you've been somewhere sunny," she said.

"Yes. The Caribbean."

"That must've been nice."

I took a sip of coffee, but it was too hot to drink.

"My brother just killed himself. I went down to tell my father."

She glanced in the rearview mirror and pulled away from the curb. I leaned my head back and closed my eyes, regretting that I'd said anything.

Partway up the mountain, I tried the coffee again. It was still hot but drinkable. I looked at the driver. She had already finished hers. She noticed me looking at her.

"I had a boyfriend who killed himself."

"I'm sorry."

"I'm sorry for you, too."

When we came to a stop at the front of the castle, she reached a hand over the seat. I thought she was reaching for the fare, so I pulled out my wallet.

"I'm Susan," she said. "Thanks for the coffee."

I offered her my hand. Her skin was cool and rough, and although her hand was small, her grip was strong. I got out of the cab and handed her the fare through her window, but she pushed it away.

"You take care of yourself," she said. "Thanks again for that coffee."

I watched her car pass through the gatehouse. When it was out of sight, I turned and looked at the castle. It was still and dark and lifeless, except for three mourning doves that cooed on the curtain wall.

I was relieved to find the apartment empty. I didn't think I had the energy to do anything more than undress and fall into bed. A progressive fatigue had been working on me all day, and now it had escalated to exhaustion.

The bed was cold. I fanned my arms and legs under the down comforter, like a child making a snow angel, until the sheets warmed. My last thought was how nice it would be to awaken in the castle, to reenter this new life, free from all the encumbrances of the past.

I awoke in stages. I heard soft voices, which at first seemed part of a dream. The room was dark. I opened my eyes and stared up at the dark canopy above the bed. One voice was Perry's, although it was more nasal than usual. The other was a young girl's, familiar yet unplaceable.

"They were both named after saints," said the girl. "Stephen was the protomartyr. That means the first martyr. Thomas was a doubter, which is both a good and bad thing, but he's not a very good uncle."

"I see," said Perry.

At the word *uncle* I sat up and turned on the light at my bedside.

There at the footboard, still wearing winter coats and hats and looking as though they'd just come from an afternoon of ice fishing, were
Perry and my niece, Catherine.

Catherine came to the side of the bed.

"You sleep too much," she said.

She nudged my shoulder with her mittened hand and skipped
out of the room saying, "C'mon, get up, we're having fresh fish for
dinner, which I caught."

Used to the long Caribbean days of the last week and a half, I
thought it was the middle of the night, but it wasn't quite six in the
evening. I pulled on clothes while Perry stood mute at the foot of
the bed.

"How long has she been here?" I asked.

"Three days," said Perry.

The next morning I stood in front of the library's cavernous fireplace
with a cup of coffee and watched the flames curl around the logs.
There was a numbness in me that I was ashamed of, but like a seda-
tive already swallowed, there seemed no way to reverse it. Here was a
chance to do the right thing, to become the good uncle I'd never been.
I thought of Dante's hell, how the hottest places were reserved for
those who in times of great moral crisis maintain their neutrality. I
didn't want that for myself.

Perry came in with a cup of tea. He sneezed and blew his nose
into a tissue, then tossed it into the fire. He looked at me and managed a weak smile.

"Well, it looks like we have another roommate."

"Looks like it," I said. "How did all this happen?"

As soon as it was out of my mouth, I recognized it for what it was:
not a question just about Catherine but about my entire life.

Three days earlier Perry had been tying flies in the library when the dogs started barking outside. He heard a vehicle pulling up in front of the carriage house. When he walked around to the front of the castle, he saw a woman and a girl standing hand in hand at the main doors like figures added later to a painted landscape.

I imagine Mary was a bit derailed when she learned I wasn't there, but she had nothing else to fall back on.

She drove off, leaving Perry and Catherine standing in the cold.

"Why didn't you ask her to stay?" I asked.

"I did," said Perry. "I might have. It all happened so fast. She acted like she was already late for wherever she was going. She barely stayed two minutes."

"What exactly did she say?"

"Just what I said. That she had to go away for a while. That she needed to leave Catherine with us for a while."

"How long is 'a while'?"

I imagined Mary joining Karen in her asylum, roommates, taking turns staring out the window, pacing the room barefoot, picking at trays of cold food, neither of them able to piece together the succession of events that had conducted them there.

"I don't know," said Perry. "The whole thing took me by surprise too. She was very forceful. By the time I knew what was happening, she was gone."

Catherine appeared at the library doors. She was wearing flannel pajama bottoms and a huge sweatshirt I thought I recognized as Stephen's.

"We're out of bagels," she said.

"We'll get more today," said Perry. "How about some toast?"

"Bagels are better," said Catherine. She stared at us, then gave a little shrug and left.

It occurred to me that I hadn't given any thought to how Catherine felt about all of this. First her father kills himself, then her mother dumps her off at a castle in Montana with a bad uncle and a complete stranger.

I walked into the kitchen and refilled my cup of coffee. Catherine was standing by the toaster, waiting for the toast to pop up.

"Did your mother say where she was going or when she'd be back?" I asked.

"She'll be back," said Catherine.

"I know she will," I said. "I was just wondering if she said when."

When the toast popped up, I jumped. I put my hand on Catherine's shoulder as she buttered her toast.

"You can stay as long as you need to," I said.

Catherine took a bite and looked at me with a hint of sympathy. "What else would I do?"

The next day a chinook blew down from Canada, and the temperature leaped into the forties. A chilling rain fell for several days, all the more depressing because it should have been snow. Instead, it dissolved the snow we had, and soon the lawns and gardens around the castle had turned ashen, mottled, and colorless. Perry's cold got worse. For two days he hardly moved from the library couch, and Catherine seized on the opportunity to become his nursemaid. She brought him bowls of soup and slices of toast, glasses of juice and cups of tea. When he was awake she read to him from *The Complete Tales and Poems of Winnie-the-Pooh*. When he fell asleep she covered him with a quilt and closed the library doors so he wouldn't be disturbed.

When she wasn't nursing Perry, Catherine would bundle herself up in a huge down coat and wool hat and, taking a flashlight along, explore the interior of the castle. During those days of the chinook, I gathered from her reports that the interior of the castle was colder than the temperature outside.

When Catherine was around, I studied her. I wanted to make some headway, but either she was purposefully making it hard on me or I just wasn't very good at it. One day I had a small epiphany. I was in the library reading *Tender Is the Night* when Catherine returned from exploring. I wondered if I couldn't engage with her because she reminded me of Karen.

Over the next few days I developed a hypothesis. Maybe all victims of suicide—if the victims are not the people who kill themselves, but the ones they leave behind—acquire some shared personality traits: the rough exterior, the drive to succeed, the desire to be loved paired with the absolute fear of it, the almost religious vow to never again become vulnerable. They were all traits that Karen protected like cash under a mattress. And, I thought, although still embryonic, these traits had already started calcifying within Catherine's little shell.

Two questions loomed: Could this be stopped? And if so, what part would I play in the process?

The chinook was eventually chased off by a blast of Arctic air that plummeted temperatures but left us with bright blue skies. I woke up one day to find Perry and Catherine in the kitchen making breakfast. Perry's cold had left with the chinook. Catherine was standing on a chair at the counter, dipping thick slices of french bread into a saucer of egg and milk, giving them a quick flip, then sending them over to Perry, who tossed them into a frying pan. Catherine was chattering away about herself, I thought, and Perry as usual was merely listening and nodding. I said good morning and poured myself a cup of coffee. I sat at the bar but was hardly noticed.

"Catherine was very smart," said Catherine.

I realized she was talking about saints again.

"She out-argued fifty of Caesar's best orators and turned them all into Christians. But that outraged Caesar, and he ordered them all to be burned in the center of town. They were afraid for their souls because they hadn't been baptized, but Catherine told them not to fear, the shedding of their blood would be their baptism. They were thrown into the fire, but not a hair on their heads or a shred of their garments was singed."

She flipped another piece of bread to Perry. He shot me a glance that said, *Since when do nine-year-olds talk like this?*

"She was a virgin," continued Catherine. "I don't know what that means, but all the good saints were virgins."

"A virgin," said Perry.

"Yeah," said Catherine. "I'm not sure what it means, though."

Then it must have dawned on her that worthless as I was as an uncle, I might know something about this. Or maybe she was just being nice and trying to include me in the conversation.

"Uncle Thomas, do you know?"

Perry flipped his piece of bread. It sizzled as the wet side hit the hot skillet. I took a sip of coffee and thought about hedging, but knew I shouldn't. There was something about Catherine that demanded she be treated as an equal.

"That's a woman who's never been married," I tried.

She thought for a moment, tilting her head a little as if she'd been prepared for a deception. But then she nodded, and I could tell my definition met with her approval. She turned back to the counter and dropped another piece of bread into the egg mixture.

"That makes sense," she said to Perry. "Catherine said she was the bride of Christ."

Perry nodded, but I knew he was wondering, like me, where this strange little girl had come from.

After breakfast, encouraged by the weather, I decided to make an effort. I asked Catherine what she'd like to do for the day.

"I don't know," she said. "Whatever."

"Well, what do you normally do?" I asked.

"*Normally,* I go to *school.*"

Perry and I looked at each other. School? Should she be going to school? Mary hadn't said anything about it. Wouldn't taking her to school imply a degree of permanence? But if she didn't go, she would fall behind. What would a good uncle do?

"School," I said. "Of course, school. We'll set that up tomorrow. But what do you want to do *today?*"

We took a walk around the convent, just Catherine, the dogs, and me, while Perry went back to bed and slept. Catherine, a city girl, at first kept close to me, until we'd passed through the grove of cottonwoods and found the deer trail that circled the convent. Then she strode off in front, trying to keep up with the dogs, her body language saying, *Okay, I can see the trail. I don't need your help anymore.*

As I watched her trotting along, I thought of Karen and started daydreaming. I imagined we'd gotten married as planned.

We are happier than two people have ever been, have ever had the right to be. We engage in none of the petty arguments and quarrels that most newlyweds have, never taking each other for granted, always being extravagant with our love. Every day for us is a new day to give thanks for each other, to give thanks that we have known love, really known it, that we have not squandered or abused it. If possible, we are happier still when we find out we are going to have a child. Throughout the pregnancy, the fresh awe we feel at the miracle that is taking place inside Karen's body never loses its overwhelming power. We spend endless hours talking about our baby, what it will be like, what it will look like. We are like children on Christmas Eve, too excited to wait until morning to unwrap our presents. At night in bed we take turns reading to Karen's womb, already feeling that we are a family.

But in the delivery room, tragedy strikes. Karen dies while giving birth to our daughter, and I'm left a single father. Now it's nine years later. I've raised Catherine alone, and although it has been difficult, impossible really, I've done a good job. People who know me often tell me I'm a saint, citing the sacrifices I've made, how it's more than they could have done themselves. Everyone who knows me has enormous respect for me, for raising such an intelligent and savvy daughter with no mother.

And Catherine and I are more than just father and daughter; we're best friends. She tells me everything, all her hopes, all her fears, and I confide in her as well. Every night in our house is a slumber party. We put on our pajamas and read together in bed. We talk and laugh and play games. Not until she's fast asleep do I get up and go to my own bed. Despite not having a mother, Catherine believes herself to be the luckiest girl she knows. And, although a widower, I believe a man has never been more blessed. Every day I meet her at the bus after school, and we walk home together. We hold hands and talk about what kinds of days we've had. Catherine, out of the blue, often says, "You know, Dad, we're lucky to have each other." And I say, "Yes, we're lucky."

I was pulled out of this fantasy by a bark. A hundred yards up the trail, Catherine was looking at something on the ground. She was scolding the dogs, trying to keep them away. I jogged up and ordered the dogs back, and they reluctantly obeyed.

"It's a little baby bird," said Catherine. "It must have fallen out of its nest."

"That's a pine siskin," I said. "And I think it's full grown. That's as big as they get. I don't think they'd be nesting at this time of year."

"Well, shouldn't he have flown south?"

"I don't know if they do that."

"Well, we should bury it."

"Okay."

Catherine scooped up the little bird in her gloved hands, and we continued walking. By now the dogs had lost interest and had run ahead again. I was thinking how the recent warm weather would make it easy to dig a little hole for the bird when Catherine, without so much as breaking her stride, tossed the bird into the trees, not even looking to see where it landed.

When we entered the clearing, she stopped and looked down at the valley floor. Snowless now, it appeared dirty and lifeless, the lake a large puddle of spilled ink on sun-yellowed paper. The absence of snow in the meadow made me think about what it would look like in the spring. I wondered if it would be full of wildflowers—glacier lily, lupine, mountain sorrel, fireweed, wild geranium, maybe even Jacob's-ladder.

"That's where you'll be going to school," I said, pointing down toward the town.

Catherine thought about that. She turned and walked after the dogs, again getting ahead of me.

I caught up to her again at the convent's gates. I stood next to her, and we looked in.

"What's in there?" she said.

"I don't know. Nuns."

"What's a nun?"

"You should know," I said.

"Why should I know?"

I realized that Catherine's interest in saints wouldn't necessarily require a knowledge of Catholicism.

"Never mind," I said. "Dumb assumption."

She looked up and smiled, then walked on toward the castle. I wondered if all I needed to do to gain her respect was to admit my shortcomings.

When we got back, we sat on a bench outside the french doors of the apartment and took off our boots. As Catherine bent down and untied her laces, I heard her say, "Salvation comes from the cross."

"What's that?" I asked.

She said it again, "Salvation comes from the cross."

"Yes?" I said.

She pulled off her boots and stood up.

"That's what it said at the entrance to the convent," she said.

"Above the gates?"

"Yes."

"Who taught you Latin?"

I suddenly felt uneasy.

"No one."

"But that was in Latin," I said. *"A Cruce Salus."*

Catherine looked at me. She gave a little shrug.

"It looked like English to me."

She opened the door and started inside. As she did, she said it again, "Salvation comes from the cross."

That night after Catherine was in bed, Perry and I sat in front of the fire in the library. Perry had brought a dusty bottle of port up from the cellar. He poured two glasses and handed one to me. He asked me how I was doing, and I assumed he was referring to Karen.

"I'm fine," I said. "I'm better now than I ever was when I was with her. I really can't fathom now how I let it go on so long."

Perry looked amused.

"What?"

"I was thinking more about Catherine."

"Right, Catherine. I don't know. It's hard to know what's she's thinking. I suppose I'll take her to school. Maybe a little normalcy will help."

Perry refilled my glass. I rested it on my knee and watched the flames behind it throw curtains of light through the wine, reminding me of times I'd seen the northern lights.

"Tell me the truth," said Perry. "Is Catherine's mother coming back?"

I wanted to say with confidence that she was, but ever since Catherine had arrived, I'd had a nagging feeling that Mary wouldn't come back, at least not any time soon.

"She's a good mother," I said. "And strong. Whatever this is, it's temporary."

"I like Catherine," said Perry.

"So do I. But it would be nice to know how long she's going to be here. So we're not just living day to day."

Perry poured more wine and stared into the fire. He drifted off to some dark place. When he came back, his eyes were focused.

"Day to day is the only way to live, Thomas."

That night in bed I thought about what Perry had said. I'd been looking at the small picture, how Catherine's presence and Mary's absence would affect the minutia of our day-to-day lives. The larger frame, Perry's concern, was this: If she stayed long enough, she would have to watch him die.

The next morning I took Catherine into town and enrolled her in school. She was able to start right away, so I left her, promising to return in the afternoon. The principal and I walked her to her class-room. When she hesitated for a moment at the door, I knelt down beside her.

"Are you going to be okay?"

"Of course," she said. "Why wouldn't I be?"

She walked into the room and disappeared among a mob of fourth graders that I thought looked especially intimidating.

The principal walked me to the front door and put his hand on my shoulder as I was about to leave the building.

"She'll be fine," he said. "We'll take good care of her. We have an excellent counselor should she need to talk to someone."

I thanked him and left. Despite my own aversion to shrinks, I thought the counselor might be something Catherine would want to take advantage of.

When I got back to the castle, I whistled for the dogs and set off around the convent. The air was crisp and stung the insides of my nose as I walked, almost jogged, along the stone wall. When I reached the massive wrought-iron gates and looked up, I was at first blinded by the sun hanging low in the sky. But the words were there. In Latin, not English. There'd been no simple mistake. *A Cruce Salus.* There it was, etched in stone. Not in English.

*D*uring the rest of that winter, I developed what even I had to admit was a mild drinking problem. I worked my way through the castle's wine cellar like a man on a quest. The wake-up calls came in rapid succession. One evening Perry asked me for the bottle of wine that I'd just opened. I had no recollection of opening a bottle, but we eventually located it on the mantle in the library. It was already empty.

On another night, or maybe it was the same night, I fell asleep on the library couch with a glass of wine in my hand. When it spilled onto my chest, I awoke thinking that I'd been shot. Not long after, there was a morning when I discovered an empty bottle of 1972 claret on the dresser in my bedroom. I had no memory of drinking it, and worse, of tasting it.

The final slap came on a Sunday afternoon in April. The weather had been warm for a week, and most of the snow around the castle had receded. Now it had turned cold again, and a misty rain was falling. We were all in the library, Perry dozing under an afghan on the couch, Catherine restless and bored. I picked up a school library book from out of Catherine's backpack. On the cover were a crow and a weasel, dressed in Indian clothing, both of them on horseback. I leafed through the pages, admiring the artwork, then walked over to where Catherine was sitting by the window, staring out at the rain, sucking on several strands of her hair.

"How about you read this book to me? It looks interesting."

Catherine stopped sucking on her hair and stared at me.

"What?" I asked. "You don't want to read it? Do you want me to read it to you? Have you already read it?"

She continued to stare, tilting her head and narrowing her eyes.

"Yes, I've already read it," she said at last. "Last night. Out loud. To *you*."

After that, I didn't drink for a month, although there were times when I wanted to. I caught myself several times passing by the stairway to the wine cellar, once even reaching for the doorknob, simply out of habit. Sometimes at night I would dream of drinking. It may have been the sudden onslaught of spring that saved me, but I like to think it had more to do with Catherine's saints.

While Catherine was at school, I took long walks in the woods with the dogs. Then I'd sit by the pool with a book and a glass of water and let the sun bake the toxins out of my body. Perry assured me that the warm days and uninterrupted sunshine were unprecedented, but he didn't seem inclined to capitalize on them. He spent almost all his time indoors, alternately restless and sleepy.

Late one Saturday morning at the beginning of May, I was sitting on the patio by the empty pool when I heard sounds coming from inside the convent. It was the sharp sound of plastic on plastic. It was a nostalgic sound, something I remembered from college. Then it came to me. The nuns were playing Wiffle ball.

The cottonwoods beyond the patio were speckled with green buds. I imagined them opening over the following weeks, releasing their musky perfume. The air already smelled of warm earth and sprouting plants. I breathed it in along with the aroma of coffee rising from the mug I held in my lap and the distant, efficient smell of chlorine coming from the pool, although I don't think it had been used in years.

I thought I could hear music coming from the castle. Perry would often put on an opera while napping in the library. But today it was Verdi's *Requiem*. I knew it because it was Karen's favorite.

Exaudi orationem meam,
ad te omnis caro veniet.
Requiem aeternam dona eis, Domine,
et lux perpetua luceat eis.
Kyrie eleison,
Christe eleison,
Kyrie eleison.

Hear my prayer.
All flesh shall come before you.
Grant them eternal rest, O Lord,
And let perpetual light shine upon them.
Lord, have mercy.
Christ, have mercy.
Lord, have mercy.

The serenity of the music was occasionally interrupted by the sound of a Wiffle ball being hit on the other side of the convent wall, but for me it all blended into one piece. It struck me how different a requiem is from an opera. A greater intimacy and spirituality, a mixture of despair and hope—a hope in a future life where our sins will be forgotten and life will be better.

I was just drifting off to sleep, the colors and rhythms of the music and the Wiffle-ball game all jumbled in my head, when the dogs bounded onto the patio and licked at my elbows. Catherine arrived moments later. She was wearing shorts that hit the tops of her knees. Her legs were white like ivory and looked too skinny to hold her up. When she took the seat next to me, the dogs finally settled down at our feet and panted.

"What's that noise?" asked Catherine.

"Wiffle ball," I said. "The nuns have a game going."

I had no way of knowing for sure that the nuns were playing Wiffle ball, but by this point I'd convinced myself. For over an hour I'd been imagining them spread out on a makeshift diamond in their black-and-white habits, bent at the waist, pounding fists into palms, maybe even talking a little trash.

Until the recent warm weather, we hadn't heard anything from inside the convent. We'd had no evidence that it was even inhabited. And now this. A nice game of Wiffle ball.

Catherine scratched one of the dogs behind the ear with the toe of her shoe, giving no indication that she found anything odd about a sect of cloistered nuns having a game of Wiffle ball.

"How was your walk?" I asked.

"Good," she said, not looking up from her scratching. "I ran into a saint. I think it was Saint Anthony."

I tried to read Catherine's narrow face, but she was already off on something else. Catherine rarely stayed with one subject for long. She jumped from one topic to another like a nervous nuthatch flitting about in a dogwood tree, as if staying in one place too long would be dangerous.

"Where's Perry?" she asked.

"Still sleeping, I think. Maybe he's up but doesn't want to come out in the sun."

For reasons I didn't understand, but related to his illness, too much sun was something Perry had to avoid.

"Is he going to die?" asked Catherine.

She looked at me now, studied my face, her own little polygraph test.

"Yes," I said. "But we all are."

"But him a lot sooner."

"Maybe. Maybe not."

The last three days had been a bad stretch for Perry. Whenever his blood test results indicated his disease was becoming more active, he would have to take high doses of cytotoxic drugs—basically, chemotherapy. For days afterward he would only leave his bed to go to the bathroom or vomit.

"He has lupus," said Catherine. She said the words slowly, concentrating on each one. "But that's not what's going to kill him."

It was as good an explanation as any. I'd heard Perry try to explain to Catherine why he was sick, but I suppose she wasn't satisfied with his explanation. In truth, I'd never felt I had a very firm grasp on it myself. All I knew was that lupus disrupted the body's normal immune system so that it couldn't tell the difference between foreign substances and its own cells and tissues. Within Perry's body, his immune system was attacking his own organs. People didn't die from lupus, but from kidney or some other organ failure.

"I don't really know," I said. "I think his kidneys are going bad, and some of his other organs, too."

Catherine closed her eyes, still scratching the dog's neck with the toe of her shoe. Huge cumulus clouds were drifting overhead. Verdi's *Requiem* drifted across the patio like low-lying smoke. I listened to the nuns playing Wiffle ball on the other side of the convent wall, each hit, each connection of bat with ball, like small-caliber gun shots, and the music a choral background.

When I looked at Catherine, I saw that her lips were moving. I thought for a moment that, incredibly, she might be singing along to the music.

Lacrimosa dies illa,
qua resurget ex favilla,
judicandus homo reus.

Huic ergo parce Deus.
Pie Jesu, Domine,
dona eis requiem.
Amen.

On this day full of tears
when from the ashes arises
guilty man, to be judged,
Lord, have mercy on him.
Gentle Lord Jesus,
grant them rest.
Amen.

But then I thought she might simply be saying a prayer. It could have been both.

That night when I tucked Catherine into bed, I asked her to tell me about the saint she'd seen.

"You should be telling me a story," she said.

"Maybe if I was a good uncle. Now what about this saint you saw?"

"Saint Anthony," said Catherine. "At least I'm pretty sure. That's who I think it was."

"Where did you see him?"

"In the woods. On the other side of the convent. My father had something to do with it."

Catherine lay back on her pillow and closed her eyes. For a moment I thought she'd decided to go to sleep, but then she started talking. She sounded as if she was reading from a book. I wondered if she'd swallowed an encyclopedia of saints, and all she had to do to see it was close her eyes.

"One day in church, when Anthony was twenty years old, he heard a voice: 'If you want to be perfect, go sell what you have and give it to the poor.' And he went right out and sold all his possessions and then lived like a hermit in the desert of Egypt for twenty years."

"How did he survive?" I asked.

Catherine opened her eyes. "He gardened and made hats."

She closed her eyes again. I watched the furrows on her forehead.

"Saint Anthony encountered a lot of temptations, but he resisted them all. He also had a lot of visions. Visions of Satan and of angels and of demons that tormented him. Once when he was deep in prayer, he saw the whole world covered with snares all connected together. He prayed, 'How can anyone escape these traps?' And he heard a voice that said, 'Humility!' Then he was carried into the air by angels, but a bunch of demons blocked their way. They told the angels about all the sins Anthony had committed from childhood on. But the angels didn't care. They said, 'Don't speak of these things. By the mercy of Christ they have been wiped away.'"

Catherine opened her eyes and looked at me.

"How do you know all this?" I asked, but Catherine ignored me.

"Do you want to know what was most important about Anthony's life?"

"Okay."

"It was that he left his hermitage. Three different times, when problems arose, he traveled to Alexandria and made great conversions. He knew when to reenter the world and help out."

Catherine eyed me, but I wasn't going to give her the pleasure of responding to her preaching.

"Good story," I said. "Maybe tomorrow night I'll try to be a good uncle and tell you one. Maybe about a little saint who thinks she knows everything."

I pulled the covers up to her chin, kissed her on the forehead and told her good night. But when I'd turned off the light and stepped out into the hallway, I stopped and leaned back into the room.

"Catherine?"

"Yes?"

"How did you know it was Saint Anthony? Did he tell you who he was?"

She waited awhile before answering, then flipped on the light at her bedside and stared at me.

"It was a *statue*," she said. "It didn't *say* anything."

I nodded, told her good night again, and left the room. Out in the hallway, I thought I could feel the subtle rotation of the earth. I'd taken only a couple steps when I returned again. This time I didn't go in but stood in the doorway, at the threshold between the light of the hall and the dark of the room.

"Can I bother you again?" I asked.

Catherine didn't answer, didn't turn on the light, but I took her silence as consent.

"I'm still curious how you knew his name. Was there a plaque or something?"

When she spoke this time there was no trace of annoyance.

"No," she said, taking her time. "There was no plaque. I don't know how I knew. I just did. I can show it to you tomorrow if you want. Maybe there was a plaque."

"Okay," I said. "Let's do that."

I told her good night for the third time and left her to sleep. As I descended the stairs I felt a strange uneasiness, as if I'd gone on vacation and couldn't remember whether I'd turned off the iron.

I found Perry in the library, sitting by the fire, drinking port. He looked drained and waxen. I sat down next to him.

"How's our girl?" he asked.

"Okay. How are you?"

"Feeling better," he said, although I'd never seen him look worse.

I told him about the statue Catherine had discovered in the woods and asked him if he'd ever seen it.

He shook his head and stared into the fire.

"I do remember hearing as a child about a statuary inside the convent. Although, I don't know. It could have been something I dreamed. I have a memory of it though—a large garden with stone paths and tall hedges that form all these nooks and alcoves. And all these saints, hundreds of them, standing around in the alcoves, out in the open, beneath large poplars, so that even if you're there alone you feel a presence, something besides stone."

Perry smiled and ran his hands through his thinning hair. He leaned back in his chair and stretched.

"I haven't thought about that for a long time."

"I'll bet it wasn't a dream," I said.

"Well, now that you bring it up, it's a very vivid image. I can almost feel the stones of those paths under my feet. It must have been late fall or early winter. There was a dusting of snow on the benches and in the cracks between the stones. There was a crisp breeze blowing, and I wasn't dressed warmly enough."

He leaned toward the fire, elbows on his knees.

"It's amazing what your imagination can do."

"That sounds a little too vivid to have been a dream. Maybe you were in there once."

"If so, I don't know when it would've been."

I slept with my window open that night for the first time. Although the nighttime temperatures still dropped to near freezing, the air held a fertile freshness, an innate warmth that smelled like hope. A slight breeze rustled the trees in the garden below my window, and somewhere far off I could hear the faint tinkling of wind chimes. I slept and dreamed of the Caribbean.

We are at Casa La Verdad, all of us, Stephen, Ellen, my father, even my mother. For months we've been preparing the resort so that it will be ready for guests. Stephen and I have re-drywalled and painted all the bungalows. We've weeded the paths and repaired the cracked cement, fixed railings, mended benches, reattached fallen gutters and downspouts. Mother and Ellen have cleaned and restocked the kitchen, scoured and waxed the dining-room floor, restocked the pantries and freezers. Father has resurfaced the swimming pool and filled it. He's restocked the wine cellar and polished the bar. Together, all of us have worked for two weeks straight repainting the exterior of the villa and the bungalows.

Now everything is done. Tomorrow the resort will be filled with guests. We stand together on the patio by the pool and look around at all we have accomplished. Ellen, Stephen, Mother, and Father all decide to take a swim in the ocean, but I'm content to sit by the pool with a drink and watch. They take inner tubes down to the water, and after swimming past the breaking waves, they float together, bobbing lazily on the rising and falling swells, linked together by their feet. From my spot on the patio, they look like a cell that has divided once, and then again.

I close my eyes and listen to the birds singing in the trees above me, relaxing for the first time in months, feeling my heart rate slow and slow until it seems minutes between beats. When I open my eyes, I see that my family has drifted far out from the shore, too far I think for them to get back easily. I stand up and wave my arms, but they don't notice me, don't notice, it seems, that they have drifted so far out. They float farther away, their relaxed figures atop the inner tubes becoming smaller and smaller, still unaware that they are drifting away. I look around for some way to get their attention. My heart pounds, threatening to break through my ribs, and I think the sound of it alone must be enough to alert them to their peril. I run down to the beach, but as I reach the water's edge, the tubes are caught up in a strong current. They speed away and soon vanish.

I stagger back to the pool, collapse onto a chaise longue, and cry. When I stop, my throat is raw and my head throbs.

Then Martin is there, standing over me.

"Why are you crying?" he asks.

"They're gone," I say.

"That should make you happy," says Martin. "Now you're alone. Isn't that what you've always wanted?"

I look up, but his face is dark and featureless. When he turns to go, I notice that he's carrying a suitcase. He walks into the forest and disappears without looking back.

I awoke with the impression that it was still early in the night, that I hadn't been asleep for long. I stared at the canopy above the bed and breathed. I listened to the sounds the castle made, the soft clicking noises the stone walls emitted as the night air cooled them. Outside the breeze had died and the distant wind chimes were still.

I got up and walked to Catherine's room. I knelt by her bed and watched her sleep, listened to her breathing. I was suddenly aware of a fear—a fear that in some fetal form must have been inside me for months, only now coming to term, its ugly head crowning—the fear that Mary would soon return and reclaim Catherine.

I pulled her blanket up around her chin and went to her window that she, like me, had left open. I leaned out and breathed the crisp air. There was a half-moon, waning, clear and bright, lighting the grounds below, covering everything in silver leaf. I looked up at the moon, something stirring inside me, something like prayer attempting to rise up in my throat, but when I opened my mouth no words came out—only breath.

The next morning after breakfast, Catherine led us to the spot in the woods where she'd seen the statue of Saint Anthony. It was another fine spring morning, still chilly from the cold night, but the sun was already promising to take the temperature into the sixties. At one point I saw a flash of red at the edge of my vision, and I stopped on the path and peered into the trees. Far off I saw a massive woodpecker clinging to a fir tree only a few feet from the ground. When I moved ahead to try to get a better look, it was gone. I was sure I was looking at the same tree where I'd seen it moments earlier, but now there was nothing but bark, speckled with a bluish lichen.

Walking on I saw that Catherine and Perry had stopped and were standing in a small clearing to the side of the path. When I joined them, Catherine held out her hands.

"This is where it was," she said. "But it's not here anymore."

She turned to leave, continuing on the path around the convent.

"Wait," I said. "Are you sure this is where it was?"

"I'm sure. It was right there, but now it's gone."

I have said that it might have been Catherine's saints who saved me from my own self-absorption that spring, but it may also have been Catherine herself and the comfort of her routine. Every weekday I drove her down the mountain to school and picked her up again in the afternoon. Other parents were always doing the same, mostly mothers of kids who lived out of town where there wasn't any bus service. Over time I learned which children belonged to which mothers. At some point I crossed an imaginary threshold and became one of them. Although no one knew my name, there were always smiles and waves as we circled through the roundabout in front of the school, dropping off our children.

One day, as one of these mothers waved to me from the window of her car, I detected something I hadn't noticed before. I realized that it had been there all along. It was behind all their smiles and waves. It was pity.

It occurred to me for the first time that they assumed I was Catherine's father. I imagined them wondering about Catherine's absent mother. Was she working? Had she left? Was she dead, leaving me alone to be both father and mother to Catherine? I imagined they were all a little bit in love with me, a single man raising his daughter on his own, having been dealt some heartbreaking blow, sorrow now the staple of his existence. I realized also that if these assumptions existed outside of my own imagination, I had no inclination to correct them.

After school we would stop at a small market before coming home. Sometimes I would have a list and a plan for dinner. Other times I would ask Catherine what she thought we should have, and we'd make up the menu as we walked the aisles. But whether it was planned or impromptu, it didn't escape me that we were shopping for one meal at a time.

One day after shopping, Catherine made me stop at the nursery we passed every day on the edge of town. They'd recently put out hundreds of flats of flowers, turning their parking lot into a mountain meadow bursting with color. Catherine skipped between the rows like someone in love. We went home with four flats and planted them in a long-unused bed at the edge of the patio.

The next day as I was sitting by the pool reading, I looked over at the flowers. They didn't look as good as when we'd bought them. In fact, each time I looked up from my book to check on them, they looked worse.

By the time I left to pick Catherine up, I was sure they were beyond hope. On the drive down the mountain, I rehearsed what I would say. It was too early for flowers up here. We should have waited. Maybe the soil was no good. We can try again with fertilizer in a couple of weeks. But when the time came, I was afraid to say anything. They were just flowers, but I thought any kind of death now might be too much for Catherine.

When we got home, Catherine went right to the flower bed.

"I'm sorry," I said.

"For what?" she asked.

"I think they're dead."

"They're not dead, you silly. Don't you know anything? They're having a little transplant shock. They'll be fine by tomorrow."

I'd heard of transplant shock, and for a moment it sounded like a good explanation, but these flowers seemed too far gone. If only they could be as resilient as Catherine.

The next day, after dropping Catherine off at school, I went into the library to find a new book. Perry was asleep on the couch covered by an afghan, one arm draped on the floor. During those first weeks after my arrival, I'd been careful to be quiet whenever I came upon him sleeping, but in time I learned that Perry slept like a newborn. It was an apt metaphor. He slept away almost his entire existence, and he could do it anywhere, no matter what was going on around him.

I straightened the afghan, chose a book, and went out to the pool. The bed full of flowers caught my eye. I smiled as I touched one of the blossoms with the tip of my finger. Catherine had been right. They looked as good as when we'd bought them.

I settled into a chaise longue facing the sun, and the dogs arranged themselves at my feet. I was only a few pages into my book when Perry appeared and sat down next to me.

"I thought we might fill up the pool," he said.

He stared into the empty concrete crater, still mottled with debris.

"Sounds reasonable," I said.

As if he'd only been awaiting my approval, Perry clapped his hands and leaped up. He disappeared into a garden shed at the back of the castle and soon reappeared dragging a hose. The dogs sprang to their feet when they saw the hose and moved cautiously toward it, sniffing the air, edging closer, then springing away whenever Perry flipped it in their direction. When he had it straightened out, with one end dangling over the side of the pool, he disappeared again. In a minute a stream of water poured out, splashing onto the cement below.

Perry returned and stood at the edge of the pool. We watched as the water spread across the blue concrete like spilled mercury.

"How long do you think it will take?" he asked.

"I don't know. Days. Weeks."

When I picked Catherine up that afternoon, I told her that I had a surprise.

"If it's that the flowers recovered, that's no surprise."

"Well, you were right, but that's not the surprise."

Back at the castle Perry was still standing at the edge of the pool. I wondered if he planned to stay there until it was full. I made Catherine close her eyes until she was standing right at the edge.

"Okay, open," I said.

Before she could react, there was a loud crack from inside the convent. We all watched as a Wiffle ball cleared the wall and landed in the tall grass beyond the patio. The dogs both raced to the spot where it had landed, and after rooting around for a few seconds, one of them emerged with it in his mouth. He trotted back proudly as if it were a pheasant. After circling around us several times, he settled down a few feet away and began chewing on it. The other dog lay down nearby with his head between his paws and watched.

We all looked up to where the ball had come from and watched in wonder for a while, until it became clear that nothing miraculous was going to happen. Perry returned his attention to the bottom of the pool where the water was gradually rising. After a while he turned toward the castle and announced that he was going inside to take a nap.

I looked again at the dogs and the attention they paid to the Wiffle ball. Since it had appeared, we hadn't heard anything from inside the convent. I imagined all the nuns gazing at the spot on the wall where the ball had disappeared, at first in awe of the swing that had sent it flying so far, then wondering if it would somehow come back. Now the sound of the nuns' play had returned, the sharp crack of plastic on plastic, interrupting the otherwise quiet afternoon.

Catherine stepped next to me and put her hand in mine. I realized that the nuns might not know we were here. They were probably aware of the castle, in years past had heard the riotous parties, but now hadn't heard anything in years. They'd probably forgotten all about it. Since I'd arrived in the middle of the winter, we'd done nothing to alert them to our presence. Our two worlds were no more than a home run apart, and yet the wall that separated us might as well have been an ocean.

I had an urge to retrieve the Wiffle ball from the dogs and throw it back over the wall, to show the nuns that there was another world outside theirs. Maybe they would view it as a good omen. But by now the ball was gnawed to shreds and partially consumed. I thought that to return it now couldn't be viewed as a good omen, certainly not evidence of a friendly outside world.

When we were children and wanted to hear a bedtime story, it was our mother who came to us. We would get into our pajamas, brush our teeth, and use the toilet; then we'd all crowd into Ellen's bed. With Ellen's huge down comforter pulled over our heads, we'd wait for Mother to find us. We used Ellen's bed because it was the largest, but also because Ellen liked the security of having us in bed with her. When the story was over and Stephen and I went off to our own rooms, maybe some of that safeness remained, the warmth from our bodies lingering long enough for her to fall asleep.

We huddle together in the darkness with our knees up to our chins, Ellen between Stephen and me. After a while we hear our mother's footsteps on the stairs; then we hear her down the hall, poking her head into Stephen's room, her voice playful.

"Where are my children?"

The three of us squirm and giggle and shush one another. There are more footsteps, and we hear her again, closer this time, banging around in my room, looking behind the door, fluffing the sheets of the bed.

"Where are my children?"

We giggle more, barely able to contain ourselves. Then she appears in the doorway that joins my room with Ellen's. She's still wearing an apron, her hands smelling faintly of lemon dish detergent. She comes over to the bed and pulls the comforter off our heads.

"There you are!"

We shriek, delighted to have been discovered. Of course it's a game we enact almost every night. Still, we never grow tired of it, never lose the thrill of being found.

She doesn't read to us from books. Instead, she tells us stories about one of her childhood friends, Janis McManis, who is a girl detective. Janis always inadvertently stumbles upon some minor wrongdoing or unsolved crime and uses her sleuthful skills to unravel the mystery. Sometimes the stories go on for nights or weeks.

Mother begins by sitting down on the edge of the bed and saying, "Now where were we?" I think she genuinely doesn't remember where she left off the night before, but of course, the three of us are quick to remind her.

"That's right," she says.

She pauses for a moment and says, "Now close your eyes."

When we do we are transported back into the world of Janis McManis, girl detective.

Mother's a good storyteller. She doesn't stumble or pause more than the story's dramatics call for. There's no indication that she's making anything up as she goes along. It seems that the stories are scripted, memorized, and rehearsed. It's years before I realize that although my mother did grow up with a girl named Janis McManis, all the stories she tells are made up.

What an injustice it was to my mother that she was not the favorite storyteller in our house. She told us stories almost every night, while our father remained in the living room reading to himself. But no matter how much we loved to hear about Janis McManis, it was my father and his one story, a story he told us only once a year on Christmas Eve, that we wholly anticipated, like orphans waiting to be adopted. In the end, my mother's Janis McManis stories were merely turkey sandwiches; my father's story, the whole Christmas meal. Of course, my father had an unfair advantage, for although Janis McManis was pretty and smart and funny and always getting into interesting predicaments, there was no way she could compete with an ugly, one-eyed ogre.

It's Christmas Eve, far past our normal bedtimes. We've eaten our dinner of oyster stew and homemade bread still hot from the oven. We've been to church and returned. We're in the living room in our pajamas, waiting for our father. Outside it's snowing, but it's so dark that everything beyond the walls of our house has disappeared. Inside, however, we are safe and warm. The room is dim, lit only by the soft glow of the fire and the lights of the Christmas tree.

After what seems like an eternity, our father appears, wearing a long, red and white striped nightshirt, a matching nightcap on his head. The fuzzy, red ball of the cap dangles by his right ear like a piece of fruit. It's an outfit that for the rest of the year remains buried in a bottom dresser drawer. He enters the room, and it immediately seems smaller and more intimate. We wait like puppies while he takes a large pillow from the couch and drops it on the floor in front of the fireplace. We continue to wait while he lies down on his back with his head on the pillow and smoothes the long nightshirt over his legs. When he finally has himself situated, we drop to our knees around him, hardly able to believe that this moment has arrived, already a bit of sorrow creeping into our hearts, knowing how soon it will be over.

When the three of us have stopped squirming, my father waits still longer. His eyes are closed, his breathing deep and regular, but he won't start until my mother comes in. She arrives, still wearing her apron, and settles into a nearby chair. And my father begins.

"He decided to run away from home…"

His voice is rough and raspy, but it's perfect for this tale. We've heard the story so many times now that we could each tell it ourselves, but we receive it like communicants, the story like Christmas itself, always the same, always brand new.

This was the story my father eventually wrote down and published. It was called *The Christmas Ogre*. It's still in print, still haunting us. The great irony is that it is one of my fondest childhood memories, and at the same time, in the aftermath of our mother's death, it gave my father the financial means to make his complete escape from us.

The night Catherine told me the story of Saint Anthony was the beginning of a bedtime routine. Each night we would take turns telling a story. It made me feel more like a good uncle. In story we were able to connect in ways that we couldn't otherwise.

When it was my turn, I most often told her stories about Janis McManis, girl detective. I wasn't as good a storyteller as my mother had been, but to my surprise, Catherine was satisfied with Janis McManis. Night after night, whenever it was my turn to tell a story, she listened carefully and never interrupted. When I finished she often commented favorably on the story's outcome.

"She likes the order," Perry said once. "Mystery stories are very ordered. You start out with a neat little ordered world, then something happens—a crime, some mysterious event—to upset that order. Then very methodically, very logically, the mystery is solved, and you're back to your nice little ordered world again. There's no ambiguity. There's always closure. There's always resolution. Good and evil get sorted out."

When it was Catherine's turn to tell the story, she would tell the story of a saint. After a while I realized that her stories had the same quality of order as mine. A person hears a calling to follow Christ. He's persecuted but holds fast to his beliefs. He accomplishes great acts of charity or conversion, performs some miracles, then gets burned at the stake or decapitated by the emperor. Later he's sainted. All neat and tidy. Beginning, middle, end.

Over time, however, Catherine's stories felt like more than a bed-time diversion. They acquired more of a frame, and became more than stories. They became actual encounters with statues she ran into while walking around the convent. As spring metamorphosed into summer and the end of the school year drew near, her reported en-counters with the statues increased, as if the warm weather were mak-ing them sprout from the ground like tulips.

I wondered whether I should do something.

"It's all she talks about," I told Perry.

"You think it's unhealthy," he said.

"I don't know about unhealthy. It seems a little obsessive. A little out of touch with reality."

One warm evening at the end of May, I was lying next to Cather-ine in her bed, our heads on the same pillow. Her window was open and a fragrant breeze blew the curtains into the room like roiling waves. I listened to her little voice, smooth and confident, like oil on water.

That day she'd run into Saint Valentine on the far side of the con-vent. She didn't speak of the things I associated with Saint Valentine. There was no romance, no divine arrows, no love.

"Valentine was a priest," she said. "One day he was called before the emperor, Claudius. He tried to get Claudius to believe in Christ, but Claudius only got angry. Claudius turned him over to one of his assistants, and told the assistant to lock him up in his house. When

Valentine came to the house, he said, 'Lord Jesus Christ, true light, enlighten this house and let all here know you as true God.' The assistant said, 'I wonder at hearing you say that Christ is light. Indeed, if he gives light to my daughter who has been blind for a long time, I will do whatever you tell me to do.' Valentine prayed over the daughter, and she was able to see again, and the whole household was converted. Then the emperor found out about it and ordered Valentine to be beheaded."

I'd had my eyes closed as she talked. When she finished I looked up at the ceiling.

"And you saw his statue today? In the meadow?"

"Yes. He was beautiful. He was looking out over the valley."

"And what do you think all this means?"

"I don't know," she said. "Maybe someone in the castle is going to fall in love."

I laughed. The thought of Perry or me falling in love was ridiculous.

"Why do you think that?"

"I don't know."

"But according to your story, Saint Valentine doesn't have anything to do with love."

"Not really," she said. "That came later. He was martyred, that means killed, on February 14, and that's the day when birds are supposed to mate. So over time he started being associated with love stuff. Mostly it's all Hallmark."

I mussed her hair. "Where do you get all this stuff?"

Catherine smiled and rolled away onto her side, her little signal that story time was over and she was ready to go to sleep. I kissed the back of her neck, then rolled out of bed and turned off the light.

Before leaving the room I said, "Perry or me."

"Excuse me?" she said.

"Perry or me. Someone in the castle is going to fall in love soon. That would be Perry or me."

"It's not going to be me," she said.

The next morning before Catherine came downstairs, I called her school and arranged a meeting with the counselor for later in the afternoon.

That day, while Catherine was at school, I took a walk around the convent. I thought it was just a walk, a little exercise with the dogs, but when I was honest, I had to admit there was something else. I was feeling guilty about my impending meeting with Catherine's counselor. It felt like betrayal. Part of me was hoping I'd come across one of Catherine's statues so I could call off the meeting. I didn't want to have to tell someone outside the castle that Catherine was hallucinating or lying or coping in some crazy way. What I wanted was to believe her.

The walk produced no statues. Nothing but a cedar waxwing in the branches of a wild dogwood and an unidentifiable hawk circling high in the sky above the convent. When I got back to the castle, I lay down on a towel next to the pool, now full of water though still icy cold. I closed my eyes and, although not intending to, fell asleep.

I dream I'm lying by the pool, but now I'm in a chaise longue, wearing my swimming suit. I've been reading, but I've set my book down and closed my eyes. Just as I'm about to drift off, something moves in front of the sun. When I open my eyes, there's a figure standing above me. Because the sun is over her shoulder, at first I can't tell that it's Karen. But when I shield my eyes, I see her. She's wearing a hospital gown. Her hair has been cropped short and is uneven, as if she's cut it with a dull knife. She doesn't speak, but her face is stricken with hurt and betrayal. I remember that I'd promised to pick her up at the asylum, that she'd only planned to stay for a few days. Somehow I've forgotten, and now she's been there for months, abandoned and alone. The look on her face makes it clear that there can be no forgiveness, that my sin of neglect is mortal. I want to get up and touch her, let her feel a tender embrace. I think she expects this, is waiting for it. But when I try to rise, I find my arms and legs are bound to the chaise longue with restraints. They're buckled so tightly that my fingers and toes are beginning to tingle. But Karen isn't aware of the restraints. She sees only that I've chosen to remain in the chair, that I can't trouble myself to get up. The hurt on her face deepens, and as she turns to leave, I try to call out to her, but I'm also gagged, with something that tastes like a dirty sock.

If I believed in such things, I would've thought that while I slept there had been a subtle shifting in the planets, that they were now aligned ill-favorably for me. Everything that happened over the next few hours made me think that I should've stayed in bed.

After waking, the vision of Karen still fresh in my mind, I went inside and showered. Afterward, standing in front of the mirror shaving, I cut my Adam's apple so badly that the water in the sink turned crimson. I held a towel to my throat, but the moment I took it away the bleeding resumed.

I dressed awkwardly, keeping the towel pressed to my throat, trying to keep the blood from dripping on my pants and shirt. By the time I left, I was able to replace the towel with a bandage, but as I drove down the mountain and looked at myself in the rearview mirror, I saw that the bandage was already soaked through with a reddish brown circle.

Then, as I rounded a sharp bend in the road, I had to slam on the brakes to avoid hitting a moose. He was standing right in the middle of the pavement, unperturbed by my screeching tires. I waited a minute, then honked the horn. He looked at me as if I were some curious oddity, certainly not a threat. After a while I eased the car forward until it was a couple of feet from his flank. I imagined he could feel the heat from the engine. I considered continuing forward, nudging him with the bumper, but when I thought about what he could do with a single sweep of his head, I decided against it. I sat there long enough for an entire song on the radio to begin and end, before the moose looked off to the side of the road and began moving. As he ambled out of the way, he looked at me with such disdain that as I drove on, I wondered what I'd done to deserve it.

This feeling of unwarranted condemnation intensified when I entered the school office and encountered an abrasive secretary. When I stepped to the counter and announced myself, she glared in such a condemning way, I had the uneasy feeling that she was aware of Karen and our failed relationship.

She directed me to the counselor's office, then turned back to her desk.

When I stepped into the counselor's office, I faltered. Catherine's prophecy suddenly didn't seem so implausible. Sitting on a small couch against the far wall was the blind waitress from the café. Before I could apologize for getting the wrong room, she looked up from the book she'd been running her fingers over and spoke in that hushed, calming voice that made me lean closer.

"You must be Thomas," she said. She stood and walked over to me, reaching out her hand.

"Yes," I said.

"I'm Clare." She put her hand on my back and directed me to a chair in front of her desk. When we were both seated across the desk from each other, she said, "So."

It took me a moment to realize that I was supposed to talk.

"I'm sorry," I said at last. "It's just that I've seen you before."

"At the café," she offered.

"Last winter," I said.

"I thought I recognized your voice. You're living up at the castle."

"Yes," I said, although I knew what we were doing was more like existing than living.

"So you're a waitress and a counselor," I observed.

"Mostly a counselor. It's my uncle's café. I'm only half time here, so sometimes I help him out when he's short-handed."

Her hair was pulled back and tied in a ponytail. Her face was clean, angular, and honest. And her eyes, although unseeing, were intense and focused. I had the immediate impression that she was smart and straightforward but also a little guarded, not willing to offer more than was necessary.

"So," she said. "What brings you to see me?"

She had such an easygoing, amiable nature that I found myself telling her more than I'd planned. I told her about Catherine's obsession with saints, about claiming to see statues at various places outside the convent. I told her about Stephen's suicide and that Catherine thought Stephen had something to do with the statues appearing. I told her about Mary leaving Catherine with Perry and me, about not knowing where she was or when she'd return. I even told her about Karen.

When I finished, she looked straight at me, and for a moment I forgot that she couldn't see.

"I'm sorry," I said. "I didn't mean to do that. This wasn't supposed to be about me."

Clare shifted in her seat, but her eyes stayed focused on mine.

"It's less about you than you think."

I suppose I'd expected an answer, some concrete advice about what I should do. I guess I was even prepared for some psychiatric mumbo jumbo, answering all my questions with more questions.

—So what do you think is going on?

—What do *you* think is going on?

—I don't know. I was wondering if this was normal.

—Do *you* think it's normal?

—I don't know. I was just wondering if there was cause for concern.

—Do *you* think it's something you should be concerned about?

—I guess so. I thought it might be some kind of cry for help.

—Do *you* get the impression she's crying out for help?

And on and on.

What I didn't expect was that she would suggest a visit to the castle. She stood up and moved from behind the desk. Her wool dress lapped at the tops of her knees.

"I could talk to her here," she said, "but I have a feeling we'd make a lot more progress if she could show me where she's seen these things."

"Fine," I said. "You're welcome anytime."

"How about tomorrow. It's Saturday. Catherine and I could take a walk."

"Great."

"Okay," she said, moving me toward the door. "I'll see you tomorrow, then."

Driving home that afternoon, I asked Catherine if she'd ever met the counselor.

"I don't think so."

"You'd know. She's very pretty. Her name is Clare."

"That's a pretty name."

"Yes, it is."

"There was a Saint Clare."

"Really?"

"Yes, really."

"Are you going to tell me about her?"

"If you want."

"I want."

"She was born in 1194. She was a virgin like Saint Catherine. When she was eighteen, she heard Saint Francis of Assisi preaching, and she was so moved that she gave away everything she had and joined him. She lived in a convent in Assisi and became the leader of a community of women who wished to live like Saint Francis. They lived with almost nothing. Their lives were simple and disciplined. It was believed to be harder than the life of any other nuns of the time.

"Clare never left her convent at Assisi. She was one of the great nuns of her time. She was devoted to serving her community and practicing Saint Francis's ideas, including his love of the world of nature. For the last twenty-seven years of her life, she suffered various illnesses, sometimes being bedridden, but she was devoted to her nuns and to the town of Assisi. She died in 1253 and was canonized only two years later."

"Clare's coming to see us tomorrow," I said as we pulled up in front of the carriage house. "Not the saint, the counselor."

"To talk to me or because you're in love with her?" asked Catherine.

"Don't think your little prediction is going to come true."

I wrapped my arm around her neck and gave it a squeeze.

"She's just coming to talk to you about the statues you've been seeing. She's interested, that's all."

When we reached the doors of the apartment, Catherine paused with her hand on the knob and looked up at me.

"Sorry," I said. "But it's going to have to be Perry. I've sworn off falling in love."

That night Ellen called from the Caribbean. She spoke more loudly than usual, making me think at first that something was wrong.

"Where are you?" I asked.

"At a hotel bar in town."

After a few minutes I determined that nothing was wrong, that Ellen was speaking loudly to overcome the noise of the bar. In fact, it seemed she had no real reason for calling. We made small talk. I asked how the restorations were going.

"We haven't really gotten started yet," she said.

"It's been five months. What have you been doing?"

"Not much, I guess. We take long walks. I've thought about going back to New York, but the thought of it makes me tired."

"How is he?" I asked.

"Okay. He drinks a lot."

I thought that was the pot calling the kettle black.

There were long pauses in our conversation. I sometimes wondered if Ellen had put down the phone and gone to the bar for another drink.

"Why don't you come down here?" she asked.

I paused, not sure how to tell her why that was impossible.

"Catherine's here," I said.

Ellen didn't say anything for a moment. I could see her standing in the dark corner of the smoky hotel bar, wearing a yellow, sleeveless sundress, her arms and face tanned and smooth.

"Who's Catherine?" she asked at last.

"Our niece. She's here."

"Oh, Thomas. Where's Mary?"

I had the urge to pour out all the details of the last five months, to lie down in bed with the phone and talk to Ellen all night. Instead I said, "When I got back after leaving you, Catherine was here. We don't know where Mary is."

There was another long silence. I thought Ellen really had gone back to the bar for another drink, but then she spoke, her voice soft, no longer trying to compete with the noise.

"What will you do?"

Funny, but it hadn't occurred to me that I had to do anything, at least not in those terms. Ellen's questions made me stop and think. Maybe there was something I was supposed to be doing, some simple thing I was overlooking that would begin to piece our fractured world back together.

All I said was, "We're taking it day by day."

"Wow," said Ellen.

Wow didn't seem to call for any response, so I said nothing, waiting for Ellen to say something else.

"I've been thinking about that Thanksgiving," she said finally.

It's midmorning. The turkey has been stuffed, and it's in the oven. After setting the table, dusting, and vacuuming, Stephen, Ellen, and I are released to go play until relatives and friends arrive. We go across the street to a park, where a group of neighborhood kids has already gathered to play football. It's a bright, cloudless day, the sky pale blue at the horizon, but above our heads deep indigo.

We divide into teams, and Ellen and I find ourselves on the side opposing Stephen. He's the quarterback. I place myself in a rushing position, knowing that the only way to prevent him from connecting with his receivers is to put on the pressure, make him throw while back on his heels. But I don't have much success. He throws time and time again, connecting with his teammates at the last second, just when I'm sure I have him sacked.

Toward the end of the game, however, I break through his blockers and find myself right on top of him. I'm as surprised as he is, and I hit him harder than I intend to. He barely has time to turn his back and cup the ball at his stomach before falling on it with me crashing down on top. When I get up, he lies there unmoving for a minute before rolling over. He doesn't take my offer of a hand up, but looks at me with a pained expression. I walk away feeling a little bad about hitting him so hard but also satisfied at finally sacking him.

He plays the rest of the game stoically, no longer seeming to take any pleasure in his completed passes, which he continues to make seamlessly.

It isn't until we're back home that I realize what's happened. Without taking off his jacket, Stephen seeks out our father, and within minutes they're out the door on the way to the hospital. When they get back two hours later, Stephen's ribs are bandaged. Two of them are broken, one of them in two places.

Stephen eats dinner as best he can. It's obvious that breathing is painful. Afterward he pops more of the pain pills he's gotten at the hospital and goes into our father's study to lie down on the sofa.

I find him there in a blurry state, not asleep, but not fully awake either.

"Why didn't you say something?" I ask. "Why did you keep playing?"

"I don't know," he says. "You would have felt bad."

He turns his head to the wall and falls asleep. Twelve years old and already becoming someone I don't fully understand.

"After that, I thought he could endure anything," said Ellen.

"Me, too," I said.

"I miss him."

"Me, too."

I heard Ellen sniffle and imagined her wiping her eyes with the back of her hand. I didn't like the idea of her standing all alone in a strange bar crying.

"God," she said with a kind of half laugh, breathing in through her nose and sniffling. "I don't know what I'm doing down here."

The natural response would have been to tell her that everything was going to be fine. What I wanted was to be there with her. It seemed that in many of my relationships, words were becoming more and more inadequate.

"I miss you, too," said Ellen at last.

"Me, too."

"I better go."

"Okay."

It was dark outside when I got off the phone with Ellen. I stood alone in the kitchen for a long time, fighting off an odd feeling that I couldn't name but that wouldn't go away, something like dread but more comprehensive. The kitchen was dark, the only light coming from a lamp left on in the living room. I moved my hands in front of my face as if what I was feeling was something physical that I could push away.

After several minutes I went to the library to see if there was an open bottle of port there. Perry was asleep on the couch in front of the fireplace, and Catherine was curled up next to him. All the lights in the room were on, and the fire burned hungrily, as if the last thing they'd done before falling asleep was bank it full. I pulled a blanket over them and listened to their breathing. There was no bottle on the cart at the end of the couch. I turned off the lights as I left the library and descended the cold stone stairs of the cellar to get one.

The next morning I awoke disoriented. For a moment I thought I was in my childhood bed, in my parents' house, but that everything in my room had been removed while I slept, replaced with things I didn't recognize. The feeling was compounded when I looked at the clock and saw that it read 4:20. It was obviously morning, but it took me a moment to realize that the power had gone off. I got up and looked at the lichened convent wall. The warmth in the air and the Chablis sunlight gave me the impression that I'd slept late.

Downstairs I found no sign of Perry or Catherine except for an old percolator-type coffee maker on top of the stove. It was cold but still half full, so I replaced it on the burner and turned on the flame. As I waited for the coffee to warm up, I walked around the apartment, looking for a clue as to where Perry and Catherine had gone. The apartment was unusually empty. I went into the library and found that even the blanket I'd thrown over them the evening before had been folded and laid over the back of a chair.

When the coffee was hot, I poured myself a mug and stepped out onto the patio. I walked across the cool stones in my bare feet to the edge of the pool and dipped a toe in. The water was still chilly, but I thought in another week or so it might be warm enough for swimming. I looked toward the convent and listened for signs that the nuns might have a game of Wiffle ball going, but there was only quiet. I imagined they might be praying.

There was a breeze at my back, and I thought I heard voices. I walked through the side garden, now brilliant green with new growth. I walked slowly to avoid spilling my coffee, careful not to step on any sharp stones in my bare feet. The morning air was warm, almost hot already, thick with birdsong—nuthatches and chickadees and finches and pine siskins all chattering, indiscernible one from the other. Amid the birdsong I thought I heard voices again, and I continued along the path to the front of the castle. There I saw Perry and Catherine standing in the middle of the gravel parking area with fly rods in their hands.

Perry stripped line from his reel and cast toward the castle while Catherine watched. The line arced out, out and back, beautiful green curves floating effortlessly against the blue of the sky. He worked out more line, putting his shoulders and legs into it, until his fly was hovering over the pond between the parking lot and the castle, extending so far behind him that I thought it might hit the gatehouse. He stripped more line until I thought there was no way it could stay aloft. With each cast the fly grew closer and closer to the castle wall, until at last I heard a faint snap as the fly flicked against the stone.

Catherine turned and saw me but returned her attention to Perry. As he reeled in the line, there was a smile on her face that could have turned an orphanage into a place children desired to go. I stood several yards off as Perry stood behind Catherine and positioned her elbow and forearm into the proper posture. He gripped her wrist and showed her how it should move, or not move—I couldn't tell which.

Just as Catherine began her first cast, a car came through the gatehouse and stopped twenty or so feet behind us. The three of us turned in unison and looked at the car as if it were something from another planet.

Clare stepped out of the passenger side, and a taller woman with a mane of thick, dark hair emerged opposite her. Clare was wearing white pleated shorts and tennis shoes and had her sandy hair pulled back in a ponytail. She looked childlike, a little waifish, all the formality and business of the office left behind. I thought she looked closer to Catherine's age than my own. But as she walked toward us, the lines in her face and her freckles became more distinct; I saw that her beauty was a woman's, not a little girl's. She walked directly toward us, unguided, but in a moment her companion was at her elbow, not touching, but close enough to be felt.

Ten minutes later I was alone by the pool, picking through the book I'd been reading the day before. I read the same paragraph half a dozen times before I put it down and stared at the curve of the convent wall where Clare and Catherine had gone. It gave me a warm feeling to see them walking hand in hand, Catherine leading Clare in a strange reversal of roles.

But now a vague emptiness was growing in my stomach. I went inside to find something to eat, but after standing in front of the open refrigerator for several minutes, I finally closed it, acknowledging that what I was feeling was not hunger.

I wandered around the apartment, from kitchen to living room to library, looking for something to occupy me. I sat down in a leather club chair, but no sooner had I leaned back and propped my feet up on the ottoman than I was up again, like a young child squirming through a church service. The power was back on, so I occupied myself by resetting the clocks.

The aloneness I'd felt in the morning again filled the apartment. I left by the door leading to the interior of the castle and closed it behind me. I stood there for a while, letting my eyes adjust to the darkness, feeling the damp coolness settle on my skin. I reached out for the heavy door to the castle's tower and began to climb.

I stopped a few flights up and looked out a narrow window overlooking the parking area at the front of the castle. There below me, like little ceramic fishing figurines, were Perry and Clare's friend Juliana, casting their lines across the gravel as if they were twin maestros conducting a single orchestra. Their lines moved together in such uni-son it seemed impossible to me that they weren't connected, that there wasn't some trick involved. After a few minutes they stopped and reeled in their lines, half facing each other, talking, sometimes laugh-ing. Their voices drifted up through the air like pollen.

Back downstairs I ran into them coming in from the patio. They were like children about to ask permission for something.

"Hey," said Perry. "We thought we might make a quick run over to Logan Creek."

"Okay," I said.

"I'm not sure how long Clare was planning to stay," said Juliana with a note of apology in her voice, "but maybe if she wants to leave before I get back..."

"I can run her home," I said.

"Perry said you wouldn't mind."

"I don't."

They were gone in an instant, and once again the apartment was empty.

I went back to the pool and waited for Catherine and Clare to get back. They were gone longer than I expected. When they returned the afternoon air was dry and warm. The three of us stood by the pool in a small circle, Catherine and Clare still holding hands like sisters. Perry and Juliana still hadn't returned from fishing.

"I'm sure they'll be back any minute," I said. "They should've been back by now. We can run you home if you don't want to wait."

Clare brushed the hair from her face.

"I hate to be a bother, but Juliana has no concept of time."

I laughed.

"Neither does Perry. Catherine and I can run you home. We need to pick up something for dinner anyway."

As we walked through the garden on the way to the carriage

house, Catherine took my hand and flashed me a smile. She was still holding on to Clare with her other hand. We walked through the garden and across the parking lot that way and didn't separate until we got to the carriage house where I needed both hands to lift the door.

When we got to Clare's house in town, I walked her to the door while Catherine stayed in the Jeep.

"So?" I said. "What do you think?"

"About what?" asked Clare.

"About Catherine. What do you think?"

Clare looked at me with her mysterious eyes, not vacant, but deep, bright, and knowing. "Are you familiar with doctor-patient confidentiality?"

I waited a minute to see if she was serious. When I saw she was, I said, "You're kidding."

"She's my patient," said Clare.

"But she's nine. The whole reason I wanted you to talk to her was because I was concerned."

"You're angry."

"I am not," I practically yelled.

A hint of a smile appeared on her face. It made her look even more beautiful, and it made me angry. At the same time I was aware that I was being childish. I willed myself to speak calmly.

"Can you tell me anything?"

"She's a good kid," said Clare. "And from what I can tell, you're a good man."

"That's pretty thin."

"I'd like us to be friends," she said. "I'd like to spend more time with Catherine."

"So there *is* something wrong."

Clare smiled again and bent her head. A strand of her hair, broken free of the ponytail, lay across her cheek.

"Look," she said. "I'll be honest. I don't think you have anything to worry about. I find her fascinating in a lot of ways. I'd consider it a privilege to get to know her better."

"Professionally or personally?" I asked.

"Both."

"Fair enough. But my gut reaction is that she needs a friend more than she needs a doctor."

"See that?" said Clare, opening the door and stepping inside. "I was right. You *are* a good man."

When we got back to the castle, Juliana's car was gone and Perry was asleep on the couch in the living room. Catherine and I carried the groceries in and began putting them away, but after a minute Catherine excused herself, saying she was going to take a nap too. As she climbed the stairs to her bedroom, it seemed as if her pockets were full of rocks. I finished putting the groceries away by myself, then went into the library to read for a while before fixing dinner.

I realized I'd fallen asleep too, when I awoke with a start from a dream about my mother. It was still light outside, but I had the impression I'd slept hard for hours. I went to the living room and found Perry still asleep on the couch. He was curled on his side in a fetal position, his mouth hanging open. I put my hand in front of his face to make sure he was still breathing, then climbed the stairs to Catherine's room.

On the way into her room, I tripped over her tackle box, and it clattered across the floor. I yelled, but Catherine didn't stir. She was curled into a little ball, hugging a small pillow to her chest. I laid my hand on her back and felt the rise and fall of her breathing.

Downstairs I went back to the library and stood in front of the large arched windows where months ago I'd learned of Stephen's death. Despite the depth and length of my nap, I thought I could lie back down and go to sleep again. I wondered if Clare or Juliana had sprinkled the three of us with sleeping powder or if their presence after so many months alone had worn us out.

In the dream I'm young, perhaps ten or twelve. It's the first day of a new school year, and I've left the house excited and hopeful. It's a warm day in September, and the world seems safe and full of promise. Once at school, however, things begin to go wrong. I can't find my homeroom. I keep walking into the wrong classrooms, and I'm met with belligerent stares. I do find my locker, but the combination I have doesn't work. I try it five or six times, but then I notice that the numbers on the dial are not in order and are larger than they should be, some of them in the thousands. Finally I give up and head for the office. On the way I realize I've misplaced my new notebook and pencils. I keep turning down long hallways that lead nowhere, with no doors or windows, just solid brick at their ends. Throughout the dream I keep thinking of my mother. I want only to get home to her, knowing that with her, everything, all this craziness, will get sorted out. Finally I find a door that leads outside, and I run all the way home, through traffic and woods and street after street of row houses that all look the same. When I get there, my mother meets me at the end of the driveway, already aware of my distress, and wraps her arms around me, pulling the side of my face into her breast. I break down and sob, not because of the lostness I felt in the school, but because in my mother's arms I am safe and know it will always be so.

I stood at the library window with my nose running, tears smearing the view. In Spokane I'd cried at the news of my mother's death. I'd cried at the funeral and during the weeks afterward. But I could see now that they'd been tears of anger. Tears of rage and injustice. I cried now, for the first time, out of simple sadness. I cried because I missed my mother, because never again would I feel the comfort of her arms. My safest place was lost, the world was now a colder, less hospitable place.

When Perry and Catherine woke up from their naps, we shared a subdued dinner of rice and fish—trout that Perry and Juliana had caught earlier in the day at Logan Creek. After dinner, Perry and Catherine went to the kitchen to do the dishes, and I stepped outside into the darkness of the patio with a glass of wine. A large moon, three-quarters full, was coming up behind the ski mountain. Despite the warm spring, stubborn patches of snow had clung to the mountain's ski runs until a week or so earlier. Now the slopes were bare, bright green with new growth, and as the moon rose, the entire mountain was bathed in a silvery light. I walked around the tiles at the edge of the pool, balanced between the firm stones of the patio and the dark water. For several steps I closed my eyes, imagining being blind, but I couldn't take more than a few steps before I felt myself falling toward the water.

I stayed outside until the moon arced its way across the sky and was directly overhead. When I went back in, the dishes were done, the kitchen counter wiped clean, and Catherine and Perry had already gone up to their rooms. I climbed up to the third floor and saw that Catherine's light was still on, so I went in and sat down on the side of her bed.

"So, how was your walk?" I asked.

"Good."

"What did you talk about?"

"Nothing much. Normal stuff."

"Did you see any saints?"

"No. There weren't any."

"Did Clare ask you lots of questions?"

"Not really," said Catherine. "We mostly just walked."

I kissed her on the forehead and pulled her sheet up closer to her chin.

"Do you like Clare?" I asked.

"Do you?"

"That's not what I asked. She'd like to come see you again. She wants to be your friend. Would you like that?"

"I guess I would if you would," she said.

"I guess I would too."

"Okay. Maybe all three of us can be friends?"

"I think we can," I said. "But don't get your hopes up. Just friends."

"Just friends," said Catherine. "I think Perry and Juliana have already taken care of my Saint Valentine prediction."

"You may be right. So that takes the pressure off me, right?"

"I guess so. I just thought it was going to be you."

"I know you did," I said. "But let's not worry about me, okay?"

I stood up and went to her door and turned off the light. "Okay?"

"Okay," said Catherine, but I thought she could have said it with much more conviction.

We didn't see Clare again until the next Saturday, but on Wednesday morning Juliana reappeared, and she and Perry went fishing again. I spent the day by the pool, reading. It was warm, the warmest day we'd had so far, and after a half-hour or so in the sun I had to move to a corner of the patio that was shaded by a tree. I looked at my arms and legs and realized I was turning brown. I thought of Ellen by the pool at the resort. Probably at that very instant she was doing the same thing I was, the only difference being that her book would be an old paperback mystery, and her drink would not be an iced tea. The thought that we were doing the same thing at the same time, although thousands of miles apart, could have made her seem even farther away, but instead it made me feel closer. I closed my eyes and imagined that not only were we doing the same thing but we were thinking the same thing. That at that very instant Ellen was also thinking of me lounging by the castle's pool, a book in my lap, a drink at my elbow.

I'd just come back from picking up Catherine from school when Perry and Juliana returned. I was in the kitchen looking for something to cook for dinner, and Catherine was at the kitchen bar having an after-school snack. We heard a splash, a shrill scream, another splash. We stepped to the open french doors and watched as Perry and Juliana splashed in the cold water. When Perry climbed up onto the diving board and cannonballed toward Juliana, I could see that his swimming suit was the pair of boxers he'd been wearing. When Juliana climbed onto the board a moment later, Catherine and I got a good eyeful of her underwear as well. She had a full figure, not too much or too little of anything, everything right where it should be, her thighs and calves well-defined and muscular. She bounced off the board and spread her arms and legs out wide and screamed, then pulled into a cannonball before hitting the water.

After Juliana surfaced, Catherine walked toward the pool, but before she made two steps, I grabbed her by the arm.

"Get back here," I said.

"Give me a break," she said. "It's just underwear."

She pulled away and skipped toward the pool, stripping off clothing as she went. By the time she got to the diving board, she was down to her panties and a thin sleeveless T-shirt. She paused for a moment on the diving board, then with a decisive little nod, she bounced off the end of the board like a kangaroo.

I watched the three of them splash around together for a minute, then felt self-conscious and went back inside and continued to search for a dinner idea. When I couldn't come up with anything that sounded interesting, I stepped back out onto the patio and called to Perry.

"Are there fish?" I yelled.

He'd just enough time to yell to me that there were brookies in a cooler in the car before Juliana put her hand on his head and forced him under the water.

I brought the cooler back to the kitchen and put on an apron. After washing the fish, I rubbed them inside and out with brandy. Then I minced an onion and added parsley, chives, chervil, and tarragon. I sliced up a handful of mushrooms and squeezed their juice onto the herb-and-onion mixture, stuffed the trout with it, and set it aside.

In a small skillet I added diced tomatoes, the mushrooms, more onion, and sautéed the mixture until it turned to a thick sauce. I sprinkled it with paprika and set it aside with a lid to keep it warm.

Next I dipped each fish in egg and coated them with a mixture of bread crumbs and parmesan cheese. I lined them up in a buttered baking dish and stuck them in the refrigerator to soak up the flavor of the herbs until it was time to bake them. After I'd washed up all the pans and bowls, I hung up the apron and went down to the cellar to look for the most expensive-looking wine I could find.

When I came back upstairs, Catherine was sitting at the kitchen bar with one of her school books open in front of her. She chewed the eraser on the end of a pencil and ran her fingers through her damp hair, smoothing out the tangles.

"Where did the lovebirds go?" I asked.

Catherine pointed toward the library with her pencil.

"You look cold," I said. "Do you want some hot chocolate?"

"Okay."

I put water on to boil. Juliana appeared from the library, pulling the huge double doors closed behind her. She walked over to us and sat down next to Catherine at the bar.

"He's asleep," she said. "I must have worn him out."

When Perry woke up, I stuck the fish in the oven and turned on a low flame under the skillet of sauce. While the fish cooked, Juliana and Catherine set the table with candles and napkins and a linen tablecloth. After ten minutes I pulled the fish from the oven and poured on the sauce.

After dinner I left the table and let the others clean up. I lay in bed with my clothes on and listened to the faint clinking of dishes being done in the kitchen. As the voices from below tendrilled up the stairs, I tried to determine what was bothering me. What had that meal been all about?

Normally after one of Karen's breakups, we wouldn't see each other for several days or a week, as she hid herself away in her apartment and refused to answer the phone. I would cook and clean and cook and clean and drink entire bottles of wine that I had no business buying. Then Karen would finally take one of my calls and agree to see me. I would spend several days trying to convince her of the rightness of our being together. Slowly she would yield, and for weeks or months she'd seem happy, affectionate, the strange turmoil inside her put to rest.

After a while I heard footsteps on the stairs, and Catherine came into the darkness of my room. She stood by my bed for a few minutes, perhaps waiting for her eyes to adjust to the darkness.

"Are you awake?" she asked.

"No."

She climbed into bed and lay beside me. Her breathing was heavy from the climb up the stairs. She waited until it slowed before talking.

"Do you want to hear a story?"

I smiled. "Do you want to know what you've done to my life?"

"What?"

"You've made it better."

Catherine didn't respond, but I could imagine she was smiling. When she spoke, her voice sounded too mature for her age.

"Do you want to hear a story?"

"Yes," I said.

"This is the story of Saint Juliana."

"You're kidding."

"No, I'm not."

"There was a Saint Juliana?"

"Sure."

There was a warm breeze blowing back the curtains at the window. Outside, in the garden below, I could hear the wind rustling the leaves of the trees. I listened for the sound of the wind chimes at the front of the carriage house, but they were muted. Catherine moved closer so that her arm was touching mine.

"Juliana was beautiful. She had thick, dark hair like our Juliana. She was supposed to be married to a man named Eulogius, but she refused to become his wife unless he accepted Christ. So her father had her stripped and beaten, then he handed her over to Eulogius to be his wife, but she told him she still wouldn't marry him.

"Eulogius said, 'My dear Juliana, why have you rejected me this way?'

"Juliana said, 'If you will adore my God, I will consent; otherwise I will never be yours.'

"But Eulogius said, 'I can't do that because the emperor would have me beheaded.'

"Juliana replied, 'If you're so afraid of a mortal emperor, how can you expect me not to fear an immortal one?'

"At this Eulogius had her beaten and ordered her hung up by her hair for half a day and molten lead to be poured on her head. But none of this did her the slightest harm, so he had her bound in chains and shut up in prison where she argued a long time with a demon who tried to persuade her to obey the wishes of her father and Eulogius. When she was brought out of the prison, everyone saw that she had the demon in bonds. She dragged him from one end of the marketplace to the other, then finally tossed him into the sewer.

"When news of this reached Eulogius, he had Juliana stretched on a wheel until all her bones were broken and the marrow spurted out, but an angel of the Lord shattered the wheel and healed her. Then Juliana was put into a tub filled with molten lead, but the lead became like cool bath water.

"Finally, Eulogius had her beheaded, and afterward he went to sea with thirty-four men. That night a storm came up, and they were all drowned. Later, when the sea cast the bodies up on the shore, they were devoured by birds."

When Catherine was finished with the story, I lay still and stared up at the canopy over the bed.

"You're going to give me nightmares."

"Sorry. Do you want me to sleep here tonight? So you're not alone?"

"Okay. I think that would be good."

Catherine got up and went to the bathroom. While she was gone, I changed into pajamas. When she crawled into bed, she lay on her side with her back to me.

"Good night," I said.

"Good night," said Catherine. "Try not to have nightmares."

I rolled over so that we were back to back, like human bookends. I stared over at the window and watched the curtains flutter in the breeze. After a long time I sensed that Catherine was still awake.

"There was a Saint Just About Everybody, wasn't there?" I said.

Catherine didn't respond for so long that I thought I'd been mistaken, that perhaps she'd fallen asleep, but then her voice came out of the darkness.

"There wasn't a Saint Perry."

When I was thirteen years old, I had a voyeuristic experience that I've never been able to shake. Our home in Baltimore was in a quiet neighborhood of medium-sized houses with manicured lawns, unfenced dogs, and children my own age. A young couple had moved into a house on our street. I don't remember, or never knew, what the husband did for a living, but he was never around. He kept long hours wherever it was he worked and would often be away for days at a time. I don't remember much about the wife either, except that I thought she was pretty, and she seemed sad…and she had an unforgettable name, Ada, which I don't know how I learned. They moved away less than a year after they'd arrived, and I experienced my first broken heart because I'd been in love with her from afar for months.

Shortly after they move in, I'm walking home following some after-school activity. It's winter and already dark. I'm short-cutting through yards and ducking through hedges when I find myself in the backyard of the new couple's home. They're having new gutters installed, and scaffolding is set up across the back of the house. In one of the upstairs rooms, I catch a glimpse of Ada as she passes in front of the window. Without even thinking, I drop my book bag in the middle of the yard, climb a ladder to the scaffolding, and inch across it on my hands and knees until I'm in front of the window. I watch Ada folding a pile of laundry that sits in the middle of the bed. There's something about her face, about her movements, that seems resigned, like a zoo animal gazing through the bars of its cage.

After several minutes she comes across a large sweater, and instead of folding it and putting it away, she raises it to her face and smells it. She inhales, holds her breath, and closes her eyes. When she lowers the sweater, there's a wistful smile on her face. She drops the sweater to the bed and pulls the shirt she's wearing over her head and replaces it with the sweater. When she does, I see that she is braless, and although it's only for a moment, I get a clear view of her small breasts. I lose my balance, and as I grab at the plank to steady myself, a large splinter wedges into my palm.

Whether or not the memory is accurate, I can still see those breasts, although now when the memory recurs, the image of Ada is dim or faded, as if I'm looking through a screen door. What's strange is that what I felt after the initial pain of the splinter subsided was not arousal, but sadness. I climbed down from the scaffolding and continued home, one coin from my lifetime bank of optimism forever spent.

In the months that followed, I would sometimes see her wearing that large, baggy sweater, and I cherished my secret knowledge of what lay beneath. I felt that I alone understood her, her loneliness, her sorrow, her sad disappointment that life didn't always work out the way you expected.

Maybe I could have developed an equal empathy by talking with her, but I don't think so. I've always believed that my understanding of her deep sorrow, or my perception of it, could only have come from spying on her, from watching her when she didn't know she was being watched.

* * *

In a way, I was having a similar experience with Clare. Whenever she was around, I found myself watching her in a way that was almost voyeuristic. Watching her didn't make me sad in the same way watching Ada had, but there was a degree of sorrow. It was unclear to me, however, whether it was coming from Clare or from within me.

I not only watched Clare, I studied her—how she walked, carefully yet unselfconsciously, gracefully; her uncanny ability to look you in the eye, to make you believe that she was seeing you; her refreshing but startling directness; her childlike innocence and optimism; her absolute loyalty to those she cared for; her hair like champagne when it was struck by the morning sun; the Celtic cross her father had given her, which she wore around her down-scaped neck; and, undoubtedly, the unconditional way she loved Juliana and, more and more, Catherine, too.

I told myself that she wasn't my type—she was too slight, too wispy, too quiet. But there was this strange triangle: At times I thought Catherine reminded me of Karen. And there were times when I thought Catherine and Clare could be sisters. Wasn't it logical, then, that there were similarities between Karen and Clare?

I examined Clare secretly, minutely along her entire length, but I kept my distance. I don't mean physical distance—I was often close to her, required to hold her elbow and guide her to a car door, through an unfamiliar room, or along a rocky trail. It was a different kind of distance. It's possible to be touching someone and remain miles away.

But over time her presence began to unseat me, and I knew I couldn't have it both ways. I looked at her one day by the pool and realized that she was a different woman from the one I'd met on my first day in town. I said stupid things whenever she was around. She gave no sign that she noticed, but how could she not?

* * *

Clare returned with Juliana on Saturday, and again she and Catherine walked hand in hand around the convent. It was a hot, breezeless day, the air torpid, smelling of smoke. I watched from the kitchen window until they disappeared around the convent wall, then I picked up the book I'd been reading and went out to the pool.

After reading only a few pages, I got overly hot. When I dove into the pool, I heard the dogs barking. They sprang from their little haven of shade next to the pump house and stood at the edge of the pool yipping and whining. I glided listlessly down through the cold water until I reached the bottom, then I rolled onto my back and lay there looking up through the water. The sun was a huge fried egg, its insides liquid and wavy. At the pool's edge I could see the blurred heads of the two dogs, tilting left then right, like a curious Cerberus between our two worlds. When I rose to the surface, they barked and licked at my wet face, but as soon as I was out, dripping on the flagstones, they lost interest and retreated to the shade of the pump house.

When I'd settled back into my chair, Juliana appeared from the castle wearing a bathing suit. She pulled a chaise longue up next to mine and sat down.

"Do you mind?" she asked.

I said I didn't and asked, "How is he?"

"Stoical. Aggravating. Infuriating."

I smiled.

"I feel like it's my fault," she said. "I didn't know about the sun. Here I've been dragging him out fishing during the sunniest days on record."

"He didn't look dragged," I said.

Since Wednesday Perry had taken a turn. He slept most of Thursday, his skin blotchy with a mottled rash. On Friday he walked around the apartment, bored with his bed and room, but the effort it took was painful for Catherine and me to watch. He looked like an old man stricken with arthritis, his joints inflamed and painful. Awake, he was stoical, as Juliana had observed, never complaining. But asleep, the act dissolved. He tossed and groaned whenever he moved.

"I don't understand it," said Juliana. "Do you know what's happening?"

"Not really. His insides are getting eaten up. His immune system is attacking his blood."

Juliana stood up. She went to the edge of the pool and looked into the water. She was wearing a simple, black one-piece bathing suit cut high on her hips. My eyes fell on her muscular legs. I wondered if she'd been born with them.

"Have you ever been in love?" she asked.

There was a sudden burning in my head. I wanted to dive back into the pool and sink again to the bottom, to view the world through ten feet of water. But I stayed where I was, kept my eyes on the back of Juliana's thighs.

"Yes," I said after too long a pause.

Juliana dove into the pool. With an almost imperceptible spring from her toes, she launched herself into a perfect little arc and entered the water without a splash. I watched her glide through the water, halfway between bottom and surface, without kicking, without using her arms. She surfaced on the far side with her head back, the water cascading off her thick hair like oil. She breast-stroked back, the two sides of her body in perfect symmetry. When she reached the edge, she dipped her head back, wetting her hair again, then crossed her arms on the edge of the pool.

"Was it love at first sight?" she asked.

I put on a pair of sunglasses to shield my eyes from the glare coming off the water behind her.

"No. It was strong attraction at first sight. It took a few weeks to fall in love."

Juliana looked at me. There were little rivulets of water running from her hairline along her nose to her mouth. Occasionally she covered her upper lip with her lower and sucked in the water. It was a gesture that was both pensive and pouty.

"What about you?" I asked.

"I've never been in love."

"Until now?"

"What makes you think I'm in love with him?"

"I didn't say you were. It was just a question."

I stood up, took off the sunglasses, and dove into the water. When I surfaced on the other side, Juliana was swimming toward me. I rested my arms on the hot rocks of the patio and looked off toward the convent. Juliana laid her arms out on the patio next to mine.

"I think I am in love with him," she said. "Do you think that's crazy?"

"No. I don't think it's crazy."

"It *is* crazy. I've only known him a week. But do you know why it's not completely crazy?"

"Why?"

"Because I see how much you love him. And how much Catherine loves him."

I know people can fall in love at first sight because that's the way it happened for Stephen and Mary. I don't think I'm being dishonest when I say I've never held a grudge against him for taking her away from me. Any bystander could have seen, the moment they met, how the long-dormant gears within them engaged and began to turn, revolving slowly, roughly at first, but then accelerating, soon spinning smoothly, the only sound a distant, efficient whir.

It's difficult to begrudge such a supernal connection, and of course it's dramatic to say that he took her away from me. Mary and I had been on only two official dates before I made the mistake of letting Stephen meet her. But, of course, their meeting was inevitable: Stephen and I lived in dorm rooms across the hall from each other; we were brothers, practically twins. In the end it was better that it happened sooner rather than later.

It fell to Stephen to bring me the news, but by then I already knew. To their credit they tried to be sensitive. Mary didn't visit Stephen in his room. They didn't sit together in the dining hall if I was there. It was inevitable, however, that on such a small campus, I would run into them. At first there were awkward moments, silences. I believe there were even times when, for lack of anything else to say, we discussed the weather. Over time, however, the awkwardness faded. Stephen and Mary were so right together that it wasn't long before I forgot that she and I had ever dated. In time we settled into a comfortable friendship, fueled by our mutual love of Stephen.

I didn't realize I was crying until Juliana apologized.

"I'm sorry," she said. "I didn't mean to bring up bad memories. I probably made you think of an old girlfriend."

"No. Not an old girlfriend. I was thinking about my brother."

"Perry told me he died recently. I'm sorry."

"It still doesn't seem real," I said.

* * *

By the time Catherine and Clare returned from their walk, Juliana had gone back inside to check on Perry. I was still in the water when the two of them walked hand in hand up to the pool's edge.

"How was your walk?" I asked.

"We're roasting," said Catherine. "All we could talk about for the last twenty minutes was getting back and jumping in the pool."

Catherine led Clare into the house, and in a few minutes they returned wearing bathing suits. Catherine guided Clare to the edge of the pool's deep end, then dropped Clare's hand and said, "There." Then Clare dove into the water with an unsettling trust.

I sat on the edge and watched the two of them swim. More and more I thought they looked like sisters. Most astounding was that they acted like sisters. In the brief time they'd known each other, they'd developed a mysterious kinship. I felt certain that a stranger passing them on the street would mistake them for sisters. I watched for several more minutes as Clare swam laps and Catherine dove, trying to pick something off the bottom of the pool.

Back inside the castle, I ran into Perry and Juliana leaving for the hospital. Apparently Juliana had talked him into changing an appointment he'd had for the following week.

"Do you want me to come?" I asked.

"No," said Perry. "They're just going to take some blood and send me home. It won't take long."

After they'd gone, I lay down on the living-room couch with my book. Despite the day's warmth, inside the apartment the air was cool, insulated by the castle's thick stone walls. I pulled a fleece throw over my body and shivered. Outside I could see Catherine and Clare sitting on the edge of the pool with towels thrown over their shoulders. Beyond them an afternoon breeze rustled the leaves at the tops of the cottonwood trees. I watched for some time, ignoring the book in my lap, feeling lonely, but expectant, as if I were on the cusp of some change toward which I could either fall forward in faith, like Clare into the pool, or not.

That night I ended up taking Clare home again. When Perry and Juliana returned from the hospital, they disappeared up to Perry's room. Catherine, Clare, and I were at the patio table eating BLTs and twice-baked potatoes when Juliana reappeared. She pulled Clare to the edge of the patio, where they had a brief conversation, then Juliana went back inside and Clare returned to the table and sat down.

"I hope you don't mind running me home again," she said. "Juliana wants to stay."

"Of course not," I said. "We can go anytime."

We cleared the table, and Clare retrieved her bathing suit from the bathroom.

"Ready," she said.

We moved to the door, but Catherine didn't follow. She stood in the middle of the living room and watched.

"C'mon," I said. "Let's go."

"Oh, I think I'll stay. Lots of homework to do, you know."

I looked at her for a moment.

"Okay. Whatever you say."

Outside Clare slipped her arm through mine, and we walked together to the carriage house.

"I'm sorry about that," I said. "But Catherine doesn't have any homework; there are only three days of school left. She thinks she's being clever, getting us alone together."

"I know. It's a good thing."

"It is?"

"I mean it's a healthy thing for Catherine. She's trying to piece her world back together. To match things up the way they're supposed to be. It means she's coping."

When we arrived at Clare's house, I walked her to the door and waited until she'd opened it. We stood for a bit longer, long enough for the moment to become awkward.

"I better get going," I said.

"Thanks for the ride," said Clare.

That night after Catherine had gone to bed, I went up to her room. On the way, I saw that Perry's door was open, so I looked in. He and Juliana had fallen asleep on top of the covers with a cribbage board between them. I picked up the board and the cards and threw a sheet over them and continued up to Catherine's room. I sat on the edge of her bed. She patted her pillow, indicating that I should lie down next to her. I was lying there looking up at the ruffled edge of the bed canopy, trying to remember whose turn it was to tell a story, when something occurred to me.

"I forgot to ask," I said. "Did you see any saints on your walk today?"

"I forgot too," said Catherine. "We did. It was a statue of Saint Thomas."

"My namesake. Did Clare see it too?"

"Sure. I mean she didn't actually see it, but she touched it. Have you ever noticed her fingers?"

"They're long," I said.

"Really long," said Catherine. "I bet she can play the piano."

I didn't encourage Catherine to tell me what she knew about Saint Thomas. Instead I yawned and feigned fatigue and told her I was going to bed. Catherine didn't seem to mind. She rolled over on her side and let me tuck her light sheet up around her neck. But when I went to the door and turned off her light, she stopped me.

"Uncle Tommy?"

"Yes?"

She paused long enough that I thought she'd changed her mind. But then she spoke again.

"I'm glad Juliana is here tonight."

I stood there fighting the urge to climb back into her bed, to curl up behind her and wrap my arms across her tiny chest. To somehow assure her of what couldn't be assured, that somehow we were going to come out on the other end of all this. Instead I remained in the doorway, wondering what I'd done to deserve her. And, more important, what I would do without her.

"I'm glad too."

I pulled the door half closed and went downstairs to call Clare.

It took five rings for her to answer.

"I hope it's not too late," I said.

"No."

"I didn't want to bother you, but I just put Catherine to bed. She said you saw a statue today."

There was a brief silence.

"That's true. We did."

"And you saw it?"

"Yes. Catherine said it was a statue of Saint Thomas."

"Why didn't you say something when I took you home?"

I thought I heard her take a deep breath before she spoke again.

"I was going to. I would have. I just wasn't ready. I needed some processing time."

"Okay," I said. "Have you had enough time to process now?"

"You're starting to sound belligerent," said Clare.

"I'm sorry. I didn't mean to."

I lowered my voice.

"What do you think we should do?"

"Well," said Clare. "I don't work on Monday morning. Why don't you pick me up after dropping Catherine off at school, and I can show you where we saw it."

"Do you think you can get back to the same spot?" I asked.

"I think I can get pretty close. It was a thick part of the woods, shaded and cool, then we entered a small sunny clearing, and that's where the statue was. I dropped my Chapstick right in front of it as we were leaving."

"That was smart."

"I thought so," said Clare.

After hanging up, I stepped out onto the patio. It was fully dark now, and a large moon was rising from behind the convent. I walked over to the pool, lay down on one of the chaise longues, and closed my eyes. Minutes later I awoke with a start from a brutal dream or vision— I was unsure which because I wasn't aware that I'd fallen asleep.

I rise from the chaise longue and go back inside the apartment. On the way up to bed, I pause outside Perry's room, and again I look in. Perry and Juliana have thrown off the sheet I pulled over them and are now lying side by side with no clothes on. Juliana's arms wrap around Perry like a protective cocoon. I walk to the side of the bed and look down at them. Their bodies are both brown, no tan lines anywhere, their skin soft and smooth like a baby's—no moles, no freckles, no blemishes of any kind. Light from the moon comes in the window and lends an unreal hue to their bodies. I realize that for the first time in months, maybe years, Perry's body is free of the bruises and mottled blotches that plague him. I realize at the same time that Juliana has something to do with this, that she's somehow healed him.

Juliana winces, and I step back in terror as a purple bruise begins to form on her shoulder. She moans in her sleep as another appears on her back, and then another and then more, until her back and arms and legs are covered with blemishes. Some are leaking a thick, yellow pus. As I'm about to dart for the door, Juliana's eyes spring open, and she looks at me. Seeing the look of disgust and terror on my face, she says, "What? You've never done anything nice for somebody?"

Sunday morning dawned warm and hazy, the air thick with an unusual humidity. When I entered the kitchen, I found Catherine and Juliana cooking breakfast. Juliana was wearing a pair of Perry's boxers and a gray, sleeveless T-shirt. I crossed the kitchen to the coffee-pot and touched her bare shoulder.

"Good morning," I said.

Juliana's smile reminded me of Ellen.

After breakfast Juliana went back upstairs to Perry's room, and Catherine and I tried to decide what to do with ourselves. We took a walk, then went into the library and started a game of Monopoly that lasted the rest of the day. It was getting dark when I landed on Park Place where Catherine had a hotel, and I handed her all my cash.

On Monday morning Catherine woke me up by jumping into my bed. The morning air was hot, but the humidity was gone and a breeze was blowing through the trees outside my window. I thought I detected the faint smell of smoke.

"Wake up," said Catherine.

"What time is it?"

"It's after eight. We need to go."

I pushed myself up and sat on the edge of the bed.

"Do I smell smoke?"

"There's a forest fire on the back side of the ski mountain," said Catherine. "It's over ten miles away, but the wind is carrying the smoke this direction."

"Is that what Juliana told you?"

"Yes."

She seemed a little offended that I wouldn't believe she could come up with these facts on her own.

I pulled on a pair of shorts and a T-shirt and slipped my feet into a pair of tennis shoes. Then I stood up and stretched.

"Alrighty. Let's get you to school."

Catherine looked at me. "Is that what you're wearing?"

"Yes, this is what I'm wearing. Is there a problem?"

"You look slobby. What if you run into someone you're trying to impress?"

"If you're talking about Clare," I said, walking out of the room, "first of all, I'm not trying to impress her, and second of all, she can't see what I'm wearing."

I hurried down the stairs so that Catherine had to take them two at a time to keep up.

"She can see more than you think," Catherine shouted behind me. "And yes, you are."

In the kitchen Juliana was cooking breakfast. Perry was sitting at the bar, already halfway through a plate of bacon and eggs and pancakes. He looked renewed, like someone who's just taken a hot shower and put on clean clothes after a week in the woods. I said good morning and grabbed a cup of coffee. When I turned around, Juliana handed me a plate full of food.

"Thanks," I said, "but Catherine and I are late. It looks delicious."

As we headed for the door, Catherine scooping up her backpack, Juliana called out, "You have to have something."

She quickly assembled two egg sandwiches, wrapped them in paper towels, and handed them to us.

"There," she said. "You can eat that in the car."

After dropping Catherine off, I drove to Clare's house. As I got out of the Jeep and brushed the crumbs from the sandwich off my shirt, I noticed a small, pea-sized stain of egg right in the middle of it. I thought about Catherine's comment, and then I did feel slobby. My fingers were greasy from the sandwich, and I hadn't shaved in two days.

The inside door to Clare's house was open, so I rapped on the edge of the wooden screen door and called inside.

"Hello. Anyone home?"

Clare answered from the back of the house. "Come on in. I'll just be two minutes."

I stepped into a small living room and looked around. The house was a clapboard two-bedroom left over from the railroad era. It was in a part of town that had once been considered the wrong side of the tracks but in recent years had experienced a face-lift. They were the kind of houses real-estate agents billed as "charming starter homes."

Clare's house was clean and sparse. All the furniture was old and comfortable, from the era when the house had been built. I chose a pale green overstuffed chair with a matching ottoman and sat down.

Back in what I guessed was her bedroom, I could hear Clare moving around, humming a measure or two of a song I didn't recognize. When she came out, she was dressed in cut-off bib overalls and a white T-shirt. She looked like she was about sixteen years old.

"Ready," she said.

I stood up and folded my arms across the egg stain.

We stepped outside, and a hot gust of wind blew Clare's hair across her face like a blond veil. She pulled it aside with two of her long fingers as I took her by the elbow and led her to the Jeep.

"What do you do during the summer?" I asked as we drove out of town.

"Not much. Fill in at the café a little. Mostly I relax. Juliana and I take some trips together."

Juliana was a ski instructor on the mountain during the winter months (which explained her legs) but didn't work the rest of the year.

"There's a hot springs over the Canadian border," said Clare. "We like to go up there in the summer. Sometimes we have the place all to ourselves."

Clare sat at an angle in her seat as she talked, her body half turned to me, her knees drawn up with her hands clasped around them. I wanted to reach over and put my hand on her knee, to let it rest there while she talked so she would know I was listening. I wanted her to know that I was perfectly content just listening.

Back at the castle we found a note on the kitchen table from Perry and Juliana: *Feeling better. Gone fishing.*

After returning from our walk around the convent, we went inside. While I fixed iced tea, Clare sat at the kitchen bar and fanned her neck and face with a magazine. Since finding her Chapstick, any kind of small talk seemed inappropriate. I kept trying to think of something to say, something that would make sense, but everything seemed banal.

I handed Clare her glass, and the telephone rang. I picked it up, welcoming the intrusion. I listened to the voice on the phone as I watched Clare drink down her entire glass of tea. When I hung up, she was absent-mindedly sucking on an ice cube. I watched her. The action seemed inappropriately erotic.

"What's wrong?" she asked.

There was a strange buzzing in my head, currents of electricity tingling across my scalp.

"We've got to go," I said. "I'll take you home."

Clare stood up.

"What's wrong?"

"That was the hospital. I need to find Perry."

"What's happened?"

"I have to get him to the hospital. His platelet count is low."

"What does that mean?"

"It means that if he jars his head, even a little bit, the blood vessels around his brain could hemorrhage."

I picked up the Jeep keys from the kitchen table and took Clare by the elbow.

"I don't need to go home," she said. "Let's just find Perry. Where did they go?"

"I don't know."

On the way down the mountain, my old driving habits came back. I gripped the wheel and took the turns on the mountain road too fast for the Jeep's high center of gravity. Clare was pushed back in her seat, her fingernails digging into the armrest, making permanent crescents.

"I'm sorry," I said, easing off. "This can't be much fun for you."

"It's okay. Let's just get there in one piece. Where is it we're going?"

"I guess we'll try Logan Creek. That's where they've been going. Hopefully they didn't decide to try someplace new."

At the bottom of the mountain, I turned up the highway and headed north. Now that we were on an open stretch of road, I pushed the accelerator to the floor and didn't back off until we approached ninety. After several miles I turned off onto a rutted dirt road, and we slowed to a crawl. We bumped up the narrow road through a clearcut recently replanted with seedlings. I wondered if Perry was already dead. I imagined his brain like a delicate vase inside a box that someone has neglected to pack properly. The Jeep bounced sideways into a rut, and Clare said, "Oh."

I told myself that Juliana's hulk of a car would have navigated the road more gracefully than the Jeep, but I thought how easy it would be for Perry to slip on a rock while wading into the creek. Even if he caught himself before falling, the slipping alone could be enough to rupture the blood vessels around his brain. I imagined that he would stand for a few seconds, aware that something cataclysmic had happened. He would look over the sparkling water at Juliana, already feeding out line for her first cast. Then he'd fall. His waders would fill with water and pull him under the creek's surface. The way the doctor had made it sound, I didn't think he'd even have time to drown.

We'd been gradually climbing since we left the highway. Now the road crested a small hill, and we entered a thick forest of evergreens. Clare noticed the change and rolled down her window. She leaned a little toward it and smelled the air.

"Are we close?"

"I think so. I've only been here once, but I think almost."

"What's happened to the road?"

"It's smoother here," I said.

"No," said Clare. "It's not just that. It's quieter, too."

"It's covered with fir needles. There're a lot of trees here."

"Describe them."

I didn't answer for a minute. It hardly seemed time for a tour.

"They're trees," I said. "I don't know. Mostly Douglas fir. Some tamarack and ponderosa pine. The ponderosas are big. Their branches don't start for fifty feet up. They have reddish bark. When it flakes off, it looks like pieces of a jigsaw puzzle."

"You're joking."

"I'm not. Haven't you ever touched one?"

"I don't know. I've never noticed that about the bark."

A Forest Service gate came into view, and I spotted Juliana's car parked in front of it. I hadn't prayed in years, but as I pulled the Jeep to a stop in front of the gate, I said, "Thank you. Now let him still be alive."

I jumped out and looked at Clare before closing the door.

"The creek's a couple hundred yards off," I said. "I'm going to run. You'll have to stay here."

"Okay."

I slammed the door, ducked under the gate, and ran down the road. After a hundred yards or so, I heard the water. I turned into the woods toward the creek. When I broke through the trees at the water's edge, I was on a small rocky beach halfway between Perry and Juliana. Juliana was downstream, casting into a shallow riffle where a small stream entered the creek. Perry was upstream about fifty yards, up to his chest in the icy water, casting into a deep pool on the creek's far bank.

I walked upstream and screamed, "Perry!" It was a few minutes before I was close enough for him to hear me over the rushing water. When he did, he reeled in his line and walked toward me. I wanted to warn him that one slip could be fatal, but I decided that trying to warn him over the noise from the creek would only cause confusion. I waited on the bank, watching him take step after step along the rocky bottom until he'd made it safely to the edge.

Perry reached me at the same time Juliana waded up from the shallows.

"Hey," said Perry. "What're you doing out here?"

I didn't want to alarm Juliana, so I simply stated the clinical facts.

"The hospital called. They want you to come in. Your platelet levels are at four thousand." (The doctor had told me that normal levels were around twenty-five thousand.)

"Oh," said Perry.

"What does that mean?" asked Juliana. "Is that bad?"

We both looked at Perry.

"It means I'm a good candidate for a brain aneurysm," he said.

"Oh, sweet crap," said Juliana.

We went back slowly, Perry walking between Juliana and me with his head held as if he'd slept on it the wrong way. Back at the cars, we decided that I should drive Perry to the hospital in Juliana's car and that the girls should follow us in the Jeep.

"I don't get it," said Juliana as we stood between the two vehicles. "Are you saying a bump in the road could cause an aneurysm?"

"It's possible," said Perry.

She climbed into the Jeep, her face rigid and angular.

The time it took to get to the highway was immeasurable. The ruts seemed to have deepened; the washboard was worse. Each rock was a boulder, each pothole a chasm. The speedometer on the Delta 88 never moved, resting all the time on zero as if it were broken. I glanced over at Perry every few seconds, but he stared straight ahead, his eyes glassy and distant. When we approached rockier parts of the road, he would mumble "Easy, easy," barely moving his lips.

By the time I picked up Catherine from school that afternoon, Perry's platelet levels had risen. There was still concern, but I sensed a tangible easing of tensions among the doctors and nurses who attended him. As I waited at the curb in front of the school, I rehearsed how I would tell Catherine about Perry. What I really wanted was to suggest that we go camping. Maybe we could drive down to Yellowstone? Maybe Clare could come along? Wouldn't that be fun?

I didn't see Catherine approach. I jumped when she opened the door and sat down. She tossed her book bag into the backseat and looked at me.

"What's wrong?"

"Nothing."

"Yes there is," she said. "Something's wrong."

"How do you know?"

"I don't know how I know. I just do."

She narrowed her eyes. I had the sense that she was better equipped for the future than I was.

"Perry's in the hospital," I said after a time. "But he's okay."

Catherine wrinkled her forehead. "What's wrong?"

"His blood tests showed that his platelets were down, so they're bringing them back up."

"How're they doing that?"

Catherine pulled her knees up on her seat and turned toward me—a way of sitting in the car that was almost identical to Clare's.

"They're pumping him full of steroids," I said.

"What's that do?"

"I don't know. I guess it helps balance things out in his blood."

"Is Juliana with him?" asked Catherine.

"And Clare, too," I nodded.

"So he's okay."

"He's fine. He's resting. Would you like to go see him?"

"Yes."

What I didn't tell Catherine was that hours earlier an Indian intern with a heavy accent had come into Perry's room and performed a bone-marrow biopsy on him. This involved laying Perry on his stomach, anesthetizing a small area of skin at the base of his spine, and inserting a wide-bore needle into his hip bone. Mercifully, Clare and Juliana had gone down to the cafeteria, because the needle got stuck and Perry started screaming at the intern. Later Perry had to apologize for telling him to "go back to India and torture some cows." Through it all I stood in the corner of the room clenching my teeth, a rolled-up magazine gripped in my hand. Finally the intern gave up and called a doctor. While we waited for him to arrive, the huge needle hung limply from Perry's back.

The next morning on the way back to the hospital, Catherine and I listened to radio reports on the spreading wildfires. There were now more than a dozen separate fires in our area. A few were contained, but most were out of control. They were jumping roads and fire lines and rivers and burning thousands of acres of forest. None of the fires posed an immediate threat to the castle; still their presence filled us with a sense of anticipation, like my father must feel in the face of an approaching hurricane.

At the hospital we found Perry and Juliana lying on the bed together watching *Flipper* reruns. Catherine pulled up a chair next to the bed and put her hand on Perry's arm.

"How's the sicky?" she asked.

"Looks like I'm going to make it," said Perry.

"I've seen this before," said Catherine, gesturing toward the TV. "My father said it wasn't very well written. He said it would have been better if they'd let the dolphin write it."

"Is that so?" said Perry.

"Yes," said Catherine. "Dolphins are very smart."

We all watched the television, aware now of the predictable dialogue, aware that we were not talking about Stephen. I sat down on an orange vinyl chair in the corner of the room and closed my eyes. After a while I thought I could hear a faucet dripping. It became louder and louder, drowning out the television. I looked at the others to see if they noticed, but they showed no sign that they did. I realized that what I was hearing was the drip of the IV in Perry's arm. I turned and watched the liquid dripping, dripping, and the sound of it pulsed in my ears. I closed my eyes, and the dripping became like thunder. I imagined the drips working their way through Perry's body. How did they know what to do? I pictured the steroids as little armored warriors entering a conflict *in medias res*, Perry's blood the battleground. Then Catherine touched me on the arm.

"Time to go."

When I dropped Catherine off at the front of the school, she hesitated before going in. Halfway between the school doors and the Jeep, she stopped and turned to look back at me. I took off my sunglasses. She stood there motionless for some time, a strange knowing expression on her face, but I couldn't guess what she was thinking. I was about to get out and suggest she skip school, when she flashed me a pensive smile, then turned and disappeared through the school's shadowed front doors.

I returned to the hospital and played backgammon with Perry while Juliana ran errands and shopped for the next night's dinner. Perry was scheduled to go home the following afternoon, and we had decided to throw a combined Welcome Home/Last Day of School party. After the heaviness of the last couple of days, it seemed like a good idea.

"You smell like smoke," said Catherine the next afternoon when I picked her up from school.

"I had to drive through some to get here," I said. "Do you see what I go through for you?"

"Smoke," she said, unimpressed.

"Yes, smoke. That's not good enough for you?"

"Well, it was just smoke. It's not like you went through an actual fire to get here. Did you see flames?"

"No. But they couldn't have been far off. It was very thick smoke."

Catherine rolled her eyes and pulled her legs up onto her seat. I stared at her, not starting the Jeep.

"What?" she asked.

"I was just looking to see if you looked like a fifth grader."

"I'm not a fifth grader."

"Well, what are you? You're not a fourth grader anymore."

"Something in between," she said.

* * *

Catherine wasn't in the habit of holding my hand, but she took it as we walked through the front doors of the hospital. We walked past the nurses' station, and as we turned down the corridor to Perry's room, she gave my hand a firm squeeze. Clare was standing by the window at the end of the hallway, already changed out of her work clothes, dressed in shorts and tennis shoes, looking ready for our party. The afternoon light hit her face and cast half of it in shadow. Catherine's steps quickened, but I resisted, practically dragging my heels, wanting to savor the sight of her there as long as possible.

Catherine couldn't stand it any longer. She dropped my hand and ran, saying, "Clare, Clare." When she reached her, Catherine took one of Clare's hands in both of hers. She looked up into her face and said, "You look so beautiful standing here. Like an illuminated saint."

"Do I?" asked Clare.

"Absolutely," said Catherine.

When I approached, the two of them turned in unison. For a moment I felt that I was envisioning a single person at two stages of life.

"Hello," I said. "You're here early."

"I left work early," she said. "There's nothing for me to do on the last day of school. And I suppose I was a little anxious. I guess I'm in the mood for a party."

"Good," I said. "We are too."

Juliana and Perry emerged from Perry's room. Perry was dressed and ready to go.

"Well," said Juliana. "I guess it's girls and boys. Perry wants to ride home with Thomas."

She flipped her hair in mock indignation, stepped between Clare and Catherine, and took their hands. She leaned down toward Catherine and whispered.

"They need to have boy-talk," she said. "They're probably going to talk about us, but that's okay because we're going to talk about them, too."

Catherine smiled as Juliana led them away.

"See you at the castle," sang Juliana as they marched off, their arms swinging between them like pendulums.

I picked up the duffel bag at Perry's feet, and we walked after the girls.

"So how're you feeling?" I asked.

"Pretty good, actually," he said. "Kind of juiced up."

"Everything back to normal?"

"For now."

We stopped at the hospital pharmacy where Perry was given a Mason jar–sized bottle of prednisone, and then we walked out into the heat. The sky was hazy with smoke.

"I didn't know it was this bad," said Perry.

"It's getting worse."

On the way up the mountain, we drove through smoke so thick I turned on the Jeep's headlights, but that only made things worse. Perry told me about a dream he'd had the night before.

"It was more a vision than a dream," he said. "Or it started out as a dream and turned into a vision. When it was over, it took me a few minutes to convince myself I'd been asleep.

"I was walking through a forest on a spring day. I came across a small cottage surrounded by thick vegetation. All the windows were open, so I looked in. I suppose it was then that it began to feel more like a vision.

"Inside the cottage on a bed made of bamboo was a woman in labor. The air in the room was hot and humid, and the smock she was wearing was soaked with her sweat. Outside where I was standing, it was a typical Montana spring day, but in there, even though all the windows were wide open, it was tropical.

"I watched for a long time as the woman progressed in her labor. She didn't seem to be terribly in pain or even all that uncomfortable. On the contrary, she was taking the whole thing in stride, as if giving birth by yourself was normal. But then the baby's head crowned, and the woman screamed.

"Her face changed then," said Perry. "It was Juliana. She kept screaming and screaming, and I realized that the baby was stuck, and if it didn't come out soon, they would both die.

"She stopped screaming and looked over at me for the first time. 'Perhaps you could help,' she said. I looked at her for a moment, and I was struck by how strong she was. Then I crawled through the window and asked what I could do.

"She laughed. I suppose it was a stupid question. But she was patient with me and nice, even though she was in terrible pain. She smiled and touched me on the arm and asked if I could pull the baby out, as if that were the simplest thing in the world. 'Just pull it out,' she said."

"And did you?" I asked.

"Yes," said Perry. "But it wasn't a baby anymore. It was a little doll, like a GI Joe. It was a fully clothed adult male, and when I held it up in front of my face, I realized it was me. What do you think of that?"

We passed through the gatehouse and stopped in front of the carriage house.

"Spooky," I said.

"Worse than spooky," he replied. "I feel like I've been given the gift of a glimpse of the future, and I'm supposed to do something with it."

"Like what?"

"I don't know. Something."

We walked through the garden, ripe with white narcissus, to the patio where the girls were swimming. Something about the scene—

the faint smell of chlorine in the afternoon air that had turned humid, the comforting sound of female laughter, the bright sun reflecting off the wet tiles that lined the pool—took me back to a distant summer spent on the Maryland shore.

Stephen and I have just returned home from college. We've been home for less than a day when our parents announce, uncharacteristically by their own admission, that they've purchased a condominium at an upscale resort on the Maryland shore and are planning to spend the entire summer there. It's their wish that Stephen and I come with them. They tell us that Ellen is already there, having driven straight from her freshman-year finals at Boston University. Since Mary is in Europe and the alternative is another stifling Baltimore summer, Stephen and I agree to go. Stephen has graduated and in the fall will be entering General Theological Seminary in New York City. For him it's the perfect interlude between two stages of his life. For me, after a rather uneventful sophomore year in which I excelled at nothing and refused to choose a major, it seems like as good a place as any to spend the summer. Our parents, already packed, leave that same afternoon. Stephen and I follow the next morning.

When we arrive in the early afternoon, no one is there. We're both surprised by the condominium. It's two stories and larger than we imagined. The downstairs is spacious and open, the living room and kitchen separated by a tile bar. There's a large deck off the front, overlooking the pool and tennis courts below. Upstairs is a master bedroom and two smaller bedrooms joined by a shared bathroom. Ellen has taken the bedroom with a view of the ocean.

After dropping our bags in the other bedroom, Stephen and I go back downstairs and step out onto the deck. Directly below us, on a chaise longue by the pool, Ellen is tanning in a dark green bikini. In a week or so when her tan has deepened to a sufficient depth of bronze, she will switch to a white suit that will suffice for the rest of the summer. Stephen takes a nickel out of his pocket and drops it off the edge of the deck. It lands with a little slap on Ellen's flat belly. She doesn't bolt upright as I'd expected. Instead a slight smile appears at the corners of her mouth, then she opens her eyes and looks up at us. She says, "Hello, brothers," then closes her eyes, removes the nickel from her stomach, and goes back to the business of tanning.

Until Perry shows up, it's a strange summer. Despite our parents' insistence that we come to the beach with them for the season, we rarely see them. They eat all their meals in the clubhouse and spend hours walking together on the beach. They've even taken up tennis and play doubles with another couple every morning. Stephen, in the early days after our arrival, describes their behavior alternately as a midlife crisis and empty-nest syndrome.

On the other hand, it's possible that Stephen and I are playing an active role in the distance we feel from the rest of the family. On several occasions we leave the condo in the morning while Mother and Father are still there, sitting at the breakfast bar or on the front deck sipping coffee, and my father asks, "Now where are you boys off to so early?"

I rarely have any idea where we're off to. Stephen usually directs the day, and I'm more than happy to let him. In reality, Stephen rarely has much of an agenda in mind. We spend the days body surfing and taking walks on the boardwalk and looking at girls. We pass many hours at the club's outside bar playing dominoes, a game we play for money, a dollar a point, which Stephen, to an uncanny degree, wins. By the middle of the summer when we stop playing, I owe him close to three thousand dollars.

It's Perry who transforms the summer. He arrives in mid-July, unexpected and uninvited, but welcomed. Stephen and I return from the beach one afternoon to find him playing a game of rummy with Mother and Father at a glass-topped wicker table on the condo's deck. Perry's back is to us, so he doesn't see Stephen and me approach. As we pass through the sliding-glass doors and step out onto the deck, my mother lays down her cards and pronounces gin.

"You are no lady," says Perry.

He still hasn't seen us, but when my mother looks up and smiles, he turns around.

"Your mother cheats at rummy," says Perry. "You might have warned me."

My mother smiles, as if an insult from this handsome young man is the crème de la crème. Father, too, is smiling, and I see that he approves not only of Perry but of me for having a friend of this caliber. My mother informs me that I'm in the doghouse for not telling them that Perry was coming. But before I can defend myself, before I can tell them I had no idea myself, my mother is already back to cooing over Perry.

"It's so nice of you to come see us," she says. "Thomas has been telling us about you for two years now, but frankly we were beginning to wonder if you existed."

Perry smiles and greets Stephen and me with something that is halfway between a handshake and a hug. The sound of children's laughter is coming from somewhere below, mingling with the distinct sound of AM radio coming from the direction of the clubhouse. Perry steps back and looks at us. I'm suddenly aware of an invisible change, almost imperceptible, like the quiet moment when the tide begins to ebb.

The summer from then on has a different flavor. What's funny is that our routines don't change much. The major difference is that

Stephen now spends most of his time studying a Greek primer in preparation for entering seminary in the fall. He's never done well with languages and wants to give himself as much of a head start as possible. Now, instead of letting Stephen direct my days, I let Perry, who proves better at it than Stephen.

We play a round of golf every morning, which always commences with a screwdriver at the clubhouse and ends there with french fries and martinis. When we return to the condo in the early afternoon, we stumble upon the same tableau. Father and Mother, still dressed in their tennis clothes, are dozing in chaise longues in the shade at one end of the deck. At the other end is Stephen curled up with his primer in a club chair he's dragged out from the living room. Below us beside the pool, Ellen is tanning, her skin glistening with oil. The only variable is whether we'll look down to find her lying on her back or on her stomach.

I'm not sure why this is, but the days have taken on a sense of purpose. Although hardly anything has changed, I no longer have the feeling that we're killing time. With Perry everything seems intentional. The feeling of randomness to my days, and I suppose even to my future, has dissipated like a brief summer thunderstorm.

As far as I can recall, no one ever asked Perry how long he was staying. Maybe we assumed that if we didn't ask, he would stay on and on, which in the end is what he did. Oddly, I think his presence made us more intimate with each other than we'd been for the first half of the summer. I have many vivid memories from the second half of that summer, but two stand out.

It's near midnight during our last week at the beach. Perry, Stephen, Ellen, and I are sitting on the deck, watching an impossibly large moon rise up from the ocean. It's been a dreary, rainy day spent inside playing endless games of dominoes, cribbage, and rummy, but now the skies are clear, and what seems like an artificially warm breeze blows in off the ocean. For the first time that summer, I'm wearing socks. As the moon rises, as if birthing itself from the ocean, the presence of the socks strikes me as wildly inappropriate. I take them off and toss them through the open sliding-glass doors behind me. I look at the others to see if they've noticed, but they are all mesmerized by the moon, which shrinks several sizes as it ascends. Stephen clears his throat and speaks. At first I think he's going to comment on the socks, but he only asks if we're planning to play golf in the morning.

"I suppose we are," says Perry. "Would you like to join us?"

"I guess I would," says Stephen.

No one speaks for a few minutes. I'm both happy and sad that Stephen will forsake his Greek for the morning and spend the day with us.

"Me, too," says Ellen. "I want to come too."

"We have a foursome," says Perry.

As the moon rises into a few straggling wisps of clouds, there's a pang in my chest, something between hunger and heartburn. I close my eyes and see the four of us lined up at the clubhouse bar in the morning, a bright orange screwdriver in front of each of us. Then we're walking together down a wide fairway lined with huge maples and oaks. We've each driven our balls an impossibly long way off the tee, and we're eager to see whose ball has gone the farthest. Still we walk rather slowly, not wanting to rush things, each of us very conscious of enjoying each moment of this round of golf, knowing that each time we strike the ball is a moment of our lives both given and taken away.

* * *

The other event occurred earlier in the summer, shortly after Perry's arrival. Perry and I have just returned from a lunch of martinis and french fries at the clubhouse. We get back to the condo in time to see my father ushering my mother in the door, cupping her head with a bloodstained towel. By the time we get inside, they've been joined by Stephen in the bathroom, and it's too crowded for me to see what's going on. What I can see is that Mother is sitting on the closed toilet seat with Father and Stephen hovering over her. There's blood on her white tennis blouse and skirt, and more on her shoes.

"What happened?" I ask.

"I hit your mother with my racket," says my father.

"It was an *accident*," my mother insists. "It was my fault, really."

"It wasn't your fault." He reaches for a fresh towel from a shelf behind the toilet. "I could've put your eye out."

"Oh, pooh," she says. "Your backhand isn't that strong."

"Is she okay?" I ask. "Where is all that blood coming from?"

"I'm fine," says my mother. "It's just one of those head cuts that bleeds like crazy. What do you boys want for dinner?"

She looks up at the bathroom light and squints. What color she has left in her face drains away, and her head bobbles on her shoulders.

"Oh dear," she says, lowering her head, "I always knew I'd die young."

By the time she regains consciousness, we have the bleeding stopped and have fixed two butterfly bandages to the cut. We lay her on the divan in the living room, but she insists that she's going to get up and fix dinner. The fact that she has hardly cooked a single meal since arriving doesn't seem to concern her. Tonight she is going to cook dinner if it kills her. In the end she finally agrees to let us order out for pizza, but only after she attempts to walk to the kitchen while none of us is looking, and almost faints again.

* * *

Our last day at the condominium is sunny and warm, but there's a change in the air that hints of fall. We've stayed longer than many of the other summer residents, and already there is a quietness about the place that feels lonely and remote. All day, as we pack and clean, I have the strange sensation that I've stepped into a huge, vacant ballroom on the morning following an all-night party.

Around noon Perry finds me sweeping off the deck and comes to tell me that he's on his way. He's already tracked down everyone else and said his good-byes. Our farewell is brief and casual, knowing we'll be seeing each other again on campus in a few days. I watch him turn and leave, a single duffel bag slumped over his shoulder, then return to my sweeping. But not more than ten minutes later, I'm taking a bag of trash down to the trash bin behind the building, and I spot Perry and Ellen standing together in the parking lot by his open car door. I watch as Ellen brushes Perry's bangs away from his eyes, leans up, and kisses him. It's not a long kiss, but time seems to slow, and I notice the mirage-like waves of heat rising from the roof of Perry's car. I'm halfway back to the condo before I realize I'm still carrying the bag of trash. I return again to the trash bin and, on my way, run into Ellen.

"What are you doing here?" she asks.

I hold up the bag.

"Taking this to the trash."

Ellen eyes the bag and scratches at some peeling skin on her shoulder.

"Did you see me kissing him?"

"What was *that* all about?"

"It's no big deal," she says. "We stayed up late last night by the pool and talked. We sort of connected. I wasn't planning to kiss him. Saying good-bye in front of Mom and Dad didn't seem right. It was just spontaneous. But I have to say in retrospect that it seemed like the right thing to do."

"You might not ever see him again," I say.

"You might not either," Ellen says.

All that afternoon at the party I tried to orchestrate time alone with Clare. I didn't have anything in particular that I wanted to say. I just wanted to be alone with her. Whenever she surfaced from the pool, I felt compelled to be there with a towel. But the others were always around. I wondered if they were intentionally keeping us apart. For a long stretch of time, she and Perry sat on the edge of the pool and talked. I imagined that they were talking about me. I realized I was being paranoid, and yet I was convinced that I had to put an end to the conversation. Short of sitting down between them, however, I couldn't think of anything to do.

Alone in the kitchen at one point, refilling a bowl of chips, I experienced a wave of vertigo that made me weak in the knees. When I reached for the countertop, I upset the bowl of chips and sent them scattering to the floor. Down on my knees, picking up the chips one by one, I wondered if my entire life was pointless. I had no purpose, no direction, no ambition. What was this I was doing and calling living?

Leaving the remaining chips on the floor, I went to the sink and splashed cold water on my face. Outside I saw Perry and Juliana sitting at the edge of the pool kicking their feet, sending ripples arcing out into the water. Behind them Clare was sitting upright on a green patio chair while Catherine stood behind her and braided her hair. A fine, white smoke from the barbecue drifted across the patio and over the grass toward the convent.

Sometime later, leaving the bathroom to return to the party, I ran into Clare, for the first time not in someone else's clutches.

"Hello," she said, pausing with her hand on the bathroom door. "I haven't seen much of you today."

"You've been busy talking to everyone else," I said. "I thought maybe you were avoiding me."

Outside there was a loud splash and the dogs' excited barking.

"I guess I have been."

"Well," I said more loudly than I'd planned, "I didn't expect you to admit it. A lie would've been fine."

She smiled and touched me on the forearm.

"I promise we'll talk," she said. "I just wasn't up to it today. I guess I didn't want to think about things."

As she turned to go into the bathroom, I noticed that the braid Catherine had tied in her hair was already beginning to unravel.

"So," I said, unable to stop myself. "I guess you and Perry haven't been talking about anything serious."

"We've been talking about you."

"More truth," I sighed. "That was another perfect opportunity for a lie."

"I prefer the truth."

"So, what did he tell you about me?" I asked.

"Lots of things. Things I pretty much knew already."

"Like what?"

"Like that you're hard to get to know. That you've always felt a little on the outside of things. That you're a little lost."

"Perry told you those things?" I asked.

"Basically," she said. "Now if you don't mind, I really have to pee."

She went into the bathroom and closed the door. I stood there until I heard the soft sound of her tinkling before going back outside and rejoining the others.

* * *

I have a patchwork memory of the rest of that day, resembling the jumbled clippings on an editing-room floor more than a cohesive film. The five of us sat around a table on the patio until it got dark. In the middle of the table a feeble flame burned inside a small green bucket, and I noticed the sharp smell of citronella. I remember the conversation bouncing between the trivial and the serious, but I can't recollect what we talked about. I recall climbing the spiral stairs to my bedroom, taking each step as if under water, clutching the handrail like a geriatric patient. I paused at the doorway to my room and scrutinized the distance between myself and the bed.

I awoke in the middle of the night from a deathlike sleep. Soft blue moonlight was filling the room, although when I turned my head and looked out the window, the moon itself wasn't visible, only a single star, or planet, suspended above the convent like an observant eye. The castle was quiet, even more than it should have been in the middle of the night. My mouth was painted shut. When I sat up to take a drink, the pungent scent of myrrh filled the room. This was doubly strange, because as far as I knew, I'd never smelled myrrh before, and yet I was sure that was what it was. I didn't remember undressing, but when I got up and walked to the open window, I was naked. Outside the night was still, but as I leaned my head out the window, the smell of myrrh became distinctly stronger.

Below me on the grass, just outside the convent wall, was a young girl, fourteen or fifteen years old, dancing in the moonlight. She had long, dark hair and olive skin. She was wearing a white, almost silver, translucent gown, hemmed below her knees, and she was barefoot. My first thought was that she was a young rebellious nun sneaking out after curfew, but then as she spun with her arms above her head, I noticed that she was five or six months pregnant. I began to wonder if she was from the convent at all. I watched her for several minutes, dancing and skipping through the wet grass before she disappeared behind the convent wall. I staggered back to bed, the smell of myrrh fading.

Then there was a young girl sitting in a chair next to my bed with her legs drawn up under her, the bright morning sunlight striking her tanned knees. Because her hair was piled on top of her head in a way I'd never seen, because my eyes were still half-glued shut and my brain was operating at half speed, it took me a moment to recognize her.

"You're sick," said Catherine.

I found this information very comforting, like stepping into a warm, firelit tavern after walking in a cold rain all day. Suddenly the previous night and day made more sense; all along I'd been getting sick.

"I know. I think I must have a fever."

Catherine stood up and put her hand on my forehead, then nodded and disappeared down the hall. In a few minutes she came back with a glass of water and aspirin.

"Take these," she said.

She stood by the bed until I swallowed the aspirin, then she stuck a thermometer into my mouth.

"I'll be back in four minutes. Keep that under your tongue."

If the castle had been strangely quiet when I awoke in the middle of the night, now it seemed especially noisy. I lay on my back with my arms at my sides, the thermometer pointing straight at the ceiling, and listened to the muted din that rose up through the floorboards. There was a sharp tinny clicking, like the sound a radiator makes when it's heating up. There was the low whistle of water running through pipes. Periodically there was the sound of a door opening and closing on squeaky hinges on the castle's ground floor. There were soft footsteps, also coming from far below, and voices so muffled by the distance they traveled that I couldn't discern whether they were male or female. Underlying all this clatter was the biting smell of smoke that rose and fell in its intensity, so that at times I thought I was imagining it and at others I was sure the castle itself must be on fire.

When Catherine returned and I mentioned the noise, she said, "Yes, we have guests." She held the thermometer in front of her face and tilted it up and down until she could see the silver band of mercury.

Our guests were Clare and Juliana. They'd left not long after I'd gone to bed but were back in minutes with the news that a mile away, our road was closed by a fire barricade. Thick waves of smoke poured across the road, and a quarter of a mile down the mountainside, a long band of flames was visible, leaping into the air above the trees.

I stayed in bed all day, drifting in and out of feverish sleep, dreaming wild, disconnected dreams. Sometimes when I awoke, Catherine would be in the chair by my bed, ready with a glass of water or juice and more aspirin and usually the thermometer. Although she never told me what my temperature was, I gathered by the look on her face and by the number of times she checked it throughout the day that it was high. When I awoke alone, I lay still and listened to the sounds from below. The muffled voices, the opening and closing of doors, the sound of running water, the splash of someone diving into the pool, all melted together so that even while it was happening, it all seemed like a nostalgic memory.

Throughout the day, penetrating both my waking and sleeping, was the acrid smell of smoke and the faint sound of Mozart drifting up from the library, as if every Mozart CD in the castle were being played continuously one after the other. All in all it was a rather pleasant experience. In truth, I didn't feel all that bad. At times I felt euphoric. The day passed neither quickly nor slowly, but timelessly.

I awoke in the middle of the night drenched in sweat and realized that my fever had broken. Clare was in the chair beside my bed. The soft moonlight on her face made her look like a little girl. It was still uncanny to me how much she and Catherine looked like sisters. When she sensed I was awake, she reached out her hand and put it on my forehead.

"You're soaking wet," she said.

"I think my fever broke."

"I hope you don't think it's weird that I'm here. I couldn't sleep."

"I'm glad you're here."

She surprised me by reaching under the sheet and taking my hand. As she did, her fingers grazed my bare hip, sending a shiver down my legs and up my back. I closed my eyes and let the coolness from her palm penetrate my hand and move up my arm.

When I awoke in the morning, both my fever and Clare were gone. Outside my window, perched on a cottonwood branch, was an enormous Steller's jay staring at me. When I propped myself up, he flew off, as if my waking were what he'd been waiting for. When I stood up I marveled at how my muscles and joints felt—not stiff and achy like I'd been sick in bed for thirty-six hours, but warm and relaxed as if I'd just had a massage. I stood naked in the middle of the room and stretched my arms toward the ceiling, the scent of frying bacon wafting up from downstairs.

On the way down the stairs, I'd imagined I would tell the others about the young woman I'd seen dancing around the convent, but when I saw Catherine standing at the stove, chest level to a frying pan full of eggs, my resolve slipped away. I felt an urgency to keep the experience to myself, as if sharing it might diminish it or, worse, defile it. Maybe it had been a dream. I poured myself a cup of coffee and, sitting down at the kitchen bar, said good morning to Catherine.

She was dressed in khaki shorts and a tank top and had her hair piled on top of her head in a way Clare often wore hers. She was wearing one of Perry's aprons that would have reached to his knees, but on Catherine it fell all the way to her bare feet and brushed the floor.

"Feeling better?" she asked.

"Like a new man," I said.

Catherine flipped two eggs onto a plate with bacon and toast and set it in front of me. She frowned at my mug of coffee and went to the refrigerator to pour me a glass of juice.

"Thanks," I said as she placed the juice in front of me. "Where's everyone else?"

"Perry's still asleep," she offered.

She fixed herself a plate and sat down next to me.

"I think Juliana's in the tower trying to find Perry's high-school yearbooks, and Clare is swimming."

Catherine forked an entire egg into her mouth, and as she chewed, a dribble of yellow yolk ran down her chin.

"And," she said, wiping her chin with her napkin, "in case you're wondering, I'm going to take the dogs for a walk around the convent, so if you were thinking about taking a swim too, you two would be all alone out there."

"Thanks," I said. "I'll give it some serious thought. What about the fires? Is it safe to walk around the convent?"

"There was a fireman here this morning. He said the fire wasn't moving this way, and the road should be open again tomorrow. He said they'd give us plenty of notice if we had to get out."

Outside it was hot with only the slightest hint of a breeze drifting across the patio from the north. For the first time in days I didn't smell smoke. I stood outside the french doors and watched Catherine and the dogs until they disappeared behind the wall of the convent. I walked across the patio in my bare feet and sat down at the edge of the pool and watched Clare swim. She was a beautiful swimmer, gliding through the water like a seal. She'd only made a lap and a half before she stopped in the middle of the pool and treaded water.

"Thomas?" she asked.

"Now how could you have possibly known that?"

"Trade secret. Are you feeling better?"

"Much. An angel came to me in the middle of the night and ministered to me."

"I'm sure you were hallucinating."

She finished a few more laps, then she walked up the steps at the pool's shallow end and picked up her towel. When she'd finished drying off, she walked over to me.

"Should we go for a walk?" she asked.

The fact that Clare always took my arm when we walked created an intimacy between us that I had to remind myself was artificial. I knew well enough that if she hadn't been blind, she wouldn't have walked with her hand cradled around my elbow the way she did. It was a necessity that I was both grateful for and that at some level tormented me.

Without discussing where we would go, we walked through the castle's gatehouse and started down the road. I'd thought that Clare's suggestion of a walk meant we would finally talk about Catherine's mysterious disappearing saint. Instead, she talked about her childhood.

She had not always been blind. She had been born in Africa; her parents were Presbyterian missionaries. When she was seven years old, there'd been an incident with African guerrillas. I remember that *incident* was the word she used, because later it seemed an exercise in understatement.

"We were living in a small village in the mountains. We'd been there for about six months. We lived in a one-room hut with a dirt floor. I can remember my parents sitting at our little kitchen table drinking warm beer and talking after I'd gone to bed, discussing one or another of the villagers, how they thought they were making progress, how they might finally be breaking through. I liked living there. It wasn't until I moved to the States that I realized I was white, or that there was even a difference.

"One day a band of guerrillas entered the village and began stealing food and making threats. They grabbed my parents and made them kneel down. Two soldiers pointed their machine guns at the back of their heads. There was so much screaming and shouting between the villagers and the soldiers that it wasn't clear what they wanted. And I was no help. I screamed obscenities at the soldiers, demanding that they let my parents go. Somehow I knew that they wouldn't hurt a seven-year-old girl. I wasn't a very good missionary daughter.

"A young soldier held my arms behind my back, and I screamed at him to let me go while I kicked at his shins with my bare heels. Then there was a bright flash of light that originated behind my eyes and an explosion at the base of my skull, and the world went dark. I learned later that the young soldier had hit me with the butt of his rifle, but at the time all I was aware of was that at any moment my head was going to explode.

"I fell face forward into the dirt, but I didn't lose consciousness. I heard a familiar voice nearby telling the young soldier that he would burn in hell. It was the voice of Ratu, an African minister from a nearby village who'd been visiting my parents. I felt his hands on my shoulders as he lifted me to a sitting position. There was a patch of liquid warmth at my neck, spreading over my shoulders and down my back. Just as I realized that it was blood from the wound at the back of my head, I heard two shots ring out, one after the other. Moments later they echoed back off the distant hills.

"I felt Ratu shudder and whisper, 'Lord have mercy,' as he lifted me to my feet and led me away to our hut. Ratu laid me down in my bed, and I told him I couldn't see. I felt him place a wet cloth at the back of my head and hold it there.

" 'What's happened?' I asked. 'What's happened?'

"He continued to cradle the back of my head with the cloth as he described to me how two angels, clothed in white and so bright with light that they were blinding to look at, had descended from the sky and wrapped my parents in their arms, then carried them with them to the heavens.

" 'I heard gunshots,' I said to Ratu.

" 'No,' he said. 'The angels only clapped the soldiers on the head with their wings and knocked them down. There were no gunshots.'

" 'Then my parents are okay?' I asked.

" 'More than okay,' said Ratu. 'They have been given the great privilege of living in a mansion in the sky with our sweet Lord Jesus.' "

My eyes were fixed on Clare's face as she talked, and I practically ran us right into the barricade that closed the road.

"What is it?" asked Clare when I stopped.

"The barricade," I said. "End of the road."

I turned to Clare and hugged her. I stroked the hair at the back of her head and thought I could feel the scar from where she'd been hit with the rifle. For a moment she acquiesced, her body softening. But then she stiffened, turned away, and began walking back up the road without me. When I caught up to her and took her arm in mine, she continued.

"Do you know the Bible?"

"I used to."

"Remember in the Bible when Saul was on the road to Damascus, and he was blinded by the Holy Spirit?"

"He was blind for three days," I said. "Then someone came and healed him."

"That's right," said Clare. "Well, somehow I got it into my head that the same thing was going to happen to me. Not in three days, but in three years. I believed that my blindness was a gift, an opportunity to look inward, to become a more spiritual person. That's the way missionary kids tend to think. I believed that on the three-year anniversary of my blindness, some strange person would appear and restore my sight."

"And when that didn't happen?" I asked.

"I realized for the first time that Ratu had lied. I understood that my parents had both been shot in the back of the head. That there'd been no angels. Then I thought that angels had been there after all. That the soldier who blinded me, and Ratu who lied to me, had been angels in disguise. That my blindness *was* a gift. But a gift in the sense that it spared me from seeing my parents murdered right in front of me."

"And what do you think now?"

"I think we all get to suffer. And maybe those who suffer the most live the most."

"So we can't really live unless we suffer?"

"I don't know," said Clare. "There might be other ways."

"Like?"

"Like loving someone and knowing you could lose them. Like raising a child."

When I was fifteen years old, a freshman in high school, I made the game-winning catch in our school's homecoming game. This was miraculous for several reasons: First, in such an important football game, I can't figure out why a freshman would be on the field at all. More miraculous still was that I was the intended receiver of the game-winning pass. My guess is that the coach was betting that everyone else was thinking that I was by far the least likely receiver on the field. Most miraculous of all was that I not only made the catch, but

I managed to hold on to the ball as I was knocked into the end zone by a kid twice my size and my collarbone was snapped in two as he landed on top of me. I remember turning to catch the ball and noticing the white stadium lights, like multiple moons circling an alien planet. The air was cold and crisp and had a smell that made me think it was going to snow. When the ball landed in my arms, I remember thinking what a perfect experience it was, like I was born to do this, that I could be happy the rest of my life catching footballs. Then I felt the impact on my left shoulder and an odd sense of euphoria as my feet left the ground and I watched the white goal line pass under me. I even believe there was a smile on my face as I fell toward the grass, clinging to the ball like life itself. Then the stadium went black.

This strange sensation of euphoria returned on the evening after my walk with Clare to the fire barricade. The five of us were sitting at a table by the pool, the remains of a steak dinner scattered in front of us. Although late, it was still light. The sky was a mixture of white and purple, and above the mountains hung a single row of huge cumulus clouds, their undersides highlighted gold. The smoke was visible in the air, making everything shadowy and soft. I watched a moth fly dangerously close to the citronella candle in the middle of the table, and my chest filled with air; then my arms and legs, even my fingers and toes, were buoyed up, as if all my blood had changed to helium. I had the feeling that something was about to happen, or that it already was happening and I just had to figure out what it was.

I looked across the table at Perry, and I had a vision of him walking across Death Valley. Naked, he is walking through thick waves of heat rising from the sun-baked sand. When his body abruptly ignites, he continues to walk. Chunks of flesh and muscle burn up and fall sizzling from his bones, but he keeps walking until he's nothing but a charred skeleton, and still he walks until his blackened skeleton disappears over the horizon.

I took a sip of wine and closed my eyes. When I reopened them, Perry was back to his old self, covered with clothes and flesh and blood, but behind him a dark, ashen figure was approaching from one of the gardens. It wasn't until he stood right next to the table that I realized this was not another hallucination, but one of the firemen coming to report that the road had been reopened.

After the fireman left, a discussion ensued about how many glasses of wine Juliana had had and whether or not she was fit to drive. I listened with detachment as she argued for her sobriety, knowing all along that she and Clare would end up spending one more night. She stood up and walked heel to toe on one of the cracks in the patio, her arms stretched out to her side. The telephone rang. I got up to answer it as Juliana continued her tottering performance.

I was feeling a little off balance myself, but the sound of my father's voice had a sobering effect. I could hear the sound of a television and a roomful of voices, the ringing of a cash register.

"Dad? Isn't it late at night there?"

"I couldn't sleep," he replied. "This was the only time I could get into town to use the phone."

"Dad? What's going on?"

"Well," he said and paused. Then I heard a voice nearby say, "Excuse me."

"Well," he said again. "Ellen's had a little accident."

"An accident? What do you mean? Is she okay?"

"She's okay. She was bit by a shark. She was—"

"Bit by a shark!" I said. "She was *what?*"

"She was swimming in the ocean, and she was...well, you know..."

What my father couldn't bring himself to say was that Ellen had been swimming in the ocean and without realizing it had started her period. The shark bite was high on her thigh and had required a hundred and thirty-five stitches.

"When did this happen?" I asked.

"About two weeks ago."

"Two weeks! Why are you just now calling me?"

"Because we thought she was okay. But now there seems to be an infection. She's got a fever, and the doctor here doesn't know what to do."

"Why don't you take her to Miami?" I insisted. "Take her to Miami."

"I've tried, but she won't go. She says she won't leave the island."

"Well, she's got to," I said. "Tell her she doesn't have a choice."

"There's really nothing I can do. She's made up her mind."

His voice was weak and helpless. I realized I was gripping the phone so tightly that my fingers were tingling. I relaxed my grip and shifted the phone to my other hand.

"I thought you might have a suggestion," continued my father. "You've always been close to her."

I looked out the window at the group seated around the table on the patio. It had grown dark. Catherine had moved to Clare's lap and had her head resting on her shoulder. The dim light from the candle on the table cast a soft glow on their faces.

"Tell me more," I said into the phone. "Do you think she's going to be okay?"

"I really don't know. I don't know what to do."

His voice wavered in a way I'd never heard before, and I realized he was afraid. Afraid of losing yet another of his children. I also realized that throughout the entire conversation I'd practically been yelling at him.

"It's okay," I said in a softer voice. "It's okay. I'm coming down there."

At thirty-six thousand feet, somewhere over the arid expanse of Wyoming, I started making a list on my cocktail napkin of things I'd forgotten to tell Clare and Juliana before leaving. I had one side of the napkin full and had turned it over before I realized how ridiculous I was being. As I crumpled up the napkin and placed it on the corner of my tray table, Dori, the long-legged first-class flight attendant, came by and refilled my glass of champagne and replaced the napkin with a fresh one.

"You miss them," she said.

A little of the champagne spilled over the edge of the glass.

"Excuse me?"

"Your family," she said. "I'm just guessing. I would say it's a little girl. Your wife and your daughter. Am I wrong?"

"I'm afraid so. I'm not married."

"Hmm," said Dori. "That's strange. I'm usually right about these things."

"Sorry."

She picked up the crumbled napkin. "Well, it just goes to show you."

I resisted the urge to ask, "Show me what?"

She was the worst kind of flight attendant—overly friendly, overly helpful, annoyingly attentive, unable to recognize those travelers who want to be left alone, and yet good-natured and well intentioned so that if you do let loose with a snappish remark, you immediately feel guilty.

Early on in the flight, shortly after the seat-belt sign had been turned off, she'd appeared at my seat with an open bottle of champagne.

"You're lucky," she said.

"Excuse me?"

"To be here."

She looked around the nearly empty first-class cabin. "It's like sardines back in coach."

I reluctantly acknowledged that she was right. The flight had been overbooked; I was lucky to have gotten on at all. But being bumped up to first class seemed especially auspicious. Then, unasked, she returned again and again with the bottle of champagne. Apparently I had the one other person in first class to thank for that.

"He just wanted the one glass," said Dori, bending close to my ear. "You might as well drink the rest of it. It'll just go to waste."

On the way off the plane in Houston, Dori pulled the ticket from my breast pocket and examined it.

"Your connection is at C-28," she said. "Same concourse but at the other end. You've only got twenty minutes, so don't dawdle."

I took the ticket back and thanked her. Before I could push past her, she tilted her head and pursed her lips.

"I just can't figure it. I really had you pegged for a wife and daughter."

On my first trip to my father's island, I'd noticed a large number of young girls who were pregnant, many of them appeared to be no more than twelve or thirteen. When I'd asked Martin about it once, he'd said, "All the locals do is shack up and collect the dole." But this hadn't sat well. The pregnant girls I'd seen had appeared happy, not pushed down by circumstances. It made me think that there was more to their lives than collecting a welfare check.

One day I'd watched four young Puerto Rican girls sitting on a bench waiting for a bus. Two of the girls were visibly pregnant, and I suspected that one of the others might have been as well. They'd come to town to shop for baby clothes, and as they waited for their bus, they pulled the little items from their bags and passed them around for the others to see. As I watched, I hadn't thought of the extra money the United States government would be giving them the following year. What I thought was, *These girls have the ability to create life, and they know it.*

As I walked out of the airport through the thick Caribbean heat toward Simon's taxi, I passed a young girl going into the airport. She looked about fifteen years old and six months pregnant, with long dark hair and smooth skin. As we passed each other, our eyes met for a moment, and she smiled. It may have been her smile, although I believe I'd noticed the resemblance already, that made me think of Cordelia Zangrilli, a girl Stephen had gone out with in high school.

It's a moonless evening in Baltimore in the middle of winter, and Stephen has failed to show up at the dinner table. This isn't cause for immediate alarm; however, as soon as dinner is over, I'm sent out to look for him. It's been snowing on and off all day, and now, as I pull on my parka and walk out into the night, a gusty breeze is blowing. It kicks up pockets of snow and swirls them through the air, so that it's impossible to tell whether it's snowing or not. I walk to the end of our street and cut through a small wood. The path is so dark that it would have been impossible to follow if I hadn't been on it a thousand times. On the other side of the wood is a large grassy field that is being turned into a new housing development. On one end of the field, where houses will not be built for months yet, Stephen and I, along with some other neighborhood kids, have built an underground fort, using stolen two-by-fours and plywood from the nearby building sites. As I approach the fort, I can see a soft glow around the entrance from the candles that burn inside.

I climb down through the hole and find Stephen on all fours, his forehead pressed to the dirt floor. From the quantity of melted wax at the base of the candles, I guess that he's been here for hours, that he probably came directly from school.

I sit down and lean my back against one of the dirt walls.

"What are you doing?"

It's cold, although not as cold as outside. Stephen sits up, leans against the wall across from me, and sticks his ungloved hands under his armpits. It's obvious that he's been praying, but I'm not sure whether I expect him to confess this, or even if I want him to.

"Cordelia may be pregnant," he says. "I'm praying that she isn't."

There's a moment of almost religious silence before I blurt out, "You've had sex with Cordelia?"

Of course I've failed to understand the gravity of the situation, and Stephen is annoyed. It's possible that by the time he's sixteen, Stephen will be a father. He's spent hours in prayer, making a deal with God, and all I can focus on is the fact that he's entered a mysterious and forbidden sexual inner sanctum, and I haven't even touched a girl's breasts yet. I don't even consider it within the realm of possibility. We walk home in silence, Stephen always a half step ahead, not even acknowledging me enough to show his disgust.

Unlike Dori on my flight to Houston, Simon was astute enough to know that I wasn't in the mood to chat. We said hello to each other when I first climbed into the cab, then we drove the narrow, winding roads to Casa La Verdad in silence. Simon kept his eyes forward, never glancing into the rearview mirror, all the while humming under his breath.

It wasn't until we came to a stop in front of La Verdad's main villa, billows of dust rising up from behind us and curling into the open windows, that Simon looked to the rearview mirror.

"Here we are," he said in his thick Caribbean accent. "Welcome back."

I was aware that I was expected to exit the cab, but for several minutes I didn't move, and Simon, to his credit, respected my inaction.

"Sorry, Simon," I said eventually. "I guess I needed a moment."

"Quite all right," said Simon. "I understand."

"Have you seen Ellen?" I asked. "Do you know how she is?"

"I've taken her to the doctor two or three times. And once I have brought the doctor out here to her. I am not a doctor myself, just a driver, but Miss Ellen appears to me to be a strong woman."

"Thanks, Simon."

I got out and handed him the fare.

"You're a good driver."

As I walked through the large double doors of the villa and stepped onto the cool tile of the foyer, there was a loud clap of thunder. I turned around as marble-sized drops of rain began pummeling the dusty road. I watched as the road where Simon had just driven away turned into a streambed. When I turned around again, Martin was standing in front of me.

Uncharacteristically for that time of year, the rain continued for the rest of the evening and throughout the night. I awoke several times to a torrential beating on the metal roof above me, a beating that came in erratic waves. Outside was the constant sound of running water, trickling and gushing, so relentless that I thought the resort might float out to sea. The rain pervaded my sleep, too, all my dreams water dreams.

The next morning the rain had stopped. I stepped out of my bungalow into a renewed world. The rubber tree in front of my porch was full of singing birds, hundreds of them, and although the birds themselves were nondescript—small, grayish, sparrow-looking things—their song was colorful and uplifting. I stood on the bungalow's stoop breathing in the clean morning air and thought about how nice it would be if I were here on vacation.

The evening before I'd gone to Ellen's bungalow to check in on her but had found her sleeping. My father told me that Ellen slept a lot, but the doctor had assured him that it was a natural response to fighting infection. I stopped at her bungalow again that morning and knocked on the screen door. When I got no response, I stepped in and walked over to her bedside and, pulling back the mosquito netting, placed my hand on her forehead. I'd done the same thing the previous night. Then, her head had been hot, and although she didn't wake at my touch, my hand on her forehead seemed to aggravate her. She'd turned away from me with an animal-like moan. Now her head was cool, and she didn't stir when I touched her. I pulled back the sheet and raised the bottom of her nightgown. The wound was bandaged from the top of her thigh to her knee, so I couldn't see the stitches. Beyond the bandage her skin was bruised a purplish yellow. I covered my mouth and nose, although there was no odor except for the faint smell of coconut butter. I pulled the nightgown back down and covered her with the sheet. On the bedside table, on top of a dog-eared paperback, were two brown bottles of pills, one marked *penicilina,* the other *morfina.* I moved them aside and picked up the book. I flipped through it and read a sentence. *Taggert thought about his gun. He wished he had it now, but he always left it at the office, because of the children.* I put the book down and left the bungalow and walked toward the main villa in search of Martin and my father and coffee.

I sat down and told them I was going to take Ellen to Miami to see a real doctor.

"She won't go," said my father. "She won't leave the island."

"Why not?"

"We don't know. But she's made up her mind."

"Well, we'll have to change it."

"We've tried," said Martin. "She would have to be drugged."

"Then we'll drug her."

I carried a tray of juice and toast back to Ellen's. I was glad to see that she was awake. She was staring out the window where a thick band of sunlight poured in, lighting up a patch of the weathered floor. When the screen door clicked behind me, she turned her head and smiled.

"Hey, you," she said in a dreamy voice. "What brings you to our little island?"

I set the tray on the bedside table and kissed her on the forehead. "I heard a shark tried to eat you."

Ellen smoothed the sheet over her leg. "Just a flesh wound."

I tried to make my voice both sympathetic and firm. "Ellen, you're going to lose your leg."

She sighed and looked at me. "Thomas, you can save yourself a lot of time and energy. I'm not going to Miami."

"How about Houston?"

She didn't find this funny. She turned her head and stared out the window. "Just leave it alone."

I suddenly had the sensation that someone was in the room with us. I turned and looked around, but we were alone. When I turned back to the bed, Ellen was still facing the window.

"I'm worried about you," I said, touching her shoulder. "What do you want me to do?"

She turned back to me. Her eyes were unfocused. I wondered if she was using the morphine. "Promise me you'll drop this Miami business. It's a waste of time."

I rubbed her shoulder where a taut muscle covered the bone. "Can I at least know why?"

"Promise," she said.

I promised.

Ellen put her hand on mine where it still rested on her shoulder and gave it a squeeze.

"I'm glad you're here," she said.

"Me, too."

I looked down the length of her body. She was so slight under the sheet, almost as if she wasn't there. I moved my hand down her arm and could just feel her faint pulse at her wrist. Again I felt a presence in the room. The feeling was so strong this time that I stood up and turned around.

"What is it?" asked Ellen.

"Nothing."

I put my hand on her arm again, but this time I couldn't find her pulse.

"What am I going to do with you?" I asked. "Why won't you let me take you to a doctor?"

Ellen looked away for a minute. When she looked back, her eyes were focused.

"What is it?" I asked.

"I don't know quite what to say. I had a dream."

"A dream."

"A dream. Except I wasn't asleep."

"An awake dream," I offered.

"Yes," agreed Ellen. "An awake dream. I don't know what else to call it but that."

"A vision?"

"No. It felt more like an awake dream."

"Describe it to me."

It was ten or so days after the shark attack. For the last several days, as the infection had set in, Ellen had been running a pendulous fever, anywhere from ninety-nine to one hundred and five. On the evening of the dream, the pain in her leg had been especially bad, and before going to bed, she'd swallowed three of the little purple pills of morphine—three times the suggested dosage. She awoke hours later in the middle of the night, her arms and legs and back itching from the morphine, and she heard the faint but distinct sound of music coming from somewhere outside.

"It was beautiful," said Ellen. "A cello or an oboe, I couldn't tell which. And there was a harp, too. I wanted to know where it was coming from, but of course with my leg I couldn't very well be traipsing all over the resort in the middle of the night.

"But the music was so compelling that I forced myself up and hobbled over to the screen door and looked out. I don't know why I didn't go out onto the stoop. It was stupid. I watched it all through the screen. Like through a veil of smoke."

"Watched what?" I managed, although I already had a guess what she'd seen.

"There was someone swimming in the pool. A young girl with dark hair and dark skin, probably a native from somewhere nearby on the island. She was skinny-dipping. When she got out of the pool, I saw that she was pregnant. I expected she would put her clothes on, but she didn't seem to have any. Instead she danced to the music, which had become a little louder. After dancing for a while, she started to walk off toward the beach, but as she was about to step off the patio into the sand, she turned and looked at me and she spoke."

"She spoke to you?"

"Well, not exactly. Not with words. She didn't speak out loud. It was like she placed a word, just a single word, in my brain. It was as clear as if she'd said it right into my ear."

"What was the word?" I asked.

"Stay. She said, 'Stay.' "

While Ellen had been talking, she'd had her eyes closed. Now she looked at me for my reaction, but I didn't say anything. I felt cold.

When it was clear I wasn't going to talk, Ellen added, "Oh, and there was something else. A smell."

"Myrrh," I said.

"Yes, myrrh," she said, as if hearing the word for the first time. "It was myrrh."

After leaving Ellen's bungalow, I went out to the pool to see if Father had filled it, but it was still empty.

After checking on the pool, I found Martin and had him radio Simon for me. He arrived soon after and drove me to a hotel in town where I went into the bar to use the phone. I hadn't asked Simon to wait, but as I picked up the phone at the back of the room, I saw that he'd followed me in. At this time of the morning the bar was empty. There wasn't even a bartender, although I could hear movement coming from a room somewhere behind the bar, some clinking of glass as boxes of booze were moved around. As I dialed I watched Simon reach over the bar for a half-pint glass and fill it with beer from a tap.

My first call was to an old high-school friend, Gage Roberts, now a physician with his own practice in Baltimore. Because it was Sunday, I asked information for his home phone number. It was some time before the call went through, but when it did the connection was good.

"This is a surprise," said Gage. "Are you in Baltimore?"

"I'm in the Caribbean," I said.

"Rough," he said. "Don't tell me you went down there for your honeymoon and never came back?"

"No. My father and Ellen are here."

"Hey," he said, "I'm sorry about not making it to your wedding. Did I even send you a gift?"

"It's okay. You didn't miss much."

There was a brief silence during which I heard the tinkling of ice in a glass.

"So," he said.

"So. I need a favor."

I described the details of Ellen's accident, what I knew about the treatment she'd received, and her current condition. Gage interrupted several times, asking me to elaborate on certain things, to clarify others. Now that I was finished, however, he said nothing.

"Gage?" I said.

"I'm not sure what you're asking me, Thomas," he said after a while. "What is it you want me to do?"

I hadn't thought this far ahead.

"I don't know what I'm asking you."

"Hold on," he said after another pause. "Let me move to another phone."

The whole time we'd been talking, there'd been a collage of background noise coming from his end: the clinking of dishes in a sink, the sound of children's voices, the din from a too-loud television, the slamming of doors. Now, as he moved to a private room, the noise stopped.

"You want me to do something illegal," he said.

"I don't know. I don't know if that's what I'm asking."

"Look, the penicillin's not doing the job. For one thing the dosage is too small. But at this point even if you upped the dosage, I don't think it would do any good."

"Okay," I said, relieved that he was taking control.

"What Ellen needs is one of the new big hitters. I'm going to send you some Ceftriaxone. I've got a whole cabinet full of free samples at the office. I don't imagine you can get it down there."

"I don't imagine."

"Okay. It's administered by muscular injection. Can you handle that? I'll include a bag of syringes. One gram, twice a day, for about two weeks, but call me in a week and let me know how she's doing. The fever should be down by then."

"Okay," I said.

"Okay. Give me your address. I'll send it Next Day Air."

"Thanks, Gage," I said. "This makes me feel better."

"You're welcome. Consider it your wedding gift."

The next call I made was to the castle, where Catherine picked up the phone.

"Hello, Uncle Tommy," she said before I'd had a chance to speak.

"How'd you know it was me?"

"Who else would it've been? How's Aunt Ellen?"

"She's okay. She'll be getting better soon."

"How about Grandpa? Did you tell him I sent a kiss?"

"Yes, I did. I even delivered it. How's everybody there?"

The night my father had called to tell me about Ellen, I'd asked Clare and Juliana if they would mind staying at the castle until I got back. They'd agreed, I think even a little offended that I'd thought it necessary to ask.

"Oh, fine," said Catherine. "Perry's acting a little weird."

"Weird how?" I asked.

"You know, he doesn't sleep at night. He wanders around the castle looking for things to do. Last night I got up to go to the bathroom and ran right into him and about had a heart attack. He didn't even seem to recognize me."

"That's the prednisone he's taking," I said. "The doctor said it would have some side effects."

"Yeah. And he has an insatiable libido."

She said the words as if she was reading them off an index card.

"Really," I said. "Who told you that?"

"Why do you think that someone had to tell me?"

"Because you don't know what an insatiable libido is."

There was silence on the line. I could see Catherine standing in the kitchen in a pair of shorts and the oversize T-shirt she slept in, twirling the long phone cord back and forth around her forearm, looking around the kitchen in frustration, willing herself to be older.

"Juliana," she finally admitted.

"Juliana told you that Perry has an insatiable libido?"

"Yes. So what is it?"

"It's a libido that won't be filled up. Like a bucket with a leak."

"That only explains half of it. What about the libido part?"

"Libido is desire," I said. "It's like a need."

"So he has a need he can't fill up?" asked Catherine.

"That's right. That's the prednisone, too. I'm sure he'll be back to normal once he stops taking it."

"I hope so. It kind of weirds me out."

"How's everyone else?"

"Okay," said Catherine. "We all miss you."

"I miss you, too," I said. "Is Clare around? Can I talk to her?"

"She's doing laps. But I can get her if you want."

"No, that's all right. I'll talk to her next time I call."

"When will that be?"

"Probably tomorrow or the next day," I said. "I have to come back into town to pick up a package, so I can call you then."

There was a long pause, then Catherine said, "Clare says it's okay to miss her."

"Miss who?"

"My mom. Clare says it's natural."

"It is," I said. "It's perfectly natural."

"She says I shouldn't try to replace her."

"No," I said, trying to keep my voice steady. "No, you shouldn't."

I had an overwhelming urge to be there in the kitchen with her; to pick her up in my arms and tell her that everything was going to be all right. Even more I wanted the power to make her believe it; the power to believe it myself. In the absence of this power, however, I cried. I cried with my back to Simon, unable to speak into the phone. Catherine, on the other end, whether aware of my crying or not, began to cry herself.

"Oh, God," I finally said into the phone, and it occurred to me that this might be both an expletive and a prayer.

"Uncle Thomas?" said Catherine. "Are you all right?"

Something about the utter selflessness of this question made me chuckle.

"Yes," I said, sniffling. "I'm fine. How about you?"

I could hear Catherine blowing her nose and imagined that she had reached for the dishtowel that hung from the handle of the oven.

"I'm fine, too," she said. "I love you."

"I love you, too. I wish I was there and not here."

"Me, too. I mean I wish I was there and not here."

"That would be nice," I said. "Tell everyone there I miss them. And I'll be home as soon as I can."

"Okay," said Catherine.

"Okay," I said.

Without any explanation, Simon took a different, longer route back to the resort. We circumnavigated the southern part of the island where I'd never been before. Here it was drier and dustier, the vegetation less lush and hunkering closer to the ground. At one point the road turned from pavement to sand, and we ambled along. We passed the gate to one of the military installations, and the road returned to pavement. Wild horses were grazing in an open field on the other side of the fence. As we passed the gate, the security person—a short, dark man with a thick mustache—acknowledged us from his chair by pointing his finger at us and nodding. It was a generic gesture, the kind of thing he did a hundred times a day. Still, I took it personally. I had the keen sense that he was pointing not at me *and* Simon, but at me alone. And although I didn't know why he'd singled me out, it was obvious to me that he had.

This sense of being singled out stuck with me for the rest of the day and had the dual effect of making me feel both predestined and out of control. As Simon drove along a winding road that bordered the ocean, and a cool, salty breeze blew in the open windows, I found myself yearning for something I couldn't quite name, but I think bore a resemblance to deliberateness. That, at least, seemed close. By the time we arrived back at the resort, I'd decided two things: First, I would share with Ellen my own experience with the young pregnant girl dancing around the convent. Second, I would have that long-overdue conversation with Clare concerning the statue of Saint Thomas she'd seen on her walk with Catherine.

Back at the resort I walked out to the pool, but no one was there. I shielded my eyes from the sun and looked up the beach both north and south for signs of my father returning from his walk, but in both directions the beach was deserted.

During the drive with Simon around the island's south coast, there'd been a refreshing breeze coming off the ocean. Now the air was motionless and heavy with humidity. I pulled off my shirt and started toward my bungalow. On the way I looked in on Ellen and found her sleeping restlessly under a floral sheet.

I awoke later in my own bungalow, lying on top of the covers, the mosquito netting pushed aside. I hadn't intended to sleep, only to lie down with my eyes closed for a few minutes, but now there was a breeze blowing through the window, and I thought I must have slept for a long time.

The next afternoon, after a quick trip with Simon to town and back, I gave Ellen the first of her injections. She was sleeping soundly when I entered her bungalow, and she failed to wake up when I rubbed her shoulder and gave it a squeeze. I hummed while I prepared the needle, the same tune Simon had been humming on our trip back from town, hoping that it would wake her up, but by the time I had the needle ready, she hadn't even stirred. I shook her shoulder again, this time forcefully, but again I got no response. I considered giving her the injection in her sleep. It would either wake her up or it wouldn't. Either way I figured it would be better than being awake from the start.

I pulled away the sheet and attempted to maneuver her pajama bottoms down. Just as I'd gotten them past her hips, Ellen slapped me across the back of my head.

"Hey!" I said. "I'm not trying to molest you."

"Being stuck with that needle doesn't seem much better," she said, attempting to pull her pajamas back up.

"It won't be that bad."

"Easy for you to say."

I picked up the needle and looked at it.

"Or maybe it will be, I don't know," I said. "But you don't have a choice."

"Don't you always have a choice? I mean, if you go back far enough, can't you always find some time when a different choice would have changed things?"

"That sounds like your therapist talking," I said. "You could beat yourself up thinking like that."

"You could," she said. "But the point is not to think about all the decisions you made that might have been wrong. The point is to acknowledge that we have choices. No one's out there running our lives but ourselves."

"No. I suppose no one is. I don't know if I'd want someone running my life. Who says they wouldn't do a crappy job?"

Ellen turned away and looked out the window. The stark white curtains wavered in the breeze.

"Sometimes I wish someone would run my life," she said.

I put my hand on her shoulder. I could feel her scapula, hard and bony under her skin.

"Hey. Do you want to do this later?"

Ellen looked at me, her eyes brimmed with tears.

"That would only be choosing not to make a choice," she said.

I held up the needle between us.

"What's your choice?"

She looked at me and her eyes narrowed.

"Stick me."

"Good choice," I said. "Now choose a cheek and roll over."

When I was done with the injection, Ellen rolled back over.

"Was that so bad?" I asked.

"It burns a little, but not so bad."

"What about this?" I said, tapping her bandage. "Do you want me to change it?"

"I guess so. It's been since yesterday morning."

Outside Ellen's bungalow I stretched my arms over my head and several vertebrae in my back clicked into place. I walked down to the beach and stood for a while. Out on the horizon a cruise ship drifted along like a colossal Precambian water creature.

I thought of all the people on board, isolated in a manufactured synthetic world, playing shuffleboard, shooting skeet, grazing at endless seafood buffets, staying up late, dancing and drinking champagne, sleeping in, and I was suddenly aware that I was living the same kind of life. I wondered how much longer I could avoid reality, trapped inside my own emotions. I picked up a conch shell and tossed it into the water. I wanted to simply vow to live again, but I knew it wasn't that simple, not as simple as getting a shot.

*B*ack in Montana I stepped out of the airport into a hazy world. It was like viewing everything through a gauzy veil. It was unsettling not to be able to see the mountains or any other landmarks to help ground myself. It didn't help when I climbed into the back of a taxi and told the driver where I wanted to go, and he responded, "I'll see what I can do," as if odds were involved.

As we left town and started up the mountain, the smoke thinned, but above us were scattered pockets of orange on the mountainside, like sunspots bursting on the surface of the sun.

"How bad is it?" I asked the driver.

"Bad," he said. "We need rain."

At the turnoff to the ski resort, two fire engines blocked the road. When a firefighter approached and the driver rolled down his window, I heard the rhythmic thumping of a helicopter in the sky above us. The fireman leaned down and asked the driver where we were going.

"The castle," said the driver.

"Not possible," said the fireman. "Trees have fallen across the road a couple miles up. We won't have a chance to clear it for a few days." He looked into the backseat at me and said, "Better make other plans."

As he walked away, the driver turned in his seat and faced me.

"Well," he said. "Where to now?"

I thought for a minute, then reached for my wallet and pulled out money for the fare.

"Thanks," I said. "I guess I'll walk from here."

He paused, as if wondering whether he had any responsibility to stop me. But then he got out of the cab and opened the door for me.

We stood together on the dark pavement and looked up the road.

"You be careful," he said.

Moments earlier I'd felt daunted at the prospect of having to walk the five miles to the castle, but now I felt bolstered up by this unlooked-for and unlikely sympathy.

I thanked him and threw my duffel bag over my shoulder and started up the road. Before I'd gone a hundred yards, the fireman who'd spoken to us shouted to me.

"I wish you wouldn't do that."

"I'll be okay," I shouted back. "I'll be careful."

He frowned and waved his hand, indicating that he thought I was foolish, but there was nothing he could do to stop me. As I turned to head back up the road, I noticed that the cab driver was still standing next to his cab, like a teen waiting for his date to be inside before driving away.

I'd stayed two weeks at La Verdad, until I was sure Ellen was getting better. Every morning I would wake her by sitting on the edge of her bed and rubbing her back for a few minutes, then humming while I prepared the needle. Throughout our childhood, Ellen had made herself vulnerable to me, but it had been vulnerability on her terms. She revealed things to me that she revealed to no one else, but there was an element of manipulation. She could share her most intimate secrets, but afterward it wasn't a sense of proprietorship or power I was left with, but rather obligation.

Now, however, in her sickbed in the Caribbean, she was vulnerable in the purest way. There was resignation in her eyes. All her defenses were down, but at the same time she wasn't scared. She was glad to be in my care. Glad to be alive.

Every morning when I came to her with the needle, Ellen greeted me with a smile. After four days her temperature began to drop, and by the end of the week it was back to normal. One morning, after giving her the injection, I lingered by the side of the bed. Ellen's face was tan and smooth and still smelled faintly of coconut oil. She closed her eyes for a few moments, then looked at me. It was a look I'd never quite seen before. Some hard thing inside her had dissolved.

I wanted to ask her what had changed. I wanted to know if it was something she'd decided, if there was effort and will involved, or if it was something that had just happened. I wanted to know if it was possible to remake ourselves, or if we could only wait to be miraculously remade. The funny thing is, I don't know which answer I would have preferred.

A few days later I went to Ellen's bungalow in the morning and didn't find her. I found her by the pool in a chaise longue turned toward the sun. She was lying on her stomach in her scant yellow bikini, a paperback mystery propped in front of her, a Bloody Mary on the table at her elbow. I sat down next to her.

"I guess I'm not needed here anymore."

She rolled over. Her leg was unbandaged. My eyes were drawn to the massive, zigzagging scar.

"You're needed," she said. "But maybe you're needed somewhere else more."

She ran her finger unconsciously up and down the wound.

"You don't seem to be too bothered by that," I said.

Ellen looked down at her leg. "I guess I'm not. I guess I'm kind of attached to it."

I smiled.

"Seems weird, I know," she said, "but it's like it's a part of me, yet it's not me. It's like something that's attached itself to me as a reminder."

"A reminder of what?" I asked.

"I'm not sure. I'll let you know when I figure it out."

The two weeks at La Verdad had sped by, but now it felt as if I'd been gone from the castle for months. I didn't see any flames as I walked up the road, although at times the smoke was thick and burned my throat and eyes. It was beginning to get dark when I passed through the gatehouse. The castle was shrouded in smoke; the whole world turned black and white.

I walked around to the pool, and the dogs raced up but didn't bark. Through the glass doors I saw that inside the apartment, Perry, Catherine, Juliana, and Clare were sitting around a table playing cards. Two disparate thoughts struck me at once: First, that the cards must be in Braille, and second, that I was not ready to go in, that I would not go in until they were all asleep.

It was dark enough now that they couldn't have seen me from inside. I pulled a chair over from the pool and sat about twenty feet from the french doors and watched. I couldn't tell what it was that they were playing, only that every time someone discarded, they would announce for Clare's benefit what the card was.

The smell of smoke was strong but no longer acrid. Now it was sweet and soothing, like piles of fall leaves burning in a backyard. I stayed outside until they'd all gone to bed and the last light had been turned off.

I think I've gotten to my room and into bed without making any noise, but then Clare is standing in the doorway, lit from behind by the hall light so that I can see the silhouette of her body through her nightgown. After hesitating for a moment, she steps into the room and sits in the chair by my bedside. After a while, she reaches under the sheet and takes my hand. Her voice in the darkness is quiet, yet startling at the same time. "Thomas," she says, "I'm afraid I'm falling in love with you."

"It's okay," I respond. "I'm in love with you, too. I have been, in some way, ever since first meeting you at the café."

I pull her into the bed and kiss her eyelids and the nape of her neck, but as my hand begins to slide up the back of her thigh, she makes me stop.

"Let's just sleep," she says. "Hold me, and let's sleep."

I awoke from this dream to find someone standing in the doorway, as if I was still dreaming. It was Clare, lit from behind just as in my fantasy, like I'd conjured her. When I sat up, she spoke.

"You're home."

"I'm home. Hello."

"Hello. Can I come in?"

"Sure."

She sat in the chair by the bed and ran her fingers through her hair.

"It's nice to have you back."

"It's nice to be back. How did everything go?"

I studied her face in the dim light and remembered the first time I'd seen her at the café. How could I not have known then that she was beautiful? I reached out my hand to touch her cheek, but as I did, she spoke, and I drew back.

"Fine. We have a little mystery to solve."

"Another one? I don't think we solved the first one."

She got up from the chair. "I know, but they may be related. I'll tell you about it in the morning. You're probably exhausted."

She walked to the doorway and put her hands on the threshold. "It really is nice to have you back."

She turned down the hallway, and in a moment I heard the door to her bedroom click closed.

The next morning I awoke to a hazy sunlight filling the room. Downstairs the apartment was empty. I looked outside to the pool and checked the library but found no one. I was about to walk out to the parking lot to see if any vehicles were missing, when I heard something in the cellar. I walked down the stone steps and found Clare standing in the dark in front of the vaults. I flipped on the overhead light and stood next to her.

"Good morning," she said in her soft, whispery voice.

"Good morning," I said. "Where is everyone?"

"Fishing. Perry said he'd heard about a stream he thought they could hike to from here."

"What are you doing?"

"Is it true that Perry wants to be buried down here?"

"I think so. He's mentioned it."

Clare ran her fingers over the hinges, over the thick, brass handle, along the surface of the inlay, made of some darker, smoother wood.

"I think it would be a nice place to be buried," she said. And then she surprised me by saying, "I wonder if that would be possible."

I looked at her. Her champagne hair was a little mussed and hung down over her forehead.

"You would want to be buried here?" I asked.

"I think I would."

She removed her hand from the door and turned to face me.

"But I don't suppose it would be possible."

"I don't suppose," I said.

Clare turned back to the vault, and we stood there awhile longer. I had a vision of all of us buried there. Perry and Juliana. Catherine. Clare and me. All of us sealed for eternity in the bowels of the castle. It was gothic and sad and premature, but also logical.

"Well," said Clare at last.

"Well," I said. "What's this about a mystery?"

"Yes," she said, putting her hand on my elbow. "Let's get to it."

We went outside and walked around the convent. About halfway around, Clare stopped and tilted her head and listened for something, getting her bearings by sounds and smells. The morning breeze carried the smell of pine. The sun lit her upturned face so it looked like a watercolor. Without even thinking, I leaned down and kissed her. There was the briefest hesitation, then she took two steps backward and glared. She even raised a finger into the space between us, as if she were scolding a disobedient child.

"Don't do that," she said. "Don't."

"Why?" I asked.

"Just don't."

"I'm sorry. I didn't even think about it. I just did it."

Clare hugged her arms across her chest and bit her lower lip. She looked up into the trees.

"I'm sorry, Thomas," she said. "It's too soon."

"Too soon for you?" I asked. "Or too soon for me? Maybe you're just scared."

For the first time since I'd known her, I saw something on her face that looked like genuine anger. She took a decisive step toward me.

"I'm not scared," she said. "Let's not make this be about me, because it's not about me. It's about you."

She took another step forward and sighed. "Look, Thomas, I care about you. I hope that's obvious. I wouldn't say the things I'm about to if I didn't."

I looked around for something to sit on. I felt like I should be sitting.

"Maybe I've given you some wrong signals," she said. "If that's the case, I'm sorry. But the two of us together would not be good."

"Am I allowed to disagree?"

"No," she said. "We would be *okay* together," she continued, "and it would be nice for a while, but you only have so much of yourself that you're willing to give to a relationship. That would be fine for a while, but in time I'd want everything, and that's when things would fall apart and both of us would go away angry. You're always surrounded by your own distance."

"I think you're wrong."

"Stop. I'm not wrong. You want to be loved, and you want to love, and that's admirable. I think you have a great capacity to love, but only up to a point. Beyond that it gets too scary. You'll be vulnerable only to a degree. You'll always be holding something back. You'll always have this reserve of emotion that no one ever gets to see. This safe reservoir that you can retreat to. I'll be honest with you; I could fall in love with you if I was stupid enough to let it happen. But I'm not."

The air around us was still. There was no birdsong.

"So, I'm a lost cause."

"I don't know if you are or not," said Clare. "But look around you. You're pathetic. You and Perry both. You're hiding out in a castle. A fortress. What a perfect place for the both of you. No one gets in. No one gets out."

"But Catherine came in. And you and Juliana."

"All of us uninvited," she said.

I turned away and put my hands flat against the wall of the convent. I rested my forehead on the cold stones.

"I think you're being unfair," I said. "I loved Karen. I'm capable of it."

"I don't doubt that you did, but you didn't love her fully. Loving her completely might have been the one thing that could have saved her."

"Are you saying what happened to her is my fault?" I said, turning around. A familiar edginess was creeping into my voice.

"I don't think it was anybody's fault. And I don't have all the information, but from what I know, I think I can make a few accurate conclusions. Karen was scared to death of love. After her mother killed herself, she vowed to never let anyone have that kind of power over her again. I've seen it plenty of times. She promised herself that she would never allow herself to get hurt like that again. Then you came along, and she found herself doing what she promised herself she would never do. She began to care for you, and that made her vulnerable. It was a constant conflict for her. Loving you terrified her. It was her own love that betrayed her."

This was almost the exact diagnosis that Karen's doctor at the asylum had given me, but I wasn't about to give Clare the satisfaction of knowing that.

"At some point," Clare went on, "Karen realized you weren't all there, that there was this distance around you that she would never penetrate, and that's when the problems started. She hung on for a long time, reasoning that you might come around. But in the end it was too much for her. I'm surprised that it took until your wedding day before she lost it altogether."

I had never reacted well to scoldings, and that's what it felt like I was getting. I was glad Clare couldn't see my face, because I was sure I looked wounded. I felt very alone, a feeling I wasn't unfamiliar with, but that now felt colossal in its scope.

"You make it all sound so bleak," I said.

"It is bleak," said Clare. "It's all very bleak. And it'll stay bleak until you realize that it wasn't something that happened to you. You made choices. You weren't solely a victim, so stop acting as if you were."

"Thank you for your diagnosis, counselor," I said.

"Now you're feeling hurt."

Clare stepped forward and reached out her hand to touch the side of my face, but I stepped aside so that her hand met with nothing but air. There was an immediate look of hurt on her face, but also a sad knowingness, an expression that said, *See, you can't even allow someone to reach out to you in kindness.*

It was the cruelest thing I could have done, and yet once done, I could see no way to undo it. I stood there dumbly, wondering what kind of an olive branch I could find that would have the power to overcome this kind of enmity.

And yet, Clare moved immediately beyond it, as if she expected nothing more from me. She extended her elbow, confident that I wouldn't make the same mistake twice, offering me a second chance. I reached out and took it.

"Well," she said. "Maybe it would be best if we moved on."

We continued along the wall of the convent, the whole episode for her already in the past. We walked slower than we had before, Clare paying special attention to every sound and smell.

I felt an empty sadness. Not because I couldn't have her, but because I was incapable of letting anyone have *me*. We passed a partially decayed stump where several Oregon juncos were flitting around. I *was* pathetic. And this sadness was another way I was feeling sorry for myself. I'd been doing it to a degree ever since my mother's death.

I'd let myself feel unfairly determined when in reality, I had the power to make choices. It was a realization that began on the beach in the Caribbean and now solidified.

I bowed my head and closed my eyes, letting Clare, unaware, lead us along the path for a while. I knew I couldn't convince her of this change with words. I would have to show her that I'd given up feeling victimized and powerless.

"You still haven't told me what this mystery is," I said. "What are we looking for?"

"I'm not sure what we're looking for, but I'll tell you the mystery. Almost every day while you were gone, Catherine and I would take a walk around the convent. And every day at the same place, where the path moved away from the wall, we would stop, and Catherine would make me wait while she would walk over to the wall and do something."

"What did she do?" I asked.

"I'm not sure. That's what I'm hoping to find out. Sometimes I would hear some paper crinkling. Other times I heard what sounded like a squeaky hinge."

"Didn't you ask her what she was doing?"

"I did," said Clare. "She said she was praying."

"Praying."

"Yes, praying. When I pressed her on it she wouldn't elaborate, except once she said, 'Sort of praying.' "

"Sort of?"

"Yes, sort of."

"And where was this?" I asked.

Just then the path turned a little to the right around a small grove of spruce.

"I think right here," said Clare. "This is where we'd stop."

"Well. There's a grove of trees here obscuring the wall. Let's go have a look."

I took Clare by the hand, and we ducked into the trees. A faint path wound through the trees and ended at the wall.

"Well," I said.

"What is it?" asked Clare. "What's here?"

In the wall in front of us was a hole about twelve inches wide. I took Clare's hand and guided her to it.

"An opening?" she said. "It goes all the way through."

She traced the perimeter of the hole with her hand, then reached into the center.

"What's this?" she asked.

"It's a wheel," I said. "With a clothesline around it. The rope must be attached to another wheel inside the convent, but what it's for I can't imagine."

"I don't understand."

"It looks just like a clothesline," I said. "Like ones you'd see between buildings in a city. But I don't imagine the nuns use this for their laundry. It makes no sense coming to the wall like this."

"Are there clothespins?"

I looked in through the opening.

"Yes, every four or five feet."

"She's been *sort of* praying," said Clare in a whisper.

"What?" I asked. "Do you have it figured out?"

"I might. I have a theory."

She reached her hand in through the hole and pulled on the line, and the wheel creaked.

"There's your squeaky hinge," I said.

"Thomas. I think I know what this is. I believe I once read that convents in Italy had things like this in their walls."

"What were they for?" I asked.

"People from the village would write down their prayers on a piece of paper, pin it to the line, and then send it in to the nuns. Then the nuns would act as intercessors for them. They would pray the people's prayers, supposedly more effectively because they were closer to God."

"You think that's what Catherine has been doing?"

"I'm sure of it."

"Well, what do you think she's been praying for?"

"I can think of any number of things."

*S*ix months into our relationship, Karen and I decide to take a trip. It's early summer, just after school is out. On the morning we load up the car, the Colorado air is hot and arid. We can feel the dryness in our nostrils and eyes. We drive north out of Boulder and angle up through Wyoming to the southwest corner of Montana and camp in Yellowstone. The next day we drive to Spokane, where we spend a week with friends of mine from college.

I'm aware before the trip begins about the adage regarding taking trips together—that it's a true indicator of the health of a relationship. Without ever saying so, I believe we're both conscious that this trip is a test. But despite the self-imposed pressure, everything goes fine. We have no fights, no real arguments. We have several better-than-average conversations in the car, and in Spokane Karen likes my friends and enjoys being with them. The drive home is relaxed, neither of us uncomfortable with the long silences that dominate. When the trip is over, I feel better than I ever have about our being together.

But something has happened that I'm not aware of. When we get back to Boulder, Karen has me drop her off at her apartment instead of staying at mine. I'm only mildly concerned. We've been together constantly for five days, and it's understandable that she might feel the need for a little space. But the next day she appears at my front door in the morning to tell me she doesn't think we should see each other anymore. She's ready to leave it at that, to walk away forever, but I persuade her to come inside and explain what's wrong.

We sit on the couch, an inch of space between our knees, as I plead with her.

"Just tell me what's wrong," I say. "I love you. I'll do anything for you."

"Do you mean that?"

"Yes."

"Then let me go," she says. "Let me go."

But this I can't do.

It's obvious I'm torturing her, but I can't let her run away from what we have. I'm convinced that with perseverance we can overcome these invisible obstacles and emerge on the other side, whole and happy and together.

To Karen I must sound like a senile old man. I tell her the same things over and over, repetition my only weapon. Finally we come to an agreement. I'm aware it's more because I've worn her down than because she believes it's a good idea.

It's a sort of compromise. It's not over; there's still hope. Karen doesn't want to see me for a month. This includes talking on the phone. And although I agree, I'm baffled.

"What will this accomplish?" I ask. "What will it prove?"

"It will prove that I can live without you," says Karen.

"And what is the point of that?"

"If I'm going to live with you, I need to know I can live without you. Or at least know what it will feel like."

I'm still baffled, but I have no choice but to agree. I stand up from the couch as she walks to the door. She stands for a moment in the open doorway, and I can hear a squirrel chattering in a tree outside. I feel there's something that still needs to be said, but nothing comes to mind. This is new territory for me. I have no past experiences to build on.

"See you in a month," says Karen.

Then she's gone, and the chattering squirrel is silenced.

A week after I returned from the Caribbean, I was sitting on the patio, watching Clare swim laps in the pool. I'd wondered how Clare could know when she'd reached the end of the pool, how she knew when to dive and turn, but I'd finally figured it out by counting her strokes. She made the same number of strokes during each lap—twelve.

Just as I made this discovery, a firefighter who had visited us previously walked through the garden and onto the patio. She took off her helmet as she approached the table and held it behind her back.

"Good morning," I said.

"Morning," she said. "Just here to let you know the road's open."

"Thanks. Would you like a cup of coffee?"

"Is it hot?" she asked.

"I think so."

"That would be nice. I can't remember the last time I had a cup of coffee that wasn't lukewarm."

I handed her a mug, and she cupped her hands around it and took a sip.

"It's the little things you miss," she said. "I don't mind sleeping on the ground, and I don't mind the food. I don't even mind not showering for four or five days straight. You want to know what I miss?"

"Hot coffee," I said.

"Yeah, hot coffee. The other thing is brushing my teeth in a sink."

"Would you like to borrow one of our bathrooms?"

"No, thanks. The coffee is enough."

She thanked me again when she stood up to leave. As she drained her mug and set it on the table, she looked over at Clare, still swimming, fluid and rhythmic.

"Is that woman blind?"

I nodded. "How can you tell?"

"Her strokes are so even."

We watched for a while.

"It's always so simple," she remarked.

"What is?"

She put the helmet back on. "Everything. Anything mysterious. Once the mystery is taken away, it's usually quite simple."

When Clare climbed out of the pool, I walked over and handed her a towel.

"How about breakfast?" I asked. "I was thinking about making french toast."

Inside, Clare sat at the bar while I pulled out bowls and pans and half a loaf of french bread, but when I opened the refrigerator, I remembered aloud, "We don't have any eggs."

"We're out of just about everything except wine. If the road doesn't open soon, we'll have to start eating each other."

"I don't think it'll come to that," I said. "How about plain old toast?"

I'd considered not telling the others that the road was open. Maybe just for a day or two more. But we would need groceries. I put the last two slices of bread into the toaster and pushed the handle down. As I did, Juliana walked into the kitchen wearing a T-shirt of Perry's.

"He won't get up," she said.

I went up to Perry's room and sat on the edge of his bed. He was lying on his back with his eyes open, but they were glassy and vacant. His skin was a washed-out yellow, the color of a bruise.

"You've looked better," I said.

"I've felt better. I think if the road was open, I'd let you take me to the hospital."

"This is your lucky day."

Juliana, Catherine, Clare, and I spent several hours in a fluorescent-lit waiting room, the hum of the lights like an unseen mosquito. When a doctor appeared, he gave us the familiar spiel. Perry's platelets had plummeted again, they were giving him large dosages of steroids to try to bring them back up to normal levels, and he would have to stay in the hospital for a few days.

"Can we see him?" asked Juliana.

"Sure," said the doctor. "We've moved him to a private room. Just check in at the nurses' station."

Juliana took Clare by the elbow and went off toward the nurses' station, but as I followed with Catherine, the doctor caught me by the arm and requested a word in private. He glanced at Catherine and then at me.

I took Catherine's hand in mine and gave it a squeeze.

"It's okay," I said. "What is it?"

He waited a moment and glanced at his clipboard.

"Perry's kidneys are failing. He'll need to go on dialysis for a while."

"How long is a while?" I asked.

"Until we find a donor. He's going to need a transplant. I've put him on a waiting list."

Catherine and I, still hand in hand, walked down the stark hallway toward Perry's room.

"What's dialysis?" she asked.

"I don't know, exactly. It's something that people with bad kidneys have to do. I think it removes toxins from your blood, which is what your kidneys are normally supposed to do. I know it's not any fun."

That night I slept soundly at first, so when I awakened in the dark, I thought it must have been near morning, but when I looked at the clock, I saw that it was a little past midnight, and I'd only been asleep for an hour. When two o'clock came and went and I'd still not fallen back to sleep, I got up and dressed, left the castle, and drove to the hospital.

Walking into the hospital in the middle of the night, I was reminded of the night I'd tried to rescue Karen from the asylum. But, of course, *rescue* had been *my* word. She hadn't wanted or needed my rescue. I wondered if I was any less deluded now, if the thought that had been nagging me all night was any less misdirected.

I stepped into the blue darkness of Perry's room and closed the door. Just as when I'd stepped into Karen's room, the television was on. Perry, however, was not standing at the window, but tied down in bed by a maze of tubes and wires. I was all the way to the bedside before I could tell that he was awake. I sat down in a vinyl chair.

"Why aren't you sleeping?" I asked.

"Pump yourself full of steroids and prednisone and see if you can sleep," he said. "What are you doing here?"

"I couldn't sleep either. I thought I'd come down here and hold a pillow over your face until you stopped kicking."

"I wouldn't kick much."

"Don't be so sure. Your survival instinct might kick in."

"I don't know."

He looked away, past the television, to the darkened window.

"I can feel my kidneys," he said. "When I hold my breath and concentrate I can feel them."

"What do they feel like?"

"There's a little pressure. Like there's gas in there that's expanding. But I can feel more than that. I feel like I can detect individual cells shutting down, like they're tired and they've decided to quit. When I hold my breath and concentrate I can feel cells throughout my kidneys shutting down. Like millions of tiny lights going out."

He looked back toward the window.

"I'm glad you showed up tonight," he said. "I have a huge favor to ask."

"Name it," I said.

The breakup scene with Karen eventually becomes familiar. Over the next year we repeat it again and again. A pattern develops. Months pass, and all seems well. Karen is happy and at ease. Then for no apparent reason, with no warning signs, she tells me that she can't go on. That it's over. That it has to be over.

Miraculously, each time I'm able to dissuade her. Sometimes it takes hours, sometimes days, and although I'm aware of the anguish it causes her, at the same time it's obvious she loves me, and this gives me the license to act in what I believe is her own best interest.

The breakup scenes happen so often that I can hardly distinguish one from another. One episode, however, stands out from the rest, because even at the time I was aware that we were acting out a tired cliché.

One Saturday morning I walk to her apartment. There's a drizzling rain falling that makes all the houses and trees seem out of focus. My plan is to suggest to Karen that we rent some foreign movies and spend the entire day in bed. For a day we'll forget about term papers that need writing and novels that need reading and stacks of under-graduate papers that need grading, and we'll disappear into a world where there's just the two of us.

She takes a long time to answer the door. When she does, she opens it only halfway and stands in the opening.

"We can't go out anymore," she says.

I'm dripping wet from the rain. There are drops running down my face.

"Can I at least come in and get dried off?"

I take a step forward and Karen yells, "No!" She slams the door, but before she can get it closed, I stick my foot in the opening.

Later I'll discover that she's broken a bone in my foot, but at the time I'm aware only of the task at hand—to again make her see that the love we share is strong enough to overcome whatever is tormenting her.

We stand that way for a long time. Karen with her shoulder pressed against the door, me with my foot preventing its closing. But as we argue (mostly me trying to persuade her), I remember the words actually running through my mind, *At least I've got a foot in the door.*

I left the hospital tired and confused. The idea that had caused me insomnia, that had compelled me to come to the hospital in the middle of the night, was that, if possible, I would give Perry one of my kidneys. But Perry never gave me the chance to make the offer. Before I could, he told me that he'd decided against having the transplant.

"You're going to have to explain," I said.

"Ultimately, it will only prolong my death. It won't prevent it. I'm tired, Thomas. I've been tired for a long time. Drawing this out is senseless."

At that hour of the night the hospital was starkly quiet, but the silence was interrupted by someone wheeling a cart down the corridor outside the door. One of the wheels chirped like a trapped bird on every rotation.

I knew Perry well enough not to argue.

"What's the favor?"

"I want you to explain it to the others," he said.

The chirping faded down the hallway.

"Why not tell them yourself?"

"If it comes from you and they see that you support my decision, they'll be less likely to argue."

Driving back up the mountain to the castle, I felt an acute disappointment. It wasn't because Perry had decided against the transplant. On some level I could understand that. What I was disappointed about, and this was unsettling, was that I wanted to give him a kidney. My motivation was suspect. Would I be doing it for Perry? Or partly for myself—to feel benevolent and magnanimous and noble? Or worse yet, was I doing it for Clare, so that she would see how selfless and devoted I could be? So she would see that she'd been wrong, that I could love completely, to the point of giving one of my own organs to someone I cared for?

I went to bed that night with this question spinning around in my head: Was it possible to do anything that was completely selfless? Or were even our most philanthropic acts ultimately rooted in our need to feel better about ourselves?

I fell asleep at last, just as the sky outside was beginning to breach with a brilliant pink. But I felt none of the hope a sunrise sometimes brings. I felt only sadness, as if some green sprig of life deep inside me had at last withered and died.

I got mixed reactions at breakfast the next morning when I told the others of Perry's decision to refuse the transplant. No one spoke, but

Clare, I think, understood in the same way I had. She listened carefully as I told them about my late-night hospital visit. When I was finished, she bowed her head toward the table.

From the look on Catherine's face, I could see she didn't entirely understand, neither the implications of such a decision nor what it meant for Perry at the most immediate level. What she did understand was that there was a deep, almost religious solemnity to this moment, and now wasn't the time to ask questions.

Juliana's reaction was the most unvarnished. Without saying a word, she stood up and left the apartment. Moments later we heard the grating sound of her car wheels crossing the gravel parking lot, then silence again as she passed through the gatehouse and descended the mountain.

I looked around the room and realized what we needed to do.

A week earlier, after discovering that Catherine had been sending clandestine prayers to the nuns, I'd gone to her at bedtime and asked her about it.

"I wasn't being sneaky," she said. "I was just being private."

"That's fine," I said. "I didn't say there was anything wrong with it. I was just curious."

"Do you think it's silly?" she asked.

"Of course not. I think it's a good idea. I just don't want you to be disappointed if you don't get what you're asking for."

"Aren't you going to ask me what I've been asking for?"

"I wasn't going to. I figured you'd tell me if you wanted to."

Catherine was sitting up with a pillow propped behind her back. Now she pulled up her knees to her chest and smoothed out the floral sheet over her kneecaps.

"It's called a Catherine wheel," she said at last.

"You've named it?"

"No. That's what they're called. After Saint Catherine, because she was martyred on a wheel."

"How do you know that?"

"I must have read it somewhere. Do you think that's a coincidence?"

"I don't know if anything's a coincidence anymore."

Catherine stretched out her legs and lay down. I pulled the covers up to her chin.

"Sleep tight," I said.

I kissed her on the forehead, stood up, and switched off the light.

"Uncle Tommy?" said Catherine.

"Yes?"

"Will you stay here until I fall asleep?"

"I'd love to."

I went back to the bed and crawled in next to her, and although her little body was warm under the covers, as I snuggled up next to her, I felt her shiver.

I got up from the kitchen table and pulled a pad of paper and pencils from a drawer. Back at the table, I set paper and pencil in front of each of us.

"Let's all take a walk to the Catherine wheel," I said.

Catherine and Clare picked up their pencils. When I picked up mine, I hesitated. I knew what I wanted to ask. I just didn't know how to ask it. Finally I simply wrote, *I have a friend who is dying. Please pray for him.*

When I looked up, Catherine had finished writing and was folding her paper into little squares, but Clare hadn't written anything.

"I'm going to need some help," she said.

"I'm sorry," I said. "Let me do it for you."

"Thank you, but I think I'd rather have Catherine do it."

Catherine slid her chair over next to Clare's. "What do you want to ask?" she said, sitting up on her knees.

Clare leaned over and whispered in Catherine's ear, and Catherine smiled.

"That's a good prayer," she said.

She wrote on the paper, folded it into tiny squares, and placed it in the palm of Clare's hand.

"There," she said. "Let's go."

The day was clear and bright and almost smokeless. When we approached the Catherine wheel, the dogs flushed twenty or thirty chickadees from the spruce trees around it. Inside the enclosure of trees, the smell of pine was sweet and warm in my nostrils. We stood in front of the wheel for a moment. One by one we pinned our prayers to the line and sent them squeaking in to the nuns. When they were gone from sight, Catherine took one of Clare's hands and one of mine and led us away.

We continued around the convent. When the path narrowed, Catherine dropped our hands. We walked single file until we reached the wrought-iron gates at the entrance, where the path widened again. Catherine took Clare's hand again, and they walked side by side in front of me. As we passed the gates, I glanced up at the archway where the words *A Cruce Salus* were carved into the stone. Since visiting the Catherine wheel, I'd been feeling something I could only think of as a warm empowerment, but now I felt a chill.

I believe the foot-in-the-door incident is the last of them. Afterward there's a period of restraint on both our parts, then a long period when we're harmonious and close. I begin to forget that there have ever been obstacles to our happiness. It's during this period that we agree to get married. At the time it seems like the final victory in our long battle. Once married, we both feel, there will be no more threat. That ultimate commitment will nullify the fears.

But again I'm projecting my thoughts. In Karen's reality our engagement is the final torment. I'm too blind to see it, but she's constantly at odds with our decision. Looking back now, I see that time after time she tried to tell me she was uneasy, but I was so confident that marriage would solve our problems, I didn't hear.

Karen even phones on the night before our wedding, perhaps to tell me she's decided not to go through with it, but I never give her a chance. I interrupt her with my excitement about our new life together, how happy we're going to be. I tell her to get to sleep so that she'll be well rested for the wedding.

"I love you," I say before hanging up.

"I love you, too," she says.

It's the last time she says it to me.

When we neared the castle, the dogs ran ahead to get a drink from the pool. As they reached it, we heard the crack of plastic from inside the convent, and moments later a Wiffle ball sailed over the wall and landed in the center of the pool. The dogs barked and jumped around at the edge of the water. I jogged ahead of the girls, stripping off my shirt as I ran. When I reached the patio, I pulled off my shoes, hopping toward the water. I half dove, half fell into the pool and, opening my eyes underwater, surfaced under the ball.

When I climbed out, the dogs bounced around at my knees, barking. Catherine and Clare had reached the patio and were standing hand in hand like twin sisters. When I stepped toward the convent, the dogs fell silent. Once again feeling miraculously empowered, I gripped the ball and threw it over the wall.

*T*wo weeks later I awoke one morning with the feeling that someone was in my room. I sat up in bed and waited for my eyes to adjust to the dim, gray twilight. As the objects in the room came into focus—a chair, a bureau, a lamp—I remembered what it was that had awakened me. I'd been sleeping dreamlessly, or so I thought, when I heard a voice—powerful, authoritative, and male—right next to my ear. It said, "Go to the window." And that's when I woke up.

I pulled on a pair of jeans and went to the window. There was a flash of whiteness on the ground below, then it was gone. Although this time I caught only the briefest glimpse of her, I was sure it was the girl again. The same one I'd seen earlier in the summer. The one I was sure Ellen had seen swimming in the pool at La Verdad. The one with the long, dark hair and olive skin. The silvery, translucent gown. The bare feet. And, of course, the bulge of pregnancy in her belly, although she wasn't any more pregnant than when I'd first seen her, as if her pregnancy had fallen into stasis, a ghost forever imprisoned in her second trimester.

In that moment I had a clear premonition that Perry wasn't going to die. There was no logical connection between the phantom pregnant girl and Perry, no reason to believe they should be linked in any way. And yet, there it was. As I backed away from the window, I was convinced that Perry would recover.

In an instant everything made sense. The pregnant girl, Catherine's sightings of saint statues outside the convent wall, her discovery of the Catherine wheel, even her presence at the castle; all of it pointed to this: Perry's life would be spared. It was astonishing that it had taken one of us this long to see the signs.

I went downstairs, eager to share my epiphany with the others, but it was far too early for anyone else to be up. I stepped out onto the patio and knelt down to scratch the dogs behind the ears.

"Your master is going to be okay," I told them. "Perry's going to be okay."

Back inside I pulled eggs and bacon and cheese and mushrooms from the refrigerator. I banged pots and skillets together as I pulled them from the cabinets, then let the doors slam shut. I hummed a show tune I'd heard on a radio ad the day before, but the noise didn't wake the sleeping. How could they sleep? How could they slumber when the world was so full of good news?

Catherine and Clare came down as I was lifting the bacon from the frying pan. They were both wearing long cotton nightshirts that fell to their knees. Catherine's shirt had a large, grimacing raven on the front—the mascot from the college Stephen and Perry and I had attended. I didn't know where she'd gotten it—whether it was mine or Stephen's, or even Perry's. Clare's shirt had a phrase of Latin on it in small, black lettering. When I'd first seen it earlier in the summer, the Latin had thrown me off kilter, but now it had no effect. It read: *Si Hoc Legere Scis Nimium Eruditionis Habes: If you can read this, you're overeducated.*

I watched Catherine get Clare a cup of coffee. As they sat down at the table together, Catherine looked at me and said, "What's so funny?"

"Nothing's funny," I said. "I just have some news."

But the moment I said this, I was aware of how ridiculous it would sound. It had sounded logical when I'd voiced it to the dogs. But now, in the face of voicing it to rational human beings, it seemed preposterous. Was Perry really going to live?

Thankfully, I was spared. Juliana came through the french doors, wearing waders and a fishing vest. She was carrying a string of trout, which she plopped down on the bar in front of me like an ancient hunter-gatherer returning home to her mate with her kill. She plodded over to the coffee machine and poured herself a cup, splashing some of it onto the counter. After gulping down half the cup, she looked around and announced, "I've been up all night."

She refilled her coffee and sat down at the table.

"I have an announcement to make," she said. "Actually two announcements."

She rubbed her hands over her face and through her thick black hair. "I'm not thinking all that clearly."

"Where have you been all night?" asked Clare.

"Well," said Juliana, "Where to begin? I was up half the night arguing with Perry. Then I went fishing because I needed time to think."

"Go on," said Clare.

"Well, the first part is that Perry has asked to be put back on the transplant list. He's decided to do it."

"That's great," said Clare.

"Yeah," I said. "That's wonderful."

"I knew he would change his mind," said Catherine. "I was sure of it."

A moment passed when nobody spoke. I was sure we were all recalling the past two weeks and the many tiny slips of paper we'd sent to the nuns. In that moment of recollection, two distant memories presented themselves to me.

In the first I am sitting on the second-story roof of Karen's apartment outside her bedroom window. We've been drinking beer, and now it's after midnight. Suddenly Karen challenges me to throw a beer bottle down to the street below. Although there's little traffic and only the occasional pedestrian, it seems an exceedingly reckless thing to do, and I tell her so. Karen doesn't even try to hide her scorn as she stands up and launches her bottle into the darkness. As the bottle pops on the pavement and the sound of shattering glass echoes up and down the street, I'm aware that another milestone in our relationship has been passed, all milestones of my failures.

In the other, I'm in my midteens. It's summer and again after midnight. Stephen and I have been out walking when we come across a street dance in a neighborhood not far from ours. There, standing on the sidewalk alone, body swaying to the music, is a girl I've been distantly in love with all summer. I've seen her at the grocery store and at the park. Once, she even walked in front of our car while we were stopped at a traffic light. Each time Stephen has had to endure my lovesick blabber.

Stephen nudges me with his elbow.

"Your lucky day."

The girl looks in our direction and smiles, but I just stand there.

"What are you waiting for?" asks Stephen. "Go ask her to dance."

"I'm going to. I'm just going to go pee first. Make sure she doesn't go anywhere."

Of course, by the time I return, the girl is gone.

I broke eggs into a glass bowl and beat them as the others talked.

"How did you talk him into it?" asked Clare. "I thought he was dead set against it."

"He was," said Juliana, "until I told him I was pregnant. That's part two of my announcement."

Later that morning, as Juliana napped and Clare and Catherine took a walk around the convent together, I drove to the hospital and sat with Perry while his blood was pumped through a dialysis machine. Since entering the hospital, Perry had been despondent, but now he was energized.

"Do you believe in miracles?" he asked.

"I used to. Until my mother died. After that I didn't believe in anything. Now I don't know what to believe."

"But don't you think something's going on?" asked Perry. "I mean when I look back at everything that's happened in the past six or seven months, it feels more than random. It feels purposeful."

"Maybe it is random," I said. "Maybe we have the need to attach meaning to it."

"Maybe. But it feels like more than that. It feels like something's going on. I don't know how else to explain it, but it feels like something intentional is happening that we don't have any control over. Does that make any sense?"

I stood up and walked to the window. In the parking lot below, an old man was helping an old woman to their car. It looked as if at any moment, if there was the slightest breeze, both of them would topple over.

"No," I said, "it doesn't. I mean, it does. I've felt the same way. And I don't know how to explain it either, but something's happening."

I turned around and looked at Perry.

"Do you know what I'm going to do?" he asked.

"What?"

"I'm going to stay alive until my baby is born."

Leaving Perry's room I walked to another part of the hospital and met with Perry's doctor, who explained what was involved in donating a kidney. There would be a regimen of tests—blood tests, EKGs, MRIs, chest x-rays, more blood tests, a CAT scan, possibly an angiogram. All this just to determine whether I would be a suitable donor.

"You're going to need support through this," he said. "You're going to need family or friends nearby. I know I haven't made all this sound like a walk in the park, but it's going to be even worse than I've made it sound. Tests will be scheduled for 6:00 a.m., then we'll keep you waiting for three hours before we do anything. We'll take so much blood from you that you'll think you're in Transylvania, and just when you think there's nothing else we could possibly hope to determine from your blood, we'll ask for more."

I looked down at my shoes, and they seemed alien. I tried to think when and where I'd bought them, but for the life of me, I couldn't remember.

Dr. Bilke picked up a pencil and made a note in a file folder on his desk. There was something about this action that made me feel self-conscious, as if my suitability as a donor was being judged not on the chemical makeup of my kidneys but on the way I responded to questions.

"Well," he said, "I hope for Perry's sake you're a match. At this point, unless someone from his family steps forward, you're his only hope."

Dr. Bilke stood up and shook my hand.

Then, as if to emphasize what he'd said earlier concerning the regimen of tests I would have to undergo, he sent me down the hall to check in at the nurses' station for the first of my tests, which aside from the mountain of paperwork I was asked to fill out, proved to be simple enough—to determine that I had two kidneys.

Later, when I passed the cafeteria, I caught the smell of turkey and gravy, and I was taken back to that same Thanksgiving when Stephen broke his ribs.

* * *

It's the day after Thanksgiving. Stephen is lying on the couch in our father's den under a large purple and burgundy afghan. When I approach, I think for a moment that he's not breathing. But as I get closer, his eyes open and his mouth, which has been hanging open, closes, and he licks his lips. I notice the distant look in his eyes. Instead of reasoning that this is the natural effect of the pain medication, I find myself longing for that distant place.

"How're you feeling?" I ask.

Stephen's eyes move from me to the ceiling, and his forehead furrows.

"Do you ever think about your own death?" he asks.

I'm at first disarmed by the question, and then a little indignant. I'm only ten years old. I don't feel my own death is something I should have to think about yet. But Stephen is mature beyond his years. Looking back, there was always a part of Stephen that was inaccessible to me, but this was something I considered to be my shortcoming, not his. I always had the sense that I failed to reach him at that more meaningful level. When he died, it didn't escape me that I learned more about him from his suicide note than I'd known in years.

Stephen doesn't notice that I have no answer for his question, or perhaps he's not expecting one. Perhaps he's already lowered his expectations of me.

"How about heaven?" he asks. "What do you think heaven is like?"

"It's perfect," I say. "There's no death, no stealing, no hate, no murder. None of the bad stuff we have down here."

Stephen closes his eyes. Again I'm uncomfortable with the level of the conversation.

"How many of those pills have you been taking?" I ask. "I think they're making you a little wacky."

Stephen opens his eyes and looks at me in a way I will become very familiar with over the years. It's a look of sympathy and disappointment, and a longing for something more for me.

"Do you want to know what I think it will be like?" he asks.

"Sure."

"I think it will be like waking up. It will be like living your entire life underwater, and then one day coming to the surface and emerging into the air and sunlight for the first time. We'll realize that things we thought we were seeing clearly were actually only blurred images of the real thing. We'll understand that we've lived our entire lives in watery shadows, that none of the things we've seen or done even come close to what God desires for us. I think the sharpness and clarity of things will blind us, that it will take our eyes and our hearts some time to adjust. But we won't ever adjust. Just when we think we've seen something the way it really is, it will become even clearer, and we'll see that what we thought was the real thing, although infinitely clearer than anything we'd ever known, was still only a shadow of the real thing. This will go on forever."

"Sounds depressing," I say.

"It won't be. Nothing could be further from the truth. It will be the most fantastic thing you've ever experienced. You see, you won't know there's anything clearer than what you're seeing, so each time something new is revealed, it will be completely overwhelming and unexpected. Nothing in the physical world will change. It will all happen right here on planet earth. But *we'll* be changed. We'll be so transformed that everything will *appear* different."

Stephen looked at me to see if I understood, but I didn't. I couldn't imagine heaven being anything but repetitive and boring.

After a minute he looked away and closed his eyes.

"Besides," he says, "we'll be in the presence of God."

Years later, on a humid summer afternoon, we are standing together at our mother's graveside, while a minister reminds us that our mother is now in heaven and, thus, better off. I watch Stephen's face and try to read what he's thinking, try to determine if he still believes in his twelve-year-old vision of heaven, and if it's giving him any comfort. I'm angry with him, and I know it's irrational. All through the service I rehearse what I will say to him later when I pull him aside at the reception. I will say, "So I guess Mom is seeing things clearly now." Then I'll turn and walk away, not giving him any opportunity to respond.

I almost do it. I go as far as to pull Stephen aside at the reception, but when we're alone, I see for the first time that Stephen is completely devastated by our mother's death. I realize that no matter how much I grieve, my grief will never compare to Stephen's. As firstborn, he's had a relationship with our mother that I will never understand.

Instead of saying what I've planned, I kiss him on the cheek and embrace him. As I do I feel his body begin to shake. He sobs, and I hold him as hard as I can, as if I can somehow stop the pain.

When I got back to the castle, there was a note on the kitchen counter from Juliana saying that they'd run into town to get groceries, and then were going to visit Perry. I thought about the Catherine wheel. It had become a place of solace for me, shaded by tall spruce trees full of a coolness and the smell of evergreens and pitch. When so much in our lives was random and unknown, the wheel felt like an anchor or focal point. In a world where so much was uncertain, it felt reassuring and sound. However, I'd never gone there alone.

Dark storm clouds were forming in the southern sky when I stepped out onto the patio. A gusty breeze blew through the tops of the cottonwoods. By the time I reached the Catherine wheel, the sky was darker, but the wind had stopped. When I walked into the spruce grove, I stepped into a stillness, like walking into a long-deserted country church.

I took a pencil and piece of paper out of my pocket and wrote "Please pray for…," but then I paused. I lifted my face to the sky for inspiration, and large drops of rain began to fall. Soon my hair and shirt were soaked through, but I still hadn't decided on what prayer to send the nuns. I scratched out the word *for* so that the note read "Please pray," and I wheeled it in.

For three weeks I spent every day at the hospital—for tests, for meetings with Dr. Bilke and the transplant team, sometimes to take my turn keeping Perry company while he was on dialysis. Then one morning I awoke to the realization that it was all done. There would be no more prodding, no poking, no letting of blood. No filling out forms and signing authorizations in triplicate. There would be no three-hour waits for a nurse to finally appear and inform me that it would be just a few more minutes, a period of time that was closer to three-quarters of an hour. The only thing left now was to hear back from the hospital as to whether my kidney was a suitable match.

It was a warm, cloudless day. I started it by sleeping in, then I went downstairs and wandered into the library. I wanted nothing more than to find a good book and spend the day by the pool. When I came across Greene's *The Heart of the Matter,* I pulled it from the shelf and headed outside.

There was no sign of Catherine or Clare or the dogs, so I settled into a chaise longue and started reading. Wilson was still on the balcony of the Bedford Hotel waiting for his gin and bitters when I looked up and saw Perry's dogs returning from a walk around the convent. I watched the curve of the wall where they'd first appeared, and in a moment Catherine came tramping into sight. She was wearing a light cotton sundress that swung around her bare ankles. Her gait was purposeful, yet at the same time reckless, as if, and this seemed quite fitting to me, she somehow had all the concerns and responsibilities of an adult, yet still maintained a child's faith and carefree optimism.

"What have I done to deserve this?" I whispered.

Catherine jumped up onto the patio.

"Good morning, Uncle Tommy."

The answer came as clearly as if someone had whispered it into my ear. *You've done nothing to deserve this. Nothing.*

"Well," I said as she sat down in a chair next to me, "you seem very chipper this morning."

Catherine looked at me and narrowed her eyes. "Nobody says chipper anymore, Uncle Tommy."

"No? Well, we should bring it back into vogue."

"I don't think so. I think it probably went out for a good reason."

"Okay. How *are* you feeling this morning?"

Catherine squinted up at the sun.

"I'm glad," she said after a while. "I'm feeling very glad."

"Well," I said, "I suppose that's as good as chipper. What are you so glad about?"

"About my mother," said Catherine. "I ran into a statue of Saint Mary just now, and now I know it won't be long before I see her again."

At the mention of Catherine's mother, my throat tightened, something that happened to some degree whenever I heard Mary's name.

"It's because your feelings associated with Mary are complex," Clare had told me once when I'd confessed this to her. "I can think of any number of reasons why her name might fill you with anxiety: You dated her once, she was your brother's wife, she's Catherine's mother, she might appear one day and take Catherine away from you. That's your greatest fear. On the other hand, you're also afraid she won't come back, because you don't want Catherine to go on hoping in vain, to be devastated when she realizes that her mother is never coming back. I'd say you have a right to a certain amount of anxiety."

I'd been sitting on the edge of Clare's bed where she sat with her back against the headboard, her knees pulled up underneath her nightgown. I stood up and walked to her window. It was a warm summer evening, and I realized for the first time that unlike the East where I'd grown up, Montana had neither crickets nor lightning bugs. As this realization sank in, the night seemed vacuous, as if something elemental was missing.

"But she *is* coming back, isn't she," I said, turning around and going back to Clare's bed.

We'd spoken about this before. Although Catherine rarely brought up her mother with me, with Clare it was a frequent topic. Catherine believed that Mary was going to return. This wasn't just a child's wishful thinking, Clare assured me. It went well beyond childish hope. Catherine believed that certain things about the future had been revealed to her. And for reasons that weren't clear to me at all, Clare believed there was substance to Catherine's beliefs.

"I've told you," said Clare, "I think she is."

There was a rustling at the tops of the trees, and the dogs raised their heads and pricked their ears. Not until the trees fell silent did they again lower their heads onto their paws.

"Mary," I said. "The Mother Mary?"

"No," said Catherine. "This wasn't the Blessed Virgin. This was another Mary."

"Mary Magdalene," I suggested. "Was she a saint?"

"She was," said Catherine. "But it wasn't her either. This was Mary the Egyptian, also known as the Sinner."

"She was a sinner and a saint?"

Catherine stared into the pool. I watched her shoulders lift, then fall.

"Mary was born in Egypt and went to Alexandria when she was twelve. For seventeen years she lived as a prostitute, never refusing her body to anyone. Then one day some people from the area were going up to Jerusalem to pay homage to the holy cross, and Mary asked the sailors if she could go with them. When they asked for her fare, she said, 'Brothers, I have no fare, but take my body in payment for the passage.' So they took her aboard. When she arrived in Jerusalem, she went with the others to the church to worship the holy cross, but an invisible force pushed her back from the door. Again and again she got to the entrance and got pushed back, while the others went in with no trouble. Then she realized that this was happening to her because of her dreadful crimes. She beat her breast and cried tears of regret. Then she saw an image of the Blessed Virgin Mary. She began to pray tearfully to her, asking her to pardon her for her sins and to be let in to worship the holy cross. She promised that she would renounce the world and live chastely. Having offered this prayer and having put her trust in the name of the Blessed Virgin, she went again to the door of the church, and this time she was able to go in."

Catherine sat down next to me.

"What's that you're reading?" she asked.

I picked the book up off my lap. *The Heart of the Matter.*

"Is it good?"

"I've just started."

Catherine sighed. "Do you want to hear more about Mary?"

"Yes."

"When she finished worshiping the cross, someone gave her three coins, and she bought three loaves of bread. She heard a voice that said, 'If you go across the Jordan, you will be saved.' So she crossed the Jordan and went into the desert and stayed for forty-seven years without seeing another human being. The loaves she brought with her turned hard as stone, but they kept her alive for all those years.

"Then one day a priest named Zozimus crossed the Jordan hoping to find some holy father there. He saw a figure walking around naked, her body blackened by the sun. It was Mary the Egyptian. Over the years her clothes had worn out, but her hair had grown long and taken their place. When she saw Father Zozimus she ran, and Zozimus chased after her.

"Finally she stopped and said, 'Father Zozimus, why are you pursuing me? Forgive me, I cannot face you because I am a woman and naked, but lend me your cloak so that I can see you without being ashamed.'

"He was surprised that she knew his name, so he gave her his cloak and laid down on the ground and asked her to bless him.

" 'It is you, Father, who should give the blessing, since you are a priest.'

"When he heard that she knew both his name and his job, he marveled still more and asked again that she bless him.

"Then she said, 'Blessed be God, the redeemer of our souls!' She extended her hands in prayer, and he saw her lifted off the ground. The old man began to suspect that this might be a spirit pretending to pray. 'May God forgive you,' she said, 'for thinking that I, a sinful woman, might be an unclean spirit.'

"Now Zozimus pleaded with her to tell him about herself. Her answer was, 'Excuse me, Father, because if I tell you who and what I am, you will flee as if frightened by a serpent, your ears will be contaminated by my words, the air will be polluted with filth.' But the old man insisted, so she told him all that had happened to her. When she'd finished her story, Father Zozimus knelt at her feet and prayed.

"Then Mary said to him, 'I beg you, Father, to come back to the

Jordan on the day of the Lord's Supper and to bring with you the body of the Lord. I will meet you there and receive the sacred body from your hand, because since the day I came here, I have not received the communion of the Lord.'

"The old man returned to his monastery, and the following year, when Holy Thursday was drawing near, he took the sacred Host and went to the bank of the Jordan. He saw the woman standing on the other bank, and she made the sign of the cross over the river and walked across the water. Marveling at this, the priest fell down at her feet. She said, 'Don't do that! You have the sacrament of the Lord on your person, and you shine with the dignity of priesthood.'

"After receiving the sacrament she said, 'I pray you, Father, that you will come again to me next year.' Then, once again making the sign of the cross over the Jordan waters, she went over and returned to the desert."

I looked at Catherine. She pulled her dress up above her knees so the sun could hit them.

"That's a remarkable story," I said. "But I must have missed something. What's all this got to do with being reunited with your mother?"

"You didn't miss anything. I haven't told you about my dream yet."

"Tell me about it."

"Well, last night before I knew anything about the statue that I saw this morning, I had a dream about Mary the Egyptian."

"What happened in the dream?"

"Everything I've just told you," she said. "I saw the whole story of her life in my dream like it was really happening."

I realized that only months ago talk like this would have sent me scampering to Clare, but now I believed her.

"That's some dream," I said. "But I still don't get it."

Catherine looked at me and rolled her eyes.

"In the dream," she said. "My mother played the part of Mary the Egyptian. It was her face on that naked, blackened body."

That night I found it impossible to fall asleep. Finally I got out of bed and went to the window. After looking out into the darkness for a few minutes, I closed it and went back to bed. Twenty seconds later I got up again and reopened it. I hadn't been aware of making any noise, but when I turned around again, Clare was standing in the doorway wearing a knee-length T-shirt.

"You can't sleep," she said.

"No. Am I keeping you awake too?"

"You weren't making any noise, if that's what you mean. But I could tell you were upset at dinner tonight, so I guess you are keeping me awake."

"How could you tell I was upset?"

"Well, for starters you only said about half as much as you usually do."

"You mean I said two words instead of four?"

"Exactly."

"I wouldn't say I'm upset."

Clare came into the room and lay down in my bed. She propped her head on one elbow and patted the sheet.

"Come here," she said. "Why don't you tell me what's bothering you?"

I lay down next to her. I could smell her scent. It was a smell I'd grown to love. Not perfume—I don't think she ever wore any—but ozone and chlorine and fresh fruit.

"I'm not upset," I said.

"Okay, then what are you thinking?"

"I guess I'm a little upset."

"I think we've made a breakthrough," said Clare.

"It's this whole thing with Catherine and the statues and the dreams and her feeling like she has a piece of the future right now."

"You don't believe she does?" asked Clare.

"No, that's just it. I think I do believe. That's the problem. I believe it, but I feel like I'm on the outside of it. Everyone else seems to be comfortable with all this, like they're a part of it."

"You feel left out."

"I guess I do. Catherine's got a piece of the future, but I feel like I don't even have a piece of her piece of the future."

"And everyone else does?" asked Clare.

"I guess that's what it feels like."

"Well," said Clare, rolling onto her back. "I don't think that's the case. It's all very mysterious to me, too. But Catherine does tell me things I think she holds back from you."

"Why is that?" I asked. "Am I that inaccessible?"

"You're getting a lot better. Maybe she thinks you'd be skeptical, and to be fair, you would be. Maybe it's just that I'm a woman. For whatever reason, she's chosen to tell me more than the rest of you."

"You mean she doesn't tell Juliana the stuff she tells you?" I asked.

"No, she doesn't. If Juliana had the energy to think about anything besides her baby and Perry right now, she'd probably feel the same way you're feeling. Does that make you feel better?"

"I feel a little bit like I'm being a baby," I said. "But I'm not. That's not what I'm doing. I just want to be in on things. Not just for my own sake, but for Catherine's sake and everyone else's. I feel like my whole life I've been observing a stage play, and I've been watching from the catwalk above. I don't want to do that anymore. I want to be on the stage with everyone else. Fighting and arguing and making up and loving and the whole messy business."

At this Clare reached over and touched my cheek with the palm of her hand, then she moved her fingers down my face and across my lips.

"That's the most accessible thing I've ever heard you say."

I closed my eyes and let her fingers caress my face. She ran them across my eyebrows and down the sides of my nose and kept coming back again and again to my lips. Maybe it was this simple. Maybe all I had to do was let someone touch me.

At some point I realized that Clare was no longer touching my face. I opened my eyes and looked at her lying next to me.

"I'm sorry. Did I fall asleep?"

"I think so," said Clare. "But don't apologize. That's why I came in here, remember?"

"Well, since I'm awake now, why don't you try to explain this whole Mary of Egypt thing to me."

"It's pretty simple. Catherine believes that the nuns caused her to dream about Mary the Egyptian."

"Whoa," I said. "She believes what?"

"I know," said Clare, "but listen. It makes perfect sense when you think about it. For months now she's been asking the nuns via the Catherine wheel to intercede for her. She's been asking them to ask God to reunite her with her mother. Then last night she has this elaborate dream in which her mother plays the starring role. It's not that strange to see something like that as a message from God. But Catherine is not in direct contact with God; she's been going through the nuns first, so, for Catherine, God first sends the dream to the nuns, then the nuns send it over here, and Catherine dreams it. It makes sense."

"Okay, I can see that. But I still don't know what the dream means. Or what Catherine thinks it means."

"Well, that's a little more complex," said Clare, "but not much. Catherine thinks there's a correlation between the life of Saint Mary the Egyptian and Mary her mother. She thinks she knows, in general terms at least, what her mother's been doing for the past seven months, and what's going to happen in the future. In general."

"What's the correlation?"

"As Catherine sees it, there were three basic parts to Mary's life: Her seventeen years as a prostitute, her forty-seven years of wandering naked in the desert, and finally, crossing the Jordan and receiving the sacrament."

"Catherine thinks her mother has become a prostitute?" I asked.

"Actually, the prostitute years correlate with her marriage to your brother. Catherine thinks that her mother prostituted herself to the church, doing anything it asked of her, to the exclusion of being a good wife to Stephen, which she now realizes should have been her primary role. She thinks, and I think she's right about this, that Mary probably blames herself for Stephen's death."

"Okay. That makes sense. So now for the past seven months, Mary has been wandering in the desert?"

"That too makes perfect sense," said Clare.

"Yes it does. So what's next? When does she cross the Jordan? Is that when Catherine thinks she'll see her again?"

"When she crosses the Jordan, she'll be right with God again. The next natural step would be to make it right with her daughter."

"Does she know when that's going to happen?"

"Not exactly," said Clare. "But here it does get a little more specific. Catherine believes that her mother is going to have to cross a body of water to get to her, and that she's going to be there, like the priest Zozimus, to watch it."

"The moat."

"I suggested that to her. She said that in the dream it was a much larger body of water than that."

"Well," I said. "That's going to be a bit tough in Montana, isn't it?"

"Yes, it is," said Clare. "And Catherine is well aware of that."

I closed my eyes, and without beckoning it, there stretched before me a large body of water. It was neither a river nor a lake nor even an ocean. Its surface was smooth, glasslike, and I imagined if I were to touch it, it would be warm. It had a deep, bronze hue, as if the setting sun had descended into it and was lighting and warming it from beneath. Then I heard a woman's soft voice, and I realized that the body of water I was seeing was not water at all, but a mirage.

"I'm sorry," I said, without opening my eyes, "what did you say?"

"You fell asleep again," said Clare. "Maybe I should go."

"No," I said, opening my eyes. "I'm sorry. Tell me what you were saying."

"I was asking you if Catherine had told you about the lion."

"What lion?"

"The lion in the story about Mary. Obviously she didn't."

"No."

"Well, there was a lion. After serving Mary the sacraments, Father Zozimus again returned to his monastery. A year later he returned to the spot in the desert where he'd first met her, a journey that took him thirty days to complete. But when he arrived, he found her lying there dead. He began to cry and said to himself, 'I wish I could bury the saint's body, but I fear this might displease her.'

"As he was thinking about this, he noticed something written in the sand beside her head. It read, 'Zozimus, bury Mary's little body, return her dust to the earth, and pray for me to the Lord, at whose command I left this world on the second day of April.' Then the old man realized that she had died the previous year immediately after he had served her the sacraments, and in one hour she had traveled to the spot where she lay, an expanse of desert that had taken him thirty days to cross.

"Zozimus tried to dig a grave but couldn't. Then he saw a lion coming toward him, and he said to the lion, 'This holy woman commanded me to bury her body here, but I'm old and cannot dig, and anyway I have no shovel. Therefore, you do the digging, and we will be able to bury this holy body.' The lion began to dig with his paws and in a while had dug a suitable grave. When he was finished he went away, and the old man returned to his monastery."

"And what's that part supposed to mean?" I asked. "Does Catherine think she's finally going to be reunited with her mother only for her to die?"

"She doesn't think so," said Clare. "She doesn't know what that part of the dream is all about."

"Now I'm getting skeptical. It seems like she's reading things into the parts she wants to but is discounting the parts she doesn't like."

"It could appear that way, but I don't think she is. There was one thing I didn't tell you."

"What's that?"

"In her dream, when the old man returned and found Mary dead, her face had changed."

"Changed how?" I asked.

"It wasn't her mother anymore."

"Who was it?"

"She wouldn't tell me."

I didn't remember saying good night or even falling asleep, but when I awoke in the morning to a dim, gray light filling the room, Clare was still in bed with me. She was lying at the edge of the mattress with her back to me, a pillow crammed between her knees. There was an unfamiliar cool humidity in the room and a flowery fragrance that made me think of spring snowmelt. I wondered if Clare's presence could be responsible for the sensuous aroma, but then I looked to the window and realized that for the first time all summer, it was raining.

Should I have marveled that Clare had stayed all night? It *was* marvelous, but at the same time, it seemed natural. But even this naturalness had a feeling of wonder to it. Over the last three weeks, Clare, along with Catherine, had been my constant companions, going with me to the hospital whenever I had to undergo tests, sitting with me, reading to me, telling me jokes, talking about almost everything, anything to quell the boredom. One day after an angiogram, I was required to lie still for eight hours so that clots from the procedure wouldn't break loose into my bloodstream. All day Catherine bounced between Perry's room in another wing of the hospital and mine, but Clare stayed with me, telling me stories from her childhood in Africa. When she ran out of stories, she read to me from Braille *National Geographic* magazines. Once, after falling asleep for a while, images from an arid African landscape bouncing through my head like antelope, I awoke to find that Clare had gone to sleep in her chair, her head fallen forward in an awkward position on the bed by my arm. There was a thin sliver of drool at the corner of her mouth like a little meandering stream.

Over those weeks Clare and I had quietly covered new ground. We'd settled into a new place that was at once unfamiliar and comfortable. Nothing had been spoken, and neither of us, I think, had any illusions about where we stood with each other or what the future would hold, but there was this new, quieter place, a new context in which to be together.

Now I watched her sleeping as the rain tapped on the window. Even in her sleep she seemed sure of herself. Over the past weeks I'd seen new facets of her personality. She was smart and confident and surprisingly tough when she needed to be. But she was also genuinely kind. From the outset of the testing process, she'd grilled Dr. Bilke and the other team members about every aspect of the transplant procedure. Every time a nurse stuck a needle in my arm and withdrew a vial of blood (and sometimes this happened three or four times a day), Clare wanted to know why they were doing it and what it was for. Before allowing any test to proceed, she had to know everything about it. Within the first few days, I began to detect slight grimaces on the hospital staff's faces whenever Clare approached. She knew she was being a thorn in everyone's sides, but she didn't care.

In the beginning I thought that this was Clare's scientific side kicking in, but after a few days I began to see that it evolved from a genuine concern for my well-being. Later I realized that there was even more to it than that. She was scared. Clare loved me. Maybe not in the way I had hoped, but still, it was love.

When Clare woke up she rolled over and faced me. There was a slight puffiness under her eyes that made her look a little sad.

"Good morning," I said.

"Good morning," she said. "Is it raining?"

"It is."

I was expecting Clare to be a little embarrassed at staying all night, but if she was, she didn't show it. She looked toward the window and sighed. Then quite unexpectedly she leaned toward me and kissed me, connecting partially with lips, partially with cheek.

"How're you feeling?" she asked.

The words *whole* and *complete* jumped into my head. I would have spoken them if they hadn't been so inadequate.

"I feel good. How about you?" I asked.

"Do you think it's going to rain all day?"

"I don't know. It has that feel about it."

"Then I feel like going downstairs and starting a fire in the library," she said. "Then sending you into the basement to find a thirty-year-old bottle of wine while I curl up on the couch under a blanket. Then when you get back, having you read to me all day."

I leaned toward her to return the kiss, but the telephone rang downstairs and I stopped to listen. Somebody picked up the phone. It was a brief conversation, and when it was over, we heard footsteps on the stairs. In a moment Catherine was standing in the doorway. She didn't seem surprised to find Clare there. I thought it pleased her.

"Good morning," she said.

"Good morning," we answered.

"That was the hospital," said Catherine. "The lady said they just green-lighted the transplant."

After dinner that night, the four of us sat on the patio by the pool before going to bed. It had rained for most of the day, but now the rain had stopped and the sky was clear. Over the mountains to the west there were still cottony wisps of clouds receding toward the horizon. As the sun dropped below the mountains the clouds became inflamed, like great waves of fiery red hair.

It was a coolish evening. Cooler than it had yet been that summer. There was a subtle difference in the air, a quiet shifting. I didn't think it was the smell of fall. Even here in the mountains, that was several weeks off. But something was different.

Both Clare and Juliana were wearing long pants and sweaters, but Catherine was still wearing her summer uniform: knee-length denim shorts and an oversize, white V-neck T-shirt. She had her arms wrapped around her legs, but she didn't seem uncomfortable.

"Aren't you cold?" asked Juliana. "I'm getting cold just looking at you."

Catherine had been staring at a spot on the table in front of her. At the sound of Juliana's voice, she raised her eyes to another spot on the table and shook her head.

This kind of spaciness was not typical of Catherine, but since setting the date for the surgery earlier in the day, everyone had been distant and sedate.

"Maybe it's time for a party," I said.

"I think that's a good idea," Clare said.

"It will be a Coming Out and Going in Party," I said.

"Here at the castle?" asked Juliana. "What about Perry?"

"We'll get Dr. Bilke to let Perry come home for a night," I said.

"What if he won't?" asked Juliana.

"Then we'll sneak him out," I said.

Juliana looked to Clare.

"What do you think?" she asked.

"I think Thomas is right," Clare said. "A little festivity would do us all good."

"Okay," said Juliana. "I guess you're right. What do you think Catherine?"

"We can make a kidney-shaped cake," said Catherine. "Or will that gross everyone out?"

* * *

That night before going to sleep, I went in to check on Catherine. She was already in bed, the lights off.

"Are you asleep?" I asked from her doorway.

"No," she said. "You can come in."

I went in and sat on the edge of her bed. She was wearing an enormous sweater made of a thick weave of blue cotton. I'd seen her in it before, but had never known her to sleep in it.

"Are you okay?" I asked.

"Yes. Am I not acting okay?"

"No, you're acting fine. There's just a lot going on, so I wanted to check."

"I'm okay."

"Okay," I said, feeling that I wasn't very good at whatever it was I was trying to do. "Are you excited about going back to school?"

"Not really."

"Why not?"

"I don't think I should go on the day of the surgery. Do you?"

"Not if you don't want to."

"I don't want to," said Catherine. "I think I should be at the hospital."

"Of course," I said. "I think Perry and I will both feel better knowing you're there."

There was a sound from the direction of the convent. At first I thought it was singing, but in a moment it sounded different, like a tree filled with sparrows, all chirping in unison. Catherine sat up on her elbow and listened.

"What is that?" I asked.

"It's prayer," said Catherine in a whisper. "They're singing their prayers tonight. The nuns believe that when prayers are sung, they are better able to float up to God, and he hears them better."

We listened until the music became faint, as if the wind had changed and was now taking the song in another direction, away from the castle.

Catherine lay back on her pillow. I was about to kiss her on the forehead, but something stopped me. I had the gut-twisting feeling that leaving the room now would be like going to sleep still mad at a spouse. Something was unsettled. Then I noticed that the nuns' prayers had stopped.

"What's wrong?" I asked.

"Nothing," said Catherine. "Nothing's wrong."

"Are you worried about the surgery?"

"No. Not like everyone else is."

"How is everyone else worried?"

"Everyone else is worried because they don't know what's going to happen. You're all pretty sure everything will go smoothly, but you can't know for sure, so you're worried."

"I think that's probably true," I said. "But that's not how you're worried?"

"I'm more sad than worried," said Catherine.

"Sad."

"Yes. I'm sad because I know what's going to happen."

A siege of chills shot up my back and down my arms.

"Really," I said. "What's going to happen?"

Catherine closed her eyes and sighed. After a moment she looked at me through narrowed eyes as if sizing me up, a quick evaluation to see if I could handle what she had to say.

"What is it?" I said again. "What's going to happen?"

I could tell she was reluctant to speak, as if speaking it would cement its fate.

Catherine bit her lower lip and stared up at the charcoal canopy above her bed. She reached out and took my hand in hers.

"What is it?"

"He's going to die," said Catherine.

Her hand tightened a little in mine. I looked at her, and she looked away. After a short time, a wave of fatigue washed over me. I thought about going to my room to see if Clare was there waiting for me, but instead I leaned over and kissed Catherine on the forehead and crawled into the bed next to her. I turned off the light at the bedside, and we fell asleep still holding hands.

I'm walking down a long tunnel that's gradually narrowing. As the walls and ceiling begin to close in, I realize that it's not a tunnel in any conventional sense. When I reach out and touch one of the walls, I find that it's not solid, but neither is it liquid. It's something in between. The tunnel is made up of a viscous slime, a mucus or goo. Then I realize I'm inside a living organism, traveling through an intestine or vein or other bodily passageway. At some point it becomes clear that the organism I'm in is human. Somehow I'm traveling inside someone else's body.

All at once the passageway opens up, and I find myself in a large chamber that pulses and throbs with the rhythm of a heartbeat. At the center of this chamber is a hole or pit. When I walk over and look in, I see that Perry is at the bottom of it, knee-deep in sludge and sinking. He reaches out his hand to me, and I lie down on my stomach and reach toward him, but my arm is short by about six inches. I stand and look around the chamber for anything I might be able to use to reach Perry, but there's nothing but the smooth pulsing walls.

I realize then that I'm naked and that there's no flesh across my stomach and chest, leaving my ribs and organs exposed. I reach into my chest and break off the longest of my ribs, and again lie down and reach out to Perry. By now he's sunk up to his waist in the sludge, and he looks desperate. I reach down with the rib and see with relief that it will be long enough. But when Perry reaches up and grabs it, it crumbles into dust. A fleeting look of betrayal passes over Perry's face. Then he disappears into the muck.

Then music, women's voices, like a Greek choir chanting quiet admonitions to the actors on stage. I'm lying in an enormous bed, so soft it seems to be made of clouds. Clare walks into the room and stands next to it. The sheer, white nightgown she is wearing appears to be a blend of chiffon and sunlight. When she pulls it over her head and drops it beside her, it dissolves into the floor. She climbs into the bed, and her soft champagne hair drifts across my face as she begins to plant delicate kisses at the corners of my eyes and the edges of my ears. As her kisses begin to wander, down my neck, onto my chest, I expect to feel that surge of blood, that familiar rush of arousal, but instead there is only numbness. Clare continues to kiss down the center of my chest, then suddenly she stops and raises her head. "There's something missing down here," she says. "You're not all here." I raise my head, prop myself up on my elbows, and look down at myself. Where there should be stomach and pelvis is a gaping hole. Inside, where there should be blood and organs is nothing but a thick fog.

This was the framework of my sleep—my failure and inadequacy—neatly laid out by my subconscious. And yet, despite Catherine's prophecy and the disturbing dreams of the night before, I awoke feeling peaceful, the way I'd felt after encountering the phantom pregnant girl. I eased out of Catherine's bed, walked across the hall, and looked out my bedroom window, half expecting to see her dancing outside the walls of the convent. But aside from a large raven perched atop the stone wall, there was no sign of life.

When I stepped outside, the dogs appeared from beneath a hedge and sat at my feet. When I knelt down, they licked at my outstretched hand.

"Okay," I said. "We'll go for a walk."

At the word *walk* the dogs jumped up and ran in the direction of the convent, and I followed. As I walked that strange, euphoric sensation I'd awakened with, like a drug-induced high, slowly wore off. I watched the dogs zigzagging down the trail in front of me, their noses to the ground, and Catherine's words from the night before started to replay in my head.

He's going to die.

Catherine spoke with such authority that it was impossible not to believe her. But if I believed that Perry was going to die, then why go through with the transplant? Why put myself at risk for nothing? Why not tell him I'd changed my mind, that I thought his original decision not to have the transplant was the right one?

I'd just about decided to do that when one of the dogs trotted up to me with something in its mouth. This alone was enough to get my attention, because these dogs were not retrievers. If they picked something up in their mouths, it was for the sole purpose of tearing it to shreds. I was even more intrigued when the dog dropped whatever it was at my feet. It was a pale blue ribbon, still tied in a bow as if it had fallen unnoticed from someone's hair. I picked it up and raised it to my nose and inhaled. The faint scent of myrrh filled my head like a balm. Of course I would go through with the transplant. I stuffed the ribbon into my pocket and started back to the castle, but I'd only taken a few steps when I ran blindly into a statue.

Later I lay on the library couch, holding a washcloth full of ice on the bridge of my nose, and tried to explain to Catherine and Clare how I'd possibly broken it by running into a saint. I was tempted, and I don't know why, to alter the facts. To say that after stuffing the ribbon into my pocket and starting back to the castle, I'd turned around and walked backward for a few steps to make sure the dogs were following, and when I'd turned forward again I'd run into the statue. But in reality, and this is the way I told it, I'd been facing forward the whole time. I *had* been in a hurry to get back, but I'd also been watching where I was going. One second nothing was there; the next I walked right into the statue. I felt a ricochet of heat through my sinuses and fell backward onto the ground. Everything went black. I put my hands to my face as a throbbing pain spread across my forehead to my temples and then wrapped around to the back of my head like fingers. I was sure that when I reopened my eyes, the statue would be gone, leaving me to believe that I'd been hallucinating and had merely run into a tree. But when I looked, the statue was still there, the Patron Saint of Broken Noses.

"Which saint was it really?" asked Catherine.

She took the ice pack off my nose and examined the damage.

"I don't know," I said. "How am I supposed to know?"

"You're starting to look like a raccoon," said Catherine. "But I don't think your nose is broken. I had a friend from school who broke her nose, and it looked much worse than yours."

"How are you feeling?" asked Clare.

She sat down on the edge of the couch and brushed back the hair from my forehead. I was surprised by the way I responded.

"Happy, I guess," I said. "I feel happy."

"Yes," said Clare after a moment. "That's the way I felt too, after I saw my saint."

"That's the way you should feel," said Catherine. "And lucky. The saints don't show themselves to everyone."

"Who do they show themselves to?" asked Clare.

"I don't know," said Catherine. "To people like us."

"And what kind of people are we?" asked Clare.

Catherine stood up, opened the washcloth, and looked in at the remaining ice.

"People who are willing to see," she said at last. "Now don't move," she said, pointing a stern finger at me. "I'm going to get more ice."

As soon as Catherine left the room, Clare surprised me by bending over and kissing me on the lips. It was a real kiss, her lips firm and moist and lingering.

"What was that for?" I asked.

"I don't know," said Clare. "Maybe I was wrong about you."

"I think you were probably right about me."

"Maybe I was. But I look back at that person who first came into my office all those months ago, and I don't even think of that person as you. The only thing you have in common with him is your body."

I sat up and put my hands on Clare's shoulders and moved my face close to hers.

"I'm going to kiss you," I said.

"I'm not arguing," she said.

We kissed for a long time, until I bumped my nose against hers and winced. When I looked at her, I saw she was crying.

"Sorry," she said, wiping her eyes.

"About what?"

"About bumping your nose."

"Why are you crying?"

She sniffled and looked away. When she turned back to me there was something mournful in her eyes, something that at once both invited me in and warned me away.

"Women cry for a lot of reasons, Thomas. Sometimes we don't even know why."

Facing me in the mirror the next morning was a man with a swollen purple nose and two black eyes. I couldn't even brush my teeth without unbearable pain, but under the pulsing ache was a current of bliss. The night before, after putting Catherine to bed and telling her a story, I'd run into Clare in the hallway outside my bedroom. She'd seemed to be lingering there, unsure of where to go. I walked up to her and took her by the hand.

"Come sleep with me," I said, leading her to the door.

She followed without a word, but when we got to the door she stopped.

"I don't think that's a good idea."

"I do. I think it's a very good idea."

"Please, Thomas. Let's take this slowly, okay?"

"Okay," I said after a moment. "I think that's a good idea too."

Clare kissed me lightly on the lips and walked down the hallway to her room. I went to bed feeling lucky because there was a "this," and we were taking it somewhere, and a few weeks ago that alone was more than I ever could have hoped for.

I stepped out of the bathroom just as Clare was reaching for the door.

"Good morning," she said. "How are you looking today?"

"You're lucky you can't see me."

"Sometimes I wish like crazy I could."

I reached out to her and ran my hand through her hair and squeezed the back of her head.

"I'm sorry," I said. "Did you sleep all right?"

"Not so great. I almost changed my mind and came to see you."

"That would have been nice."

That morning at breakfast we began making plans for Perry's Coming Out and Going In Party, but the girls were less enthused than I would have expected. Juliana seemed distracted, Clare appeared pensive, and Catherine was more interested in positioning a fried egg on a piece of toast than making party plans. When the telephone rang, I detected a wave of relief.

"Well," I said, coming back to the table after talking on the phone. "It looks like there won't be a party after all. That was the hospital. They want to do the transplant tomorrow, if that's okay with everyone."

"Is it okay with you?" asked Clare.

"I don't see what difference it makes," I said. "I guess I'd rather get it over with."

"My feelings exactly," said Juliana. "Let's get it over with."

"Okay," I said. "Tomorrow it is."

"When do you have to go?" asked Catherine.

"Right now," I said. "They want to get me ready."

Catherine looked panicked.

"Do we have time to make a last visit to the Catherine wheel?" she pleaded. "I think we should."

I looked at Juliana and Clare, then turned to Catherine.

"Of course," I said. "I wouldn't think of letting someone take out one of my kidneys without first putting it in the hands of someone I trusted."

I gulped down the rest of my coffee.

"I'll go upstairs and get packed," I said. "Then we can all go together."

Moments later I was tossing socks into an open suitcase on the bed when I heard someone enter the room behind me.

"What's wrong?" asked Clare.

I didn't turn around, just continued to toss more socks than I could possibly wear into the suitcase. After a moment Clare moved closer and wrapped her arms around me from behind, turning her head so that the side of her face was on my back. She tightened her arms and squeezed some of the air from my lungs. When she loosened her grip, I turned around and locked my arms behind her back.

"You're amazing," I said.

"How so?"

"You can't see me, but you can see me better than anyone who's ever known me."

"Would it surprise you if I told you I was falling in love with you?"

She looked up into my eyes, her face so close to mine I could feel the warmth of her breath on my neck. I forgot, as I had so many times before, that what she saw before her was not me, not my bruised purple and yellow face, but only darkness. I moved my hands up her back and pulled her head into my chest.

"Yes," I said. "That does surprise me."

"Why?" asked Clare in a whisper. "Is it that surprising?"

"Maybe you shouldn't. Maybe I'm a fake."

Clare pushed back from my chest but kept her hands clasped at the small of my back.

"Why a fake?" she asked.

I reached back and unclasped her hands, and turned and walked to the window overlooking the convent.

"This whole Catherine wheel thing," I said after a moment. "What if it's just an insurance policy?"

"The fact that you have that concern would indicate to me that it's more than that."

"Maybe," I said. "Maybe not."

Clare was still standing near the bed where I'd left her, but now she walked to me at the window and again wrapped her arms around me from behind.

"I think you're being too hard on yourself," she said.

"Maybe," I said. "Maybe not. It's just that I don't understand all this. Don't understand what we're doing. In some ways it feels like a child's game we're playing. But it's not a game. There's a lot at stake. And that makes it seem dangerous."

"Thomas," said Clare in a whisper so soft that her voice seemed to travel through water before reaching my ears, "I don't pretend to understand all this any better than you, and I wouldn't presume to know all your motivations. But this I do know; if we insist on understanding everything, we'll never get it. We need to simply do our best to live into it, and accept that we may never know what it all means."

I turned around and faced her, intertwined my fingers behind her back.

"How do you live into something you don't understand?" I asked.

"We're already doing it," she said. "We just keep doing what we're doing. Sometimes actions precede faith."

"It scares me," I said. "It feels very out of control."

"I think that's the way it's supposed to feel."

I looked into Clare's face. For the first time I noticed that the faint freckles under her right eye resembled the Pleiades. Without warning, an astronomy lesson from college came back to me, and I laughed a little at the stark clarity of it.

"What's so funny?" asked Clare.

"I just noticed that you have a group of freckles under one of your eyes that looks like a constellation."

"The Pleiades."

"You've been told that before."

"My dad used to call me his little Pleiades."

"Do you know their names?" I asked.

"Whose?"

"The seven daughters of Atlas. There was Maia, Electra, Celaeno,

Taygeta, Merope, Alcyone, and Asterope. They were metamorphosed into stars."

"Why?"

"I think Orion was chasing them. Zeus took pity on them and placed them in the heavens as stars."

Clare looked over my shoulder out the window.

"Metamorphosed," she said softly.

I kissed her forehead. As I did I heard the faint but distinct sound of a plastic bat connecting with a Wiffle ball.

As the four of us walked around the convent to the Catherine wheel, the sounds from the Wiffle-ball game continued. The air was still, and there was no birdsong. Catherine was leading the way, holding Clare's hand, when she stopped. In front of us, a distance off, there were several shadowy figures standing motionless in the woods.

"What is it?" asked Clare. "Why have we stopped?"

"Saints," said Catherine under her breath. "Lots of them."

Catherine continued walking, leading us through the woods. As we neared the statues, I noticed the porous stone, like petrified skin, mottled in places with a sage green lichen. They were spread randomly throughout the woods. Every thirty or forty yards, we'd come across another one. As we neared the Catherine wheel, they were more numerous and closer together. Passing by each one, Catherine would whisper its name.

"Saint Austell," she said. "Sixth century. Saint Justus. Saint Gemma. Saint Brendan. Saint Pancras of Taormina, first century. Saint Rigby. Saint Dwyn. Saint Mybard. Saint Kirby, sixteenth century. None you've heard of."

When we arrived at the Catherine wheel, the saints became thick, as if the wheel itself had been churning them out like a factory.

"Saint Kolbe," said Catherine running her fingers along a statue's stone cloak. "A Franciscan priest."

She approached the Catherine wheel and pinned her prayer to the line. She pulled on the line, and the wheel creaked. We took turns—first Clare, then Juliana, then me—sending our prayers to the nuns, and when we were finished, Catherine led us home through the maze of saints.

My room was on a different floor than Perry's, but I checked on him before settling in.

"Last chance to change your mind," he said.

The skin under his eyes was a hollow yellow, as if he, too, had run into a saint. I walked to the window and looked out over the pond.

"Things didn't exactly turn out the way we were thinking, did they?" I said.

"You mean our feeble attempt to hide out in a castle?"

"Life's funny," I said, sitting on the side of his bed.

"Funny strange or funny ha-ha?" asked Perry.

"Both, I guess."

Perry reached out his hand and put it on top of mine.

"Thomas, I want you to know that whatever happens, I'm going to be okay."

I nodded.

"I mean if this doesn't work out, I'm going to be okay."

I nodded again.

"Do you know what I've been thinking about all these weeks in the hospital?"

"No."

"I've been imagining myself in another hospital room. Standing where you are now. With Juliana. Watching our child being born."

"It's going to happen," I said.

Perry narrowed his eyes and stared up at the ceiling.

"Then," he continued, "I imagine us getting married and living together, but not at the castle. I imagine us living in a little house in an old section of town behind the high school. Isn't that crazy? The little yards with grass and white picket fences and big cottonwood trees. The big covered front porches with the swings. I can see myself sitting on the porch in the summer, holding my child. There's a comforting hum of a neighbor's lawn mower and the distant barking of a dog. Kids are playing hockey in the street."

"It could all happen," I said.

"Yeah," said Perry. "Or not. There's another version. The one where I'm not around. Juliana the single mom. People in the neighborhood notice what a good mother she is. How attentive she is to her daughter. How much she loves her. She's strong and firm and playful, but there's always an undercurrent of sadness. People notice this about her. They've heard the rumors. That her boyfriend got her pregnant, then died before the baby was born and left her to raise it alone. But despite all this, they don't feel sorry for her, because Juliana won't allow it. Because she feels she's lucky. She has three good friends. A man and a woman and a little girl. Friends who are more like family than a real family. Friends who would lay down their lives for one another. The man might as well be the child's father. Her real father wouldn't treat her any differently. Probably not as well."

Perry stopped, his eyes both vulnerable and serious.

"That's not such a bad vision either," I said. "Except that you're not in it."

"Thomas, you're doing more than anyone could ask of another person, but I'm going to ask more anyway."

"What is it?"

"I want you to promise that if my first vision doesn't come true, you'll make sure the second one does. I probably don't need to ask, but it's what I want second most in the world."

"No," I said. "You're right. You didn't need to ask."

Visiting hours had ended, but Clare and Catherine lingered in my room, fidgeting about like hens, rearranging the flowers on the nightstand, straightening the sock drawer, smoothing the sheets on the bed. As much as I loved them, I wanted to scream at them to leave. I felt bad about this. They were only following their natural instincts, and I was thankful beyond words that I would have them at my side through this. But at the moment I needed to be alone, to face alone what was before me. I needed to turn off the lights and sit alone in the darkness and think about what was ahead and about all in the past that had led to this moment. I needed to pray, inept as I was at such things, at the very least to acknowledge to some unknown thing, whether it existed or not, that my future was out of my hands and that at some level, I was comfortable with it.

When Clare fluffed the pillow on my bed for the fourth time, I reached my limit. I was about to throw them out when I was saved by a nurse who told them it was time to go.

Catherine and Clare both kissed me, then wrapped their arms around me and squeezed.

Clare whispered in my ear, "We're going to be back first thing in the morning. We'll be here when you go in and when you come out and every minute in between."

"I know you will," I said. "I'm counting on it."

After they'd left, the nurse got me situated in bed and in a very business-like manner, hooked up an IV to my arm. I thought she was going to leave without saying a single word, but at the door she paused.

"Would you like this light on or off?" she asked.

"Off. I like the dark."

She flipped off the switch, and the room was cast in a bluish light from the hallway.

"Thank you," I said.

"You're welcome. My name's Grace. I'm here all night. I'll still be on in the morning when you get prepped for surgery. If you need anything, you just let me know."

"Such service. I feel like I'm at the Ritz."

"Well, just between you and me, we don't treat all patients alike. Some slob comes in stone drunk and bleeding from the head, I don't always hear the first time he rings begging for more pain killers. But say some handsome young man came in here to give one of his kidneys to a dying friend. Well, that young man might find out that for someone like him, the kitchen is open all night."

"I had no idea."

"Well," said the nurse, "it's not a fair world."

"No," I said. "It's certainly not."

When I awoke the next day after surgery, Clare and Catherine were sitting at my bedside. They were holding hands and talking to each other in whispers and for a long while didn't notice that I'd opened my eyes. Clare was dressed in blue jeans and a white T-shirt. Her hair was pulled back into a ponytail, her bangs hanging over her forehead, long enough now to touch her eyes. Occasionally, as she spoke to Catherine, she would brush one of the strands from her face; then it would fall back to where it had been.

I watched and waited for one of them to notice that I was awake. I noticed a burning sensation in my back. At the same time I realized that this was the last chance I would have to make love work for me, and I was frightened I would mess it up.

Where had Clare come from? Where had this love I felt for her come from? After Karen, I hadn't thought it was possible again. And yet, here it was. I was in love with Clare. It was a love that felt pure, intense, messy, and unexpected. I loved her champagne hair, the faint freckles under her eyes, the way her eyes, though unseeing, were so full of light. The way she laughed at unexpected moments and made passé things fresh and new. I might have fallen in love with her most of all because she promised me a way out of myself.

And then Catherine. This extraordinary girl I didn't ask for and didn't deserve, who had pulled me back from the valley of the shadow of death, from life on the periphery, and given my life more purpose than I would ever have aspired to on my own. I decided I would fight

Mary for her. I would do whatever it took to make her mine both emotionally and legally.

The television hanging in the corner near the ceiling began to change shape. It went from square to octagon to triangle and back to square. I looked away and focused on where my toes wiggled under the sheets.

Who was I kidding? If Mary returned, and I knew like Catherine that she would, then it would be Catherine who would choose. And I knew what she would choose. But even if I lost Catherine, there would still be Clare. Or was her love for me entwined with her love for Catherine? What if by losing one of them, I would lose them both?

"Oh," said Catherine, "you're awake."

I managed a weak smile.

"How's Perry?" I asked.

"Still in surgery," said Clare. "But everything on your end went fine. How're you feeling?"

"I'm not sure," I said. "A little ungrounded."

Three days later I was released. Juliana spent the days at the hospital and gave us regular updates on Perry's recovery. A week after the surgery I was lying on the couch in the library with an ice pack under my back when the telephone rang. Clare was sitting nearby in a club chair with her eyes closed. I heard Catherine answer the phone in the kitchen. In a moment she came into the library. She stood in the doorway with her hands at her sides.

"That was Juliana," she said. "Perry's new kidney has started functioning on its own."

Clare blew the air out of her lungs and smiled.

I looked at Catherine, but she only shook her head and left the room. I followed her upstairs and found her lying in bed curled on her side facing the window. I went over to her and put my hand on her shoulder.

"What's wrong?"

Catherine shook her head.

"The doctor said that once the kidney starts functioning on its own, it's a very good sign that the transplant is going to work."

Catherine didn't respond.

"What's wrong? Do you want to take a walk to the Catherine wheel?"

"No."

I put my hand on her forehead. I thought she felt a little warm.

"Are you feeling sick?"

"Maybe a little."

"Why don't you try to sleep."

I pulled a blanket over her and tucked it around her shoulders. I kissed her on the cheek. "Do you want me to bring you anything?"

"No. I think I will try to sleep."

"Okay. Let me know if you need anything."

I kissed her again and left the room. Out in the hallway I paused and listened. For a moment I thought I'd heard music, something twangy and Middle Eastern. I went into my room and went to the window. Outside the sky was low and gray. I looked down at the lawn around the convent wall and tried to conjure the pregnant girl, but she wouldn't come.

The next morning I checked on Catherine before going downstairs. I found her sleeping, her forehead cool and dry. I heard the telephone ring and went downstairs to answer it.

Clare walked into the kitchen as I was hanging up.

"Was that Juliana?"

"Yes."

"Is everything okay?"

"She says he's running a fever. It could be the sign of an infection."

Later that day Catherine and I were in the library playing Scrabble when the telephone rang again. We both looked to the kitchen and heard Clare answer it. We heard her gasp and cough, as if she'd gotten something stuck in her throat. In a moment she stepped into the library.

"That was Juliana. Perry just died."

Juliana didn't come back to the castle. For the next few days, Clare and Catherine and I rarely left each other's sight. It was as if we were afraid that anyone who walked off into another room would disappear into another dimension and not be able to get back. We said things to each other like, "Who wants more tea?" and "Does anyone want to go sit in the library?" and "Maybe we should make some sandwiches."

There was an emptiness that wouldn't let us go. We had to accustom ourselves to the coming days, like a stroke victim learning to walk or speak again. We took turns holding each other and crying. My body ached from the surgery, dull and insistent, a constant companion, a reminder of what was missing.

But Perry's death also had some small satisfaction to it, an ice dam breaking free. Although we hadn't wanted to listen, Catherine had readied us. In the recesses we knew it would be hard and empty and painful and surreal. Now here it was, and it was all those things, things we knew were coming.

In the late mornings we walked around the convent. A hint of fall crispness was in the air when we first woke up, but by the time we took our walk, it was usually warm and summery. The saints were still congregated around the Catherine wheel where we'd first discovered them, imposing and idle.

Pinning our prayers to the wheel was something we did both cor-
porately and privately. We never discussed what we'd written. I was glad
because since Perry's death, I'd been sending in blank sheets of paper.

The day after Perry died, the hospital called and asked me to make
arrangements for the body. I called a funeral home, then went to the
hospital to sign things. Afterward I stopped by Juliana's house. Her car
wasn't there, but I went to the door and knocked.

"She's not there," said a voice.

In the yard next door was an old woman I hadn't noticed on my
way up the walk. She stood near the fence by a flower bed, wearing a
pair of gardening gloves and holding a small hoe. There was something in her face that made me assume she was a widow.

"Do you know where she is?" I asked.

"Gone."

"Do you know where?"

"She's had some trouble, I expect. I hadn't seen her in months,
thought she'd moved away. Then last night she showed up, loaded
some things from her house into that old car of hers, and drove off
into the night. I don't think she'll be back."

"Do you have any idea where she went?"

The old woman looked to the sky where dark clouds were rolling
in from the west.

"I don't expect she'll be back. I expect she's had some trouble. My
guess is she's carrying a baby in that flat tummy of hers. Boyfriend
probably left her, and now she's gone off to start somewhere fresh."

"Well," I said. "You're right about one thing. She is pregnant. But
the father didn't leave her. He died."

The old woman looked indignant. I thought that she probably
wasn't used to being crossed.

"Well," she said after a moment, "I know she's gone. I don't expect she'll be back."

"Thanks for your help," I said. "You have a nice day."

With Clare's help, I'd arranged for a viewing and a short service at the funeral home. Where Perry would go after that was still up in the air. I told the funeral director that I wanted Perry buried in the catacombs at the castle, but he didn't think it would be possible. He told me that at the very least we would need the family's consent. When he asked me where the family was, I had to admit I didn't know. We didn't even know where Juliana was. All week Clare had been trying to track her down but hadn't had any luck.

The day of the viewing dawned bright and cloudless. I stood in front of the bathroom mirror and put on a tie—something I hadn't done for a very long time—and examined the fading bruises beneath my eyes. They'd started as a purplish black, then turned to a washed-out gray, then a jaundicey yellow, and now, although almost gone, there was still a hint of a sallowness that hinted of anemia or malnutrition. I touched the bridge of my nose with my finger, and for the first time since breaking it, I felt no pain.

Downstairs I found Catherine and Clare already dressed, sitting at the kitchen table.

"You both look very nice," I said.

Clare stood up and touched the front of my shirt. "I imagine you look very handsome in a tie."

"He does," said Catherine.

I put my hands on the girls' shoulders and guided them to the door, but as we stepped outside, I patted my rear pants' pocket for my wallet and realized that I'd forgotten it.

"Go on to the car," I told them. "I've got to run upstairs and get my wallet."

I found the wallet on my bureau, opened it, and checked it for cash. As I stuck it into my pocket, the light in the room dimmed and a soft breeze came through the open window, carrying with it a strange but familiar aroma. The smell of myrrh.

I rushed to the window, already preparing myself to be disappointed, but as I looked down, I saw the figure of a young girl at the edge of the convent wall, dressed in white, moving across the smooth lawn as if she were floating inches above the ground.

Unlike the other times I'd seen her, this time I was given more than a fleeting glimpse. I watched her spinning and twirling on the lawn as if to some languid interior music. Her pregnancy didn't seem to have advanced a single day since the last time I'd seen her, although sometimes she'd place a hand on the base of her abdomen to support it.

Suddenly she dropped to her knees and grimaced, the pangs of a contraction seizing her. She knelt for a long time, motionless, except for a slight shaking of her head. When it was over, she raised her head and looked at me.

My chest pulsed with electricity, the air vibrated. Her eyes were unblinking and warm. Then she stood and glided off, disappearing around the convent wall.

When I turned around, the room was again bright. I stood still and thought I heard a child's footsteps in the hall, thought I'd been away too long and Catherine had come looking for me, but then it seemed as though the footsteps were coming from within the castle's thick stone walls. I listened hard, stilled my breathing, and thought the footsteps faded deeper into the depths of the castle. There was the faint sound of adult laughter, drunken laughter, and the distinct noise of breaking glass.

The moment I stepped into the hallway, the whole experience became surreal. I patted my hip pocket, not remembering if I'd gotten my wallet. When I felt it there, I pulled it out and held it in front of me, needing something solid and familiar to ground me to this world.

The funeral parlor was a flat-roofed building built in the seventies. The architecture was dimensionless and wan, the bricks a washed-out red. When we stepped inside, there was music playing, soft and soothing, meant to calm or sedate. Perry's coffin was placed at the front of a small room with benches in front of it. I'd told the funeral director that we wouldn't need anything more.

I was surprised to find a woman standing at the coffin. When we walked in, I recognized her as a nurse from the hospital. I walked up to her and said hello.

She looked at me and started to cry.

I put my hand on her shoulder and rubbed it.

"I'm sorry," she said. "I've never done this before."

I surprised myself by putting my arm all the way around her.

"I mean, I've never come to a patient's funeral," she explained.

She put a handkerchief up to her face and blew her nose.

"I spent a lot of time with him. He was my favorite patient. My name's Faith, but he always called me something different. He called me Farrah or Florie or Fawn or Fern. He was always teasing."

She looked at me and smiled. "How did you know him?"

"He was my best friend."

"Oh. You're the donor. You gave him your kidney."

"Yes."

The door opened behind us, and several people came in. I turned and looked. It was Juliana and two people I didn't know. Juliana was wearing a black knee-length dress that struck me as having been purchased in the last half-hour. She removed her sunglasses and made a quick survey of the room.

As she walked toward us, Faith excused herself and sat down. The couple with Juliana was obviously Perry's parents. His father had the same build, the same cheeks and lips. The woman didn't look like him, except for her eyes. She was unhealthily thin, her face dark and weathered. She was fidgety and impatient. It was the nervousness of a smoker who ached for a cigarette.

They approached the casket and looked in. The body inside didn't look much like Perry. His face was swollen and sallow.

Juliana looked into the casket but quickly turned away. She gave me a hug and sat down with Catherine and Clare.

Mr. Palmer turned and faced me.

"Chance Palmer," he said, "Perry's father. You must be Thomas."

I took his hand.

"Yes. It's nice to finally meet you."

"And you. Apparently I owe you a debt of gratitude. Juliana has told us what a good friend you were to Perry."

Mr. Palmer put his hand on my shoulder and led me to the other side of the room.

"Which makes what I have to say all the more difficult. I'm afraid we have some disagreeable business to take care of."

I marveled at how quickly we were getting down to business. I felt sorry for him, sorry for his whole life. He seemed like a man on the verge of some great personal discovery, of some monumental self-enlightenment, if only he could make a small paradigm shift and admit that what he had thought all of his life to be important hadn't been at all. It was as though he stood at the edge of a great cliff, and all he had to do was take one tiny step and he would fall into an entirely different world. I didn't think it was too late for him, and yet I knew he wouldn't do it.

"What about this disagreeable business?" I asked.

"Yes," he said. "I have a business associate who's been pestering me for years to sell him the castle. He wants to turn it into a spa for business executives."

"A spa?"

"A place to relax, to forget about business for a while. A place to slow down and be pampered," he said. "Anyway, now that Perry's gone, I don't see any reason to hold on to the place. My wife has never liked it."

"Of course. We didn't expect to stay."

I looked over to where Juliana was sitting with Catherine and Clare. Perry's mother had sat down nearby.

"No," he said. "I don't suppose you did."

He took my hand again and shook it, as if we'd just completed a prosperous business deal.

"Of course, you don't have to leave right away," he said. "You can have a couple of weeks."

He turned to leave, but I stopped him. "Mr. Palmer?"

He turned halfway toward me. "Yes?"

"Perry wanted to be buried there. In the cellar."

He looked at me, and I again saw him on the cliff. *Just take one step,* I thought. *Just one step.*

"I know he did," he said after a moment. "But we don't all get our last wishes."

As he walked away to rejoin his wife, I thought to myself, *That wasn't his last wish. His last wish he's going to get.*

We didn't need the two weeks Mr. Palmer offered us. On the day after the funeral, I put a postcard in the mail to my father (well aware that I would probably beat it there), letting him know that I would be coming to La Verdad. After a quick meeting in the library, we decided that we would all go to the Caribbean. Even the dogs.

It was unsettling how easy it was to disappear from our lives. With a handful of phone calls, Clare had obtained a leave of absence from her job, Catherine was withdrawn from school, and Juliana had informed the ski mountain that she wouldn't be returning next season. It didn't escape me that of all of us, I required the least effort to jettison my current life in exchange for another. I could have viewed this as a failing. I had, after all, recently attempted a very similar thing. But there was a difference this time. This time everything I valued I was taking with me.

The night before leaving, I tucked Catherine into bed and sensed that something was wrong.

"What is it?" I asked. "You've always said you wanted to see Grandpa's resort."

"I know I have," said Catherine.

"Then what is it?"

Catherine turned her head toward the window and closed her eyes. I put my hand to her forehead and stroked her hair.

"You're worried about your mother," I said at last.

Catherine opened her eyes but continued to stare at the dark window.

"How will she find me?" she whispered.

I touched the side of her face.

"You don't have to worry. I'm leaving notice with the new owners. If your mother comes here, she'll know where to find you."

Catherine turned from the window and looked at me.

"She is coming back," she said.

I took my hand from her head, pulled the covers up to her chin, and kissed her on the forehead.

"I know she is. And she'll find us."

I turned off her light and walked down the hallway to my room. The room was dark except for the light cast from the hallway, but when I entered, I could see that Clare was in my bed. I climbed in behind her and spooned up close. I breathed in the fruity smell of her hair and kissed the nape of her neck.

"How is she?" whispered Clare.

"She's worried about Mary finding us."

"What did you tell her?"

"I told her we'd leave a forwarding address."

Clare moved a hand up to mine where it cupped her shoulder and traced small circles with her finger on the back of my hand. Outside a soft wind blew. It carried a charged scent, the smell of coming rain.

"What are you thinking?" asked Clare.

What was I thinking? Something. Nothing. Too many things. I remembered a day spent with Karen.

We get up late and have coffee and fresh croissants for breakfast. We read the paper and decide to take a drive into the mountains. It's a fine fall day, and as we ascend the winding mountain road, the air turns cooler and sharper, and the leaves on the aspens turn lighter as if bleached by the summer sun. Karen has brought along a tape of Kathleen Battle arias, and she plays it loudly with the sunroof open. The crisp mountain air and Battle's celestial voice whip about our ears in a torrent. In Estes Park we find a small café where we have wine with our lunch, then we walk the downtown area hand in hand, window shopping until the sun drops below the mountains and we hurry back to the car shivering and drive home.

When I close my eyes in bed that night, the many images from the day replay themselves in my head.

"What are you thinking?" asks Karen.

"Nothing," I say.

It's the wrong answer.

"Nothing."

"I'm not really thinking anything."

"Your mind is a complete blank."

"All right," I say with more impatience than I intend, "it's not blank; it's just that I'm not thinking anything specifically."

"Then what are you thinking, *generally?*"

"I suppose your mind is always filled with erudite thoughts?"

Karen swings her arm and clubs me in the forehead. The fact that she misses my nose only fuels her rage. She storms out the door and slams it behind her. It's late at night and I should follow her, but I'm too enraged to be civil. I let her walk home alone, down dark streets filled with drunken fraternity boys and broken beer bottles. Even the next day I don't call to see if she's made it home. I wait and wait, and she waits too.

That night, when I calm down and fall asleep, I have a dream. Karen and I are in bed together, neither of us with any clothes on. I'm lying on my back and she's straddling me, but we're not making love.

She's reaching into my mouth, feeling around for something. Her face is taut. She seems to think I'm hiding whatever it is she's looking for. She becomes more enraged. She reaches deep down in my throat until her arm is into my mouth up to the elbow. I can feel her hand down in the recesses of my chest, groping around, pushing organs aside for whatever it is she's trying to find. It's then I realize what she's doing. She's trying to pull words from my chest. When she can't find any, she pulls out pieces of flesh and throws them across the room.

But when I tell Clare I'm not thinking anything, she doesn't react. I wonder if it's because I'm becoming more accessible.

"What are you thinking?" I asked.

"I've been thinking about Catherine's dream."

"Which?"

"The one where her mother returns and has to cross a large body of water."

"I'd forgotten," I said.

"Me, too," said Clare. "Until just now."

On the way to the airport the next day, the storm that had held off all night arrived. A wind came up, and the late-morning light gave way to a sullen, diffused gloom. A thick rain began to pelt the windshield. There was a clap of thunder, and the whole sky broke loose.

I dropped the girls off and parked the Jeep in a long-term lot. I'd left a note for Mr. Palmer on the castle's kitchen counter telling him where it would be. As I locked the doors and walked to the shuttle, I wondered if he would ever come get it or if, for Mr. Palmer, the trouble of picking it up would be more than it was worth.

By the time I got to the shuttle, my jacket was soaked. Inside the terminal I ducked into a bathroom and laid it over the top of a waste can. I wouldn't need it where I was going.

On the plane the girls had a row to themselves near the front. I was seated farther back over the wing. Next to me was a waifish girl wearing a faded tank top and threadbare khakis. Her leather sandals were worn and faded. Her hair, which was sunbleached, was uneven and short. There was something alluring about her. When she lifted her arm to adjust the air above her head, I got a blast of body odor. It was so potent that I put my hand to my face and turned away.

"I'm sorry," said the girl. "I probably stink."

"It's not that bad," I said.

"That's nice of you, but I know I probably stink. I've been on airplanes and in airports for thirty-six hours. At this point I can smell myself."

She adjusted herself in her seat and half turned toward me, keeping her arms close to her sides.

"I'm on my way home from India," she said. "I've been there for the last six months."

"Where's home?"

"Turkey Creek, Louisiana."

"How does someone on their way to Louisiana from India end up in northwestern Montana?" I asked.

"In a nightmare of reroutes."

She turned and looked out the window, and I studied her angular profile. The plane started to taxi.

"It's about 160 miles from Houston," she said. "About four and a half hours on a bus."

When she mentioned the bus ride, her voice wavered. I thought she might begin to cry and that if she did, I would cry with her. I wanted to wish her home. To will her through space and time.

"What were you doing in India?" I asked.

"Just checking it out. I'd heard it was the kind of place where you could figure things out. I guess I thought I needed that."

"And did you?"

"I thought so," she said.

She shifted in her seat, and I got another whiff of body odor. As the plane raced down the runway, she squeezed her eyes shut.

"I hate the taking-off part," she said. "But landing's even worse. I don't know if I can handle another landing today."

"I'm pretty sure you've got at least two more on your itinerary."

The plane hummed like a swarm of gnats. It banked and dipped into an air pocket. The air was dry and metallic. The girl next to me was still talking. I pretended I'd been listening.

"There was an American woman I traveled with for a while. I think I learned more from her than I did from India. She was a lot older than me. But we got along. She was different from the other Americans I met. She had a quiet sort of wiseness to her. And sadness. She carried her sadness like a backpack. I think what made her different was that she wasn't looking for something. Everyone traveling in India was looking for something, but not her."

"What was she doing?" I asked.

"I think she was trying to forget."

"To forget?"

"It was like the whole India experience for her was a kind of self-induced trance designed to erase something. One time we were staying in a hotel together, and one afternoon I walked down the street to a corner market to buy some fresh fruit. It was so hot I almost collapsed on the way home. It must have been 115 degrees. It was too hot to take a full breath of air. You had to take little shallow gulps, then spit it back out before it burned your lungs. All I could think about was getting back to the hotel and taking off all my clothes and lying on the bed under the ceiling fan and running ice cubes all over my body. When I got back, the room was empty. As I stripped off my clothes, I looked out onto the balcony. There was my friend, sitting in a chair facing the sun, without a stitch of clothing on to protect her from it. I watched her for a few minutes."

I nodded. "Did you ever ask her what she was trying to forget?"

"I did once. It was a couple of months after the balcony incident. It was toward the end of my trip, and I wanted to ask before leaving."

"What did she say?"

"It was kind of funny," said the girl. "At least if it hadn't been a little spooky, it would have been funny."

"How so?" I asked.

"Well, I asked her what it was she was trying to forget, and she looked at me like I was a voice from her past, like I was someone she was trying to recognize."

"What did she say?"

"She said, 'I can't remember.'"

I looked at her uneven hair and wondered how long it had been since it'd been washed.

"So she taught you to forget?" I asked.

"No. Sometimes it's good to forget, but sometimes it's important to remember. What she taught me was that you don't always have to try so hard. She taught me that sometimes it's okay just to be."

I looked at her, about to ask another question, but she yawned.

"Maybe you should take a nap," I suggested. "How much sleep have you had in the last thirty-six hours?"

"Not much," she said. "I'm not very good at sleeping on planes."

She yawned again and looked at me. "I've been doing all the talking."

"That's okay. It's been very interesting."

"Still, it's kind of rude. We haven't even been introduced."

She extended her hand, forgetting to keep her elbow restrained, and my nose was assaulted by a goatishness.

"My name's Audrey."

"Thomas."

"So how 'bout you?" she asked. "Where are you going?"

"My father owns a little resort on a small island off the coast of Puerto Rico," I said. "My sister's there too."

"That sounds pretty nice. How long are you staying?"

"To be honest, I haven't given it much thought. Maybe forever."

"Wow," she said. "Then for you this is like a major change-of-life plane ride."

"I guess it is."

Despite not being able to sleep on planes, Audrey fell asleep with her head slumped on my shoulder, where it stayed until we descended into Denver. She made a low purring sound like a kitten, a cute little kitten who has fallen into a sewer.

The descent into Denver was bumpy. The moment Audrey opened her eyes and raised her head, all the color drained from her face.

"Don't be afraid," I said. "It's going to be all right."

"I'm not afraid of crashing. And I don't think it's going to be all right."

"What are you afraid of?"

"Of puking," she muttered.

She swallowed and closed her eyes.

My altruistic vision had been much more grandiose, but I held her raggedy hair back from her face as she vomited into the air-sickness bag.

After landing I went with her into the terminal where she headed for a water fountain. She took a gulp and swished the water around in her mouth, then spit it out. She took another drink and swallowed.

I glanced down the terminal and spotted Catherine, Clare, and Juliana standing together, waiting for me. When Audrey stood up, some of the color had returned to her face.

"Thanks," she said. "I think I'm all right now."

"Are you sure? You still look a little pale."

"Yes, I'm feeling better. Thanks again. There were an awful lot of people on that plane. I'm glad I was sitting next to you."

"You're welcome. Is there anything I can do for you?"

"No. You've been great. Thank you."

We said good-bye and she thanked me again and we parted, but we were going in the same direction. Audrey smiled and was about to say something, but I interrupted her.

"Audrey," I said. "I hope this doesn't seem too strange, but I'd like to do something for you."

"What?"

"I'd like to buy you a plane ticket to Turkey Creek. So you don't have to take the bus."

"That's sweet," she said, "but there's no airport in Turkey Creek."

"Isn't there somewhere you could fly that would be closer than Houston?"

"I'm afraid not. It's the bus ride or nothing."

I looked at her matted hair and the sallow crescents under her eyes and wondered why I couldn't just leave her alone. I ran my hand through my hair and looked out a nearby plate-glass window. Outside the day had grown prematurely dark, and the window was getting pelted with what looked like a mixture of rain and sleet.

"Well, I'm sorry," I said.

"Why is it so important that you do something for me?" she asked.

"I don't know. I know it must seem strange."

"Actually, it's not all that strange. It's a fairly typical reaction.

People meet me for the first time, and they want to do something for me. I was just wondering if you knew why you felt that way."

"I guess I don't. But it's good to know it's a normal reaction when meeting you."

Audrey touched me on the forearm.

"My last name is Jackson," she said. "If you're ever in Turkey Creek, you have my permission to look me up."

"Okay," I said. "Let me extend the same invitation."

I took out my plane ticket sleeve and scribbled my father's address on it.

"It's not the Waldorf, but you're welcome to stay anytime, free of charge."

"Okay," she said. "I may take you up on that."

"What was that all about?" Catherine asked when I joined them.

"She sat next to me on the plane," I said. "She got sick when we landed."

"And that was cause to exchange phone numbers?" Juliana teased.

I looked at Clare.

"We didn't exchange phone numbers," I said. "I invited her to the resort. I'll admit it was an odd thing to do. I felt compelled to do something for her. I don't know why."

Clare slipped her arm through mine, and we started down the concourse.

"Maybe you're just a nice guy," she suggested.

*I*ve noticed that airports are worlds in themselves, separate in time and space from the outside cosmos, operating in their own self-made dimension. The airport has its own ecosystem: its own food, water, air, its own system for disposing of waste. Here it's acceptable to have a cocktail at six in the morning or to fall asleep in a chair at noon. Travel long enough, across hemispheres, as Audrey did, and it's possible within the walls of the airport to lose track of the date, the season, even what city you're in.

As we walked from one concourse to another, we were only vaguely aware of the rain and sleet that pelted the huge windows. It was that other world's tempest and not our concern. But as we arrived at our gate and settled into the waiting area, that outside world began to intrude. It began as a quiet murmur, like old women whispering to one another at the back of a church. Then it gained strength and voice and refused to be ignored.

It was Clare who noticed it first.

"What's wrong?" she asked.

"What do you mean?" I said.

"Something's wrong. People are walking faster. There's excitement in their voices. That man at the desk keeps speaking on the phone. He's worried about something."

As she spoke, the sky darkened. I walked to the plate-glass windows and looked out. There was a large plane resting on the tarmac like a wounded beast. On a platform above it was a man bending against the pelting sleet, spraying a pink, foamy deicer on the wings and fuselage. Even as I watched, another man appeared on the ground and shouted to him to give it up and come inside.

I walked down the concourse to the bank of monitors announcing arrivals and departures. I stood there in wonder while like dominoes, every departure time was replaced with the word *canceled.*

I went back and told the girls.

"What do we do now?" asked Catherine.

"We'll get a hotel," I said. "I don't think we're going anywhere for a while."

Our room had two king-size beds and tall, narrow windows with heavy mauve drapes that overlooked the parking lot of some kind of factory. Juliana pulled the drapes apart and stood at the rain-streaked window. When she turned in profile, I noticed for the first time the slight bulge of her abdomen. After a moment she turned back toward the room and placed her hand at the base of her stomach.

"I noticed there's an indoor pool," she said. "Is anyone up for a swim?"

"I am," said Catherine.

"I guess I'm not," said Clare.

"Not me," I said.

After Juliana and Catherine left, Clare went into the bathroom, and I lay down in the middle of one of the beds and closed my eyes. I don't think that Clare was in the bathroom for more than a few minutes, but in that time I fell to the edge of sleep.

"What are you doing?" she asked.

"Just lying on the bed," I said. "I almost fell asleep."

"Why don't you?"

"You look tired too. Why don't you lie down here with me?"

Clare sat down on the edge of the bed and rested her hand on my knee.

"I am tired," she said. "But I guess I don't feel like sleeping."

"What do you feel like?"

Clare looked toward the narrow windows where we could hear the sleet pinging against the glass.

"I feel like a dry martini," she said.

"Really."

"Yes, really. Maybe two."

Down in the lobby we sat in velour chairs with a faint fleur-de-lis pattern. They were arranged around a leaded-glass coffee table near a gas fireplace. The lobby was filling up with other stranded travelers. The low murmur of voices swelled like a far-off ocean. When our drinks arrived, Clare ate the olive. She took a sip and closed her eyes.

"It's been a long time since I've had a martini."

Her face was sad and far away.

"Is something wrong?" I asked.

Clare sighed and took another drink. "I'm not sure what I'm feeling. Maybe it's just exhaustion. I feel like running away to a deserted island and not thinking about anything for a while."

"Isn't that what we're doing?"

"That's not what it feels like," said Clare. "It feels like the opposite. It feels like we're jumping into the middle of something that's going to take a lot of energy."

I looked down into my drink and stirred the olive around with the sword. Why did this have to be so difficult?

Shortly after we got back to the room, Catherine and Juliana returned from the pool with a dice game they'd picked up at the gift shop. We ordered food from room service and sat down and played.

The directions described it as a game of risk and chance. A player would start by rolling six dice. The dice that counted (ones and fives; also pairs, three of a kind, and straights, etc.) could remain on the table; the others could be rolled again. The catch was that every time you rolled, something had to count and be left. The remaining dice could be rolled again. If all the dice ended up counting, the player could roll all six again. You could quit your turn whenever you were satisfied with your score. However, if at any time you rolled and no dice counted, any points you had accumulated on that turn were lost.

There was some nameless comfort about it, but when we were finished, Catherine said what I'd been feeling.

"I like this game. It's mostly luck, but you have to know when to take risks and when to be satisfied with what you've got."

That night the fatigue that had shadowed me all day fell away like a veil, and for a long time sleep eluded me. As Juliana and Catherine slept together in one bed and Clare lay sleeping next to me in the other, I lay on my side and watched her.

Clare, Clare, Clare. Why does loving you scare me? Why can't I jump from the plane and float recklessly? Why can't I live in the moment and forget the future?

But I'm haunted by a vision: In the morning I awake, and you're not next to me. I can hear only an echo of your whispery voice, buried beneath the floorboards, telling me, "Good morning," and it's clear by the way you say it that you believe the morning to be good solely because you've awakened next to me. But then the echo fades, recedes deeper under the floorboards, into the earth, fainter and fainter until it's gone. And now I've been left with less than I had before. Because I've been given more, more has been taken from me. I'm only the chaff of what I was. What is worse, I'm also spiteful. Not only have I messed up my last and best chance for love, but I've tarnished its memory with bitterness.

When I finally fell asleep, I dreamed of the Caribbean.

We are at La Verdad, a new La Verdad that over the past months we've resurrected. Every surface has been painted a dazzling white, every window has been washed, every weed pulled from every crack in the patios and walkways. The bungalows have been scoured with bleach and equipped with new linens. The stone floors of the main villa glisten with new sealant. The kitchen pantries and coolers are stocked to overflowing, and the glass shelves behind the bar bow with full bottles of liquor.

Late one morning I'm standing with my father and Ellen by the pool. I marvel at the two of them. Instead of the slight yellow bikini, Ellen is wearing a worn pair of overalls, cut off at the knees, splattered with specks of paint and caulk. Her shoulders and arms are tanned a deep bronze, not from lounging by the pool, but from working in the sun. My father is standing next to me holding a hammer at his side. He's wearing a tired pair of painter's pants, now so marred with paint and dirt, it's difficult to know their original color. His arms and back ripple with thin, sinewy muscle.

Then I'm walking alone on the beach, picturing the coming days when the resort will be filled with guests. I can hear the laughter of children, the noise of high-spirited splashing in the pool, the clinking of glasses from the open doors of the bar, the quiet tones of a card game being played under the shade of the pergola. I see myself standing with Clare at the head of the dining room overseeing the evening meal and smiling at all we've accomplished.

But as I return from my walk, I spot black smoke rising above the trees surrounding the resort. I race down the beach, and the sand itself, as if fueled by the fire, heats up and burns my feet. It only takes me moments to get back, but by the time I arrive, the entire resort has burned to the ground. There's virtually nothing left—no rubble, no charred timbers, no ashes, nothing. Only the swimming pool remains, now empty, the water evaporated.

For a moment I stand there in shock, unable to process what's happened. Then I fall to the ground and cry.

"I can't do this again!" I wail. "It's too much! I can't do it all again!"

I have the sense that someone is kneeling next to me. I feel a female touch on my shoulder. I look up, expecting to see Clare, but because the sun is right behind her, I can't make out her face. Still, I believe it to be Clare.

"It's going to be okay," she says. "We can do it again. We can make it just the way it was before. We can do it together. I'll help you."

Her hand moves to the side of my face, and as she lifts my chin, the sun is blocked by her head and her features become clear. She leans close and kisses me. I smile and am buoyed up by her gentle strength. I rise and take her by the hand. We walk together down the beach and begin to make plans to rebuild the resort.

I awoke from this dream smiling, or at least I imagined myself to be smiling, but then I was startled by a dark figure standing at the foot of the bed. I was so alarmed that I lunged for the bedside lamp and knocked it to the floor. In spite of the fact that I'd heard breaking glass, I rolled out of the bed and fumbled on the carpet with the lamp, trying to turn it on. When it was clear that it wasn't going to work, I stumbled to the bathroom and flipped on the switch. I looked back into the room but saw nothing out of the ordinary. I stood there, my hand braced on the doorjamb, watching the empty space at the foot of the bed.

Clare was sitting up.

"What is it?" she asked.

"Nothing," I said. "I just had a weird dream."

"Did something break?"

"I broke the lamp trying to turn it on."

"Are you okay?"

I looked down and saw several smudges of blood across the bathroom tile.

"It looks like I cut myself a little. I don't think it's anything serious."

"Are you sure? Do you want me to come over there?"

"No. There's still glass on the carpet. Stay where you are."

I sat down on the toilet and looked at the bottom of the foot that was doing most of the bleeding. There were some cuts in the ball, but the majority of the bleeding was coming from a deep slice in the arch that still had a large piece of light-bulb glass sticking out of it. I wasn't alarmed so much as intrigued. I thought, *For such a deep cut, it should be bleeding much more.*

"Dammit," Clare said from the bed.

I leaned forward so I could see her.

"What?"

She was sitting cross-legged on the edge of the bed, facing the bathroom, the wreckage from the lamp strewn out like flotsam on the carpet in front of her.

"Well, what does it look like?" she asked.

"Not so bad. Why did you say 'dammit'?"

I eased the shard of glass from my foot.

"It's just that there are times when being blind becomes very poignant," said Clare.

"Would you like to see the blood?"

"I just have this overwhelming female desire to come in there and take care of your foot, which is aggravating and silly."

"Why is it silly?"

I examined the shard of glass and tossed it into the wastebasket.

"Well, for one," said Clare, "I'm sure you're quite capable."

"I don't know," I said. "I think I may have cut off my toe."

"Go ahead and joke, but it's frustrating."

"I'm sorry. But there's nothing to worry about. I am capable."

"I know you're capable," said Clare. "Didn't I say you were? But when someone steps on broken glass, a woman's reaction is to comfort, and the way we do that is by pulling out the pieces of glass and daubing on some alcohol and bandaging it up and then kissing it and telling the person it's going to be fine."

Clare put her hands over her face and fell backward onto the bed.

"Oh, God!" she said. "When did I become so ridiculous?"

She raised her voice so that she was almost yelling, "And why haven't we woken up Catherine and Juliana yet?"

"Maybe we have," I said.

I found a several-year-old bandage in my bathroom bag and stuck it over the cut.

"Maybe they're just pretending to be asleep because they enjoy listening to you being silly."

Clare rolled over and faced the other bed.

"Are you guys listening to me being silly?"

When no one answered, she rolled over again and faced the bathroom.

"Good grief," she said. "I have a headache. I shouldn't have had that second martini."

When I finished bandaging my foot and cleaning up the bathroom, I knelt by the side of the bed, picking up the broken pieces of light bulb and tossing them into a waste can.

"Don't cut yourself again," said Clare.

I smiled and continued picking up the mess. When I had it cleaned up as best I could, I turned off the bathroom light and crawled back into bed. Clare's body was wooden, but when I slipped up next to her and wrapped my arms and legs around her, she softened.

"I'm sorry," I said, kissing her on the cheek.

"For what? For cutting your foot?"

"For doing something that made your blindness seem poignant."

"Don't be ridiculous."

She pushed me onto my back and nuzzled her nose into my neck.

"*I'm* sorry," she whispered.

"For what?"

"For being so silly."

"Don't apologize," I said. "I found it very cute."

"I found it cute too," said Juliana from the darkness.

"Me, too," giggled Catherine.

It should have been easy to convince myself that what I'd seen at the foot of the bed was part of a dream. But as I stared into the darkness where the phantom had been, instead of dissipating, as the memory of dreams often do, this one became more palpable.

My first impression before knocking the lamp over was that there was a dark figure standing in the blackness at the foot of the bed. But the more I thought about it, the more details I remembered. It was like a Polaroid photo coming into focus.

It hadn't been an androgynous, dark figure, but the figure of a woman. In a few minutes more, I recalled long, brown hair and olive-colored skin. She was young, wearing a soft, almost translucent gown that breathed moonlight. And she'd been pregnant. It was a strange sensation. I was able to replay the vision with more clarity and detail than when it had happened.

Like the shard of glass in my foot, this dream metamorphosis wasn't alarming, but intriguing. And although there was no apparent connection between the vision of the girl at the foot of the bed and the dream I'd been having about the resort, I thought they were linked. Either the dream I was having conjured the vision or the other way around.

I replayed the dream in my head to see if I could make sense of it. I did this over and over, but the more I thought about the dream, unlike the girl, the foggier it became. It was as if by analyzing it, I was destroying it. Like pouring salt on a slug, I drew away all the substance and was left with nothing but a shriveled carcass.

I heard a metallic clanging in the hallway, a serving tray dropped, and I remembered something about the dream that had been lost to me since waking up. The woman who touched my face after the fire and kissed me and told me that we could rebuild the resort together wasn't Clare at all. It was Mary.

*S*ometime in the night, a warm front swept across the mountains, and in the morning we returned to the airport and boarded a plane to San Juan. There we connected with a twenty-seater that had only just taken off over the bright lapis lazuli ocean before descending to my father's little island. It was afternoon when we stepped out of the terminal into the tropical heat. The dogs tugged at their leashes, grateful to be released from their kennels and the cargo hold of the plane. They couldn't have known where we were going, but they were intent on distancing themselves as quickly as possible from everything behind them. I leaned back as they dragged me across the white apron of concrete toward the street. There was no breeze, and the leaves of the banana trees that lined the sidewalk hung listlessly. Across the street from the airport stood a small, bare hill with a single tree on top. Beneath it several goats dozed in the shade.

When we reached the street, the dogs stopped pulling. They glanced back at the airport, then sat. Our exodus from Montana had been so hasty that I hadn't thought beyond this moment. We stood on the curb like a group of helpless tourists. I was on my way back to the terminal to call Simon when his taxi appeared through the waves of heat that rose from the pavement. He got out and flashed his brilliant smile.

"Welcome," he said.

Even with the delay in Denver, there was no way my postcard could have already arrived.

"How could you have known we were coming?" I asked.

"There was a plane arriving," he said. "I came to see if anyone needed a ride."

It was a logical explanation, but it didn't dilute the feeling that we were fated and fortunate.

When I introduced the girls, Simon took their hands in both of his and bowed. As soon as the introductions were made, he picked up the suitcases and loaded them into the cab.

It was soon clear that we wouldn't be able to get all the luggage and ourselves and the dogs into the cab at the same time. Simon was determined to make it work, but our luggage alone overflowed the trunk. After several unsatisfactory configurations of bodies, dogs, and suitcases, he finally relinquished hope by throwing up his hands and cursing in Spanish.

"It's okay," I said. I put my hand on his shoulder. "The dogs and I will catch another cab."

"There is no other," said Simon. "Except for that skunk Philippe who at this hour is sure to be asleep in the shade of a banana tree with his radio turned off. But I will come back for you. It will only take twenty minutes."

I smiled at his optimistic estimation. It was at least twenty minutes to the resort, one way.

"That'll be fine," I said.

After they were gone, I waited on a wooden bench, shaded by a towering palm. In truth, I didn't mind. I felt the need to pause, to arrive more slowly, to take a few deep breaths before entering this new world. I needed to let my senses sort out the island's images and sounds and smells, which had been buzzing around my head since I got off the plane.

The dogs retreated under the bench and lay down in the red dirt. Their panting fell into a steady rhythm. I stared at the goats on a distant hill, their backs sagging under the heat. There was the slightest suggestion of a breeze, and I thought I heard music—not island music, but something classical, something mournful—then both music and breeze were gone. Beads of sweat ran down my face and neck. I began to feel lightheaded and remembered a time as a child when I'd been very sick.

I'm lying in the middle of my parents' bed. I can hear my mother and father talking to each other in the hallway in hushed, urgent voices. I'm aware that a decision to call an ambulance is being made, something my mother wants to do, but that my father doesn't think is necessary yet. Strangely, I'm less concerned about an ambulance ride than I am about the water stains on the ceiling above the bed that are growing at a frantic rate. I think there must be water pouring into the attic and that at any moment the ceiling will cave in and we will all be drowned.

When my mother comes back, she's holding a damp washcloth. She lies down in the bed and places it on my forehead and begins to stroke my hair. She hums a portion of a lullaby, then asks me how I'm feeling.

I tell her about the water stains on the ceiling.

My mother looks up. She removes the washcloth from my forehead and touches it with her hand.

"Those aren't water stains," she says. "Those are the faces of angels. They're looking down on you and protecting you. They're going to make sure you're all right."

The water stains do look like angels. I watch them to see what they will do. When I awake later, my forehead is dry and my eyes are clear for the first time in days. The angels on the ceiling have left, but my mother is still in bed, asleep at my side, her hand clasped around my wrist, as if to prevent someone from taking me while she sleeps.

* * *

Positioned between the dogs in the back of Simon's cab, I rested my head on the back of the seat and breathed in the island's earthy scents. As we drove closer and closer to the ocean, the inner island's stifling heat was gradually replaced with a briny freshness. Simon sat slumped down, his hands low on the steering wheel, humming something that had a narcotic effect on me. I closed my eyes but jerked them open when Simon stopped the cab and started shouting.

"Stupid *gallinas!*" he shouted.

On the road in front of us was a group of chickens that didn't seem inclined to move. Simon honked the horn, stuck his head out the window, and cursed. The dogs jumped to the windows and barked.

Despite Simon's disdain for the chickens, he was unwilling to run them down. Finally he got out of the cab and shooed them off the road into the underbrush, swearing all the while.

Only moments after he'd resumed driving, he was again slumped in his relaxed posture humming his hypnotic tune. I leaned back and closed my eyes. I felt myself nearing the border of sleep and marveled at how quickly I could adjust to the island's rhythms. I may have fallen asleep, because at some point I had the sensation of waking and thought I could feel the memory of fingers clasped around my wrist.

When we reached the entrance to La Verdad, I had Simon stop. There was a narrow, half-mile lane off the main road that led back to the resort. It was a rutted, sandy track that wound its way through dusty scrub oak hunkered close to the ground. Because the heat was now a little more endurable and my luggage had already been delivered, I decided to walk the last half-mile. I thanked Simon, handed him some money, and told him he was a good driver.

As I walked down the lane, the dogs zigzagged in front of me, their noses to the ground. When my shoes filled up with sand, I stopped and took them off. I rolled up my pant legs and untucked my shirt and continued like a beachcomber.

It was still hot and the sand burned my feet, but there was a salty breeze blowing from the ocean. Now, instead of feeling heavy and dank, the air was light and crisp and smelled of fresh fruit. I passed a clearing where wild horses grazed in the shade of a rubber tree. On the other side of the road was a crude fence made of sticks that looked as if they'd grown up from the ground right where they were needed. The fence ran for thirty or forty yards, then abruptly stopped. As the dogs raced ahead, then back to urge me forward, I tried to conjure an image of Perry.

Since his death I'd managed to hold off the sorrow that swirled around me like a building storm. But now something shattered, and the storm burst in. I dropped to my knees in the burning sand, and the dogs trotted up and licked at my tears. After some moments they sat at my side and let me cry. I stroked their necks and buried my face in their fur as something hard and calcified inside me broke apart and flaked away.

When I was cried out, I wiped away the tears with sandy hands and looked at the dogs. They seemed to be waiting for an explanation, so I told them I was sorry, I didn't know what that was all about.

"I miss him," I said. "I know you miss him too."

Later I realized that I hadn't been crying only for Perry. There in the hot sand with my arms around the dogs, I wept for my mother, for Stephen, for Karen, and for who knows what else.

As we neared the resort and I saw the front doors of the main villa flanked by dwarf banana trees, I knew this was where I wanted to be. This was what I needed. I needed this heat. This briny air. These sun-baked hills with their scrub oak and palms and rubber trees. Although it would have been impossible to call this home after my mother's death, or after my failed wedding, or Stephen's suicide, now it seemed not only the most likely place to come but the only one. This was not a default destination.

When I walked into the coolness of the foyer, my father was there. The dogs ran up to him and sniffed at his bare knees. My father embraced me. He held me, reluctant to let go. When we separated, he stood at arms' length with his hands on my shoulders.

"I'm glad you're here," he said.

If I hadn't emptied myself of tears, I would have cried again.

That night, my father suggested we take rooms in the main villa instead of staying in the bungalows. Ellen had already moved. As I put things away in my room, I realized that staying in the main villa connoted a permanence that was absent on my previous visits. It also meant that the bungalows would be freed up to be used by guests, if any ever came.

There was no evidence of any restoration projects underway. But now, with our arrival, there seemed a loaded potential for change, as if during all these years, the restoration hadn't been static but had been quietly building up steam, and now with a full head of pressure, only needed someone to release the brake.

There was this change too: My father was childishly happy to have us there. On my past visits there'd been an undercurrent of sadness in him, as if my presence, although longed for, was also painful. I had the impression that while I was at the resort, my father wore a mask that he removed the moment I left. But now the mask had been discarded. Like a snake that's shed its skin, my father was renewed.

The next day as I lay in bed next to Clare, I heard Catherine and my father greeting each other in the hallway.

"Good morning," said Catherine.

"Good morning, indeed!" said my father.

I could hear him moving toward her, could imagine him hugging her and spinning her around. I could see Catherine kissing his bearded face, her arms wrapped around his waist. I could see him burying his face into the side of her neck and breathing in the salty smell of her hair.

Had my father regained his faith? Or had his sorrow simply had a half-life? Had it finally blown away like dry leaves?

The evening before, my father had killed the fatted calf. It wasn't actually a calf, but a goat that Martin had been sent on foot to obtain from our nearest neighbor several miles away. While Martin was gone, my father instructed Ellen and Catherine to decorate the rafters of the pergola with strings of white Christmas lights. He sent Juliana to the bar with instructions to concoct "some sort of blended cocktail." He took Clare with him to the kitchen to keep him company while he chopped vegetables. He sent me off into the woods with orders to bring back mangoes. I walked into the trees, then turned around and saw my father leading Clare through the open doors of the bar with his arm around her shoulder. Moments later the air was filled with the peals of steel-drum music, piped through the patio's speakers.

That night after dinner, with the wreckage of the meal scattered across the table, I watched my father. He was drunk, but maybe as much on our presence than on all the wine he'd had. He pulled Catherine onto his lap and told her a story about a sea turtle he'd rescued on the beach earlier in the week. I could tell he was embellishing, but after a while I stopped listening. Clare was sitting next to me leaning back in her chair with her eyes closed. She held a glass of wine in her hand that looked close to toppling. I put my hand on her arm.

"Hey," I said.

"Hey, what?"

Her voice was dreamy. She didn't open her eyes.

"I like you," I said.

"That's good." She rolled her head to my shoulder and smiled sleepily. "That will definitely help."

Several mornings later I awoke to the sound of singing birds that seemed a remnant from a dream I'd been having. I walked to the window, opened the latticed wooden shutters, and looked down onto the flagstone patio. My father and Ellen, along with Juliana and Catherine, were sitting at a small table under the pergola. There was a bowl of fruit, a plate of fresh rolls, carafes of coffee and juice. A large iguana was moving hand over hand along the vines of the pergola. It looked more like the scene from a Graham Greene novel than something my father could have produced from his decrepit resort.

I looked out to the ocean where the morning sun glistened on the glassy water. The horizon was an uninterrupted division between sea and sky, save for a small fishing boat, its unrigged mast jutted into the sky like a crucifix. On the beach at water's edge, Perry's dogs were wrestling with a rubbery piece of kelp.

I looked at Clare lying in the bed beneath a veil of mosquito netting. She was sleeping face down, partially covered by a white sheet. The morning sun banded across her bare calves. The night before we'd made love for the first time. It had been delicate and tender, yet purposeful and passionate. It was slow and present and fragile but also mournful in the sense of laying something long loved to rest.

I pushed aside the mosquito netting and sat down on the edge of the bed. I put my hand on the small of her back where tiny beads of sweat had formed and ran my fingers up her spine. She awoke with a little moan and stretched like a cat sprawling on a sun-baked windowsill.

"Good morning," she said.

"Yes, it is."

I brushed a wisp of hair from her eyes and told her she was beautiful.

Clare smiled and stretched again. "I'll take that compliment. I feel beautiful this morning."

"You should," I said.

"Is it last night?" she asked. "Or is it this place?"

"I don't know. Maybe both."

"I feel like there's a drug in the air. Or in the songs of the birds, or in the fruit, or in the water. I feel so warm and relaxed and wonderful, like I've been walking across an endless field of poppies."

I smiled and kissed her.

"I'm going down to breakfast," I said. "Do you want me to wait for you?"

"No, that's all right. You go on."

When I got down to the patio, Catherine had moved to the beach and was digging in the sand with a small shovel. I walked over to the pergola and poured myself a cup of coffee. My father stood up next to me and looked at Catherine.

"She's growing up," he said. "She's beginning to resemble her grandmother."

Ellen stood up, put her arms around my father's neck, and kissed it. For a moment his eyes burned with nostalgia. He touched the back of Ellen's neck and kissed her on the forehead.

"Ellen and I usually take a walk after breakfast. Why don't you join us?"

We didn't talk as we walked, but I sensed I'd been invited for a reason.

"Thomas," my father said at last. "This is mostly for you. I've tried to say something similar to Ellen, but I don't know that I ever did it very well. So it won't hurt for her to hear it again."

He kept his eyes trained on the sand in front of his feet. "I haven't been a very good father since your mother died."

"You don't have to apologize," I said.

It had never occurred to me that he hadn't been a good father. He was broken and angry and removed, but weren't we all? It would have been more accurate to say that since my mother's death, I hadn't been a very good son, or brother, or uncle.

My father raised his eyes to the sky, then looked down the beach. I glanced at Ellen, but she only looked at the sand.

"I guess I'm not apologizing," he said. "I guess what I'm saying is that since I've been here, I've realized that certain things happen in life, and we react however we react. Sometimes we wish we would have behaved differently; sometimes we feel lucky to even have survived. But no matter what we do, we're always an active part of history. Whether we think we are or not, we're impacting other people's lives and we're affecting their stories, which are also our stories. What's ironic is that we have very little say in how this story gets played out, and at the same time we are each more involved than we would ever want to admit."

He looked at me and frowned. "Do I sound like an old man?"

"No."

"You've brought quite a crew with you."

"I guess I have."

"I need to thank you for bringing Catherine," he said.

Tears brimmed at the corners of his eyes.

"She's already given me back more joy than I could ever have hoped for," he said. "And Juliana is gorgeous. And Clare is beautiful, both inside and out. I don't deserve two more daughters, but I feel like I've been given them. You love her?"

"I love all of them, but yes, Clare is special."

My father took Ellen's hand and smiled. He stopped walking and faced me.

"We do too. It's uncanny, but Ellen and I have talked about it, and we agree that we loved them the moment they stepped through the door, even before Simon had time to go back and get you. Maybe Ellen and I have just been lonely, but we're glad of the way the story is progressing. We feel very grateful."

"I don't have much say in how the story gets played out," I said.

"No, you don't," said my father with a gleam of satisfaction. "I guess I was making more sense than I thought. No, you don't have much say at all, not much at all. But more than you think. A lot more than you think."

Back at the resort, my father disappeared into the main villa, and Ellen and I went out to the pool, now full of water. We swam for a while, then sat on the edge with our feet in the water.

"I like her," said Ellen.

"Who?"

"Clare. Can I make a confession?"

"I love confessions."

"I've always been a little jealous of your girlfriends."

"That's not such a huge confession."

"The confession part is that I've always kind of hoped they wouldn't work out. I kind of willed breakups. Then I was glad when it happened. I guess I didn't want to share you with anyone. I'm sorry."

"Ellen, I don't think you caused any of my relationships to break up. Unless you know voodoo, and I didn't know about it."

"But I don't feel that way about Clare. It makes me happy that you're happy. I'm already thinking of her as a sister. And, like Dad said, I'm grateful."

Ellen leaned over and kissed me on the cheek.

"Thanks," I said.

"Don't get me wrong. I still don't like sharing you with another woman, but I can't think of anyone I'd rather share you with."

Martin appeared behind us and asked if we needed anything.

"What time is it?" asked Ellen.

"Half past eleven," said Martin.

"Close enough," said Ellen. "I'll have a Bloody Mary."

Ellen waited for Martin to leave, then lowered her voice.

"Have you seen her?"

"Who?"

"You know. The pregnant girl."

"Why? Have you?"

Ellen looked out to the ocean and squinted at the glare. "I guess I have."

"You guess?"

"I've seen her in my dreams. I've gotten up at night and caught glimpses of her out here by the pool. But it all seems like it's part of the dream. They're good dreams, though. I enjoy them. Not like that nasty stuff I used to have as a kid. These I look forward to. I'll be sad when they end."

"What makes you think they're going to end?"

"Everything ends. So what about you? Have you seen her?"

"Yes."

"Maybe this is all a dream," said Ellen. "Maybe one day we'll wake up, and it'll all be gone."

Ellen was still talking, but I'd stopped hearing. Something had made me look up to our bedroom window. There I saw Clare, wrapped in the sheet from our bed, staring toward the sea.

Her expression was one I'd seen before. It made me wonder what she was seeing. If not beach and ocean and sky, then what? What did she see when she stood at an open window and gazed out? Was she remembering the past or imagining the future? Or was she only trying to make sense of the present?

Something Ellen said made me realize that she was no longer talking about the pregnant girl but had segued into the shark bite and the scar on her leg. I thought I heard her mention the word myrrh, but I couldn't make myself listen. I was feeling a weighty longing for Clare, as if she were already gone.

There were six rooms on the second floor of the main villa, three on either side of a narrow tiled hallway with a solitary bathroom at the end. The bathroom was just a toilet and a rust-stained sink. The showers were outside. One morning I got up early and found Juliana sitting cross-legged in the hall outside the bathroom door.

"Are you all right?" I asked.

"Fine," she said.

The hallway was so narrow that I would have had to step over her to get to the bathroom, so I sat down.

"What's up?"

"I was thinking about names for the baby. Perry and I never decided. His only request was that if it was a boy, I wouldn't name it after him. He didn't like his name. I suppose you knew that."

"He thought it sounded like a drink."

"Exactly. Bartender, be so good as to bring me a perry. Two olives! And one of those little cocktail swords would be smashing!"

I smiled. Perry had said the same thing to me the first day I met him.

"He was funny," said Juliana. "I loved that about him. In the face of everything, he could still joke about things. He used to call the dialysis machine a sump pump."

I put my hand on her knee.

"I like your father," she said. "Maybe I'll name the baby after him."

"I'm sure he'd like that."

Juliana looked up at the ceiling where two small lizards clung.

"Hey." My voice sounded hollow. "I don't know if I ever told you I was sorry."

"For what?"

"For Perry."

"You're not going to tell me you gave him a bad kidney, are you?"

"You didn't expect me to give him the good one?"

Juliana smiled, then looked down at the line where the tile met the wall.

"I just mean I'm sorry," I said. "I'm just sorry. There was so much going on after he died. And you were gone. I never got a chance to say it."

Juliana continued to look away.

"Do you know what I've realized? I've realized that I'm very lucky. My last weeks with Perry were the best weeks of my life. I discovered Perry, knew him, knew him to the core before he died. No one is more truly themselves than when they're dying. Sometimes we only reveal the depths of our souls out of necessity. I may have known Perry better in those days before he died than if we'd spent all our healthy lives together. That's a gift."

She patted my hand.

"Plus," she said, "look at what I've got. I'm living in the Caribbean at a resort with my best friend and my boyfriend's best friend, who has sworn to take care of me and raise my child as his own."

"You know about that?"

She waited a few moments before answering. "If I told you that you didn't have to keep that promise, would it make any difference?"

"No."

"I didn't think so."

I stood up and stepped over her and walked to the bathroom. Before going in, I looked back at her still sitting cross-legged on the floor, still staring at the wall in front of her.

"It wouldn't have made any difference if he hadn't asked," I said.

Juliana looked at me.

"I know that, too," she said.

When I stepped outside I noticed with satisfaction that I was the first one up, although I was sure that Martin was already at work in the kitchen. I considered taking a swim in the pool but decided that my mood demanded something more dramatic, so I walked down to the beach and dove into the ocean. I swam for fifty or sixty strokes, then rode the swells while a great cumulus cloud sailed overhead with monumental laziness. Back on the beach I stared at the resort while the morning breeze dried me. The resort reclined in its alcove of trees as if it were a slumbering beast, a beast that in the past I would have thought bewitched, destined to sleep. But now, miraculously, I'd sensed movement. Perhaps it was nothing more than a muscle spasm, but something, however subtle, had changed.

That evening we were all sitting under the pergola watching the sun dip toward the ocean. There was a slight, forgiving breeze coming off the ocean. The radio was playing Elton John Muzak, and Catherine was exploring at the edge of the patio, trying to catch tarantulas. A single bird in a nearby palm tree was singing.

"Should I start dinner?" I asked my father. "I could throw some steaks on the grill."

He was squinting, looking out at the watery horizon.

"I was hoping for fish."

A boat appeared at the tip of the peninsula that jutted out from the resort. A small outboard motor buzzed. As it got closer, I saw a solitary shirtless figure kneeling in the rear, one hand on the motor.

"Who's that?" I asked.

"That's Albert," said my father. "Ellen's boyfriend."

"Ha!" said Ellen. "As if I could take an interest in a boy like that. There's probably a law against it."

He didn't look like a boy to me. He was tall and lean, his arms and torso layered with sinewy muscle from pulling fishing nets from the sea. His skin was a deep, smooth chocolatey bronze. He had thick, dark hair that fell over his eyes, eyes that were deep and black like onyx. He would tell me later that he was Puerto Rican, but I think he meant simply that he'd been born here. To me he looked Greek. Part Greek fisherman, part Greek god. He was beautiful.

When he got out of the boat, he pulled on a shirt and lifted a fish-net bag from the hull. As he walked toward us, the orange sun dipped behind him and cast him in shadow. I looked over at Ellen. She watched Albert approach and took a sip from her cocktail.

"God, he's beautiful," she said.

Albert smiled broadly when he entered our circle and approached my father with his bag of fish. Father introduced everyone, then pointed to Albert's bag.

"What do we have tonight?"

"Spanish hogfish," said Albert. "Nice and sweet."

"How would you recommend we cook it?"

"I would grill it. With a little lemon and pepper. Nothing else."

Father looked at me and smiled.

"Okay, Thomas, fire up the grill."

It became a daily ritual. Albert's little skiff would pull up on our beach in the evening, and he would approach my father with some aquatic gift (red snapper or grouper or Spanish hogfish). Sometimes he would have lobster; other times octopus. Once he arrived with a large bag filled with fifteen or so conch, which I helped him clean by cracking a hole in the ends with the claw of a hammer, then cutting the meat from the shell with a fillet knife. Albert showed me how to tenderize the meat by banging it with a metal hammer. We sautéed it in garlic and butter and served it over rice with lemon slices.

It was impossible not to like Albert. Impossible for all of us, except Martin. I suspected that in Martin's view, Albert was defying the culture's caste system and reaching for a woman above his class.

"He wants to get inside Miss Ellen's drawers," he said to me one day while we were unloading cases of wine from the back of Simon's cab. "Excuse my language, but he is thinking only with his nether regions."

"You mean he's a *fisherman* who wants to get inside Ellen's drawers, don't you?" I asked.

"Perhaps," said Martin.

"Ellen can take care of herself," I said, lifting a case of wine from the trunk. "I'm more worried that Albert is going to go bankrupt through all this."

Martin grunted as we carried the wine to the kitchen.

"He is one of the better fishermen on the island," he said. "The other fishermen say he has a gift. He has been spotted swimming with dolphins. He holds on to their fins, and they pull him through the water like a rag doll. They say the dolphins lead him to where the best fishing is."

Then, as if snapping out of a dream, Martin shook his head and said, "Besides, he has another job."

It turned out the island had another taxi driver besides Simon and Philippe. On the three days a week when there was no ferry from the big island, Albert would take his little boat to Playa de Fajardo, looking for tourists who were unaware of the ferry's intermittent schedule. On a good day, if he got an early enough start, he was able to make as many as four trips to and from the mainland. At twenty dollars a trip (five times what the ferry cost), it was a great deal more money than he could make fishing, even when he was catching lobster.

Albert was harmless. I thought he was good for Ellen. He brought out a playful side of her that I hadn't seen since our mother's death. It was good to see her laughing at his silly antics that were designed to get her to do just that. I once saw him walk away from her with a hurt look on his face, then fall backward into the pool. One evening when it was growing dark, I spotted him in the branches of a tree at the edge of the patio, scratching like a monkey. Ellen stood below with her arms crossed, trying not to laugh, but then snorted. I found it refreshing to see her flirting with him when she thought no one was watching.

Another reason I liked Albert was that Catherine had fallen in love with him. Whenever Ellen made herself inaccessible, Albert would turn his affections to Catherine. Since our arrival, Catherine had taken up a new hobby of collecting exotic creatures and turning them into pets. She captured iguanas, *anoles,* geckos, snakes, tarantulas, and once for a day and a half, she kept a scorpion confined in a Mason jar before it mysteriously disappeared on its own.

Albert was Catherine's biggest fan. Each evening when he arrived, he would ask Catherine what she'd found that day and then express unbridled delight when she would show it to him. Whatever she showed him, Albert would declare it to be the "best" or "largest" he had ever seen. Then he would teach her the Spanish word for it—*lagarto, culebra, escorpión.*

Once while I was walking with her along the path in front of the bungalows, Catherine suddenly knelt down and scooped up a small lizard.

"Wait till Albert sees this!" she said.

"Oh, *muy bonita*," said Albert that evening. "It is the most beautiful lizard I have ever seen. I believe it is a skink. Very difficult to catch."

Another evening Albert disembarked from his boat with a small bag dangling from his hand. When he stepped onto the patio, he stood beaming at Catherine.

"Is that for me?" she asked. "What is it?"

"Come and see," he said, placing the bag on the patio.

When Catherine opened the bag, a baby octopus, no more than four inches across, scurried across the flagstone as quickly as a mouse and headed for the pool. After she'd caught it, she held it in her cupped hands for us to see.

"Look everyone! Look what Albert brought me!"

She smiled in a way that made me think of Mary.

For weeks the weather was rigidly glorious, each day a replica of the one before—stark indigo skies, high billowy clouds, hot sun that baked our skin to a buttery bronze.

One morning I awoke early to a dim, grayish light in the room and the sound of raindrops on the patio below my window. I rolled over and found that Clare was already up and gone. I went to the window and was surprised to see that Albert's little painted skiff was pulled up on our beach. I'd never known Albert to make a morning appearance at the resort, and also odd was that I thought it was really Tuesday, a day when the ferry didn't run and Albert would normally have been running his water taxi. I was trying to decide if it was a Tuesday when I detected movement in the distance. I caught a brief glimpse of Albert and Catherine, with Clare between them, before they disappeared down the beach.

I felt compelled to follow them. I threw on clothes and ran out into the warm rain and stumbled onto the stone patio. I sat back on my heels and examined the palms of my hands, scraped and bleeding. I had a sharp, epiphanal moment, wondering if this stigmata wasn't well deserved. I patted the raw skin on the front of my shorts and continued nevertheless.

When I reached the beach, the others were already far ahead, their silhouettes gray and blurred through the rain. I followed them at a half jog, staying close to the edge of the woods so, if necessary, I could duck into the trees.

I gained on them until I was within a hundred yards, then I slowed my pace to match theirs. I wasn't close enough to hear them talking, but I had the feeling they weren't. This muteness added to the impression that this was more than a casual stroll down the beach.

We walked for a long time. After we'd gone two or three miles, Albert turned into the woods, and Catherine and Clare followed.

When I reached the spot where they'd left the beach, I found a narrow trail into the woods that didn't look like it had been used for years. I followed, pushing away low-hanging vines and scraping my bare shins on the serrated undergrowth. After a time the forest darkened, and I saw a tall stone wall, ancient, covered in lichen and vines.

I heard their voices. Through the thick undergrowth I could see the three of them standing together in front of the wall. Albert pulled out a long fishing knife and hacked at the vines. After a few minutes he put the knife away, put his hand to where he'd been working, and I heard the sound of creaking hinges.

When they left I hid behind the trunk of a large tree and waited until they reached the beach before I continued on. The warm rain had turned icy, and my joints ached. I unclasped the wooden door and looked in at an old, rusted Catherine wheel. I decided that there couldn't have been any nuns in this convent for more than fifty years, but I was beginning to wonder whether that made any difference.

* * *

When I got back to the resort, Albert's boat was gone. I returned to our room and found Clare just back from the shower. She was standing by the bed, wrapped in a towel, drying her hair with another. When I closed the door behind me, she looked in my direction and smiled. I could tell she knew.

"Good morning," she said.

"Good morning."

"You should take a shower too." She fluffed her hair with the towel. "I'm sure you're cold."

"I am. To the bone."

"Isn't it amazing?"

"What?"

"Albert's Catherine wheel," said Clare.

"Yes," I said. "How did you know I was there?"

Clare smiled. She dropped the towel and started dressing. "I smelled your deodorant."

"I didn't even put any on this morning."

"I know. It was yesterday's."

When Clare had her hair pulled back into a ponytail, she walked over to me and put her arms around my neck.

"Ooh," she said. "You *are* wet."

"I'll take a shower."

Clare twirled her fingers through the hair at the back of my neck. "Do you know what she was praying for?"

"Yes, I know."

"It's going to happen," said Clare.

"I guess I know that, too," I said.

Clare kissed me on the cheek and stepped away. I watched her as she sat on the edge of the bed and put on her shoes.

I should have gone to her and kissed her, recklessly removed her clothes, and made love to her and stayed in bed with her all day, but the moment for doing this seemed to have already passed, so I walked out into the rain and headed for the shower.

·

We didn't see Albert for days. Then one evening while we were all sitting under the lights of the pergola, his skiff appeared far out on the water.

"There's Albert," someone said. Moments later we could hear the humming of his outboard motor.

As he neared we could see that he had two passengers with him. We rose in unison and like a congregation walked down to the water. As he approached the beach, Catherine took several steps forward and stood waiting alone. Clare's hand slipped into mine, aware without seeing that we were crossing a threshold that could never be uncrossed.

Albert pulled his boat up onto the beach, then helped Audrey and Mary out. Mary stepped onto the sand and moved toward Catherine. She was leaner than when I'd last seen her, hardened by wind and sun and sand. Her face was thinner, her cheekbones more prominent. Her once-long hair was cropped short, bleached and dried out. And yet it all looked good, as if what had been burned away had never been necessary.

She didn't see anyone but Catherine. She stepped forward and stopped, and the sound of the ocean itself fell silent. Everything fell away. I became aware only of a dull pulsing in the air around us. Even Clare's hand had disappeared from mine.

Mary and Catherine stared at each other in silence, and for one frightful moment, I thought that Mary would suddenly turn, jump back into the boat, and order Albert to speed away. But she stayed, as paralyzed to move forward as she was to retreat.

In a broken but resolute voice she said, "Forgive me."

It was neither a question nor a plea. Just immaculate, snow-white words offered up like a prayer in hopes they would be heard.

Catherine took a step forward and took Mary's hands.

"Do you love me?"

Mary fell to her knees and grabbed Catherine around the waist. She buried her face in Catherine's dress and sobbed.

"My love, my love," she cried. "I love you so much!"

Catherine dropped to her knees and kissed her mother on the cheek. She hooked her chin over Mary's shoulder and cried.

Although the roar of the ocean had returned and my ears were congested by my own tears, I heard Catherine say, "Then there's nothing to forgive."

*T*here is a vein in Clare's neck, pale, greenish blue, that begins below her right ear and traverses the front of her neck, then meanders between her breasts where it vanishes. On the night Mary returned, I was tracing this vein with my finger as Clare lay on her back, staring up at the mosquito netting. The room was lit by a three-quarter moon, hanging low over the ocean like a hovering seagull. I continued to trace the vein with the tip of my finger from the base of her ear, across the front of her neck, down her sternum, between her breasts. When it ended, I continued down her stomach, across her belly button and down one of her thighs.

"Tell me about something," said Clare.

"About what?"

"I don't know. About anything. Just talk."

I talked about the first thing that came into my head, a memory from childhood.

We're on a family vacation, driving from Baltimore to the Grand Canyon. We've stopped for lunch at a rest stop on the western edge of Pennsylvania. There are picnic tables in a sparsely treed grassy area, bordered by a tall hedge dividing it from a farmer's field. It's so humid that I think any minute it will begin to rain. All through our lunch, a man and a woman and a little girl are walking up and down the hedgerow looking for something. At one point the man disappears into the hedge and doesn't reappear for fifteen minutes. After a while it becomes apparent that they are looking for a pet, a dog or perhaps a cat. We hear them calling its name, Samson, over and over. At one point the woman goes back to their car and lights a cigarette. She returns and sits down at a picnic table near the edge of the field and smokes. Every few minutes she calls out "Samson!" then continues to smoke. I watch the little girl. She walks up and down the hedge, bending down, sometimes crawling on her hands and knees, calling out for her cat. I have decided by now that it's a cat. As we continue our lunch, her calls become more and more frantic. She knows this search has a time limit, and the clock is ticking. On the way back to our car, I notice the license plate on their station wagon. Arizona. As we drive away, I look back and see that the man has joined the woman at the picnic table. He takes a cigarette from her, and this makes me immeasurably sad. I look at the little girl, still searching in the hedge, calling out for her cat, and I think that something has changed for her, that happiness from now on will be much harder to come by.

When I finished talking, Clare was asleep. I covered her with the sheet and went to the window. The moonlight reflected on the water like a brilliant silver highway leading to the horizon. Below me I noticed someone sitting in the darkness under the pergola, so I put on clothes and went down.

When I got outside, I saw that it was Mary. I pulled a chair up next to her.

"Can't sleep?"

Mary smiled. "I think I'm beyond sleep. I'm a little afraid that if I go to sleep, this will all have been a dream when I wake up. I won't be here, and my little girl won't have forgiven me."

"Is it so hard for you to believe she did?"

"It's more than I deserve."

"She never doubted that you were coming back."

"I had to go, Thomas. I couldn't love anything after Stephen died. I would have made a terrible parent. I would have hurt Catherine. I would have made her suffer as much as I was suffering. I would have destroyed her and in the process destroyed myself."

We stared out into the night. Mary's profile was dark and angular and resolute. She didn't look like someone in need of penitence, someone who would fall into despair.

"What are your plans?" I asked.

Mary ran a hand through her hair. "I don't have any plans."

She turned and stared, as though trying to remember something about me. She closed her eyes and dropped her chin. She murmured something.

"What?" I asked. "I didn't hear you."

She raised her head but didn't open her eyes. "I need your forgiveness too."

I put my hand on her shoulder.

"No you don't," I said.

The next morning I awoke to a symphony of birds in the trees outside our window. Clare was curled on her side, her back to me, her thigh sweaty where my hand rested. I rubbed her back and whispered that it was morning and the sun was up and the birds were singing, but I said it all softly, not loud enough to wake her, because I didn't want to disturb her dreams. I whispered into the downy hair at the back of her neck and told her I loved her. I felt an overwhelming need to keep her safe, to ensure that she would always be mine.

I left our bedroom and went down to the patio. I poured two cups of coffee and walked down to the beach where Mary and Catherine were standing in the water, the waves washing in around their ankles.

"Good morning." I handed Mary a cup of coffee. "Did you finally get to sleep?"

"Yes. And it turned out that none of this was a dream."

"What wasn't a dream?" asked Catherine.

"You," said Mary.

"It could be a dream," said Catherine. "We could all be having the same dream. Or worse, we could all be a part of someone else's dream."

But it wasn't a dream, and it didn't end. The long, luxurious days passed by unnoticed, until one day we heard a shout from the small room behind the bar that my father used as an office. Ellen was sunbathing by the pool, and I was reading under the shade of the pergola. We both ran to the office, expecting to find our father nursing a scorpion strike, but instead he was standing in the middle of the cluttered office holding a calendar.

"What is it?" asked Ellen.

"Do you know what today is?"

"No."

"I'm not sure I know what month it is," I said.

"It's Thanksgiving," he said. "Today is Thanksgiving."

He dropped the calendar and clapped us both on the shoulders as he walked by.

"I'll tell Martin. We'll have a traditional feast."

When he was gone, I picked up the calendar.

"This calendar is from 1971," I said.

"Does it matter?" asked Ellen.

"No," I said. "I guess it doesn't. But where is he going to come up with a turkey?"

Martin called Simon on the radio, and Ellen, Juliana, and Audrey were enlisted to go to town for supplies. Martin walked off through the brush with a burlap sack. The rest of us were put in charge of preparing the dining room. As the girls spread a white tablecloth on the long teak dining table and discovered silver that hadn't been used in years, my father led me into the bar, where he pulled a bottle of champagne from the cooler.

"Open this, would you?" he said. "Make sure everyone gets some. We want to make sure we have happy workers."

"It's hardly noon," I said.

He looked at me and frowned.

"Champagne makes things more festive," he said. "What's the matter? Do you have to be at work tomorrow?"

Later in the day Ellen and Juliana and Audrey came through the door followed by Simon, their arms loaded with bags of groceries. Ellen looked at the table and smiled.

"Simon's going to be joining us," she said. "And I'm sure Albert will too. And I think we should make Martin eat with us, although I'm sure he'll put up a royal stink."

Mary said, "I think that makes eleven."

I stepped outside and saw Martin emerge from the woods. He had the burlap sack thrown over his shoulder.

"Let me help you with that," I said.

I took the sack and lowered it to the patio. "So, what's the mystery meat?"

I opened the sack and looked in. Inside were a dozen small birds.

"Chukars," said Martin.

"They're beautiful."

"Yes. And very delicious."

It was still light out when dinner was over. Full and sleepy, I walked down to the beach. The day had turned bleak, the onset of Caribbean winter. A warm wind was blowing dried debris along the sand, some of it drifting into the water and floating away. Out over the ocean were three seagulls with their beaks pointed into the wind, hovering almost motionless, as if part of a painting. Down on the water a solitary pelican bobbed on the swells. I stared out at the horizon. For a moment there was a break in the clouds. The beach and the water lit up as though a spotlight were shining down, but then the clouds closed up and the light went out.

That night I had a strange dream.

I'm walking down the beach under the light of a half-moon, the sand before me sparkling. I'm on my way to the convent, to the Catherine wheel, to send a prayer in to the nuns who haven't been there for fifty years. I'm walking along the edge of the trees, looking for the faint trail that leads back to the convent wall, but I'm having trouble seeing clearly, as if I'm looking through a screen. I'm sure I've come far enough down the beach, but I still can't find the trail.

When I'm about to give up, I notice a rare fragrance in the air. I turn and see a woman sitting in the sand, looking out over the glittering water. I know at once that it's the phantom pregnant girl, and I freeze, knowing that the moment she becomes aware of me, she'll vanish. At the same time I'm compelled to approach, and I find myself moving forward.

Except for her dark hair blowing in the breeze, she doesn't move until I'm right next to her. She looks up and smiles and places her hand on the sand to indicate that I should join her.

I tremble as I sit. I've never gotten this good a look at her. Now, she fixes her eyes on mine, and I'm completely addled. I've never seen anyone like her. Something inside me is interrupted, as if the blood in my veins has changed direction. The deep sparkle of her black eyes transfixes me so that I barely notice anything else. But she has full lips, a nose with a high, straight bridge, creamy, poreless skin that radiates warmth, and silken, raven hair that doesn't just float in the breeze, but by its movement seems to be causing the wind to blow.

She continues to smile, a smile that is compassionate and friendly and at the same time serious. When I can finally take my eyes from her face, I notice that she's placed a large marble in the sand in front of us. I understand that she's offering it to me.

I pick it up. At first it appears to be clear, but as I look closer, I see that beneath its glassy surface is a never-ending complexity of beautiful swirls like agate. The swirls seem to move, as if they're dancing, never staying in one place, never holding to one shape for long. I blink, and the marble becomes heavier. Now it appears to be solid black, but as I look closer, I see that within the blackness there is light, light that is emitted from the center and bounces off millions of soft surfaces. When I peer into the marble, the light recedes, collapsing in on itself again and again and again.

"It's beautiful," I say.

She nods and stands up.

"Wait," I say. "What am I supposed to do with it?"

She doesn't answer. A gust of wind blows in off the ocean, and she's gone.

I awoke to a clatter. A wind had come up in the night and was banging the latticed shutters against the wall. I got up and held the shutter and looked out toward the ocean. The beach was dark, the air heavy. I clutched the shutter and breathed. I thought about Stephen and the time as children when he'd saved me from the neighbors. I remembered huddling on our front porch together and looking at the clouds and being frightened by his love for me. "Stephen," I said aloud. "What do you want from me?"

I closed the window and crawled back in bed. I curled up behind Clare and wrapped my arm across her chest.

"Are you okay?" she asked.

"It's windy," I said. "I got up to shut the window."

I closed my eyes and felt the rise and fall of her slight chest.

"I love you," I said.

"I love you, too," whispered Clare.

"No, I mean I *really* love you."

"I really love you, too," she said.

"Say it without the too."

Clare rolled over and crawled on top of me, one of her legs slipping between mine. She put her hands on my shoulders and kissed me.

"I really love you."

The next morning I ran into Catherine outside our bedroom, already dressed in a knee-length skirt and a long-sleeved cotton sweater.

"Where are you off to?" I asked.

"To the kitchen," said Catherine. "I'm helping my mother make breakfast. We're giving Martin the day off."

After going to the bathroom, I followed Catherine down to the kitchen, where she was helping Mary crack eggs into a large glass bowl.

"Good morning," said Mary.

"Good morning. What's all this?"

"Quiche," said Catherine. "Grandpa says real men don't eat it. But you can have as much as you want."

"Ha ha," I said. I looked at Mary. "Your daughter has gotten kind of cheeky."

Mary looked up and smiled, then returned to shelling crab.

"Well," she said. "She's been in your care for the last ten months. I don't see how you can blame it on me."

"Well," I said. "I'm not a very good uncle, I know. We established that quite some time ago."

I reached over the island, took a piece of crab meat from Mary's pile, and plopped it into my mouth.

"Enough of that," she said. "Why don't you make yourself useful and set the dining-room table. I don't think there's any chance we're eating outside this morning."

I stole another piece of crab and went into the dining room. The previous night's carnage had been cleared away so thoroughly that I thought the meal, too, might have been a part of my dream. I walked through the bar and opened the french doors that led out to the patio. It wasn't raining, but the patio was spotted with pools of water from a downpour sometime during the night. Across the pergola and pool area was strewn random debris—banana leaves, palms, a coconut, and a branch from a rubber tree. A gusty wind swept the surface of the ocean, whipping up whitecaps all the way to the horizon.

After a time I felt a hand on my shoulder, and Ellen was standing next to me.

"Hello, brother."

"Hello, sister."

We stood there for a long time, content not to speak, but just to be together, brother and sister, staring out at the volatile sea.

One morning I awoke to the smell of myrrh. It had been months since I'd smelled it. I got out of bed without waking Clare and went to the window. Out on the beach there was a woman sitting on the beach, her hair long and flowing. It was a windy morning, and low, gray clouds hung over the horizon. I got dressed and walked down to the beach. As I approached, I saw it wasn't the phantom pregnant girl but Audrey. She was sitting in a lotus position, eyes closed, her face raised to the wind. When she heard me, she opened her eyes.

"Good morning," I said. "You're up early."

She seemed glad to see me. She patted the sand next to her, and I sat.

"I couldn't sleep," said Audrey. "I came out here to think, then found myself wanting to pray, then found I wasn't able to."

"Why not?"

"I don't know. I don't feel like I'm any good at it."

I looked out over the water. The morning sky was a steel gray. The clouds over the horizon seemed frozen in place.

"What is it you want?"

"I don't know," said Audrey. "A connection. Over the last months I've been noticing how all of you here are so connected. To each other, to this place, to life."

"You don't feel that."

"No. Not really."

"Maybe it just takes time."

"Maybe. Maybe I want the wrong thing. Maybe I need to find my own connection."

She looked at me, her eyes sad and serious.

"Do you believe in prayer?" she asked.

I smiled and looked at the waves breaking onto the beach. "If you had asked me that a year ago, I would have said no."

"And now?"

I looked at her. Over the last months her hair had grown long and thick.

"Do you want to take a walk with me?" I asked.

I jogged up to the bar and grabbed a pencil and paper, then led Audrey down the beach. As we walked the wind died down and the clouds pressed in closer. When we turned to enter the forest, a yellow greenish light diffused in the trees. I had thought the old convent was far into the woods, but very soon we came upon the wall. We followed it for twenty or thirty yards, then I found the Catherine wheel.

"What's this?" asked Audrey.

"It's a Catherine wheel."

Audrey reached up and opened the door.

"It's a way to pray." I pulled out the pencil and paper. "You write down a prayer, then you pin it to the wheel and send it in to the nuns. They intercede. They pray your prayer for you."

I looked at her to see if she understood.

"There are nuns in there?"

"No," I said. "Not anymore."

Audrey pushed her hair behind her ears. She took the pencil and paper from me and smiled. She looked at the wheel, then at me.

"Do you mind if I do this alone? I'm sure I can find my way back."

"Of course."

I turned and started walking away.

"Thomas," said Audrey.

"Yes?"

"Thank you."

I smiled at her, then walked toward the beach.

Back at the resort I ate breakfast, then went to the bungalow where I'd been painting the day before. By noon I'd finished. I cleaned the roller and brushes, then went to the showers. The day was warm, although the sky was still charcoal gray. I stepped into the shower and turned on the water, and the handle broke off in my hand. A stream of cold water shot from the wall and hit me in the stomach. I jumped out of the stall and wrapped myself in a towel. Behind the showers I found a shutoff valve, but when I tried to turn it, it wouldn't budge. Then when I forced it, it snapped off in my hand, and another plume of water erupted.

I jogged to the main villa in my towel and went down into the basement. Against one wall of the boiler room was a myriad of black pipes and valves, their joints a patina brown. I chose the largest of the valves and turned it off.

Upstairs I ran into my father carrying a screen door from one of the bungalows. He looked at my towel and smiled.

"I just broke a faucet in the shower," I said. "I had to turn the main off."

"Why didn't you just turn it off at the showers?"

"I broke that one, too."

My father nodded, then continued on with his screen door.

I went back to the showers and got dressed, then went to the bar where my father had recently had a telephone installed. I called the hardware store in town, but quickly realized that my Spanish was inadequate.

"Never mind," I said in English. "I'll come in."

For Christmas my father had bought himself a new Land Cruiser. I took the keys from behind the bar and drove into town. At the hardware store I encountered the same clerk I'd spoken with on the phone. He seemed to be the only one working. I held up the broken faucet and told him I needed a new one. I thought my Spanish was getting pretty good, but this boy spoke so rapidly that all I caught was *si* and *no*.

"No comprende," I said. *"Nuevo?"*

I pantomimed taking a shower and turning the faucet on. I showed him how the water had shot out from the wall. Again he spoke rapidly, and all I could understand was *si* and *no*.

Again I showed him the faucet.

"Nuevo?" I asked.

This time he spoke more slowly but also more loudly, as if that might be the problem.

After two or three more manifestations of my pantomime and his responses, I understood that *si*, the faucet was something they normally stocked, but at present they were out of it. I asked him if he knew of anywhere else I could get one, and he understood.

"Si," he said. "San Juan."

I called the resort from a pay phone, and Clare answered. A jet thundered overhead leaving a wispy, white trail across the gray sky.

"What is it?" asked Clare.

"I have to go into San Juan," I said.

"Do you really?"

"They won't have what I need here for another week. I don't think we can go without water that long."

"Okay," said Clare. "As long as you're going, we need new linens for all the bungalows."

"Okay. Anything else?"

"No. Just that I love you."

"I love you, too."

I drove onto the ferry, then climbed to the upper deck and sat next to the railing. Near me on the floor were two Puerto Rican boys playing with an empty Coke can. They sat five or six feet apart with their legs spread out and rolled the can back and forth. It was the simplest of games, but oddly satisfying. I watched them for a long time, and when one of the boys noticed me, he smiled, his teeth brilliant against his dark skin. He cupped his hand to me indicating that I could join them if I wished. I was moved but told them *"No gracias,"* and they went back to playing.

When we docked I drove off the ferry and navigated the congested streets, then climbed the steep road out of Fajardo. It was late in the afternoon, and the air smelled of exhaust and metal. It was a two-hour drive into San Juan. Halfway there I rounded a bend in the road. The sun glared off the windshield, and for a moment I couldn't see the pavement. I dropped the visor and saw that my father had paper-clipped a photograph of Mary and Catherine to the back of it. It must have been a recent photo, because Mary's hair was longer now, her face that pared-down new face, unfettered. They were standing in front of a banana tree wearing similar sundresses, one with a faint pattern of leaves, the other vines. Mary was standing behind Catherine with her bare arms wrapped across Catherine's chest. They were both looking directly into the camera. Neither of them was smiling, but their faces were serene. I had always thought that there was an uncanny resemblance between Catherine and Clare, but now seeing Catherine with her mother, I didn't see how I could have thought that. In the picture Catherine looked like a smaller version of her mother— beautiful, strong, willful—with eyes that saw beyond the present.

* * *

When I got into San Juan, I bought six faucets and several shutoff valves, then I drove to a department store and bought sheets. When I came out, the day was humid and still. I drove into Old San Juan and took a walking tour of the old city before checking into a decrepit hotel. Visible from my balcony was an enormous Catholic church, built in the 1600s. I pulled a chair from the room and sat outside until it got dark. On the street below people shouted and dogs barked. Teens drove by in lowriders, their stereos thumping. I heard a woman cursing in Spanish at the dogs and the sound of breaking glass, but the barking continued. I closed my eyes and imagined the resort.

I see Ellen and Albert sitting under the lights of the pergola, talking in hushed tones and occasionally giggling like schoolchildren. Albert reaches out and touches Ellen's hand, and for a while she doesn't pull it away. I see my father in the kitchen, wearing Martin's yeasty apron, following his yellowed index-card recipe, kneading bread on the stainless-steel island for breakfast the next morning. Martin is sitting nearby, overseeing. My father wipes a hand across his face, leaving a jet trail of flour on his forehead. Upstairs Juliana is sitting in bed propped up with pillows, reading a book on natural childbirth. Occasionally she places her hand to her abdomen and smiles. In the room next door, Mary and Catherine are in bed, also propped up with pillows. It appears that Mary has been reading to Catherine, but now Catherine is telling Mary a story. I get the sense that the story is about me. The look on Mary's face is both amused and affectionate. I see Clare, alone in our room, sitting by the open window, knitting. There is a full moon, and she can sense it, can feel the moonbeams on her face.

* * *

When I awoke the next morning, the incessant barking that had invaded my dreams all night had stopped. Outside the street was quiet. I stepped out onto the balcony. The oppressive, gray clouds of the day before had gone. The sky was clear and the street was filled with a watery light. I went back into the room and checked the ferry schedule, then walked up the street to the Catholic church.

I had just planned to go in and take a look around, but when I stepped through the large wooden doors, I was surprised to find Mass in progress. I started to turn and leave, but an old woman in the back motioned for me to sit with her. Something about her gesture, welcoming and kind, made me think it would be rude to leave.

I sat down next to her, and she smiled, pleased with herself.

It was a large church but very full. There were stained-glass windows along both sides, depicting scenes from the Bible. I looked to the front where a large crucifix hung from the ceiling in front of a purple curtain. I guessed that Mass had been going on for some time. A priest was standing at the pulpit giving a sermon.

I listened for a while and gathered that his text was the scripture about Jesus going off into the desert and fasting for forty days and then being tempted by the devil.

My Spanish was still shaky, but I did get some of it. At one point the priest talked about how many days there are in Lent—forty days *of* Lent, but forty-six days *in* the Lenten season. Each Sunday in Lent, and there are six of them, is considered a feast day, what this priest liked to call "little Easters."

He said that during Lent we look inward and deal with those demons that we have perhaps ignored over the past year. It's a time to fast and to pray and walk alone in the desert and listen to what God has to say to us. And although at our weakest, we may be approached by the devil and his temptations, God will not abandon us in our weakness, he will not let us be tempted beyond what we are capable of resisting. During this season of introspection and self-denial, we are provided with little oases of comfort, little Easters in the midst of a cold, dry, wintry season.

After the service I stepped outside and walked down the cement steps at the front of the church. I sat down on a low stone wall across the street and watched as the congregation spilled out of the church. When the woman I'd sat next to came out, she spotted me and waved. She wore white gloves and held a black purse at her elbow. She walked up the street slowly, her back rounded, her head down.

One of the last people out of the church was an old man who caught my attention because I think he was the only white person in the church beside myself. He walked down the steps using a cane, taking them one at a time. He crossed the street and climbed into a car just up the street from where I was sitting. In a moment I saw the profile of his head fall onto the steering wheel and knew that he'd turned the key and nothing had happened. I walked over to the car and poked my head in the passenger side window.

"Won't start?" I said.

He looked at me and shook his head.

"I don't know what's wrong," he said in English. "I just bought this battery six months ago. Cost me fifty-five dollars."

"Pop the hood," I said. "Let me take a look."

When I lifted the hood, I suddenly felt my brother's presence, as if we were standing there together looking down at that engine, together trying to decipher the problem.

I checked the negative cable on the battery and noticed that it was loose. I twisted it a little on the post, then walked over to the driver's side of the car.

"I don't think your battery was grounded," I said. "Try it now."

The old man turned the key, and the engine turned over and started. A childish look came over his face. He turned to me and smiled.

"Thank you," he said. "It's never done that before."

"Your negative battery cable is loose," I said. "You should get it tightened."

"I will. I'll do that first thing."

As I walked back to the hotel, I felt as if Stephen were walking along with me, a smile on his face, proud of me. As I neared the hotel, the feeling became so strong that I was sure if I reached out my hand I would feel something. I paused on the sidewalk and listened. Then I did reach out my hand, but there was nothing there. The feeling began to fade, as if whatever had been there was walking away.

"Good-bye," I said in a whisper. *"Deus vobiscum"**

Then it really did feel as though he was gone.

---

* God be with you.